Praise for *New York Times* bestselling author Christine Rimmer

"Rimmer's powerful narrative brilliantly brings to life her unforgettably brave heroine, compassionate hero and fabulous co-stars. Her phenomenal handling of the heroine's spousal abuse is outstanding."

—*RT Book Reviews* on *The Good Girl's Second Chance*, 4.5 stars, Top Pick

"The book's solid plot, along with the great chemistry between Sydney and Rule, will make readers keep turning page after page."

—*RT Book Reviews* on *The Prince's Secret Baby*

"Rimmer's holiday read combines memorable yet down-to-earth characters and a wintry Montana setting in a wonderful yuletide story."

—*RT Book Reviews* on *The Rancher's Christmas Princess*

Christine Rimmer came to her profession the long way around. She tried everything from acting to teaching to telephone sales. Now she's finally found work that suits her perfectly. She insists she never had a problem keeping a job—she was merely gaining "life experience" for her future as a novelist. Christine lives with her family in Oregon. Visit her at christinerimmer.com.

Books by Christine Rimmer

Harlequin Special Edition

The Bravos of Justice Creek

Ms. Bravo and the Boss
James Bravo's Shotgun Bride
Carter Bravo's Christmas Bride
The Good Girl's Second Chance
Not Quite Married

The Bravo Royales

A Bravo Christmas Wedding
The Earl's Pregnant Bride
The Prince's Cinderella Bride
Holiday Royale
How to Marry a Princess
Her Highness and the Bodyguard
The Rancher's Christmas Princess

Montana Mavericks: The Baby Bonanza

Marriage, Maverick Style!

Visit the Author Profile page
at Harlequin.com for more titles.

HOME ON THE RANCH:
MONTANA
VOLUME 5

NEW YORK TIMES BESTSELLING AUTHOR

CHRISTINE RIMMER

HARLEQUIN® HOME ON THE RANCH

ISBN-13: 978-1-335-00501-4

First published as Resisting Mr. Tall, Dark & Texan by Harlequin Books in 2011 and Marooned with the Maverick by Harlequin Books in 2013.

Home on the Ranch: Montana Volume 5

Special thanks and acknowledgment are given to Christine Rimmer for her contribution to the Montana Mavericks: The Texans Are Coming! miniseries.

Special thanks and acknowledgment are given to Christine Rimmer for her contribution to the Montana Mavericks: Rust Creek Cowboys miniseries.

This edition published by arrangement with Harlequin Books S.A.

For questions and comments about the quality of this book, please contact us at CustomerService@Harlequin.com.

Printed in U.S.A.

CONTENTS

RESISTING MR. TALL, DARK & TEXAN

For Marcia Book Adirim.
Intrepid. Fun. Flexible.
And of course, so creative!

Chapter 1

"Lizzie, don't do this to me. You know I can't live without you."

Instantly, Lizzie Landry felt her determination weakening. *How does he do that?* she wondered. At the same time, she found herself thinking that he really would be lost without her, and she did worry that he…

She caught herself.

Oh, come on. What was her problem here? After five years with Ethan Traub, she ought to be immune to his considerable charm and shameless flattery. And she was. Pretty much. It was only that she did hate to leave him when he needed her. Which was constantly.

But no. She had to be strong. The break had to be made.

She put on her sternest, most unwavering expression. "Ethan, you've been putting me off for months, and it's not going to work this time. We have to talk about this."

The melting look in those dark velvet eyes of his faded as he scowled. She watched as his perfect, manly lips assumed a downward curve. "There's nothing to talk about," he grumbled. "You're coming to Montana with me. Eventually, if you're still unhappy with—"

Lizzie put up a hand. "I'm not unhappy, Ethan. It's been wonderful working for you. If I still had to work for *someone,* I would want it to be you."

"Great, then. We have no problem. You can *keep* working for me."

"No, I'm not going to do that. I want to be my own boss. That was always my goal—a goal it's time I reached. And you *know* that I'm ready to move on because I have told you so. Over and over and over again. Two weeks' notice. I think that's fair."

"Two weeks!" he blustered, rising from behind his desk. Bracing his knuckles on the desk pad, he loomed toward her, six-foot-four of killer-handsome, seriously imposing Texas male. "It's impossible. It's not going to happen. You'll need more than two weeks to find your replacement—not that you're going to be finding one right now. We're leaving on Thursday."

"Ethan, I told you. I'm *not* going to—"

"Oh, yeah." He cut her off before she could finish her sentence. "You are. For so many reasons."

Lizzie tried not to groan. "Please don't start on the reasons. I've heard them all."

"And now you're going to hear them again."

"Do I have a choice?"

"None." And he proceeded to tell her everything she already knew. How he couldn't get along without her, how it just wasn't reasonable for her to be talking about cutting out on him now. "You know I need time,

Lizzie. It's not going to be easy finding another assistant as good as you are. Someone flexible as to living arrangements. Someone smart. Someone calm and capable. But also fun to be around. Someone who can manage the office, the house—and have my back on the personal front..."

There was more in the same vein. Okay, yes. She'd been flattered the first time she heard it. But after months of trying to tell him she was ready to move on, listening to how she couldn't go was getting old.

She waited for him to wind down before reminding him, yet again, "Montana doesn't work for me. I'm a Texan, born and bred right here in Midland. And I'm staying here in Midland and opening my bakery as planned. You need to get used to that idea because you are not changing my mind. Not this time."

"Traub Oil needs you."

"Traub Oil managed fine without me for over thirty years."

"All right, then." He straightened to his full height. "*I* need you." He towered over her now because she remained in the chair on the far side of his desk. She considered rising to face him. Upright, after all, she was only a few inches shorter than he was and could almost stand head-to-head with him.

But no. She stayed in her seat. And concentrated on projecting calm determination. "You don't need me, Ethan. Not really. You're going to be fine."

He shook his head. "Lizzie, Lizzie, Lizzie..." And then, with a heavy sigh, he folded his long, hard frame back into his fat leather swivel chair. "How about a bonus? A...severance bonus. Stick with me a little longer, you walk away with more cash."

Do not ask, her sternest inner voice instructed. But money was money. She'd been flat-broke once. She never, ever wanted to go there again. "How big of a bonus?"

He named an eye-widening figure.

She let out a strangled laugh. "You're kidding."

"I am serious as a failed blowout preventer."

Okay, she was weakening now. Genuinely weakening. Plus, well, she did feel a little bad about letting him go to Montana without her. He had big plans for Montana. Maybe she ought to stick with him through that, at least....

There was a gleam in those dark eyes now. He knew he had her. "Think of it, Lizzie. You know you can always use a larger cushion. Startup costs multiply. They inevitably turn out to be more than you projected."

Okay, he had a point there. "How long would I have to stay on?"

He gave an easy shrug. "Oh, I'm thinking a few more months should do it."

"A few months—as in three?" She was the one scowling now.

His rueful smile could charm the habit off a nun. "Just think about it. That's all I'm asking. We'll discuss it more later."

"But Ethan, I—"

He made a show of eyeing his Rolex. "Whoa, look at the time...."

"Ethan—"

"I've got that meeting with Jamison in five. You should have reminded me."

"A minute more," she piped up desperately. "Let's just get this settled."

"Can't right now. Sorry."

"Ethan—"

"You have my offer. Think it over." He was already on his feet again.

"But I *have* thought it over and I—"

"Sorry. Really. Got to go." And, again, he was out the door before she could pin him down.

Lizzie slumped in the chair.

But only for a moment—and then she was drawing her shoulders back, smoothing her hair that tended to frizz, even in the relatively low humidity of West Texas. She was not giving up on this. Today, one way or another, she was going to finish giving her notice.

Put it in writing, her sterner self insisted. That way he would have no choice but to accept the inevitable.

But no. She just couldn't do that. Not to Ethan, who was not only her boss, but also a true friend, the one who had come through for her in a big way when she most needed some help and support.

She would get through to him. After all, he couldn't escape her indefinitely. Especially not given that she lived in his house. No matter how hard he tried to avoid her, he had to come home eventually.

The meeting with Roger Jamison went well, Ethan thought.

Roger would have no trouble holding down the fort while Ethan was in Montana. And later, if things went as Ethan planned, he would formally name Roger to replace him as Traub Oil Industries' chief financial officer.

After the meeting with Roger, Ethan could have returned to his corner office, but Lizzie would be there at her desk, guarding his door. And waiting to continue explaining how she was leaving him.

Forget that.

He was meeting his stepfather, Pete Wexler, for lunch at the club at noon. So he went on over there an hour early. He got a Coke and sat out on the clubhouse front patio and enjoyed the late-May sunshine.

Pete showed up a few minutes early and he grabbed Ethan in a hug. "This is great," Pete announced. "Good to get away from the office, get a little one-on-one time." Pete clapped Ethan on the arm as he released him. "Shall we go on inside?" He gestured toward the wide glass doors.

Ethan led the way. They got a table with a nice view of the golf course.

And as soon as they put in their order, Pete started telling him what he already knew. "You're leaving Thursday."

"Right."

"Your mother and I will try to get away Friday morning. It's important to both of us, to be there for your brother's wedding." Corey, born third in the family after Ethan, was getting married on Saturday. Corey and his bride, Erin, were settling down together in Thunder Canyon, a great little mountain town not far from Bozeman. There was already a big Traub family contingent in the Thunder Canyon area. Ethan had cousins there, and his older brother, Dillon, the doctor of the family, had settled there, too. Pete was still talking. He named off Ethan's remaining siblings. "Jackson, Jason and Rose are going to make it, too. The whole family will be there…."

Ethan sat back in his chair and listened to his stepdad

ramble on and thought about how long it had taken him to accept Pete into the family. At least twenty years.

But eventually, Ethan, like his four brothers and his sister, had come around. How could he not? Pete was a good man. A kind man, with a big heart. He doted on Ethan's mom and had consistently been there for his stepchildren.

The hard fact, Ethan saw now, was that it had taken him a couple of decades to forgive poor Pete for not being Charles Traub. Ethan's dad had been tall and commanding, a self-made millionaire before he was thirty—back in the day when a million bucks actually counted for something. He'd died on an oil rig twenty-eight years ago, when Ethan was nine.

Pete had been there for Ethan's mom, Claudia, from the day that the accident happened. And that had stirred up the town gossip mill in a big way. Ethan and his brothers had suffered no end of bloody noses and black eyes defending their mother's honor and, by extension, Pete's. At the same time as they stood up for the man, they were all secretly suspicious of Pete's motives.

But in the end, there was no denying that Pete Wexler was a rock. He was no maverick. He liked to take things slow and steady, which, in terms of TOI, sometimes drove Ethan nuts. Still, Pete adored Ethan's mom and he'd been a fine husband to her for twenty-six years now. Last year he'd had a heart attack, which freaked them all out and made them all the more aware of how much he meant to them.

Now, Pete was fully recovered and taking better care of himself. Back around the time of his heart attack, he and Ethan's mom had talked about retiring. But not anymore. Pete was feeling great lately. And for the foreseeable future, they would be running Traub Oil Industries together, Pete as chairman of the board and Claudia as CEO.

Ethan knew they depended on him, but he was through waiting to be the boss. And he was a damn sight more adventurous about the business than either his mother or Pete would ever be. He'd dedicated his life to TOI, learned the company from the ground up. And he'd been CFO for six years now. It was enough. Exploration and development was the key for him. If he wanted bigger opportunities, he needed to create them. And thus, the trip to Montana.

Their food came. They dug in.

And that was when Pete brought up the resort. "About this Thunder Canyon Resort opportunity. Your mom and I have looked over the material your brothers put together." Dillon and Corey had been pushing to get some TOI capital invested in the resort. "Do we really want to take on a failing hospitality venture at this point?"

"We wouldn't be taking it on exactly."

Pete smiled. "Sorry. Figure of speech. But you know what I mean."

"I do, Pete. And come on, I wouldn't say the resort is failing. In fact, the numbers show improvement over the past year. *And* they got McFarlane House hotels to invest. I've been in contact with Connor McFarlane, second in command at McFarlane House. He's committed to seeing the resort succeed."

"You'll get with McFarlane, face-to-face?"

"We've got a meeting set up for next week in Thunder Canyon."

"Good."

"The resort owners *have* been doing some reorganization..." Ethan waited for Pete's nod before continuing. "And they've been pulling out all the stops to broaden their market, to make the resort more accessible to a wider demographic, while not sacrificing the reputation they've built as a luxury destination."

"It's only that I see no reason to rush into anything...."

"And we won't. Sit tight," Ethan reassured him. "I'll spend more time on it, go over the books thoroughly, meet with the general manager, tour every inch of the property—all before we get down to giving a yes or a no."

Pete nodded. "I know you will." And then he started in about Ethan's plans to expand into shale oil extraction once he got to Montana. Same old yadda yadda. Extracting oil from shale was cost-prohibitive. The environmental impact wasn't good. As always, Pete reiterated all the drawbacks he'd reiterated any number of times before.

Patiently, Ethan reminded him that the higher the cost per barrel of oil, and the more depleted the oil reserves, the better it looked to be investing in oil shale. He reminded his stepdad yet again that the technology for extraction was constantly improving and TOI didn't want to end up behind the curve on this.

Eventually, Pete ran out of red flags on that subject. They finished their lunch and parted in the club parking lot, where Ethan submitted to another big hug.

"I know I tend to be a little overcautious," Pete said when he let Ethan loose. "But I want you to know that I—and your mother, too, of course—not only love you and wish we could keep you right here in Midland forever. We also realize you have to get out there and break some new ground. And we admire the hell out of you for that, son."

The smile Ethan gave his stepdad then had nothing but love in it. "Thanks, Pete. In some ways, you were always way ahead of the rest of us. It took me a while to appreciate how far ahead."

Pete was looking a little misty-eyed. "See you at the board meeting."

"Yeah, see you then."

Ethan went back to the office.

Big mistake. Lizzie was waiting.

She rose from her desk as he approached his office door, blew a strand of almost-blond hair out of her eye and tried to get his attention. "Ethan, I—"

"Not now, Lizzie. I've got important calls to make."

"But—"

"Later. Soon." He pushed open his door, went through and shut it behind him. Fast.

He spent the next few hours answering phone messages, dealing with email and clearing his desk as much as possible, because he—and Lizzie, too, whether she was willing to admit it yet—would be on their way to Thunder Canyon bright and early Thursday morning.

The board of directors meeting was happening down in the main conference room. That meant he had to leave the safety of his office and get past Lizzie again.

No problem. He waited to go until she actually had to buzz him to remind him of the meeting.

And then he flew past her desk with a "Hold any messages. I'll deal with them tomorrow."

She didn't even look up. She knew there was no

chance they would be discussing unpleasant subjects again that day.

The meeting included a catered meal and was over at a little after eight. No way was he going home that early. Not with Lizzie, who was both his assistant *and* his live-in housekeeper, lying in wait for him there.

So he called a couple of friends and they went out for a beer. The bar had the Rangers game on the big screens. Ethan stayed to watch them beat the Angels five to four.

By then it was after eleven. One of his buddies invited everyone to his place for a final round. Ethan went. And he was the last to leave.

He didn't pull into the driveway of his four-thousand-square-foot house in a newer, gated subdivision until after two. All seemed quiet, only the outside lights were on. It looked to him as if Lizzie had given up on him and gone to bed.

Terrific.

Very quietly, he let himself into the utility room from the garage. Lizzie's rooms were on the ground floor, in the back, not all that far from the garage entrance, so he took extra care not to make a sound. Everything was dark and quiet and the house smelled faintly of baked goods.

His mouth watered. Cookies? No. It smelled more like...muffins. Maybe blueberry. He really loved Lizzie's blueberry muffins. In fact, he could use one right now.

Following his nose, he tiptoed down the short back hallway toward the dark kitchen.

He got one foot beyond the doorway when the

kitchen lights popped on. He blinked against the sudden brightness and growled, "Lizzie, what the hell?"

"Ethan, there you are." She stood by the island, wearing a very patient expression and a robe that looked as if it might have been made from some old lady's bedspread. "I was beginning to wonder if you'd *ever* get home." The muffins were on the counter, behind her, looking all fat and golden and tempting. "This is getting ridiculous. You realize that, right?"

"Are those blueberry?"

She nodded, but she didn't step aside so he could grab one. "We need to talk." A weary sigh escaped her. "You want some coffee?"

He had that sinking feeling. She was determined to leave him. He knew that. She had a dream and she wouldn't let go of it. And he was running out of ways to avoid having to let her go. "I shouldn't have paid you so well," he grumbled. "You saved too much, too fast."

She shrugged. "You couldn't help it. You're a generous man." She looked down at her feet, which were stuck in a pair of floppy terry-cloth slippers the same old-lady blue as her robe. "You've been so good me. When my dad died… I don't know if I could have made it without you." Slowly, she lifted her head and they looked at each other.

He gave in. "Okay. Coffee."

She knew he was no fan of decaf, but coffee kept him awake when he drank it at night, so she brewed decaf anyway. That was the thing about Lizzie. She knew what he wanted—and what he needed—without his having to tell her.

He took a muffin, grabbed a napkin and sat down at the table by the dark bow window. She used the single-cup maker, so the decaf was ready in no time. She set it down in front of him. He waited until she took the chair across the table before he broke off a hunk of the muffin and put it in his mouth.

Fat blueberries and that sweet, buttery, pale yellow muffin. How was it that Lizzie's muffins always managed to be light and substantial, both at once? Delicious. Lizzie's muffins—like her cookies and her cakes, her pies and the fat loaves of bread she baked—always made him feel good. Satisfied. Happy with the world and his place in it.

At home.

Yeah. That was it. Lizzie made him feel at home.

She said, "I've been thinking about that severance bonus you mentioned."

He ate another bite, savoring it, before he spoke. "Three months, it's yours."

She shook her head. "It's just too long."

"*Two,* then." He pulled out all the stops and put on a sad, pleading expression. "Two months. Lizzie, you've got to give me a little time…"

A little time. Who did he think he was kidding?

There was only one Lizzie. She made it possible for him to lead exactly the life he enjoyed—no commitments, no strings. He worked hard and played hard, and when he got home, there was no one there nagging him. Just the sweet smell of something baking in the oven and Lizzie offering a nightcap. Or a bedtime cup of decaf and a fat blueberry muffin.

He not only needed to keep her from quitting, but he also needed to find a way to make her see that opening a bakery was a dream best left to die a natural death.

He needed her to keep working for him. And to keep being his live-in best friend.

He picked up his coffee and sipped.

Not much got by Lizzie. Now, she was studying him with pure suspicion in her eyes. "What kind of scheme are you hatching?"

He rearranged his expression, going for total harmlessness, as he set down the cup. "Montana will be fun. A change. Change is a good thing."

She made a humphing sound. "In spite of your plans for getting into oil shale, how likely is it that you're going to be building an office there?"

"Very likely." He hoped. "I have *family* there. Two brothers. Cousins. And my sister and my other brothers are making noises like they might want to settle down there, too."

"An invasion of Traubs."

"Well, I wouldn't put it that way exactly."

She snorted. "I would."

He reminded her, "And I *have* found a house there."

"You mean you had *me* find you a house there."

"That's right. And you did a great job." At least judging by the pictures she'd shown him online. Neither of them had actually been there yet. But the lease was for only six months. If he didn't like it, he'd find something else.

She was giving him that don't-kiss-up-to-me-because-I'm-not-buying-it look. He didn't care much for that look. She said, "How about this? You go, I stay. I hire and train my replacement while you're gone."

Not a chance. "Forget that." He ate another bite of the amazing muffin. "I've changed my mind."

"About?"

"I want two months out of you in Montana. Forget training your replacement. When the two months are up, I'll find my own assistant."

She wrinkled her very assertive nose. "Montana. Ugh."

"Don't knock it until you've been there. Thunder Canyon is like everyone's dream of a hometown in the mountains. And the scenery is spectacular." When she only sat there staring at him mournfully, he reminded her, "You get a giant bonus. For only two more months."

She slanted him a sideways glance. "Two months would be it. The end. You accept that?"

He didn't. So he lied. "Absolutely."

"Fine," she agreed at last. "Two months. I go with you to Montana. I get that big bonus and you find your own new assistant."

"Deal." He popped the rest of the muffin into his mouth and offered her his hand across the table. She took it and they shook.

He was careful to keep his gaze steady on hers and only to smile on the inside, to give her no clue that he was lying through his teeth. There was no way she was leaving him. He just needed more time with her to make her see the light.

Two months in Thunder Canyon should be just the ticket.

Chapter 2

Late Thursday afternoon, Ethan parked his rented SUV on Main Street in Thunder Canyon. The early-June sun shone bright and the air was crisp and clean, with a cool wind sweeping down from the mountains. In the distance, snowcapped peaks reached for the wide Montana sky.

He was thinking he would walk the three blocks to the Hitching Post, the landmark saloon/restaurant that had stood for well over a hundred years now at the corner where Main jogged north and became Thunder Canyon Road.

But then, a few doors down, he spotted his sister-in-law Erika. The pretty brunette stood peering in the window of one of the shops. Beside her was a gorgeous blonde. Ethan knew the blonde, too: Erin Castro, his brother Corey's bride-to-be.

As Ethan approached, Erin turned her back to the window. She sagged against it, hanging her head. When she spoke, Ethan heard the tightness of barely controlled tears. "I can't believe this. I talked to him *yesterday*..."

Erika peered all the harder in the wide front window. "I'm so sorry, Erin. I really don't think there's anyone in there. And all the display cases are empty."

Erin tipped her head back and let out a moan. "How can this be happening? Oh, Erika, what am I going to do now? The wedding is Saturday."

Erika turned around and leaned back against the window, next to Erin. "I can't believe he would just... vanish like that." Right then, she glanced over and saw Ethan lurking a few feet away, waiting for them to notice him. She frowned. "Ethan? Hey, I didn't know you were already in town."

He nodded. "Got in an hour ago. My assistant shooed me out of the house. She doesn't like me underfoot while she's trying to unpack—and why do I get the feeling something has gone wrong here?"

Erin let out another moan. "Because it has." She aimed a thumb over her shoulder at the sign that said Closed Indefinitely in the shop window. The shop was a bakery. *La Boulangerie* was written in flowing script across the front windows. "I came over to make my final payment on my wedding cake only to find that the baker, apparently, has skipped town."

Erika said, "She paid him two-thirds in advance. Can you believe that? This is fraud, plain and simple."

"It's a disaster, that's what it is." Erin raked her shining blond hair back off her forehead with an impatient hand. "I don't even care about the money at this point.

I care that it's Thursday...." A whimper escaped her. *"Thursday."*

Erika wrapped an arm around her shoulders. "We'll figure out something. There *are* other bakeries in town."

"I can't believe it. Forty-eight hours until the wedding." Erin's huge blue eyes swam with tears. "The whole town is coming. And. No. Cake."

Ethan never could stand to see a woman cry. Plus, as soon as he'd realized what the problem was, he had the solution. "Erin, dry those tears. And come with me, you two. My car's right there."

His brothers' women looked at him as if he was a couple sandwiches short of a picnic.

Erin sniffed. "Ethan, we're both glad to see you and we'd love to spend a little time with you. But right now we've got to find someone who can deliver a six-tier wedding cake by Saturday."

"I'm with you. I get it." He took Erin's arm and wrapped it around his. And he offered his other arm to Erika. "And believe it or not, I happen to know the best baker in Texas."

Erin remained unconvinced. "That's great, Ethan, but there's no *time* to fly someone in from Texas."

"I know. And that's not a problem. The baker in question is right here in town—whipping the house I'm renting into shape, as a matter of fact."

"Uh, he is?"

"Actually, *her* name is Lizzie. She's a genius of a baker. She's at my house and we are going there now."

Lizzie stood in the formal living room of the house she'd rented for Ethan, BlackBerry in hand, and checked off the afternoon's already-accomplished tasks.

Unpack 4 Ethan. Check.

Unpack 4 self. Check.

There was more in the same vein. But overall, the house was in pretty good shape. It had come quite nicely furnished and she'd hired Super-Spiffy Housekeeping to make the place shine. Also, the Super-Spiffy folks offered a shopping service. Lizzie jumped on that, too. As a result, the pantry and fridge were now fully stocked and ready to go.

Now, to figure out what to whip up for dinner. It would have to be something she could make up ahead and stick in the fridge, just in case Ethan wandered in later with an empty stomach. And cookies might be nice. Her mama's recipe for butter pecan sugar cookies maybe. He could never get enough of those.

Yeah, okay. She totally spoiled him and she knew it. But when she baked, she was spoiling herself, too. There was nothing like the smell of cookies in the oven. Or sourdough bread. Or a sweet fruit kuchen. Or a nice devil's food cake.

The smell of something baking always made Lizzie feel that all was right with the world. It brought back memories of her childhood, as vivid and real as if they were happening in the here and now, so many years later. Memories of the little child-size table she had in the back of the family business, the Texas Bluebell Bakery. Of her mama singing "Au clair de la lune" and "Frère Jacques" as she decorated a tall, splendid wedding cake or even asked for Lizzie's help to cut gingerbread men from dark, spicy dough. When Lizzie baked, she saw her *maman*'s heart-shaped delicate face, her pink cheeks and radiant smile. She saw her dad as a young man again, a happy man. He'd met her *maman* when he was in the army, stationed in France, and he'd loved her on sight. So he'd swept her off her tiny feet and brought her home to reign over the bakery he'd inherited from his parents. Lizzie's dad had lived for her *maman*.

And when her *maman* was gone…

Lizzie blinked and shook her head. No point in going there. She had a meal to prepare. And then she had butter-thick cookie batter to mix with toasted pecans, roll into sugared balls and flatten with the round base of a glass.

She was just turning for the kitchen when she heard the front door open.

Ethan appeared from the foyer, ushering a striking blonde and a curvy, big-eyed brunette in ahead of him. He spotted her. "Lizzie, there you are."

She laughed. "Ethan, what are you up to now?"

He put an arm across the blonde's shoulders. "Lizzie, meet Corey's beautiful bride, Erin Castro." He hooked the other arm around the brunette. "And this gorgeous creature is Erika, Dillon's wife. My brothers are such fortunate men."

Lizzie recognized the two from family photos. "Hey, great to meet you both at last."

Erin said, "Hi," kind of limply. Erika echoed the word. Both women looked a little…what? Unhappy, maybe, and worried. Especially Erin.

Lizzie gestured toward the living-room sofa and chairs. "Make yourselves comfortable. I'll brew a pot of coffee and see if there's anything sweet around here…" She turned for the kitchen.

"Coffee would be great," Ethan said. "And it's you we came to see."

She stopped, turned. "Me?"

The women shared a glance. Erin spoke. "Ethan seems to think you might be able to save me from disaster."

"Yikes. There's a disaster?"

"There certainly is. A cake disaster. I went to finalize payment on my wedding cake today and found out the baker has skipped town."

Lizzie let out a groan of sympathy. "But the wedding is Saturday, isn't it?"

Erin gave a sad little sigh. "Exactly."

Ethan said coaxingly, "And I told them that you're unbeatable in the kitchen. *And* that you're planning to leave me to open a bakery…"

Lizzie grinned, pleased. "You want me to do the wedding cake."

Erin let out a cry. "Oh, it's too much. Way too much to ask." She put her hands to her pink cheeks. "I'm so sorry we bothered you."

"Hold on, now." Ethan tried to settle her down.

But Erin would not be "settled." She turned to Erika. "We really have to get going. I need to work this problem out and I need to do it yesterday…"

Lizzie ached for the poor girl. "Hey, did I say no?"

Erin blinked. "But I… Well, could you? *Would* you?"

"I can, yes. And I would be honored. And you can relax. It's very much doable. Mostly it's going to be about getting the equipment I'll need together on the fly like this. But the cake itself is no problem."

"No problem?" Erin was shaking her head. "It's for *three hundred* people."

Lizzie couldn't bear to see the poor woman so worried. She went to her, took both her small, slim hands in her own larger ones. "Let me take this worry off your shoulders. Planning a wedding is stressful enough without your baker running off on you." The man—why was she sure it had to be a man?—should be shot.

A tear trembled in Erin's thick lashes. "Oh, if you could..."

"I can. And I will. You'll see. I won't let you down. I baked several multitiered wedding cakes when I worked in my family's bakery, before college. And I've done four more since then, for friends in Texas who had big, gorgeous weddings."

The tear escaped Erin's lashes and spilled down her cheek. She freed a hand from Lizzie's grasp to take the tissue Ethan had produced for her. "I know it's only a cake. It's not the end of the world. I shouldn't let it get to me like this..."

Erika moved in closer and wrapped an arm around Erin's shoulder. "It's all going to work out." She winked at Lizzie. "My instincts tell me that Lizzie is just what we need right now."

"Yes, I am," said Lizzie with a low laugh. "Now come on into the kitchen. I'll make the coffee and see if we have some packaged cookies around here because I haven't had time to bake anything yet. You can tell me all about the fabulous cake I'll be creating for you."

"Oh, thank you. Thank you..."

Over Erin's shoulder, Ethan caught Lizzie's eye and grinned in satisfaction. Lizzie grinned right back at him. He was pleased to have found a way to solve Erin's problem. And he knew that Lizzie loved it when he brought her a challenge.

The kitchen had a big round table positioned in a bow window very much like the one in Ethan's house in Texas. In fact, Lizzie had pretty much chosen the house because it seemed to her a slightly smaller version of his Midland home. She'd known he would feel instantly comfortable here—then again, Ethan felt comfortable wherever he was.

He went right to the table and pulled out chairs for the bride and for Erika as Lizzie got the coffee going and put some Pepperidge Farm Milano cookies on a plate. Within a few minutes, they were all munching cookies and sipping coffee.

Lizzie got out her notebook. "Okay, now, tell me all about your perfect wedding cake."

Erin knew exactly what she wanted. "It has round tiers—six tiers. And real flowers. I have a lot of colors. So I thought if the cake itself was all white, we could put the colors in the flowers. I have mauve, red, purple, apple green, light orange and lilac…" Lizzie jotted down the colors as she ticked them off.

Erika added, "Each of her bridesmaids and matrons gets a different color."

Erin smiled at her soon-to-be sister-in-law. "Erika's dress is red."

"That will be beautiful." Lizzie started sketching. "Filling?"

"Raspberry preserves? And I want fondant on top of buttercream icing for that beautiful smooth look…"

"The porcelain look," Lizzie said. "And the fondant holds up well without refrigeration."

"Yes." Erin frowned. "I know the fondant isn't usually very tasty…"

"Mine is—does that sound like I'm bragging?" She shrugged. "Well, I am."

Erin beamed. "Good. I have to tell you, your confidence is really encouraging."

Erika chuckled. "Now is not a time she needs a modest baker."

Ethan let out a rumble of laughter. "Lizzie? Modest about baking? Never. But then, why should she be?"

Lizzie granted him an approving nod. "White cake?" she asked Erin.

Erin said, "We wanted pink champagne cake. And can you add some vanilla mousse filling with the raspberry?"

"You've got it. I'll need to get with your florist. Gerbera daisies in your colors would be nice, trailing in a spiral up over the tiers…"

Erin blinked. "How did you know?"

Lizzie shrugged again. "I can do some pretty white fondant flowers, too, for another accent, as well as edible pearls." She turned her notebook around so that the other two women could see her sketch of the cake.

Erika made a pleased sound.

Erin was beaming. "Oh, it's perfect. Just as I pictured it." She set down her coffee cup. "And I've got my checkbook." She grabbed for the bag she'd hooked on the back of her chair. "I can pay you right now."

Lizzie put up a hand.

But Ethan was the one who spoke. "No way. Consider it your wedding present."

Erin looked stunned. "But I couldn't possibly… No, that's not right. It's too much. I know what a cake like this costs."

Ethan held firm. "You paid once for your cake. Not again."

"Ethan, you're a prince. Really. But it's way too much

work for Lizzie. It's not fair to ask her to give her time and talent away like that."

Lizzie spoke up then. "Don't you worry. As I said, I'm honored to create your cake for you. I'm going to *love* baking your cake for you, I promise you."

"And *I* promise," said Ethan, with that melting look that broke all the girls' hearts, "that I'll pick up the tab. It won't cost Lizzie a penny."

Lizzie reached over and put her hand on Erin's slender arm. "Ethan will take care of me. Count on it. He always does."

Before the two women left, Erin invited Lizzie to the rehearsal dinner the next night.

"I would love to, but I think I need to stay focused, if you know what I mean." Actually, she probably could have fit in the dinner, but she wouldn't have been much of a guest because she'd be totally concentrated on all that would need doing the following day. She'd be up at about 4:00 a.m. Saturday, and baking her butt off. Luckily, the wedding was in the late afternoon, giving her a perfectly acceptable window of time to pull it all together.

If she could get all her equipment tomorrow. Which was another reason she didn't want to commit to dinner Friday night. She could still be running around madly then, trying to scare up cake boards or the right size pans.

"The three of us, then," said Erin. "You, me and Erika. We're taking a girls' night out as soon as Corey and I get back from our honeymoon."

Lizzie liked the sound of that. "It's a date."

"I'll call you tomorrow," promised Erika. "In case

there's anything you think of that I might be able to help with."

"Thanks. That would be terrific."

And then, in a flurry of goodbyes and thank-yous, Corey's bride and Dillon's wife were gone.

With a sigh, Lizzie sagged against the front door.

Ethan stood in the arch to the living room. "You're amazing." He looked at her with affection and appreciation in those gorgeous dark eyes.

She felt really good, she realized, basking in her boss's admiration—and excited over the cake she would create. "I like them. Both of them. And this is going to be fun."

"What can I do?"

"Stick around for about an hour while I make some calls?"

"You got it."

"Then I'll let you know what I need from you."

Dark eyes gleamed. "See? You already love it here."

She had to confess, "Okay, it's not as bad as I imagined it."

"Not as bad?" His voice coaxed her.

"Ethan, for crying out loud, what do you want from me? We've only been here half a day."

"You love it."

She pushed off the door frame and stood tall on her own two size-ten-and-a-half feet. "It ain't Texas."

"Lizzie." He spoke in that dark, sweet voice he used with his girlfriends. "You love it."

A strange little shiver went through her. She ignored it and blew a loose strand of hair out of her eyes as she gestured down the central hallway, toward his big, well-appointed home office. "Go…check your email or something. I'll call you when I need you."

Lizzie booted up her own computer in her little square of office space off the kitchen and started checking online to see if she could get the equipment she needed overnighted.

No way. Not to Thunder Canyon, Montana.

She spared a wistful thought for the well-stocked shelves in her *maman*'s bakery. But all that was long gone. And even if she'd managed to keep some of her mother's pans and utensils, they would be in Texas now, useless to her anyway.

So she called a couple of restaurant and kitchen supply places in nearby Bozeman. Both were just closing, but they would be open at nine tomorrow morning. And between them, they had what she was going to need.

She made a list—not only of equipment, but of all her ingredients. And then she called Erin's florist and made arrangements to pick up the multicolored daisies Saturday morning. If she was too busy to go, Ethan would do it for her.

He appeared right then, in the doorway to the kitchen, as if she had called for him. "So? Everything under control?"

She hit Save and then Print. "So far, yes." Faintly, in Ethan's office, she heard the printer start up. "Tomorrow, if you can manage it, I need you."

"I'm all yours."

"Great. You can drive me to Bozeman. The supply stores I found open at nine. I want to be there when they unlock the doors. And we can pick up the perishables before we come back, try and get it all in one trip."

"I can get you there and help with carrying groceries and equipment. Also, I'll bring my platinum card."

"Perfect." Then she remembered. "Corey's bachelor party. It's tonight, right?"

He looked puzzled. "Yeah. So?"

"You'll be out till all hours."

"That's the way a bachelor party tends to work."

"So never mind. I can make the trip tomorrow on my own. I'll bring you receipts. Lots of them."

"Uh-uh. I'll get up in time. And I'll take you."

"I'll believe it when I see it."

He was grinning, looking way too handsome, as he took up the challenge. "And you *will* see it. Just wait."

He was sweet to want to help. She did appreciate that. And she always enjoyed his company. But it didn't matter either way. If he wasn't up by the time she had to go, she'd just take off on her own. No big deal. "Want some dinner? I can throw something together within twenty minutes or so."

He shook his head. "The party's at the Hitching Post, a local watering hole. Dillon rented a private room in the back. Dinner included."

"You guys hire a naked girl to pop out of a cake?"

"Lizzie, Lizzie, Lizzie. Give us more credit than that."

"*Two* naked girls?"

He grunted. "You know the old saying. What happens at a bachelor party *stays* at a bachelor party."

She waved a hand at him. "I know, I know. If you told me you'd have to kill me and all that. Better you just keep your secrets. I'm too young to die."

"Plus, I need you alive to make Erin's wedding cake."

"Right. That, too."

"So…the twins and Rose are staying at Thunder Canyon Resort." His brothers Jackson and Jason were fraternal twins. At thirty, their sister, Rose, was the baby of the family. "I thought I'd wander on up there, see how they're doing, maybe have a look around the resort's main clubhouse a little…"

She almost laughed. "And I need to know your every move, why?"

He lifted one hard shoulder in a half shrug. "Well, I mean, if there's anything you need from me. Anything at all…" Now he was giving her that look again. That sweet, melting look, eyes like dark chocolate.

She braced her elbows on her dinky desk and wrinkled her nose at him. "*What* are you up to?"

He smiled, slow and lazy. "Not a thing. I'm just saying you can count on me to help, that you're a lifesaver for poor Erin and I'm here for you, Lizzie."

She made a shooing motion with both hands. "Out. Go. See you tomorrow."

"You sure?"

"I am positive."

"'Night, then." He turned and left her.

She watched him go, thinking what a great butt he had.

Until she caught herself staring and made herself look away.

After that, for several minutes, she just sat there at her desk, staring blindly into the middle distance, wondering why he seemed to be pulling out all the stops to be charming and attentive to her the past couple of days.

It was kind of annoying, really. They had an easygoing, best-pals relationship. And suddenly, he was messing with the program, falling all over himself to be available to her, coming way too close to flirting with her.

Worse than whatever he was up to, was the way she seemed to be responding to it. Getting all shivery when he sent her a glance. And…staring at his butt?

Okay, yeah. It was a great butt. But still. It wasn't as if that was news or anything.

Really. The last thing she needed was to start crushing on Ethan. That would be beyond stupid.

Lizzie tossed down her pen and stood up. She smoothed her hair and straightened her plain white sleeveless shirt. *Get over yourself, Landry.* Ethan wasn't up to anything beyond being extra nice to her in hope that she might change her mind about resigning.

And she was not crushing on him. Uh-uh. No way. Not in the least.

Chapter 3

At 3:10 a.m. Friday, Ethan clapped his brother Corey on the shoulder. "You're a lucky man," he said.

"Yes, I am," Corey agreed. "I'll walk you out."

Jackson, who was good and toasted at that point, called, "Hey, where you two goin'? Party's jus' gettin' started. 'S'bad enough Dillon crapped out on us early."

The redhead on his lap giggled. "Yeah, you two. Stick aroun'…"

"I'll be back," promised Corey with a rueful grin.

Jason, across the table from his twin, shook a finger. "You guys are gettin' old," he accused.

Neither Corey nor Ethan argued. The lone bartender, left to close up the place when the party was finally over, shook his head and went on polishing the short bar at the other end of the room. He'd stopped serving at two, per Montana law. But that didn't mean the partiers couldn't bring their own and serve themselves.

Ethan waved and left the private back room of the Hitching Post with the groom at his side. They emerged midway along a dim hallway and went right.

Corey pushed the bar on the heavy door beneath the red exit sign and the cool night air came in around them. He waved Ethan out ahead of him and put down the stop on the door to keep it from latching.

They stood in the quiet parking lot under the sodium vapor lights and Corey asked, "You good to drive?"

Ethan nodded. "Not even buzzed. I couldn't afford to get blasted. I'm taking Lizzie to Bozeman bright and early tomorrow to buy supplies for the wedding cake."

Corey grinned. He was a fine-looking man and took after their mother's side of the family, with lighter hair and eyes than Ethan had. "Got news for you, big brother. Tomorrow is already today."

"Did you have to remind me?"

Corey chuckled, but then he grew serious. "I owe you. *And* Lizzie. You've made Erin very happy." His deep voice softened when he said his bride's name. And it struck Ethan strongly: Corey was deeply in love.

First Dillon. Now Corey.

The Traub brothers were dropping like flies lately.

Not that there was anything wrong with settling down. If a man was interested in that kind of thing.

Corey went on, "I told Erin all about the Texas Bluebell Bakery, about those cream cakes and éclairs that could light up your mouth, and about those pies Lizzie's French mama used to bake. Remember those pies? I loved them all. Especially the sweet-potato pie." Corey stuck his hands in the pockets of his jeans and stared up toward the sky, a dreamy look on his face. "When I think of Cécile Landry's sweet-potato pie, it brings it all back, you know? Being a kid again, before Dad died, when life was simple, when a piece of pie could just make your day…"

Ethan did remember Cécile Landry's pies. "I was partial to the strawberry-rhubarb, myself."

"Oh, God," said Corey with a groan. "The strawberry-rhubarb…"

"Lizzie still bakes a rhubarb pie for me now and then. And they're just as good as her mama's, believe me." Lizzie. He scowled. Lizzie, who thought she was leaving him….

Corey lowered his head. He peered at Ethan more closely. "You're lookin' a little grim."

"Lizzie wants to quit." The words were out before he even realized he would say them. And then he went ahead and elaborated, sounding more annoyed than he meant to. "She's got a dream, you know?"

Corey did know. "The bakery—but you were aware of that. You told me two or three years ago, after the two of you became BFFNB, that she wanted to open a bakery again someday."

"Uh… BFFNB?"

"Best Friends Forever, No Benefits," Corey explained with a self-satisfied grin.

"Very funny—and it doesn't matter that I was aware of her big dream. The point is I never really thought she would ever go through with it. What's wrong with working for me, that's what I want to know?"

"Whoa." Corey stepped back. "You're really upset about this."

Ethan felt embarrassed suddenly. Which was ridiculous. He grunted. "Well, yeah. Yeah, I am. We've got a good thing going, me and Lizzie. And have you any idea how much I pay her?"

"What's that have to do with anything?"

"Just answer the damn question."

Corey answered carefully. "I'm sure it's a lot."

"You bet it's a lot. She's got full medical and dental. She's even got points in TOI."

Corey's brows drew together. "But she wants to get back into her family's business."

"Hold on a second here," Ethan grumbled. "You're my brother. You're supposed to be on *my* side."

"I *am* on your side. But Lizzie's always struck me as the type who gets things done, who sees what she wants and makes sure it happens. She wants to open a bakery."

"It's a phase, that's all. She'll get past it."

Corey only looked at him.

"What?" Ethan demanded.

Corey spoke with exasperating gentleness. "I gotta say I've learned a lot about women since I found Erin. Before Erin, I thought I knew it all. But now I'm kind of getting the picture that I didn't know squat."

"And your point is, exactly?"

"Ethan, I'm only saying I don't think you're going to get very far with a capable, take-charge woman like Lizzie by underestimating her."

"What the hell? Who says I'm underestimating her? And who says I want to *get somewhere* with her?"

"Whoa, brother. You are really turned around about this, aren't you?"

"Turned around? I don't know what you're talking about."

Corey gave him another of those long, unreadable

looks. "Why do I get the feeling that you're about to put your fist in my face?"

Because I am, Ethan thought. Which was really all out of proportion to the situation, and he knew that. He dialed it back, going for a slow breath as he ordered his body to relax, take it easy. "Sorry. It's late. I've got a lot on my mind and a bad case of jet lag, you know?"

Corey's expression said he wasn't buying Ethan's excuses, but he let it go. "I hear you. Get a little sleep, okay?" He turned for the propped-open door to go back inside.

Ethan felt like a complete jerk bag—meaning worse than a jerk. More like a whole bagful of jerks. "Corey?"

Corey stopped in midstep, sent a glance over his shoulder. "Yeah?"

"I'm glad you found Erin. Congratulations, man."

Corey smiled then. A real smile. "Thanks. I hope you work it out with Lizzie."

What exactly did he mean by that?

Ethan decided he didn't want to know.

Lizzie was up at seven, showered and dressed and ready to face the day by seven-thirty. She headed for the kitchen fully expecting to brew some coffee, grab some toast and be on her way, alone.

But as soon as she opened the door of her room, her nose told her the coffee was already made.

She entered the kitchen to find Ethan sitting at the table in the breakfast nook. He was freshly shaved and wearing boots, jeans and a casual shirt.

"I got the coffee going," he said. He raised his full mug and took a sip. "I was beginning to wonder if you would *ever* get up."

She made a face at him. But actually, she was pleased that he'd made the effort, and that she would have his company for the next few hours. "Want some eggs?"

"Do we have time?"

"Sure. Scrambled?"

"Great."

She went to work on the food. It didn't take long. She slid his plate in front of him and put the jam in the center of the table. Then she grabbed her own plate and sat down across from him. They ate in silence, fueling up for the morning ahead. He did look a little tired, she thought. There were shadows beneath his eyes.

"How much sleep did you get?" she asked, as she took their empty plates back to the sink.

"Enough."

She sent him a glance. "Listen, I can manage the trip myself if you want to go back to bed."

"I'm taking you."

"But if you—"

He cut her off. "Look, I don't want to go back to bed. I *want* to drive you. Got it?"

"Uh, sure. Got it." She scraped the plates and put them in the dishwasher. "How was the party?"

"It was fine," he said. His tone told her that the subject was closed, just in case she had any idea of trying to get maybe a sentence or two more out of him. So she left it alone.

A few minutes later, they climbed into Ethan's SUV and were on their way.

In Bozeman, they spent about an hour each at the two restaurant supply places. After that, they visited a community co-op grocery, where there was also a deli.

They had lunch there before moving on to their final stop, which was Safeway.

They were on the road back to Thunder Canyon at one-thirty. Lizzie was feeling really good about everything by then. Ethan had been sweet and helpful the whole trip. And she had managed to find everything she needed, which was a considerable relief.

At the house, Ethan helped her carry everything inside. When the back of the big SUV was finally empty and the granite counters in the kitchen were piled high with all she'd bought, he asked, "What else can I do?"

"Not a thing," she told him. "You're my favorite boss in the whole world and you have my undying gratitude." She started emptying the bags—groceries first.

He came around the counter toward her. "I love it when you're grateful." He stopped inches away.

She could smell his aftershave, which was subtle and manly and whispered tastefully of money. Already, there was a shadow of dark beard on his sculpted cheeks. She paused with a flat of free-range eggs in her hands. "You know you're directly between me and the fridge, right?"

"Oops." He gave her one of his famous killer half smiles—and stayed where he was.

With a put-upon sigh, she eased around him and carried the eggs to the roomy side-by-side high-end refrigerator. When she shut the door and turned back to him, he hadn't budged. He was still standing there, watching her. A shiver went through her, one way too much like the one she'd felt the day before, when they stood in the foyer together, after Erin and Erika left.

There were bags on every counter. She could so easily have just started on one of them—and steered clear of him. But that seemed downright cowardly somehow. What was the matter with her, anyway? Afraid to approach Ethan? Made no sense at all.

So she marched back around him and started on the next bag, hauling out a jar of cherry juice.

"Lizzie." His big hand closed over her arm—zap. Like a light tap with a live electrical wire.

Seriously. This could not be happening.

She gritted her teeth and faced him. "What?"

"I'm leaving, don't worry." He spoke quietly now, in a low, burned-sugar voice. And he still had hold of her arm. In fact, he showed no inclination to let go. "I'll get out of your way…"

By a sheer effort of will, she ignored the scary sensations that were zipping through her and muttered drily, "Promises, promises."

"Just one thing…" His eyes were soft as kitten fur. Was he going to kiss her?

No way.

Gently, she eased her arm free of his hold and fell back a step.

There. Much better. She could breathe again. And the disorienting shivery feeling had passed. "Sure. What?"

"Tonight. The rehearsal dinner. I want you to come with me."

She frowned. "But… I already bowed out on that one."

"I know you did." Now he was all eager and boyish and coaxing. "Change your mind. Come with me. Pete and my mom will be there. And my brothers and Rose. And Erin, of course. And Erika. They're all crazy about you. It will be fun. And you can meet my cousins DJ and Dax, and their wives, Allaire and Shandie, and—"

"Ethan."

He blinked. "Yeah?"

"Is there something…going on with you?"

Now he was the one stepping back. At last. "Going on? What are you talking about?"

"Are you, um, putting moves on me or something?"

His mouth dropped open. "What the hell, Lizzie? What makes you think that?" He looked totally stunned at the very idea.

Which wasn't the least bit flattering and also made her feel like a complete idiot for even suggesting such a thing. Heat flooded up her neck. She just knew her whole face was as red as the jar of cherry juice she still clutched in her hand.

She set the juice on the counter and whirled away from him. "Um…" She pressed her eyes shut, hard, willing away her ridiculous blush as well as her own embarrassment at the whole situation. "Sorry. Never mind, okay? Just…forget I asked."

His hands, warm and so strong, closed over her shoulders—and there it was again, that quivery, scary feeling. She wanted to sink right through the floor. He said gently, "Lizzie…"

She asked again, "What is going on with you, Ethan?"

"Nothing. Come with me to the rehearsal dinner."

She shrugged off his hands and made herself face him once more. "Look, I have a lot on my mind and a lot to do, okay?"

"Well, I know. But you won't start on the cake until, like, the middle of the night or something, right? And you've got everything you need now to get the job done.

I just thought, you know, why not take a break, come out and see the family?"

He was right, of course. Now the problem of assembling equipment and ingredients had been solved, she could make it to that dinner, no problem.

But she still felt that he was up to something. Even if he wasn't putting moves on her. "You have some kind of plan. That's it, isn't it? You think that if you're relentlessly charming and helpful and drag me with you everywhere you go, I'm going to give in and decide I don't need to open my bakery, after all." She kept her gaze on his handsome face as she spoke. And she saw how he glanced to the side. Yeah, it was only for a second, and then he was meeting her eyes again. But that slight shift away was enough. She knew then that she'd hit the old nail square on the head. "Hah," she said. "That's it. That is exactly what's going on with you."

"No. Wrong. That's not true at all." His square jaw was set and his eyes flashed with annoyance.

"Don't lie to me, Ethan. I know what you're doing."

"How do you know that? Next you'll be claiming you can read my mind."

"We have an agreement. That's not going to change."

"It might." He smiled then. A slow smile. The smile of a man who never let anything stand in his way when he wanted something, a man used to getting what he wanted in pretty much everything eventually. "You never know."

"Ethan, are you listening?"

"Of course."

"I'll say it slowly. I'm not going to the rehearsal dinner, thank you." She exaggerated each word, just to make sure he understood.

He leaned against the counter and folded his muscular arms over his broad, deep chest. "And that proves… what?"

"I'm not trying to prove anything. I just don't want to go. I want to unpack these groceries and relax, go to bed nice and early. I intend to make Erin's cake spectacular. I consider it a point of professional pride."

"We both know it will be great because you're baking it."

"Thank you."

"Come on." His voice was soft again. "You have to eat dinner…"

"And I will. Here. Quietly. Alone."

"Oh, what? Like it's some kind of… Zen thing?" Now he was razzing her, pure and simple.

She kept her voice level when she answered. "Yes, Ethan. Let's call it a Zen thing—in fact, you can call it whatever you want. What you need to get through your head is that I'm not going with you to that rehearsal dinner."

"What if I said I wanted you there for professional reasons?"

"Well, that would be a flat-out lie. And I would still say no."

Those fine lips of his curled in what could only be called a sneer. "These are supposed to be *my* two months, remember? You're supposed to be doing what *I* want when I want it."

Now she was getting a little bit angry. "Suddenly, I'm your…indentured servant? Is that where you're going with this?"

He made a sound in his throat. An embarrassed kind

of sound. Good. He *should* be embarrassed. "Uh. No. No, of course not."

"Well, great. Because being your slave is not going to work for me, Ethan. Even though you're about the best friend I've got in the world, and I want you to be happy, *I* need to be happy, too. I like a challenge and I'm thrilled to go the extra mile and create this cake for your new sister-in-law. But I will not be dragged to that dinner just because it's part of your campaign to make me change my mind about what I want to do with my life. Do you understand?"

He no longer lounged against the counter. He'd drawn himself up straight. And for a moment, he looked as if he might continue the argument. But he caught himself. He raked a hand through that thick almost-black hair and muttered, "Gee, Lizzie. I didn't mean for you to get all het up."

She drew a slow breath and forced a wobbly let's-make-peace smile. "I'll say it once more. I'm not going. And can we be done with this conversation now? Please?"

Something hot and angry flashed in his eyes, his real feelings breaking the surface—and then vanishing again as fast as she had glimpsed them. "Gotta go," he said dismissively.

And he did leave, just like that. He went around her and strode out through the arch to the hallway. She longed to stop him, to try and settle things for good with him, to somehow put an end to this strange tension and unrest between them.

But at that moment, she didn't see how to settle anything. She told herself that at least she'd held her ground on the issue of the rehearsal dinner, that she'd explained to him—for the umpteenth time—that she *was* moving on and there was nothing he could do about it.

She decided, for now, just to let it be.

The rehearsal at Thunder Canyon Community Church started at four. Afterward, they all headed for the resort and the dinner in the Gallatin Room, which was the resort's best restaurant.

Ethan, as one of the groomsmen, attended both functions. At the dinner, he ended up with his big brother Dillon—the best man—on one side and his mom on the other. Both his brother and his mom asked him if something was bothering him.

He lied and said, "Not a thing," picturing Lizzie's obstinate face in his head, promising himself that one way or another, she was going to see the light within the next eight weeks and realize she loved her job with him and could never leave.

After the dinner, almost everyone wanted to call it a night to be fresh for the big day tomorrow. Not the twins, though. Jackson and Jason were raring to go. They had plans, plans that consisted of continuing the all-night bachelor party from the evening before. They headed down to the Hitching Post to listen to some live music and party some more.

Ethan went with them. Not because he was dying to party so much, but because he wasn't ready to go home. Home was where Lizzie was.

And tonight, that didn't seem all that welcoming a place.

Plus, he figured it wouldn't hurt to keep an eye on his younger brothers. They could get rowdy. Since Dillon had gone home with Erika, and Corey said he needed a good night's sleep because he was getting married the next day, that left Ethan to step up and keep furniture and glassware from getting broken. Not to mention that someone had to be the designated driver.

Jackson, especially, seemed intent on having himself the wildest weekend on record. He'd been blessedly silent for the toasts at the rehearsal dinner. But at the Hitching Post, he raised one full glass after another. He toasted the picture of the almost-naked lady over the bar. And he toasted man's freedom from apron strings and fancy weddings. He flirted shamelessly with every pretty woman in the place.

Ethan also met more than one good-looking woman that night. He flirted, too, a little. Why not?

But he didn't have the heart to ask a pretty girl if she might like to come on home with him. Since Lizzie had been making noises about quitting, he hadn't felt much like hooking up. Sometimes in life, even for a guy who liked women a lot, there were more important things than sex.

When the Hitching Post closed at 2:00 a.m., Ethan managed to coax his two liquored-up brothers into his SUV. They rolled down the windows and sang stupid drinking songs all the way up Thunder Mountain to the resort. It was past three when he finally got them into their rooms and down for the night.

Back at his house, everything was quiet and dark.

Lizzie would be awake within the hour, he knew, to get going on the cake. He considered waiting up for her, maybe brewing her some coffee so it would be ready when she needed it.

Maybe making peace with her…

But in the end, he only shook his head and climbed the stairs to the master suite.

There would be no peace with Lizzie. He knew that. Not while she was so set on leaving him.

Lizzie was up at four, as planned, and got right to work. She didn't see Ethan all morning. Apparently, it had been a long night and he was sleeping in.

Or maybe he was just avoiding her after their argument yesterday.

That was fine. She had a lot to do and no spare time for worrying about smoothing things over with him.

Everything went off without a hitch. She was putting the finishing touches on the decorations at one-thirty that afternoon.

The resort manager, Grant Clifton, was kind enough to send a van and a couple of big, strong guys to Ethan's house to pick up the wedding cake. They arrived at two. With Lizzie supervising, the guys got the cake into the van. One sat in back to protect the cake against any possible mishap during the drive. Lizzie followed them up the mountain to the resort.

She breathed a huge sigh of relief when they got the cake into the ballroom and onto the cake table without serious incident. A few of the gerbera daisies looked wobbly, though. Lizzie was carefully straightening them—each one with its stem in a tiny separate tube of water—when the bride appeared.

Erin Castro let out a cry of sheer joy. "Oh, Lizzie! I swear, it's the most beautiful thing I've ever seen!" She grabbed Lizzie in a hug.

Lizzie laughed and hugged her back. "I'm so glad it's what you wanted."

Erin hugged her harder. "What I wanted? It's more than that. It's…my dream cake."

As resort staff bustled around them, getting the ballroom ready for the reception that evening, Lizzie and Erin stood side by side, their arms around each other's waists, and admired Lizzie's creation. It was really quite something, each graduated tier white and smooth as driven snow, draped in fondant flowers and edible pearls, crowned with the bright-colored daisies.

"Perfect," said Erin.

"Good." Lizzie nodded. "My job here is done."

Erin turned to her again. "You know what? We really need you right here in Thunder Canyon."

"Need me? For what?"

"Corey told me all about your family's bakery in Midland. He said you're planning to open a new bakery there."

"Yes, I am."

"Well, how about opening one here instead?"

Lizzie was flattered. "I'm honestly touched that you think I'd fit in here."

"I don't think it. I *know* it." Erin turned and took both of Lizzie's hands. "I'm only saying, you know, just consider it, give it some thought?"

It wasn't going to happen. But then again, Lizzie was finding she really did like this charming mountain town and the people who lived in it. Why jump straight to an unqualified no? "Sure. I'll think about it."

"Great—and I've got to get moving." Erin grabbed Lizzie in one last hug. "Hair. Makeup. It never ends. So…six?"

"I'll be there. I can't wait."

* * *

Lizzie went back to the house, which she found empty.

Still no sign of crabby Ethan, which was fine. Until she figured out how to smooth things over with him, *and* make him see that he had to get real and accept that she was not giving up on her lifelong dream, well, there wasn't much point in dealing with him anyway.

They would only end up getting into another argument.

She went to work cleaning up the kitchen. And when that was done, she took a long, lazy bath. She put a lot of straightening gel in her hair, blew it dry and took a long time with the flat iron. It turned out great, falling in soft waves to her shoulders, smoother and sleeker than she'd dared to hope. She also lingered over her makeup, getting it just right.

Her dress was a vivid royal blue, sleeveless, with a V-neck and a swingy hemline. She had gorgeous dressy blue sandals with very high heels to go with it and some fabulous chandelier earrings with cobalt-blue stones.

Lizzie was a realist. She was no great beauty and she knew it; her nose was too big, her jaw a bit too strong. Her *maman* had been petite and lovely. Lizzie, though, took after her tall, broad-shouldered dad.

"Stand up straight, ma chère*,"* her *maman* always used to say. *"Be proud. There is no beauty like that of a tall, proud woman."*

Lizzie had always tried to take her mother's advice to heart. Tonight, in five-inch heels, she would tower over a good portion of the men at the reception. So be it.

When she checked herself out in the full-length mirror on the back of her bathroom door, she felt totally satisfied with what she saw. She twirled in a circle and loved the way the hem of her blue dress swung out around her.

Yeah, she would definitely do. With a last wink at her own image, she hustled into the bedroom to grab her blue satin clutch.

The light tap came at her door just as she was about to open it. Her heart rate accelerated at the sound.

Sheesh. No reason to get all breathless and fluttery just because Ethan had decided to be a gentleman after all and not make her go to his brother's wedding alone.

She pulled the door wide.

And there he was in all his gorgeous, manly splendor. Freshly shaved and showered, looking like a *GQ* cover model in a tux that must have cost a bunch. "Ready?"

She laughed and did a little twirl right there in the doorway and the dress swirled out around her like the petals of a flower. "What do you think?"

"You look terrific." He said it in a grouchy tone, but somehow also managed to sound as if he actually meant it.

"Why, thank you. You're not so bad yourself." She reached for his arm. He surprised her and gave it, tucking her fingers companionably just below the crook of his elbow, over the rich, dark fabric of his jacket.

Yes, she felt that thrill again, the hot little shiver that formed at the point of contact and kind of quivered its way up her bare arm, leaving goose bumps in its wake. But it wasn't so bad, really, now that she was getting used to it.

In fact, if she were honest with herself, she would have to admit that it felt kind of nice.

Wait. Scratch nice. It felt better than nice. It felt pretty wonderful.

* * *

It was the wedding of the year, everyone agreed.

Or at least, of the year so far.

Lizzie thought it was wonderfully romantic.

The handsome old, white clapboard church was decorated with thousands of bright summer flowers and every pew was full. Corey's brothers and stepdad stood up with him. And Erin's bridesmaids looked like summer flowers themselves, each in a different-colored bright satin gown. Erin was a vision in white as she floated down the aisle to meet her groom.

More than one sniffle could be heard from the pews during the exchange of vows. And an audible sigh went up when Corey finally kissed his bride.

The minister announced, "May I present to you Mr. and Mrs. Corey Traub."

Lizzie, in a back pew, heard somebody down the row whisper, "Who's that?" as the bride and groom turned to face their wedding guests.

"I don't know," was the murmured response.

Lizzie glanced over her shoulder to see a tall, lean man silhouetted in the open doors from the vestibule. He wore old jeans, a wrinkled shirt and a black Stetson with the brim dipped low, hiding his face, so that all she could see was a square jaw stubbled with beard.

More people were starting to whisper.

"What in the world…?"

"Never seen him before…"

There were rustling sounds everywhere as the guests turned to see what all the whispering was about.

The mystery man stepped back. He disappeared from the open doorway. And then Dillon Traub, the best man, came striding down the side aisle, slipping out after the stranger.

The organist started playing again and everyone faced front once more as the radiant bride and her handsome groom walked back up the aisle arm in arm.

The reception, in the flower-and-satin-bedecked resort ballroom, was fabulous, Lizzie thought. Dinner was served at eight.

Lizzie, as Ethan's de facto date, was seated with him and the rest of the wedding party at the main table. Everyone made a point to greet her and tell her what a splendid job she'd done on the cake.

Ethan seemed to have put aside his frustration with her, at least for the evening. It was almost like old times, she thought, like back before she'd ever even hinted that she might be moving on. He joked with her and they shared the knowing glances they used to share all the time.

She realized she'd missed their friendship lately, during the pitched battle over her right to define her own future. She'd missed the way they laughed at the same things, the way they could look at each other and know what the other was thinking.

Right after the food was served, she heard Pete Wexler asking Dillon about the mystery man who'd appeared at the back of the church. Dillon said something about a very old and dear friend who was "going through a rough time." Lizzie noticed the speaking glance Dillon shared with his wife. The look on Erika's face said she knew exactly what was going on with the guy in the black cowboy hat.

Lizzie waited for Pete to ask more questions.

But then Claudia, on Pete's other side, put her hand over Pete's and whispered in his ear. He turned to his wife. And the subject of the mystery man was forgotten.

Shortly after the exchange between Dillon and Pete, Ethan leaned close to Lizzie and said for her ears alone, "Help me keep an eye on Jackson, will you?"

"What's up with him anyway?" she asked. Jackson looked as though he'd had way too much to drink, even though the evening was just getting started.

"Basically, he's decided marriage is a crock," Ethan told her. "And he's been wasted pretty much straight through since Thursday night."

"Charming," she muttered, meaning it wasn't. Jackson had always been something of a bad boy, but tonight he had the look of a man about to cause a ruckus. "I'll watch him."

"Thanks." Ethan's voice was velvet soft.

She looked into his deep, dark eyes and thought how a woman could drown staring in those eyes—well, *some* women anyway.

But not Lizzie.

Uh-uh. She loved Ethan dearly, but as a friend and nothing more.

Or so she kept telling herself….

After the meal, before the toasts and the cutting of the cake, there was music. Corey led Erin out onto the floor in front of the long main table for their first dance as man and wife. Lizzie got a little misty-eyed just watching them; they looked so happy together.

As the floor filled with swaying couples, Lizzie visited with Erika, spent some time chatting with Ethan's mom and then with his sister, Rose.

Rose, who worked in PR for TOI in Midland, was

radiant in her apple-green strapless satin bridesmaid's gown. She said she loved it in Thunder Canyon and she was coming back the first week of July for a month-long vacation.

She sipped champagne, her long red hair shining in the light from the crystal chandeliers overhead, and she leaned close and whispered to Lizzie, "I know Ethan is mad that you're leaving, but don't let him get to you. I do wish you luck with your bakery. We all need to follow our dreams." When Lizzie smiled and thanked her, Rose added, "I have a dream myself. A couple of them, actually. I'd like to settle down right here in Thunder Canyon. And find the right guy to settle down *with*."

"Sounds like a great plan to me," Lizzie said.

"Too bad good men are so hard to find. I'm not getting any younger, you know."

Lizzie grinned. "You're barely thirty and you're a knockout. I have faith in you, Rose."

Rose dipped her pretty red head. "Why, thank you, Lizzie."

"But we'll miss you in Midland."

"Midland will just have to get along without me. I love it here." Rose raised her champagne flute in the general direction of a hot-looking guy who stood near the open bar not far from the entrance. She moved in closer to Lizzie and lowered her voice a notch. "See that guy over there? That's Hollis Pritchett, but everyone calls him by his middle name, Cade. Erin suggested I check Cade out—*and* his two brothers."

"Hey," said Lizzie. "Go for it."

"I intend to do just that," Rose replied. Then she stared out toward the dance floor and sighed kind of dreamily. "Aw, isn't that adorable?"

Lizzie followed the direction of Rose's gaze to see a man holding a small bundle in pink, swaying to the music.

"That's Jake Castro, dancing with his daughter," Rose said softly. "Her name is Marlie, I heard. She's just a few weeks old."

"So sweet..."

"Nobody knew Jake had a little girl. Until today. We're all wondering who the mother is..."

Lizzie remembered the mystery man at the back of the church. "Lots of interesting stuff going on around this town."

"Oh, yes, there is," said Rose with a wide grin. "It's another thing I love about the place. Never a dull moment, you know?"

Right then, a male voice shouted, very loud, "Hey, everybody. Everybody, hey!"

The music stopped. Lizzie turned toward the voice. She knew who it was already: Jackson.

He stood, weaving on his feet, in front of the cake table. He had his champagne glass raised high. "Listen up. And listen good. 'Cause I got somethin' important ta say..."

"Uh-oh," muttered Rose.

Lizzie hardly heard her. She was already on the move, working her way through the crowd toward the bad-acting young Traub.

"Marriage?" scoffed Jackson. "I don't like it, not one li'l bit. Marriage is jus' a way to tie a man down. What a man needs, above all, is his freedom!" Jackson blinked. He seemed to be having trouble focusing, which wasn't all that surprising. He had to be completely blasted. "Ladies and genemuns, I give you freedom!"

Right then, Dillon stepped up and muttered something in Jackson's ear.

"Quiet?" Jackson blustered. "Uh-uh. No way. You can't silence me. I got a whole lot ta say!"

By then, Dillon had reinforcements. Ethan moved in close and Jason, as well. Even the groom had left his bride and joined the group. Ethan said something and whipped the half-full glass of champagne from Jackson's fist.

That did it.

With a roar of pure fury, Jackson hauled off and punched him. Lizzie let out a cry.

But no one heard her. They were all staring in disbelief as Jackson delivered another blow—that one to Jason, right in the belly.

There was a loud "Oof" from Jackson's twin.

The brawl was on.

Dillon hauled back and busted Jackson in the chops. Ethan got in a good one, too. And Corey grabbed a vase of gerbera daisies from a nearby table and bopped Jackson on the head with it. The vase shattered. Water, glass and daisies rained down.

Jackson didn't even blink. He shook the water out of his eyes, let out a roar of outrage and popped the groom a good one.

Fists flew. For a few seconds, it was hard to tell who was hitting whom.

And then came catastrophe.

Lizzie watched in horror as Jackson, taking a well-placed blow to the chin, flew backward toward the table behind him and the beautiful, defenseless six tiers of pink-champagne, daisy-bedecked wedding cake.

Chapter 4

Claudia Traub shouted, “Boys! Stop this now!”

And poor Erin screamed, “No! Not my cake!”

And then, at the last possible second before the cake met its end, a miracle happened.

Somehow, Ethan managed to slide in between the airborne Jackson and the cake table. He caught his younger brother before he landed, and turned, redirecting the momentum of Jackson’s fall so it took them both sideways to the floor.

The table shook a little. A few bright daisies dropped to the linen tablecloth. But the cake, incredibly, remained whole.

Jason, still on his feet, was raring to fight some more. But his older brothers had more sense. Dillon grabbed him by one arm and Corey took the other.

“Easy, Jase. Ease it down now,” Dillon soothed.

By then, Lizzie had reached the danger zone.

She dropped to her knees beside the fallen Ethan and his troublemaking younger brother. "Ethan, are you okay?"

Ethan grunted. Jackson was sprawled on top of him. "Get this idiot off me." He gave a shove.

Jackson, with a groan, rolled off of Ethan and onto the floor.

Ethan scrambled to his knees. He wasn't trusting Jackson to not make more mischief. He had a tight grip on his brother's right hand and he pushed Jackson over all the way onto his stomach and shoved his captured fist up between his shoulder blades.

Jackson pounded the floor with his free hand and groaned again. "Hey, cut it out. That hurts, damn it!"

"You going to behave yourself now?"

Jackson muttered a few choice words. "Let me up."

"I'll need your promise that you're through busting up the place."

"Fine. All right. I'm done in."

Suddenly, Claudia was there. "Ethan. Now, now. It's all right. I'll look after him…."

Ethan scowled. "He's an animal, Ma. Watch out."

The fight seemed to go out of Jackson then. He went limp on the floor. "Awright, awright. I'll behave. I swear I will."

Ethan let go of him. "What a damn fool," he muttered as he stood. Shaking his head, he reached down a hand to Lizzie, who still crouched on the floor.

She took it and he pulled her up. As she rose and stood beside him, she had the craziest urge to throw her arms around him and kiss him silly.

But somehow, she kept her head. She said, "My hero! You saved the cake."

He threw back his dark head and laughed, drawing her closer, draping a big arm across her shoulders. Around them, more than one guest was laughing, too. There was even a smattering of applause.

Someone told the small band to start playing again. And everyone went back to dancing and visiting and whatever else they'd been doing before the fight broke out.

Claudia, grim-faced, helped Jackson to his feet. "Are you hurt, son?"

Jackson worked his jaw, pressed a hand to his ribs. "It only hurts when I laugh. Or breathe. Or talk."

"So shut up," Corey suggested. "At this point I wouldn't mind if you stopped breathing, too."

"Corey," said Claudia reproachfully. "It's enough."

By then, Corey and Dillon had let go of Jason, who had backed away a little and was hanging his head. Erin had run to her new husband. Erika stood with Dillon, her hand in his.

A guy in a resort uniform was cleaning up the broken glass from the shattered vase.

Pete stepped up and put an arm around his wife. "Well, boys, I have to say it. Looks like the Texas Traubs have officially arrived in Thunder Canyon. This town will never be the same."

The party lasted until late into the night.

It was after two when Ethan took Lizzie home.

He pulled the big, black SUV into the garage and turned off the engine as the door rumbled down behind them. Then he draped an arm on the steering wheel and turned to her. “It was fun.” His white teeth flashed with his smile.

“It certainly was.”

“How about some coffee?”

She felt good right then, about everything. He’d been so easy to be with all evening, not a single dark look or snide remark. It was as if she had her best friend back at last. “Sure.”

They went into the kitchen and she brewed the decaf. “Want a cookie?” She sent him a glance where he sat at the table. “I’ve got some white-chocolate chip and oatmeal-raisin, too.”

He shook his head. “Don’t tempt me. Two pieces of wedding cake’s my limit for one night.”

She turned and leaned against the counter as she waited for the coffee to drip. “Is Jackson…all right?”

He arched a dark eyebrow. “Other than being a total wild-ass crazy man, you mean?”

“I’m serious. I’ve never seen him quite so rowdy as he was tonight. I mean, he was pretty wasted. And starting a brawl at a wedding isn’t exactly what I’d call rational behavior.”

“He’s fine,” Ethan reassured her. “Going through a few changes maybe. But he’s tough. He’ll work out whatever’s bothering him, you watch.”

She gave a weary shrug. “If you say so…”

“Hey.” Ethan got up from his chair and came to her. He’d taken off his bow tie some time before and his snowy tux shirt was open at the neck. He looked totally relaxed and a little bit tired, and she found herself thinking what a great guy he was. A wonderful friend. The best boss ever. “Don’t worry about Jackson.” He stopped just inches from her.

And it was…a little overwhelming somehow—his standing so close that she could feel the heat of his body, with her backed against the counter.

Why should his being close bother her now? She'd danced with him at the reception. He'd put a companionable arm around her more than once during the evening, and it had all seemed so easy and friendly.

But now, alarms were going off inside her head. Maybe it was that it was just the two of them, alone in the quiet kitchen in the middle of the night.

Suddenly, his being close to her felt scarily intimate rather than fun and companionable. She hadn't even realized she'd tipped her head down to avoid staring into his eyes—until he touched her chin with a brush of his warm hand.

"Lizzie…" He whispered her name so tenderly, just the way a lover might. Reluctantly, she lifted her head. His eyes were waiting, dark and soft and tempting. A smile quirked one corner of his mouth. "Okay?"

She frowned. "About?"

"Jackson?" he prompted, his eyes lighting with amusement that she had already forgotten her concern for his wild younger brother.

She felt her cheeks coloring. Did he notice? "Uh, Jackson. Right."

"Don't worry about him."

"Well, okay. I won't."

His smile widened. "Good."

Behind her, the coffeemaker sputtered. "Coffee's ready," she said too brightly, bringing up her hands between them and pushing lightly at his chest. "And you're crowding me."

He seemed amused. "Can't have that." And he turned and went back to his chair.

The moment—scary, unreal and way too intimate—had passed. Lizzie suppressed her sigh of relief and turned to get down the coffee cups.

Lizzie in a blue dress.

Ethan thought she looked really good in that dress. Tall and strong and curvy. And so…capable.

How had it happened that he was starting to find "capable" downright sexy?

Strange. He'd always gone for more decorative women. Gorgeous, petite blondes with wide eyes and pouty lips, the kind of women who required constant pampering. High-maintenance women. Women nothing at all like Lizzie.

He would bring them home and Lizzie would cook them wonderful meals—meals they hardly touched to remain a size zero. The women he dated always liked Lizzie because she treated them gently. Kindly. With affection and real care. They always mentioned that she pampered them.

Ethan sat back in the kitchen chair. He watched her get down the cups and pour them each some coffee.

Friday afternoon, when he'd gotten so pissed at her for not going with him to the rehearsal dinner, she'd asked him if he was putting moves on her.

That she would even imagine he would do such a thing had shocked him at the time. After all, Lizzie meant the world to him in a number of ways.

But not in *that* way.

Or so he'd always thought. Until tonight.

Maybe it was the fear of losing her that had him

starting to see her in a different light. Seeing her as a woman—a woman who was attractive to him.

Not that he would ever actually do anything about this new awareness he had of her. Not that he would hit on her or anything. That would be beyond stupid. He really liked women, but he'd never gotten anything going with someone he worked with.

And he never would. It was not only a matter of principle, but it was also about common sense. Love affairs ended. Feelings got hurt. It became too uncomfortable, being around each other all the time. It got in the way of the job.

And then either she would quit, or he would have to ask her to leave.

He'd end up with exactly the result he was supposed to be knocking himself out to prevent: losing Lizzie.

Uh-uh. The point was to get her to see that working for him was something she wanted to keep doing.

But it sure was fun flirting with her, keeping her a little off balance, keeping her wondering what exactly he was up to.

She set his cup in front of him, carried hers to the chair across the table and sat down. She sipped, glancing up as she swallowed—catching him watching her. "What?" she demanded, a slight frown puckering the smooth skin between her brows.

He picked up his coffee. "Not a thing."

"I have an idea," Lizzie said at noon the next day, Sunday, when he came down for breakfast. She poured his coffee and set it in front of him.

"I just got up," he grumbled.

"I realize that." She stood at his side, already dressed

in jeans and a short-sleeved red shirt. The kitchen smelled of wonderful things. Muffins. Bacon. In fact, it had always seemed to him that *she* smelled of wonderful things. Any number of wonderful things—vanilla, chocolate, fresh strawberries, toasted pecans. Whatever she happened to be baking at the time.

"So where are the muffins?" he asked. "And can I have some bacon, please?"

"I've been thinking," she said, gazing down at him.

He grunted. "It's too early for thinking. Breakfast?"

"Just listen for a minute. Please?"

"Fifty-nine seconds, fifty-eight…"

She grabbed his shoulder, gave it a hard squeeze. "Say you're listening."

"Ouch. Stop. Okay, what?"

She let go. Strangely, he found himself almost wishing she hadn't. And she asked, "You're not going back to Midland, are you? This isn't a temporary thing, your being here. You're going to make the oil-shale thing work."

"No, no and yes. Breakfast? Please?"

She went to the counter, got the plateful of golden muffins, carried them back to the table and set them down. "Have a muffin." She went over and took the chair opposite him.

He grabbed a muffin and broke it in half. Still warm. He sucked in the fragrant steam that rose from the sweet, hot center. "Butter?"

She slid the butter dish closer to him.

He buttered the muffin, slanting her a put-upon glance, which she completely ignored.

She folded her hands on the tabletop. "So I was thinking that in spite of what we agreed on in Midland, you are really going to need someone when I go, at least at the office. In fact, maybe *two* someones. An assistant on the job *and* a housekeeper."

Because his plan was that she was going nowhere, he certainly didn't need to worry about who would replace her. But he couldn't say that to her as he had already agreed to let her go at the end of July. So he only grumbled, "What we agreed on is fine. I told you I would hire my own assistant. Now, about that food..."

Her hair was kind of wild around her face, the way it usually was at home. Lizzie had badly behaved hair. At the office, she tried to tame it, but it would always escape and get in her eyes or curl along the sides of her cheeks. Ethan found her hair totally charming.

Right now, though, her mouth had formed a grim line. The grim line wasn't very attractive. When she set her mouth like that, it usually meant she was about to lecture him.

Which was exactly what she proceeded to do. "You have to be realistic. You don't want to be without help work-wise *or* here at home. You're not going to like having to waste your time finding the people that I can easily find for you."

He knew exactly what she was doing. She'd realized she would feel way too guilty just leaving him high and dry with no one to step in and take her place.

What she refused to see was that he *wanted* her guilty, that he was completely shameless when it came to keeping her. If guilt would do it, guilt it would be. At least until she came to her senses and realized that staying with him was actually what she really wanted after all.

He said, "We've been through this. We have an

agreement. Just stick to your end of it and I'll stick to mine."

"But Ethan—"

"How about over easy?" He sniffed the air. "And is that home fries I smell?"

She made a low, growling sound and blew a loose strand of hair out of her eyes. "You are so obstinate."

"Lizzie, I'm starving here."

Her chair scraped the floor as she jumped up and hustled over to the stove. He reached for a second muffin.

Three minutes later, she set a plate of eggs, potatoes and beautiful, crisp bacon in front of him. "There. Shut up and eat."

He caught her hand before she could escape his side and said in the warm, low voice he usually reserved for the women he dated, "Lizzie, come on..."

She glared down at him. Her mouth had gone from grim all the way to mutinous. "I *am* leaving, Ethan. You might as well let me make sure you have what you need when I go." Her hand felt good in his. Strong. Not small, but still with a certain womanly softness. He thought how simple it would be to pull her down onto his lap. To silence her by covering her mouth with his.

But of course, he wasn't going to do that. It was one thing to be willing to play on her guilt, but it was another to get something started that could only end in a bad outcome for both of them. "What if what I need is you?"

She sucked in a sharp breath through her mouth, which was suddenly soft enough for kissing. He thought how good she looked, with her hair misbehaving and her lips slightly parted. But the kissable expression lasted for maybe only a second. Then she was scowling. "Let go of my hand, please." He did. She jerked it around behind her back, as if she feared he might grab for it again. And then she whirled and went to the counter, where she took her sweet time filling another cup with coffee. Finally, she turned, leaned against the counter and sipped. "You let me know if you change your mind about letting me find the right people for you."

"Will do." He got busy on breakfast.

She sipped some more, watching him eat. "I need to get to the store today. And then I thought I'd finish pulling the house together. I got kind of behind the curve when I took on Erin's wedding cake."

He wanted to ask how she could even consider leaving him. They were a great team and he was going to do big things. It was only going to get better from here on out—for both of them.

But all he said was, "Whatever you think. Try and get a little time just for yourself. Tomorrow, I'll need you up at the resort all day."

The next morning, Lizzie took her own vehicle up to the resort. That way, at the end of the day, if Ethan decided he wanted to hang around and do a little socializing, she would be free to take off.

Lizzie was there at 9:00 a.m. in the resort office when Ethan met with Grant Clifton, the general manager. Connor McFarlane, the resort's most recent major investor, was there, as well. Connor was heir to the exclusive McFarlane House hotel chain.

Grant, tall and lean with dark blond hair, was a local rancher-turned-businessman. Connor, who had dark hair and eyes and a brooding intensity about him, had recently married a local woman, a schoolteacher named Tori Jones. Tori, it turned out, was close friends with Allaire Traub, the wife of Ethan's cousin DJ.

Dillon stopped in at about nine-fifteen, just to make sure that Ethan didn't need him or have any questions for him. Lizzie knew that Dillon wasn't the only Texas Traub pushing for TOI to put money into the resort. Corey was, too. And he would no doubt have dropped by with Dillon—if he hadn't been off on his honeymoon.

They met in a conference room, the four men and Lizzie. For a while there was the usual getting-to-know-you chitchat about Thunder Canyon, about how Lizzie and Ethan were settling in at the house Ethan had leased, about family and friends. Lizzie played hostess, getting everyone coffee, passing the pastry around.

After an hour or so of visiting, Dillon left them. "Call me if you need me…"

Ethan promised he would.

They got down to business, poring over the extensive documentation Grant had provided, discussing revenues and expenses, income versus outlay. Lizzie had her laptop. She took detailed notes as the men worked, simultaneously keeping track of any messages or calls from Midland. For now, Ethan had to be available should Roger Jamison need his advice or guidance.

At lunchtime, they all went up to the clubhouse. They ate in the Gallatin Room and then Connor said he had to go.

He turned to Lizzie. "Great to meet you. You're already a heroine here in Thunder Canyon, whipping up that first-class wedding cake for Erin, saving the day at a moment's notice."

Lizzie laughed. “Hardly a heroine. I’m a baker, born and bred. I baked a cake. It’s what I do.”

“Well, my wife, Tori, said to be sure and tell you that if Ethan will give you an hour or two tomorrow, you should drop by the Tottering Teapot around noon. They serve lunch there—it’s all extremely healthy and organic. Homegrown produce. Everything natural, nothing with hormones or preservatives. And they offer about a thousand different varieties of tea. The women in town love it.”

“I’ll bet,” said Ethan in a tone that made it clear you wouldn’t be catching him at the Tottering Teapot anytime soon.

Connor chuckled at Ethan’s muttered remark and then added, “Allaire Traub will be there, too. And probably several other friends of theirs from town. They would love to have you join them.”

It sounded kind of fun actually. “I’ll see if I can sneak away tomorrow.”

“It’s easy to find,” Connor said. “On Main near Pine Street, in what we call Old Town.”

“We have Old Town and New Town,” Grant explained. “Old Town is the original town, built when the first settlers came here. It’s just east of Thunder Canyon Road. New Town is bigger. It’s farther east, where they started building, adding on as the town grew.”

Connor turned to Ethan. “I’m leaving tomorrow for several days of meetings at McFarlane House headquarters in Philadelphia. Didn’t you mention you were going to be traveling, too?”

Ethan nodded. “To Helena at the end of this week and Great Falls next week.” Lizzie kept track of his schedule. He would be working on oil-shale acquisition with those trips, negotiating the purchase of mineral rights to some large tracts of oil-rich shale lands.

And she would be with him, laptop and PDA at the ready, taking notes, making his life run as smoothly and efficiently as possible so that he could wheel and deal without getting bogged down in the details.

"When we're both back in town we should all make a day of it," Connor suggested, with a nod at Grant. "Let us show you the property."

Grant chimed in, "We can tour the golf course first, by golf cart. But for most of the property, horseback is the best way to go. You'll really get a feel for the land on the mountain. It's big. And it's beautiful. You do ride?"

"Yes, I do." Ethan had always loved to ride. He offered a hand to Connor and they shook. "A tour on horseback sounds good to me."

Connor left, after which Grant took Ethan around the clubhouse, all five stories and various wings. Lizzie followed along, taking notes.

There were several restaurants on-site, including the Grubstake for casual dining and also DJ's Rib Shack, which was owned and run by Ethan's cousin, the one and only DJ Traub. DJ owned the Rib Shack franchise, with rib restaurants all across the western United States. He was very successful. And he always joked that it was all because of his special secret sauce.

Beyond the Grubstake and DJ's and the Gallatin Room for fine dining, there was also the Lounge, which had a very masculine feel, all dark wood and leather booths and wing chairs. To Lizzie, the Lounge seemed like the kind of place where cattle barons should hang out, drinking whiskey, smoking fifty-dollar cigars and discussing range rights and the fluctuating price of beef on the hoof.

The spa, called the AspenGlow, was decorated in cool greens and soothing grays. It offered every variety of massage under the sun, along with facials and mud wraps and the usual hair, makeup and mani-pedis.

There was even a fully equipped infirmary, so that any guest who got sick or injured could receive immediate care. Dillon, who now ran a clinic in town, had filled in for the resort's regular doctor last year when he'd first moved to Thunder Canyon.

After the tour of the clubhouse, they got a quick look at the stables. The resort kept a number of horses for the use of the guests. Riding lessons were also available.

It was a few minutes before five and they were back at the clubhouse when Grant offered a drink in the Lounge before they called it a day. Ethan said he'd love a drink.

Lizzie took that as her cue to leave her boss and Grant alone for a little quality schmoozing time. "Well, all right, then. If you don't need me, I'll just—"

"Lizzie." Ethan reached out and hooked an arm across her shoulders, pulling her close against his side. "Come on, stick around. Have a drink."

Maybe she shouldn't have been shocked, but she was. Never in all the years she'd worked for him had he put his arm around her during working hours.

Yeah, okay. They were close friends. He'd put his arm around her several times the night before last, at Erin and Corey's wedding reception. But not at the office, not when she was wearing her admin-assistant hat.

It just wasn't done.

He was watching her face, smiling at her, a smile

that teased and challenged. He knew exactly what he was doing.

She wanted to elbow him a good one, right in the ribs. At the same time, she became intimately aware of the hardness of his body, pressed right up against hers. She not only ached to poke him in the ribs, but she also longed to turn in his arms, sighing, to slide her hands up the warm contours of his big chest and link them around his strong neck. To offer her mouth for his kiss.

But she didn't. Lizzie Landry was made of sterner stuff. She didn't jab him in the side and she didn't kiss him, either.

She held it together. "Sorry, I really can't." She ducked out from under his hold. And she sent Grant a grin, just to show the other man that she was in control and not the least fazed by the sudden too-friendly behavior of her boss. "I'm his housekeeper, too," she explained. "*And* his cook." Then she looked straight at Ethan again. He still wore that annoying, overbearing smile. "And I really need to start thinking about what to put together for dinner…"

"No problem," said Ethan. "We'll have a drink with Grant. And then I'll take you out."

Chapter 5

"This is not acceptable," Lizzie said under her breath as the host pulled out a chair for her in the Gallatin Room.

It was just Lizzie and Ethan by then. They'd had that drink with Grant and then Ethan had decided they might as well stay at the resort for dinner.

"Lizzie, Lizzie, Lizzie," Ethan chided from across the way-too-intimate corner table for two. "Come on, have a seat."

Reluctantly, she took the chair and thanked the host, who then handed her a lushly tooled leather menu that was practically as big as their table.

"Your waiter will be right with you," he said.

Ethan thanked him and he went away.

She lowered her giant menu and leaned toward the too-good-looking, totally annoying man across the table. "You keep saying you're not up to anything," she accused softly, in an effort not to broadcast her issues with him to the whole graciously appointed restaurant with its fabulous view of snowcapped Thunder Mountain. "And then you act like you're up to something."

He looked at her with reproach in those dark chocolate eyes. "I'm taking you out for a nice dinner after a long day of hard work. I'm only being an appreciative boss. Why would you think that I'm up to something?"

"Because you—"

He stopped her with a raised hand and sent a glance in the direction of the guy in the snowy-white shirt, black trousers and black vest who was approaching their table. "Our waiter's here."

Ethan ordered a very pricey bottle of Cabernet. The waiter left them. "Now, you were saying?"

"You know," she said pleasantly, "I think I'll wait to ream you a new one until we have the wine and our food."

He gave her that slow killer smile of his. "An excellent idea."

The waiter returned with the wine. Ethan tasted it, gave a nod of approval and the waiter poured. They both ordered filets and baked potatoes, with house salads to start.

Again, the waiter departed.

Ethan raised his wineglass. "To success in Thunder Canyon."

"I'm suspicious of just about everything you do lately." She lifted her glass, too. "But I see no reason not to drink to that."

"Lizzie." He pretended to look hurt. "Be nice."

"I *am* nice. Until you push me too far." She clinked

her glass with his and sipped. It was delicious, smooth and layered. “Really good,” she told him grudgingly as she set her glass back down.

He beamed in pride, as if he’d stomped the grapes himself. “I thought you would like it.” He sat back in the chair and studied her for a moment. She wondered what over-the-line move he was going to make next. But then he only asked the sort of question he often asked her when he was in the middle of deciding on an investment or an acquisition. “So, what do you think of the resort? Just your impressions after today.”

She glanced around the dining room. There was no one nearby to overhear her remarks. And she kept her voice low. “I think it’s a beautiful facility and I think Grant runs a very tight ship. From what I saw of the books, they’re doing better than they were a year ago. I think it’s impressive, the range and quality of services…”

He was leaning closer. “But?”

“It’s so ambitious. Not only the clubhouse and the endless array of high-end options, the shops, the spa, the three restaurants, the Lounge *and* the coffee bar. I noticed there are also condos up the mountain, and private cabins, too.”

“Yeah. And?”

“And it’s way out here in the middle of…” she hesitated. She really liked Thunder Canyon. Four days since they’d arrived from Midland. And already it seemed disloyal to say anything critical about the charming little town.

He prompted, “In the middle of nowhere. Right?”

She gave a low laugh. “That sounds a little harsh, doesn’t it?”

"I wouldn't call Thunder Canyon nowhere exactly. Tourists love towns like this."

"True," she said, meaning it. "It's the kind of place most people think doesn't exist anymore. The classic, homey, welcoming small town."

"And this is a destination resort," he reminded her. "That's supposed to be part of the draw, that you travel to get here, and that makes it more…exclusive. But I know what you mean. It's not that *easy* to get here. And with the economy still not exactly booming, well, luxury destinations are going to continue to take a hit."

She could always read him. "Still, you want to invest."

He took another slow sip of wine. "Am I that transparent?"

She shook her head. "Only to me. It's the price you pay for having someone who works side by side with you *and* lives in your house." It seemed a good moment to add, "Which is a good reason you might want to split the job again when I go, hire a housekeeper *and* an assistant. Get a little distance from the help. You don't need your employees knowing all your secrets."

His expression had changed, become blank. Unreadable. "I never minded your knowing my secrets. I trust you, Lizzie. Absolutely."

Tenderness welled in her. The thing was, she believed him. She knew very well that he trusted her. As she trusted him. Maybe not so unconditionally as she once had. Lately, her trust was a tiny bit shaky, because he'd refused to acknowledge her need to make her own way now, because he seemed to be putting the moves on her—and yet constantly denied he was doing that.

The waiter came with their salads.

The food provided an excuse not to say anything more for a few minutes, to let those dangerous tender feelings subside.

"Good, huh?" he asked.

"Excellent."

They ate in silence.

She tried to remember how pissed off she was at him. But it was difficult, when he talked about trusting her and she knew that he meant it. When she couldn't help thinking how generous and kind he was at heart, of the ways he'd been there for her when she'd desperately needed a helping hand.

Once, in the first few months that she worked for him, long before she started taking care of his house, when she was simply his assistant at the office and nothing more, her dad had been arrested for drunk driving. Ethan caught her crying at her desk and demanded to know what the problem was. She lied and said it was nothing.

He signaled her into his private office, shut the door, handed her a box of tissues and waited until she gave in and it all came pouring out. She confessed everything. That her dad had never been right after her mom died, that his heart was broken and he didn't know how to heal it. That he'd lost the family bakery while she was away at college and she'd never had any idea what was happening until it was all gone and they were broke. How her father had a drinking problem now and he'd just gotten a DUI. How they'd hauled him off to jail and she didn't have the money to bail him out.

Ethan told her not to worry. That he would take care of it.

And he did. He made calls and got her dad a good

lawyer. He paid for everything, made sure that Vernon Landry got community service and counseling rather than jail time. And when Lizzie insisted on paying him back, he told her she was a great worker and deserved a giant bonus exactly equal to the amount he had spent on getting her poor dad out of trouble. She signed that bonus back over to him and he said they were even.

Then, a year and a half ago, when her dad died of a stroke in his sleep, Ethan had been there, offering his broad shoulder to cry on. After the funeral, he'd given her three extra weeks off with pay and a vacation package to Hawaii. Her injured heart had started to heal there, on the wide sandy beaches under the palms.

Ironically, it was her dad's death that had made it possible for her to start planning on opening her bakery sooner than she'd ever thought could be possible. It had turned out that no matter how broke Vernon Landry had gotten, he'd always made the payments on his life-insurance policy. And Lizzie was his only beneficiary. Between the insurance payout and the great money Ethan had always paid her, she had what she needed now to make her dream come true.

The waiter cleared off their empty salad plates and brought the main course.

"You're way too quiet," Ethan said gently when they were alone again.

She swallowed a bite of tender filet, put on a smile. "Just…thinking."

His eyes were so dark, so deep and soft. "About?"

"The past."

"What about it?"

"Never mind."

"Lizzie…"

She gave him a long, solemn look. "You know exactly what you did, Ethan. You put your arm around me during working hours."

"Lizzie..."

"Don't *Lizzie* me. We have rules between us. Unspoken rules, but rules nonetheless. We never get chummy during working hours. But suddenly, you're throwing an arm around me in front of Grant Clifton, acting like I'm one of your girlfriends or something."

He didn't say anything. He only put down his fork, sat back in his chair and...watched her, a strange, unreadable expression on his face.

Although a hot flush flowed up over her cheeks, she made herself go on. "The other day, I asked you if you were putting a move on me. You denied it. You got all hurt and shocked-looking that I would even suggest such a thing. But still, since we've been here, in Thunder Canyon, you *have* been acting...differently toward me. You know you have."

He sat forward then, picked up his fork again, ate some potato. And then he took his knife and cut another bite of tender steak.

"Will you please just...say something?" She kept her voice low, but there was tension in it that she couldn't hide.

He took his time chewing and swallowing. Finally, he said with no inflection, "I apologize for crossing the line at work. I won't do that again."

"Great," she said tightly. And then she waited for him to continue.

He didn't. "More wine?" He refilled her wineglass even though she hadn't said yes.

The beautiful meal waited in front of her, almost

untouched. She picked up her fork and started eating again, her gaze on her plate because the last place she wanted to be looking right then was at the man across from her.

She felt so strange—edgy and angry. With Ethan, with the whole situation between them lately.

Was she being unreasonable, to want more from him in this exchange? He'd dealt with her issue, after all. He'd promised to keep his hands to himself during working hours, which was all she'd been going for when she started this uncomfortable conversation.

But no. Unreasonable of her or not, she was far from satisfied. He'd said nothing about his behavior the rest of the time lately, and his behavior had become seriously suspect. He darn well had to know that.

"Lizzie, come on, don't be mad at me," he finally said softly. Warmly. Gently.

She made herself lift her chin and face him. His dark eyes were waiting. He looked hopeful and worried. Was that how he actually felt? Lately, it was so hard to know with him. "I'm just…confused, that's all."

"Don't be. Everything will be fine. You'll see."

"Fine. What do you mean by fine?"

"I mean, it's all going to work out and there's no need to make a big deal out of nothing."

"Nothing. That's what's going on with you? Nothing?"

He picked up his wine but set it down without drinking any. "Look, it's just a crazy time, that's all. Everything's…changing. Maybe I'm a little on edge, okay? I'm sorry if it seems to you that I'm taking my problems out on you."

She set down her fork. It clinked against her plate.

"That is not what I said—or at least, it's not what I meant. I was talking about the way you're always getting close to me. I mean physically close. I was talking about the way you're always…flirting with me lately. The way you've been treating me like I'm one of your pretty little girlfriends when you know very well I'm not."

The hooded look was there in his eyes again. He lounged back in the chair, one muscular arm outstretched, his big hand resting on the snowy linen tablecloth. "Beyond working together, beyond what a great job you do keeping my house for me, we *are* friends, Lizzie. Good friends. We're… BFFNB."

"Uh. Excuse me?"

He gave a lazy shrug. "Best Friends Forever, No Benefits."

She blinked. "Where did you get *that?*"

"It doesn't matter where I got it. It's the truth, right?"

She shook her head. "How do you do that?"

"What?"

"Put me on the defensive when all I asked is why you're suddenly treating me like one of your girlfriends?"

Now he wore a look of endless patience. "I'm only saying that you never minded before if I was affectionate. I'm only saying, yeah. You're right. I shouldn't have put my arm around you while we were working—though if you think back, we were done working at the time, and talking about having a drink in the Lounge."

No wonder his girlfriends never lasted. He probably exhausted them by staying miles ahead of them in any argument. "You know, you could probably convince a stabbing victim that she shouldn't have gotten in the way of the knife."

"Lizzie." He gave her the melting-chocolate look from those amazing dark eyes. "What are you saying? You feel like a stabbing victim?"

"Of course not. I feel like my brain is going to explode before I ever get you to understand what's bothering me."

"But I do understand what's bothering you."

News to her. "Uh. You do?"

"Yeah. You think I'm flirting with you and you want me to stop. You don't like me flirting with you. You find it offensive."

"Wait a minute. So you admit you've been flirting with me?"

"And you find my flirting offensive."

"I didn't say that."

"So…you *do* like it when I flirt with you?"

Lizzie glared at him. And then she picked up her knife and fork for the third time. "Let's just eat. Let's just…move on. Okay?"

He tipped his head to the side and smiled in a wry way. "Sounds like a great idea to me."

The next morning at breakfast, Lizzie told Ethan she'd like to have lunch with Tori McFarlane and Allaire Traub at that tea shop Connor had mentioned the day before. "I'd like from about eleven-thirty to one-thirty for lunch. Is that too long?"

"Go," he said. "Have a great time."

"Thank you." She set down her coffee cup and gave him a warm smile.

He arched a brow. "Are you flirting with me?"

"Huh?"

"Well, Lizzie, I'm just trying to get clear on what constitutes flirting. Does a smile constitute flirting?"

"Uh, why are we suddenly talking about flirting?"

"Because I need to know. If you smile at me, are you flirting with me?"

"Well, Ethan, no. A smile is not necessarily a sign that someone's flirting with you—and I'm certainly not. You know I'm not."

"So how do you know if *I'm* flirting with *you?* Or if I'm not?"

She had the distinct feeling she was being cornered. And she had no idea how to keep it from happening. "I just… I know. That's all. I just know."

"So you *know* I've been flirting with you."

She scrunched up her nose at him. "I thought we settled this last night."

"Well, I'm just saying that you might think I'm flirting when I'm really not. Maybe I'm just being affectionate. Or friendly. Or maybe I just like you and so I smile at you—like you just did to me."

"Ethan."

"Yeah?" He slathered jam on his sourdough toast.

"It's one thing if you refuse to really talk to me about any given subject. It's another thing if you refuse to talk to me—and then bring the subject up again when I've already given up on it."

He frowned. "I have no idea what you're saying."

"You know what? At this point, neither do I."

"But if I kissed you, now *that* would definitely be flirting, right?"

"What are you getting at?"

"I've been thinking it over, that's all."

"Thinking *what* over?"

"Kissing you—and don't worry, it won't happen during working hours."

"Ethan!" She gaped. She couldn't help it.

He laughed, a low, deep rumble. "Don't look so shocked."

She knew her cheeks were hot-pink. She sputtered, "Well, it's just…that's not who we are."

"You know, I've been thinking about that, too. About who we are. About how really stupid it is to ruin a good thing—which we definitely would—with flirting and kisses." He paused. "With sex."

She felt breathless. "Well. Then, good. We won't, then. We won't, um, ruin a good thing." She could not sit still suddenly. She grabbed her unfinished plate, jumped up and carried it over to the sink.

Behind her, she could hear him. He had pushed back his chair.

He came toward her much too quietly.

She set her plate on the counter. And after that, she had no idea what to do next. Pretend he wasn't standing right behind her? Whirl and demand that he back off?

But that was the problem. She wasn't sure she really wanted him to back off.

The past few days, when it came to him, she wasn't sure of anything.

"Um. Ethan?" She spoke to the window over the sink that looked out on the side yard.

He touched her. He put his hands on her shoulders, clasping. And it felt so good. "You're trembling…"

Why deny it? "Only a little."

"Come on, Lizzie, turn around." He tugged on her shoulders, urging her to do as he asked.

And she did. She turned to face him. And she was way too aware of the warmth of him, the just-showered scent of him. His eyes found hers. Caught.

Held.

He clasped her shoulders again. “Everything’s changing.”

“Yes.”

“I’ve been lying to you, Lizzie, saying I accept that you’re leaving. I don’t accept it. I don’t want you to go.”

“I know.” Tears filled her eyes. Of all things. One got loose and dribbled down her cheek.

He said her name, so softly. With such beautiful tenderness. “Lizzie.” And then, “Don’t cry.” He touched her face with his thumb. He wiped that tear away.

“I’m not,” she lied.

And that was when he pulled her closer.

That was when his warm, firm mouth closed over hers for the very first time.

Chapter 6

Kissing Lizzie.

Ethan couldn't believe it. But it *was* happening.

And it felt so good.

He gathered her into him and he deepened the kiss. Enough to taste coffee and strawberry jam, to breathe in the warm, clean heat of her breath. She was…just Lizzie. Special and important and different from any woman he'd ever known. Firm and strong and tall in his arms. Substantial. And yet, soft, too.

Womanly in all the ways he had known she would be.

He framed her obstinate face with his hands, his fingers at her temples, brushed by her wildly curling, ill-behaved hair. Had he known her hair would be so soft? "Lizzie…"

And he kissed her some more.

She made a low, sweet noise in her throat, and she

kissed him right back. Eagerly, with the same sweet, passionate enthusiasm she gave to everything—from baking a six-tier wedding cake for his brother's wedding to arguing with him over whether he might have been flirting with her lately.

Their noses bumped. They both laughed.

And then the laughter faded. She pulled back a little. They stared at each other.

He held her by the waist then. And she had her capable hands on his shoulders.

"Oh, Ethan," she whispered. "What is happening here?"

He thought about all the reasons he shouldn't be doing this. All the ways getting intimate with her would ruin everything.

And then he thought that if she really was leaving, well, it was ruined anyway. That he would have to learn to get along without her. That August, after she left him, when she went back to Midland, was going to be hell.

Might as well have something really good to remember when she was gone.

But would *she* want that? Something temporary? Something they would both walk away from when July came to an end?

Somehow, that didn't seem like Lizzie, to have a temporary fling. Especially not with him.

Because, seriously, he wasn't her kind of guy. Lizzie went more for the solid-citizen type. She went for the guy who was looking for the right woman to settle down with, to raise a family with.

Ethan liked his life the way it was. No strings. No commitments, lifetime or otherwise.

He said, "I don't know what's happening." And he

realized he meant it. One moment, it all seemed so clear to him, that he should keep his hands off her, that getting intimate with Lizzie was the kind of uncharted territory he had no right to explore.

And then the next moment, he found himself thinking that he'd go nuts if he couldn't touch her, if he couldn't find out what it would feel like to kiss her.

"So...what should we do?" Her eyes were so green right then. So wide. And her mouth was soft, perfect for kissing.

And then he was thinking, well, why not? He'd already kissed her once.

And he really, really wanted to kiss her again.

"Ethan?" Her eyes searched his face. "I—"

"Shh. Don't talk. Not right now."

"Ethan..."

He took her mouth again. He simply could not resist. And she didn't pull away. She made a soft, surprised little sound. And then she surrendered—to him. To the moment. To...this thing between them that had always been one thing and now was becoming something else altogether.

Something magic. Something scary. Something he had never in a thousand years expected to happen with her, with Lizzie, who was the finest damn assistant he'd ever had, his favorite all-time cook and housekeeper. And most important of all, his best friend.

She kissed him back, reluctantly at first, and then with a lost little sigh as she gave in to him, to the moment. She parted her lips for him so he could taste her more deeply.

He could have gone on like that into next week. Holding Lizzie. Kissing her...

But too soon, she put her hands against his chest. She turned her mouth away from him. "Ethan…"

He knew he'd pushed her about as far as she was going to go. "All right." He loosened his hold, but couldn't quite bring himself to let go.

She did that for him, taking his wrists and peeling them away from the firm curve of her waist. Cradling his hands between hers, she held his gaze. "The more I think about this, the more I think it's not a direction you and I should be going."

"So don't think."

She laughed then, a wry sound. "Of course that would be your advice on the subject."

"I like to live in the moment."

"No kidding. But I really do think we need to…forget what just happened, forget it and move on."

He stepped back, giving her the space he knew she needed right then. And she let go of his hands. He echoed glumly, "Forget it and move on…"

Her gaze didn't waver. "That's what I said."

He didn't like the turn things were suddenly taking. He didn't like it at all. "Oh, come on, Lizzie. I kissed you. You kissed me back. We can't un-remember that."

"We can pretend to. We can *behave* as though it never happened."

He wished she was joking, but he knew that she wasn't. "That's what you want, really? To pretend it never happened?"

"That's what I want, yes."

He realized he was furious with her. So he spoke very softly, with cold, precise care. "Well, all right, then. Fine with me. You got it. I'll give you exactly what you want."

* * *

About a half an hour later, they went up to the resort in their separate cars.

The morning was similar to the day before. They met with Grant. Ethan had questions and Grant answered them. There was more in-depth study of the accounts, more discussion of what areas needed more investment and where corners might be cut.

Lizzie did her job and wished she were anywhere else but there, near Ethan. She was just too…aware of him now. She kept thinking of how lovely it had felt, to be held in his arms. How tender and perfect his kisses had been. She kept doing exactly what she had told him she wouldn't do: remembering in aching, perfect detail, every sigh, every touch, every word that had passed between them at breakfast.

He'd been right, of course. She couldn't un-remember that she had kissed him. And it was going to be close to impossible to pretend that nothing between them had changed.

Plus, he was seriously pissed off at her. Oh, he was civil enough. He treated her with calm professionalism, just like any good boss would. But she knew that closed-off look in those dark eyes of his. He was angry at her for wanting to put the events of the morning behind them.

At least Grant didn't seem to notice that anything was different. Lizzie was grateful for that.

The morning seemed to last forever. But finally, at 11:30, she had her chance to escape. She left the men in the conference room and drove back down the mountain into town.

In town, she found a parking lot tucked into the corner where Thunder Canyon Road turned sharply and became Main Street. The lot serviced both a motel called the Wander-On Inn, and the Hitching Post, the bar where Ethan had attended Corey's bachelor party. Lizzie parked in the lot and walked to the restaurant.

It was a cool, sunny day. Perfect for a stroll. The buildings were old, mostly of brick. They'd probably been there since the turn of the previous century, and then refitted to make the current shops and stores that lined the cute, old-timey street.

She found the restaurant a couple of blocks down from where she'd left the car. It had *The Tottering Teapot* painted in green-and-pink flowing script on the wide front window, which was hung with old-fashioned lace curtains on café rods.

Inside, the tables were all different sizes, covered in antique lace tablecloths, no two the same. Even the chairs were all different shapes and styles, as though the place had been furnished from any number of yard and estate sales.

Petite, pretty Allaire Traub sat at a table for five near the far wall with one other woman, a brightly dressed strawberry blonde, at her side. Allaire signaled Lizzie over.

"You made it." She jumped to her feet and pulled out a chair. "Lizzie, this is Tori McFarlane."

Lizzie greeted Tori and took the chair Allaire had offered. A few minutes later, Haley Cates joined them. Haley ran a youth program called ROOTS in a storefront Lizzie recalled passing on her way to the restaurant. The women explained that they usually met Mondays for lunch. But this week, Allaire couldn't get away until Tuesday, so here they were.

"You're welcome to join us," said Haley, "right here at the Tottering Teapot, most Mondays at lunchtime."

"Consider it an open invitation," Allaire added with a glowing smile.

They ordered from the hand-lettered menus, and their sandwiches arrived on beautiful old plates in floral-and-blue Delft and gold-leaf patterns. The dishes and flatware didn't match any more than the tablecloths or chairs did. Every piece was different. The place was cozy, friendly and unpretentious. Lizzie felt instantly welcome there.

She liked the three women, too. She learned how Haley had married a former town bad boy, Marlon Cates. She also found out that Allaire was an art teacher and Tori taught English. Tori and Connor planned to stay in Thunder Canyon through the next school year so that Connor's son, CJ, could finish high school at TC High.

"But McFarlane House headquarters are back east," Tori said. "We'll probably make Philadelphia our home base as soon as CJ's in college."

Allaire and Haley swore they weren't letting Tori go. But Tori only smiled at them and said she loved them dearly and would be back to visit often.

Rose Traub had told Allaire about Lizzie's plans to open a bakery in Midland—and Allaire had turned right around and told all her friends.

"And we've been thinking…" Allaire announced with a knowing grin.

Haley finished for her "…that you ought to stay here and open your bakery in Thunder Canyon."

Lizzie laughed. "You know, Erin said the same thing

Saturday afternoon, when I delivered her wedding cake to the resort."

"Well, you ought to listen to Erin," said Haley. "We really need someone like you, someone approachable and easy to get to know. Someone we like."

"Someone dependable," added Allaire.

Tori said, "The guy who owns La Boulangerie—the bakery a block down, at Nugget and Main?—he's a great baker. Croissants you would kill for, no kidding. But he's not a friendly guy. And then look what happened last week? He just up and vanished without a word to anyone. Luckily, you were here to save the day for Erin. But the bakery's been shut up tight ever since. That leaves the doughnut shop in New Town, the one Starbucks on North Main and that other chain bakery in the mall. Old Town needs a real artisan bakery."

"He's French, the runaway baker down the street," said Haley with a frown—and then caught herself. "Not that there's anything wrong with being French."

Lizzie laughed. "I'm glad you qualified that. My dear *maman* was French. And my dad was of French extraction."

"Well, the baker down the street was not a happy Frenchman," said Tori. "I think he had a girlfriend for a while, though, didn't he? He seemed a little happier then."

"That's right," said Hayley. "That pretty, dark-haired woman. French, too, as I remember. I wonder if she went with him…."

"No clue," said Allaire. "But you, Lizzie, you're fun *and* talented. And clearly super-dependable, too. Everyone knows that Ethan is going to be lost without you. You've totally spoiled him, and that's a fact."

Ethan. Just the mention of his name made her feel sad and tense and worried. And a little bit breathless, too. The swirl of emotions was pretty overwhelming.

Oh, what was she thinking to let him kiss her—and then to go and kiss him right back?

She said, rather feebly, "Oh, I'm sure he'll be fine."

Allaire made a low, disbelieving sound. "Corey once said that Ethan couldn't keep an assistant until you came along. They all ended up falling in love with him, pining over him all day instead of doing their work."

"I'd say that's something of an exaggeration." Hah. And now she was just like all the others. Feeling breathless and tortured at the very mention of his name.

"Well, I know he'll miss you," Allaire said. She went on, "And I mean it. If you decided to stay here, you would never regret it. Your bakery would be a success from the first day you opened the doors for business. You can count on us to make sure of that."

Tori and Hayley both nodded enthusiastic agreement.

Of course, Ethan's cousin and her friends were just being welcoming. But still, Lizzie found the wild idea kind of appealing. She did like Thunder Canyon. The country was spectacular and everyone was so friendly and easy to get along with.

But no, her plans were already made. "Sorry. I'm flattered, but I'm a Midland, Texas, girl through and through."

"Think it over," said Allaire. "That's all we're asking."

"Yeah." Tori sipped her tea. "There's no law that says you can't change your mind."

* * *

After she said goodbye to the others outside the restaurant, Lizzie had half an hour before Ethan would expect her at the resort. She was not in a hurry to spend the rest of the day at his side valiantly pretending nothing had changed between them.

So she dawdled a little. She wandered farther down the block to get a look at the Frenchman's deserted bakery.

What could it hurt, after all, to look?

La Boulangerie had a storefront much like the one that housed the Tottering Teapot: an old brick building with wide showcase windows in front and a glass-topped door of heavy dark wood. Lizzie pressed her face against the window glass to see inside.

It was nice in there, with wide-planked floors, a few tables so people could eat their treats right there, lots of shelving, the usual long glass-cased counters. She admired the gorgeous old espresso machine and a quality bread slicer. She'd really love to get a look in the back, see what the prep space was like….

Just out of curiosity, she took the alley between the bakery and the building next door. Through a window on the side wall, she got a limited view of steel tables, of rolling racks, of a couple of handsome-looking proofers—sealed steel boxes that kept yeast dough at optimum warmth and humidity. She saw two high-capacity ovens and the shiny steel doors of refrigeration units. The floor mixer was a Hobart and there was a nice, big counter mixer as well, also a Hobart, which was arguably best of the best when it came to professional mixers.

She went on to the back, where she found parking.

Plenty of it. There was a rear entrance with a steel door. No windows back there, not on the ground floor. But double-hung windows gleamed high up the brick wall. An iron fire escape zigzagged down from the roof, with a landing under the windows.

Was there an apartment up there? She smiled to herself. A baker got up early. Life would be easier if she lived above her shop.

And what would that be like, to live above her very own bakery on Main Street in Thunder Canyon, Montana?

Was it possible that the runaway French baker might be planning to sell? If he hoped to come back to town and pick up where he'd left off, she wished him a whole lot of luck. People weren't happy with the way he'd behaved.

And if he did end up selling, well, she could probably get the business and all the equipment at a really good price. Quality equipment was so expensive. The Hobart Legacy floor mixer alone would cost her upward of fifteen-thousand dollars, new....

And then she shook her head.

It was just a pleasant fantasy, really, nothing she would ever actually do. In Midland, she had her eye on a couple of locations. She had to admit, though, that neither of those was quite as attractive as this one.

But still, the whole idea was to re-create the family bakery she had lost. And that bakery belonged in Midland, Texas.

Plus, if she did decide to relocate here, she'd be living in the same small town as Ethan. That would be difficult. She'd been kind of counting on cutting it clean with him, on giving them both some serious distance while they each grew accustomed to life on their own.

Life on their own.

Sheesh. As if they were an old married couple or something—an old married couple calling it quits.

She glanced at her watch.

Yikes. Time had gotten away from her. She was going to be late getting back to the resort. So much for daydreaming—and trying to put off being around Ethan again, to delay the upcoming afternoon of playing it as if everything was business as usual.

When, in reality, it had all gone so wrong.

Ethan sat in the comfortable leather conference-room chair and tried to pay attention to Grant's really excellent PowerPoint presentation. He had a tall glass of mint-garnished iced tea at his elbow served by Grant's assistant right after they'd returned from a nice lunch in the Lounge. Ethan also had a pen and a notebook close at hand, should he feel the need to jot down a note. Hell, he had his PDA right there and could use it if the pen ran out of ink.

He really did *not* need for Lizzie to be there.

It was just that she was *supposed* to be there. But she wasn't. She was late. And Lizzie was never late.

Until today.

Ethan didn't like it. He'd given her two full hours for lunch. She'd agreed to be back at the resort and on hand in the conference room by 1:30. It was now 1:45. Annoyance moved through him, a prickly, uneasy feeling, like bees buzzing under his skin.

Was she all right? Had she been in an accident or something?

The very thought that something bad might have happened to her scared him to death. So he decided not to think about that.

No. She was fine. He was sure of it. He focused on his annoyance with her for being late, in order to keep from imagining that she might be in trouble.

It was…the principle of the thing. He paid her a fortune—especially if you counted that bonus she was getting at the end of July when she left him high and dry to go bake cupcakes for a living—and the least she could do was to be there, ready to work if he needed her for the too-short time she remained in his employ.

Grant began clicking through a series of images showing construction of the just-completed golf course, which had been started three years ago and put on hold for twenty-four months when the economy soured. "But we finished work on it this year, as soon as the snow gave us a break. And the grand opening two weeks ago brought in golfers from all over the country. It's not a large course, but it's a beauty and it really is a necessity for a year-round resort destination."

The conference-room door opened silently. Ethan wouldn't even have noticed it if he hadn't had his head turned so he could see the door from the corner of his eye.

Lizzie slipped in.

Grant sent her a smile. "Lizzie."

She gave Clifton a small wave and took her place at the long table.

Ethan let his gaze glide dismissively past her. "About time."

He was going to have a word with her about her lateness—this evening at dinner, as a matter of fact.

Yeah, okay. He'd been thinking he would eat out,

get away from the house and the tension between them, maybe try the Hitching Post. He could get a beer and burger there. Plus, he might meet someone pretty and friendly and available, someone who wouldn't make a federal case out of a few innocent kisses.

But on second thought, no. He'd eat at home and he'd get it clear with Lizzie that as long as she was his employee, he expected her to be on time.

At four, as they were wrapping up for the day, Grant asked Ethan if he planned to be back in town week after next.

When Ethan said yes, Grant suggested they go for that golf-cart and horseback tour of the property that Connor had mentioned the day before. "How about if I set it up for Tuesday, the twenty-first? Be here at the offices, dressed for riding, at nine. We can change the date if that doesn't work for Connor. I'm sure he would really like to go along."

"The twenty-first is fine," Ethan said. "But I'm flexible. Let me know if another day would be better."

Grant promised he would. The men shook hands.

Ethan and Lizzie left the offices. Out in the parking lot, he made a point of not speaking to her. She didn't say a word to him, either. They got in their separate cars and headed down the mountain.

He almost went to the Hitching Post anyway. He could use a drink in a friendly atmosphere. And then he could go home for dinner and tell Lizzie he didn't appreciate her wandering back to work whenever the mood suited her.

But he had some calls to make. He needed to touch base with his mom and with Roger, to check in with the

Midland office and make confirmation calls to Helena and Great Falls. So they ended up caravanning to the house and pulling into the garage side by side.

In the house, she actually spoke to him. Coolly, without so much as a hint of a smile. "Will you be eating dinner here tonight?"

"Yeah. Seven?"

"I'll have it ready."

"Good. I'd like a Maker's Mark, rocks, in my office at six-thirty."

"You got it."

He left her and went to his study, where he shut the door and picked up the phone.

After the calls, he took off his tie and undid the top buttons on his shirt and went over the spreadsheets Roger had emailed him from Midland.

Lizzie tapped on his door at six-thirty exactly.

"It's open," he said in a flat voice.

She brought in his drink and set it on a coaster by his desk blotter without once meeting his eyes. He waited to reach for it until, silently closing the door behind her, she left him alone again. Then he grabbed the glass, knocked back a healthy shot and hoisted his tooled boots up on the side of his desk. The whiskey burned a satisfying trail down his throat. He braced the glass on his stomach and studied his boots. Usually, kicking back at the end of the day with his boots up was a very satisfying moment for Ethan.

Not today, though. And all because of the tall, wild-haired muffin maker in the kitchen.

He had another fine, smooth sip and he asked himself, was he overdoing the lord-of-the-manor routine just a little?

Okay, yeah. Maybe.

But damn it, now he not only had to accept that she really was deserting him, but he also had to let her go without going where he'd just discovered he really wanted to go with her—namely, the nearest bed.

Five years she'd been with him, day in and day out. And until a few days ago, he'd never had the slightest clue that he wanted her. That was pretty damn strange, if you thought about it. Pretty…unsettling.

But still, he was willing to work with the strangeness of it all. He was willing to get past the unsettling nature of the whole thing. He could just accept that he wanted Lizzie. It was a fact and he was ready to deal with it.

But not Lizzie. Oh, no.

Lizzie wasn't willing. Uh-uh. Lizzie had told him right to his face that she wasn't kissing him again. She wasn't… going in that direction with him. She even wanted him to *un*-remember that he'd kissed her in the first place.

It was insulting. Seriously. He wasn't a bad guy. As a rule, women *liked* him. They *really* liked him.

Okay, he knew he wasn't Lizzie's type, the looking-to-settle-down type. But still. She could make an exception just this once, couldn't she?

After all, she wanted him, too. There was no faking the way she'd kissed him that morning—and she wasn't the kind who faked it anyway. Why couldn't she just let nature take its course? It could be really good for both of them.

Ethan swung his boots to the floor and stood from the high-backed leather swivel chair. Enough of this sitting here, stewing over this whole annoying situation.

He had a few things to say to her. And now was as good a time as any to say them.

Chapter 7

"Lizzie," Ethan said.

Lizzie felt a shiver down her spine. She had her back to him. She paused in the act of slicing sweet peppers for the salad and waited for what he was going to say next.

But he didn't say anything. Only her name, in that low, rough tone that brought to mind some hungry wild animal, growling with his lips curled back. A wild animal showing sharp, mean teeth in that moment right before he went for the throat.

"What can I get for you?" she asked brightly, setting down her paring knife and turning to face him where he lounged in the doorway. He had one big arm crossed over his middle. The other was straight at his side, his half-finished drink dangling from his fingers. She tried again, "Refresh your drink?"

He just looked at her, a look that managed to be both furious and lazy at once.

She refused to let him see that he was getting to her. Cheerfully, she informed him, "Dinner's almost ready." The prime rib was out of the oven, resting on the cooktop. She had the potatoes whipped and the green beans buttered and waiting in a covered serving dish.

He raised the glass, deftly shifting it so that he cradled it in his big palm. And he took a slow, thoughtful sip. "You were late today, after lunch."

She had known that was coming. "Yeah." She grabbed the hand towel on the counter beside her, wiped her hands, set it back down again. "I'm really sorry. I let the time get away from me."

"Two hours wasn't enough for lunch?"

She let a long pause elapse before answering that one. "Two hours was more than enough. I appreciated the extra time. I should have made it back when I said I would. I really do apologize. It won't happen again."

"See that it doesn't."

Okay, now he was really starting to annoy her. She asked with excruciating civility, "Ethan, how many times have I been late back from lunch—or at all—in the years that I've worked for you?"

He sipped his drink again, then studied the glass. "You know, I think I *will* have another drink."

It was too much. "Will you please have the courtesy to answer my question first?"

He shrugged. "You're right. You're never late. Until today."

"I'm so pleased you're aware of that. And I have apologized for today. Can we be done now with beating that particular dead horse?"

"Sure." He held out his glass.

They glared at each other. It was such a tacky power play, his insisting that she get his drink. As if he couldn't stroll on over to the wet bar in the family room and get his own damn refill.

But fine. All right. She *was* his housekeeper, and getting his drinks was her job. With a hard snort of disgust, she marched over to him and took the glass. He remained there, lounging in the doorway.

"Excuse me," she said in a tone that made it more than clear she would love to throw what was left of that drink right in his smug, too-handsome face.

"Oh. Sorry." He straightened enough that she could slip past him.

She marched into the family room, poured him another and returned to the kitchen, where he had yet to budge from the doorway. "Here you go."

"Thanks." He took the drink.

She eased around him again and returned to the counter, intent on serving him his meal and then leaving him alone to have his prime rib by himself. She picked up her paring knife and glared at the red mini-pepper waiting on the cutting board.

Behind her, he hadn't moved. And this was ridiculous. A farce. She wasn't putting up with this treatment for one more minute.

She slapped the knife down, turned on him again and folded her arms tightly across her stomach. "Ethan, you're being a complete ass. You know that, right?"

He scowled at her. "Oh, great. Now I'm an ass."

"Yes, you are." She softened her tone a fraction. "And being an ass is not like you. As a rule, you're a good, kind man. A fair man."

He had nothing to say to that. He only straightened from the doorway and went to the table, where he yanked out his usual chair and dropped into it. She'd already put his place setting there. He sipped his drink and set the glass on the corner of the place mat. His was the only setting. He gestured toward the empty spot across the table. "What is that?"

She only stared at him.

And he said, "Look, I get it, okay. I finally get that there's nothing I can do to keep you from leaving. But I don't get why you won't sit down at the damn table and eat your dinner across from me. That's just…well, that's plain mean, Lizzie. You know that it is."

She felt sorry for him suddenly, all her righteous anger with him drained away. She said gently, "Ethan, come on. The way you've been behaving today, why would I want to sit down and share a meal with you? Trying to eat my dinner with you sitting there glaring at me, it's a surefire prescription for indigestion, you've got to know that."

He slumped back in the chair. "Okay. All right. I'll behave, I promise. Just…set yourself a place, and please, can we eat?"

She studied his face for a long time, feeling all tender and sorry and sad. And then, finally, she nodded. "Just a few minutes."

"Great." A weary smile. "Thanks."

So she finished cutting up the salad and brought it to the table. He carved the roast for her and brought over the meat platter as she put the au jus in a gravy boat and set out the green beans.

The buzzer went off to let her know the yeast rolls

were ready. She transferred them to a breadbasket. "Wine?"

He shook his head. "You?"

"Not tonight."

They sat down, passed the food to each other and ate in silence for several minutes.

Finally, with care, she set down her fork. "Ethan…"

He looked up from his plate. "What? I'm behaving."

Fondness washed through her. "It's not about that."

"Then what?"

"I just want to say, in case it might be better for you, that I don't *have* to stay on until the end of July. If you're finding it hard to… I don't know, be around me now, it's okay. I understand. I could go back to Midland and see about finding you a new assistant. Or I could find one for you here. Or I could just, well, go."

He set down his fork, too. He sat very still, watching her, his eyes so dark, his expression somber. Then, very softly, he said, "No. Please. Don't go. Stay. I don't want to give you up until I have to. And don't…find me your replacement. There is no one who can replace you."

She suddenly felt misty-eyed. "Oh, Ethan…"

"I'll deal with the problem when I have to, when you're gone. But until then, do me a favor. Just keep on as we have been, help me to get started here in Thunder Canyon. That's what I want for now, that's what works best for me."

There was a definite pressure at the back of her throat, the tightness of tears rising. She swallowed them down. "It's meant so much, really. To work for you. To… be your friend. When you first hired me, I hardly knew where my next meal was coming from. I'd gone off to college secure that I had a home and the family business to return to. But when I got back, it was all gone. I was so scared, Ethan. For myself. For my poor, lost father. But you gave me a job. You gave me…a chance. And I got to find out how really capable I am. And not only that, you bailed my dad out of jail, you made it so he could get some kind of life back when I was pretty much certain he would never find his way to anything resembling peace or stability. And when he died, you were the one who was there for me. I *am* grateful to you, in a thousand ways. But I have to live my life for me, you know?"

His Adam's apple bounced as he swallowed. "I know."

"I can't stay with you if you're just going to be mean and cold to me. As much as I care about you, I'm not up for taking a lot of punishment from you for the next seven weeks. That wouldn't be good for either of us."

"I hear you," he said, his voice low and rough. "I was out of line and I know it. I'm having a little trouble getting it in my head that there's no way to change your mind about going."

"I know."

"And then there's the rest of it," he said gruffly. She took his meaning: the sudden, surprising attraction between them. "Seeing you in this different way. It has me all turned around sideways, with my head spinning."

"I know the feeling," she confessed in near-whisper.

He picked up a yeast roll from the basket, broke it in half, met her gaze across the table. "I'm used to being interested in more…willing women."

She laughed then. "Oh, Ethan." And then she didn't feel like laughing at all. She felt that little curl of heat down low in her belly, just from staring into those beautiful eyes of his. "That would be too difficult for me. I don't do casual intimate relationships, or at least I never have. And I don't feel comfortable trying that out now."

His chuckle was lacking in humor. "And I *only* do casual."

"Exactly." She gazed at him and he stared back at her and all at once, she was recalling one of the many times he'd broken up with his latest girlfriend because he said the woman was getting too serious.

"I don't do serious," he'd confided in Lizzie over a cup of decaf the night of the breakup. "I never will."

She'd rolled her eyes and told him to wait. Someday he'd meet someone really special and he'd want to get serious.

He laughed and said that was never going to happen. "Some men just don't do well in captivity. I'm one of those."

She got annoyed with him then, for equating a real relationship with captivity. She punched him in the arm and called him a bad name. He only laughed and then asked her reproachfully, "Lizzie, if I can't tell you the truth, who can I tell it to?"

"Lizzie?"

She blinked and brought herself back to the present. "Sorry. Just thinking."

"I won't be an ass again."

"I'm so glad to hear that."

"I'll keep it friendly, but not *too* friendly. Will that work?"

"Yes, it will." She forced a smile.

They picked up their forks and continued the meal.

A few minutes later, he said, "We should leave by

eight tomorrow morning. We've got a ten-o'clock meeting with a couple of land brokers in Helena."

"I'll be ready."

"It's a week and a half of being mostly on the move."

"I know, Ethan."

"So we're good, then? We're set?"

"We are, yes."

"Fair enough."

They spent Wednesday and Thursday in Helena and Friday and Saturday in Great Falls.

Sunday, they moved east. Ethan was buying up mineral rights in the more promising areas of the Bakken Shale, a large area of oil-rich shale land that covered over two-hundred-thousand square miles in Montana, North Dakota and Canada. A lot of the rights were already claimed, but if a company didn't make use of the rights, they expired. Ethan was on the trail of some of those expired leases, plus trying to get his hands on leases yet to be bought.

He also wanted to see some of the newer horizontal extraction equipment in action. They spent more than one day out in the middle of nowhere among giant, loud machines. She teased him about that. There was plenty of state-of-the-art equipment to see in Texas, after all. They also spent some nights in some not-so-attractive motel rooms in tiny towns with limited lodging choices.

But Ethan was in his element. It seemed to her that he was happier than she'd ever seen him. He loved being out in the wide-open, windy expanses of northeastern Montana, wearing old boots, a wrinkled shirt, a faded pair of Wranglers and a sweat-stained straw Resistol cowboy hat. He'd always dreamed of being a real, old-time oilman like his dad had been, back when the industry was wide-open and everyone thought the supply of black crude would never run dry.

One night, at the Golden Lariat Motel on the outskirts of a tiny town called Coyote Creek near the border of North Dakota, they sat in molded plastic chairs out by the pool after a really bad dinner at a local greasy spoon. The pool was empty. Not that it really mattered. The wind was blowing and it was too cold for a swim anyway.

"Such a scenic spot," she said drily, shivering a little in her light jacket, staring across the deserted highway at the lonely-looking gas station on the other side.

He hoisted his dusty boots onto a spare plastic chair. "This is the life, Lizzie." He sent her his cockiest grin. And then his expression changed. He gazed into the distance. "Being CFO? It wasn't working for me anymore. I was beginning to feel like I was suffocating. A man can't spend his whole life waiting for the older generation to retire, you know?" He sent her a glance.

"I get it," she said. "And I think it's great, that you're moving on. I really do. I think it's the best thing for you, to make your own place in the company—on your own terms."

He was watching her. "I'm glad you're here with me. For now, at least."

"Me, too." As she said it, she realized it was true.

His slow smile made her heart kind of stumble inside her chest. "Feel free to change your mind and stay."

"Not going to happen." She said it softly. A little bit breathlessly.

"You're a damn stubborn woman, Lizzie Landry."

"And you, Ethan Traub, are a pigheaded man."

He gestured at the dusty, empty pool, at the deserted highway and the endless, dry land around them, at a lonely tumbleweed bouncing down the center line. "I can't believe you want to give up all this."

She frowned. "Are you going to start in on that again?"

"I'm persistent. It's why I succeed at most things I do."

"You won't change my mind. It doesn't matter what you say, or how much money you offer me."

"I really hate that I've started to believe you."

"Only started?"

He didn't rise to that challenge. Instead, he asked, "And what about when I want one of your chocolate-chip muffins? Or a strawberry-rhubarb pie?"

"You'll have to have them shipped up from Midland. And it will cost you."

"Ouch. That's cold." But he didn't look especially upset about it.

He really was making his peace with the changes between them. Slowly. Reluctantly, he was letting her go.

She told herself that was for the best, that his acceptance of her leaving was what she wanted.

But her heart felt heavy suddenly. Weighted with the coming loss.

Of Ethan. Of the special relationship they shared as colleagues. As friends.

As…

Okay, she might as well admit it: as possibly so much more.

Mon Dieu, as her dear *maman* might have said. Where was she going with this? She'd been after him for months to accept that she was leaving. She was finally getting somewhere with that, finally seeing the light at the end of the tunnel, seeing the day coming when she could move on and he could wish her well as she left him.

She should be pleased. But instead, she was feeling droopy and dejected about getting exactly what she wanted.

It made no sense. Last week, she'd called *him* an ass. Well, who was being the ass now?

"Okay, Lizzie," he said in a low, teasing voice that played dangerous music on every one of her nerve endings. "What's happening inside that head of yours?"

She met his waiting eyes. Oh, she did long to tell him—that she wanted her bakery and she wanted *him,* too. She wanted to stay with him. And she *needed* to go. That she didn't do casual when it came to the man-woman thing—and yet, she was actually considering making an exception in his case.

Uh-uh. No good was going to come of telling him all that. It would only confuse him all over again. He didn't need that.

Neither of them needed that.

"Just watching the empty highway," she said. "Waiting for something exciting to roll by."

He laughed, a low, sexy rumble of sound. "Liar."

"Look." She pointed toward the two-lane road. "Another tumbleweed."

He didn't look. He kept right on staring at her. "You want to change your mind—about anything—you be sure and let me know."

Lizzie did nothing of the kind.

Not that night, or any of the remaining nights that

they were on the road. They worked all day. At night, they had dinner in diners and chain restaurants. They were joined by any number of interesting characters, by crusty ranchers and land brokers. They even met up with a few current TOI employees, landmen Ethan had sent on ahead to start lining up the mineral-rights possibilities—a landman being a professional who secures oil and gas leases, checks legal titles and attempts to repair title defects so that drilling can begin.

After each day's work, they retired to their separate motel rooms. The next morning they got up, drove to the next meeting and did it all over again.

They returned to Thunder Canyon Sunday around noon, after ten and a half days on the road. Ethan was pleased with all they had accomplished. He was already talking about getting equipment in place and hiring rig crews for the leases he was acquiring in the most promising areas.

He went to his office. Lizzie unpacked, whipped the house into shape and left to buy groceries. Ethan appeared in the garage when she returned and helped her carry everything in.

"Don't cook tonight," he instructed, as he hauled in the last armful of bags.

"Why not?" She'd been kind of looking forward to her own cooking after the endless chain of diners and greasy spoons they'd been eating in.

"I got a call from Allaire. While we were on the road, we missed the second-annual summer-kickoff barbecue last weekend at the Rib Shack. Allaire invited us there for dinner tonight to kind of make up for our missing the big event."

"Where?"

"The Rib Shack, up at the resort. It'll be a family thing. Allaire and DJ, Dax and Shandie." Dax Traub was DJ's older brother by a year. Shandie was Dax's wife. "And that's not all," Ethan said. "Dillon and Erika are coming. And Corey and Erin are back from their honeymoon, so they'll be there, too. Allaire says they're all looking forward to seeing us."

Lizzie paused in the act of putting lettuce in the crisper. *Us,* he'd said so easily. As if the two of them were a couple or something.

But they weren't. And they never would be. And she really, really needed to remember that.

The problem was, lately, it was getting harder and harder to keep in mind that in a matter of weeks, she would be in Midland and he would be here. And it was very possible, unless he happened to come down to Texas and drop in at her bakery, that she would never see him again.

Never see him again.

The words echoed in her mind. They did not make a pleasant sound.

"Lizzie, did you hear a single word I just said?"

She pushed the crisper drawer shut, pulled her head out of the refrigerator and gently shut the door. "Of course I heard you. The Rib Shack for dinner."

He seemed hurt. "You should see your face. What? You don't like DJ's ribs?"

It wasn't the ribs that had her looking glum. It was… all that stuff they'd promised each other they were putting behind them. It was losing him, which she was beginning to understand she actually dreaded in the worst way—losing him to live her lifelong dream.

Losing him. Hah. As if she'd ever even had him.

She knew very well she hadn't. Not really. Just because they worked together and lived in the same house and were good buddies, well, that wasn't the same thing at all as them being *truly* together, the way a man and a woman could be. Like Allaire and DJ. Like Dillon and Erika.

Like Corey and Erin.

Like her mom and dad had been all those years ago.

She forced a grin that only wobbled a little. "Are you kidding? DJ's ribs are the best. Melt-in-your-mouth tender. That special secret sauce to die for…"

"Lizzie…" He came to her and put his hands on her shoulders. It was the first time he'd touched her on purpose since the night she called him an ass and he'd promised to change his attitude. The first touch in days and days.

And it felt downright wonderful.

Those lean, strong hands of his, clasping her shoulders. The warmth of him. And he must have showered while she was out shopping. He smelled so fresh and clean. And she'd always loved that aftershave he wore….

"You're trembling." He said it softly and his eyes were full of warmth, full of hope.

And promises—no, not of forever.

But of a glorious, magical, perfect *right now.*

"It's nothing," she told him on a whisper that trembled just as her body did.

"And now you're lying to me. Again. The way you did that night by the empty pool at the glamorous Golden Lariat Motel."

"Oh, Ethan."

"I knew what you were thinking that night. I know…

a lot about you, Lizzie. More than you give me credit for."

"It…hurts, that's all." She shut her eyes, let out a groan. "Oh, I shouldn't have said that." And then she met his gaze again. She never wanted to look away.

"What hurts?"

"Don't make me say any more, Ethan."

"I'm not making you say—or do—anything. And you know I'm not."

She gulped to clear the clenching of her throat. "I… It's only that sometimes I think about how much I'm going to miss you. It hurts to think about it. It hurts a lot."

The light of triumph flashed in his eyes. "So don't go."

Step back, she thought. *Pull away. Do it now.*

But she didn't.

Instead, she did what she'd sworn she wouldn't. She told him the truth. "You know I have to go at the end of July. It wouldn't work now, for me to stay on, even if I didn't have dreams of my own to make happen. You're in my heart, Ethan. I couldn't go on, just working for you, with us being friends. It wouldn't be enough for me. Not now. Not anymore."

He touched her face, a caress that sent another warm shiver sliding through her. He whispered her name. And then he gathered her close and wrapped his arms around her.

And she let him, even though he hadn't said that she was in *his* heart, too. Even though he hadn't said, *Stay, Lizzie. We'll work it out, you and me.*

Really, why should he say that? She knew him, after

all. And by his own declaration, he wasn't the kind of man a woman counted on for a lifetime.

Still, she sighed in relief and joy, just at the feel of his big body pressed close, of his arms so tight around her.

And when he tipped up her chin and lowered his mouth to hers, she only sighed some more and welcomed his kiss.

Oh, my. Oh, yes…

Kissing Ethan in the kitchen.

It could easily become a habit for her.

It felt so good, so right. So exciting, so exactly as a man's kiss should feel. Why was it that no other man's kiss had thrilled her quite like Ethan's did?

He had a way of holding her in those big arms of his, a way of slanting his mouth just so, a way of tempting her to open—and that tongue of his. Really. There ought to be a law against a tongue like that. So clever, so… skilled. So very, very good at arousing her, at making her think how lovely it would be to fall into the nearest bed with him.

To stay there for the rest of the day and all of the night.

Her body felt hot and hungry. Needful in the most delicious way. And she couldn't resist pressing herself even closer, feeling more than she should have of how much he wanted her.

The man was an artist when it came to kissing.

And why shouldn't he be? asked the faint voice of reason somewhere way in the back of her desire-addled mind. *He's certainly had enough practice.*

That did it—just reminding herself of all of the girlfriends he'd had. Of the trail of broken hearts he'd left behind him in Texas.

She leaned back in his arms, breaking the sweet, endless kiss.

His long, thick black lashes lifted and he looked at her. His lips were soft from kissing her. And his eyes were heavy-lidded. He asked, gruffly, "Second thoughts? Again?"

She gave him a bright, determined smile. "Sorry. I had a moment of weakness there. My bad."

Gently, he put her away from him. And then he let her go. She tried not to feel the loss of his touch too acutely.

He said, "I'm not going to make the same mistake again."

She didn't follow. "Mistake?"

"I'm not going to act like a jerk or get angry with you. I like you. So much, Lizzie. You're my friend. A good friend, steady, honest and true. And I admire the hell out of you, I really do."

"Uh. Thanks. I think."

"And I want you. I want you so bad. But I'm not going to die if I don't have you." He winced. And then he actually chuckled. "Even if right now, it feels like I might."

She didn't know what to say to that. And as it turned out, she didn't need to say anything.

He wasn't through talking. "I'm not going to be cranky. And I'm not going to be an ass. If it's meant to happen with us, it will. I just want you to know that I'm willing. More than willing."

"Well, Ethan, I kind of figured that out already."

"Good. Then we're on the same page with this."

"I need to think it over." The words were out before she even realized she would say them. They shocked her a little and she felt her cheeks coloring. Every day she was getting closer to taking the leap. To going for it.

To making love with Ethan.

Maybe, she found herself thinking, it wouldn't be such a bad thing to live in the moment for a change, to let down her guard a little. Really, did she *always* have to be looking ahead to the future, planning for what would happen next?

For five years now, since her dad lost the bakery—no, before that. For ten years, since her beloved *maman* had died so quickly and brutally of cancer, she'd been living her life with such strict care. She'd pushed herself constantly, denying the pleasures of the moment to create a stable future for herself, a future neither death nor a loved one's heartsick inattentiveness could ever steal from her.

She'd been most careful of all in the men she dated. There had been only a few and they'd all been good marriage material.

But where had all that carefulness gotten her? None of those cautiously chosen men had worked out for her, none had stolen her heart and left her breathless the way Ethan did.

Stolen her heart.

Oh, yes. He had. He truly had. Ethan Traub had stolen her heart. She should probably be angry about that. It wasn't as though he was giving her his heart in return.

But she wasn't angry. She forgave him totally. She could love him for who he was and leave it at that.

He asked, "Whatever happened to that banker you were dating—what was his name?"

She felt, at that moment, that he could actually see inside her mind, that he knew just what she was thinking.

She answered flatly, "His name was Charles. Charles Smith. And it didn't work out."

"And the insurance salesman? And what about the guy who taught high-school geometry?"

She gave him a stern look. "Get to the point."

"They were all really nice, stable, trustworthy guys, weren't they?"

"Just say it, Ethan."

"Maybe it wouldn't hurt you to take a risk on a different kind of guy now and then, that's all."

She braced her fists on her hips and made a very unladylike snorting sound. "A risk with *you.* That's what you really mean, isn't it?" She was glaring at him, but it was only an act.

In her mind was the realization that she had reached the all-important crossroads in her life. She would have her bakery, just as she'd planned. And Ethan had accepted at last that it would happen, that he would have to let her go.

She was thinking, what could it hurt? To just…be with him, for a little while? To be with him and for once to let the future take care of itself?

He finally answered her question. "A risk with me is exactly what I'm suggesting. So if you decide you want to go for it, you let me know."

"I'll, um, keep you posted."

His smile was wry and genuine. "Hey, a guy can't ask for more."

Chapter 8

At the Rib Shack up at the resort, black-and-white pictures of cowboys and weathered buildings hung on the walls, each one tinted a faint sepia color, bringing back a feeling of the old West. There was also a large mural that showed scenes from Thunder Canyon history. Grant Clifton had told them it was painted by Allaire.

"Smells good in here," said Ethan.

Lizzie grinned at him. They'd been to more than one Rib Shack together. "Always does." Like DJ's other locations, the place smelled of the famous Rib Shack sweet-and-tangy sauce. Her mouth watered in anticipation of a big helping of messy, to-die-for ribs.

Ethan put his arm around her. Lizzie felt that quick little flash of excitement, the one that sizzled along her nerve endings whenever he touched her lately.

And this time, as that thrill went through her, she realized that she was okay with it. She accepted it. Since that afternoon, they knew where they stood with each other. He wasn't going to push her, or be an ass because he couldn't have what he wanted from her. It was up to her to make up her mind if anything was going to happen between them.

Already, one of the long family-style tables was filled with Traubs. Allaire had saved them two seats. They sat down and greeted the newlyweds. Erin and Corey looked tanned, relaxed and happy.

The food, like the seating, was family-style, big platters of ribs and barbecued chicken to pass around, bowls of coleslaw, corn on the cob and mashed potatoes, baskets of biscuits and steak fries. They loaded up their plates, tucked napkins in their collars and dug in.

At DJ's, you didn't stand on ceremony. And nobody cared if there was secret sauce on your chin.

Lizzie had a great time.

There was lots of local news to share.

First, there was the gossip about the new rib place in town, LipSmackin' Ribs. It had opened recently in the New Town Mall. DJ had been by there already. "Just to have a look," he told them.

Shandie, Dax's wife, chuckled. "I'll bet your eyes about popped out of your head."

Erin was nodding. "I heard the waitresses wear dinky short skirts and tight T-shirts that show a lot of belly—shirts with big, red lips printed on the front."

"As in lip smackin'?" Dillon asked with a groan.

Dax teased his brother. "So, DJ, you worried about a little competition?"

"Not in the least," DJ scoffed. "Tight T-shirts and

short skirts don't sell ribs. Take the word of an expert on the subject. It's all in the secret sauce."

A murmur of agreement went up from everyone at the table.

DJ also shared the news that the town's most famous crook, Arthur Swinton, had apparently died of a heart attack in prison. Arthur, long a fixture on the town council, had been embezzling from the town coffers for years, and had been caught only the year before—the same year he'd run for mayor against Grant's cousin Bo Clifton and been defeated.

"I hate to speak ill of the dead," said Dax. "But Arthur was such a weasel." He turned to DJ. "Plus, remember when he made that play for Mom?"

"Shh." Shandie, Dax's wife, sent a glance in the direction of her seven-year-old, Kayla, who was busy down the table spreading honey on a biscuit for DJ and Allaire's toddler, Alex. "Little pitchers have big ears."

Dax laughed. "Honey, you have to know Mom never gave Swinton the time of day."

"She was the greatest," DJ said.

"Yes, she was," Dax agreed. "You did not mess with Mom."

DJ went on with the story. "She slapped Arthur's face and told him she was a happily married woman. And even if she was a dried-up old maid, she wouldn't be saying yes to a skinny weasel like him."

Dax was still laughing. "And then she told Dad."

"Uh-oh," said Erika.

"You'd better believe that," said DJ. "Dad knocked him down a peg or two with a couple of well-placed hard rights to the jaw. I don't think Swinton ever got over being slapped in the face and told off by Mom—*and* beaten up by Dad."

Shandie shook her head. "Well, no matter what bad things he did, I hope the poor guy finds peace in the afterlife."

Dax grunted. "Not a chance. I have a feeling his ass is on fire about now."

"Dax!" Shandie made a show of bumping her husband with her shoulder. "That's enough."

He put his arm around her and kissed her cheek. "Your wish is always my command."

Allaire caught Lizzie's eye. "So will we see you tomorrow at the Tottering Teapot for lunch?"

Lizzie tipped her head toward Mr. Tall, Dark & Texan at her side. "Depends on whether the slave driver can spare me for an hour or two."

Ethan heaved a fake sigh. "It will be difficult, but I'll manage."

Lizzie grinned. "I'll be there."

"Great. Erin and Erika are coming, too."

Erika nodded.

Erin beamed. "We wouldn't miss it. I loved the Bahamas, but it's good to be home—and we can plan that girls' night out I promised you when you saved the day and baked my wedding cake."

"Girls' night out?" Shandie looked interested.

"I hope we're all invited to that," Allaire chimed in.

"Oh, absolutely," Erin told them.

Erika added, "The more, the merrier, I always say."

"We're thinking about maybe this Friday night, but we can firm it all up tomorrow."

"Can't wait," said Lizzie.

"Me, neither," said Erin. "It's going to be fun."

* * *

"Did you have a good time tonight?" Ethan asked Lizzie as they drove back down the mountain.

"I did."

"I think you like it here." His eyes gleamed through the darkness of the cab, and then he turned his gaze back to the road again.

"I think I do, yes." She gave him a smile.

They rode the rest of the way in silence.

At the house, she asked him if he wanted coffee or a last beer.

He gave her a crooked smile. "If I do, I'll get it myself. You are officially excused for the evening."

It was so strange, the feeling she had right then. Kind of sad and let down. He was only being thoughtful. She knew he didn't mean it as a rejection. And he certainly had a right to a little time to himself if he wanted it.

How many evenings in the years she had worked for him had he said he was fine on his own and didn't need anything more from her that night?

Hundreds, certainly. It was no big deal.

It was only that she had become accustomed lately to his constant attention. He'd been chasing her, spending every minute he could with her. And while he was chasing her, she'd told herself that she wished he would stop.

And now, true to his word that afternoon, he *had* stopped. And she wished that he hadn't.

Which was silly and unreasonable and counterproductive.

Still, it was how she felt.

Because I'm in love with him. Because he holds my heart...

Ugh. Really. She was going to have to buck up a little

here. She had some big plans for herself. She was reaching a major long-term goal. And turning into a ball of sentimental mush over Ethan Traub?

No, not in the plan.

"Well, all right," she told him in a voice that made her proud, a voice that in no way betrayed the disappointment in her heart. "See you tomorrow."

She went to her rooms, where she drew a hot bath and soaked for an hour.

The water was soothing. Still, when she climbed from the tub, she just didn't feel much like sleeping. She put on an old pair of sweats and sat on the still-made bed and channel surfed.

Nothing caught her interest. So she picked up the phone and called a girlfriend in Midland. They talked for twenty minutes, about how the girlfriend was getting along in her new job, and about how Lizzie was doing way up there in Montana.

When she hung up, she felt even more on edge and dissatisfied than before. She sat there staring at the dark eye of the TV, thinking how her friend in Midland seemed like a casual acquaintance now. Really, she had more of a rapport with Allaire and Erin, with Erika and Tori McFarlane, than she did with a woman she'd known since she was in her teens.

She supposed it was her fault, for letting her life get so filled up with Ethan, for letting him become the center of her world, her boss at work and at home, and also her best friend.

"Ugh." She tossed both the remote and the phone down on the bed. Maybe a little chamomile tea would help her sleep.

She put on her flip-flops and went out to the kitchen,

which was quiet—dark, except for the soft glow of the under-counter lights. Had Ethan gone out? She told herself she was not, under any circumstances, going to check the garage to see if his car was there.

That would just be too needy and pitiful for words.

Instead, she brewed her tea without turning on the overhead lights and went back to her room, where she sipped slowly and congratulated herself on not taking even one step down the short hallway to the inside garage entrance.

It wasn't until she turned off her bedroom light that she noticed the muted glow out on the back deck. She couldn't resist stealing a peek through the blinds: Ethan. He was sitting out there in a chaise lounge with a beer in his hand. The dim deck light didn't reveal much, just the shape of his body, stretched out in the chaise. She couldn't really see his face.

She watched as he raised the longneck in his hand and took a sip. What was he thinking, sitting out there all by himself? She longed to go and ask him.

But she didn't. She got into bed and resolutely shut her eyes.

The next morning Ethan was gone when she got up. He'd left her a note on the kitchen table saying he had a couple of meetings in town and he'd see her at the house when she got back from lunch with the girls.

She felt deflated somehow. That he was gone. That she wouldn't see him until the afternoon.

Really, she had to stop this…obsessing over him. He was finally giving her a little space and she ought to enjoy having a few hours to herself for a change.

She had her breakfast, baked a batch of double-fudge

cookies and then spent the remainder of the morning at her desk, handling general correspondence for Ethan—writing letters he'd outlined for her, answering emails that didn't require his personal touch. Beyond dealing with mail and messages, she went over the reports he'd done on their work in the field the past week and a half. He'd sent them to her computer and she proofread them for errors, getting them ready to forward to Midland.

There was also an email from the broker she'd hooked up with in Midland. One of the two storefronts she had her eye on for the bakery had just taken a serious dip in asking price. The broker said the seller was really motivated now. Was Lizzie ready to make an offer?

She wrote him back that she would think it over and have an answer for him within the next couple of days.

The morning passed quickly enough. She met her new friends at the Tottering Teapot at noon. As always when she got together with Allaire and crew, she had a great time. They got after her some more about opening her bakery in Thunder Canyon. To make them stop, she promised again to think about it—and then realized that, maybe, she really *was* thinking about it.

Which totally surprised her. Sometimes a person just never knew the secrets of her own mind….

Erin said the French baker had sent her a check while she and Corey were in the Bahamas, a full refund of her money for the cake he'd failed to bake. Erin added, "He also sent a very stiffly worded apology. I felt a little sorry for the poor guy, if you want to know the truth." A glowing smile lit up her beautiful face. "But I guess I can afford to feel sorry for him because our Lizzie saved me from one of the worst tragedies any bride can face."

Our Lizzie. Okay, Lizzie really liked the sound of that.

And yes, after lunch, she did wander down the street to check out the empty bakery again. Her heart turned over when she saw the for-sale sign in the window. She realized she had been hoping it might be there.

Her hands were shaking a little as she got out her BlackBerry and entered the Realtor's name and company: Bonnie Drake, Thunder Creek Real Estate. She punched in the contact numbers from the sign.

It didn't mean she would actually call one of the numbers.

But, well, every day she stayed in Thunder Canyon, she found herself growing more attached to the place. And now, with Ethan learning to accept the changes that were coming, she could see how it could work. They could run into each other now and then, in town or at some local event, and it wouldn't have to be an awkward moment. They could simply smile and say hi.

And walk on by.

That it could actually be that way now should have cheered her.

But it didn't. It only made her sad. She really needed to snap out of this funk.

When she got back to the house, he wasn't there. He called about two to say he was over in Bozeman meeting with a couple of landmen. He'd be back late. She didn't need to have dinner ready or wait up for him.

"Tomorrow," he said before he hung up, "be ready by eight-thirty in the morning. Breakfast up at the resort."

"That's right. It's the golf-cart and horseback tour…"

"Dress for riding."

She said she would be ready. And he hung up.

And she felt…bereft. Just draggy and sad and totally neglected.

So she spent the rest of the day baking. She made bread and croissants, a chocolate peanut-butter pie and raspberry kuchen.

Baking, as always, lifted her spirits considerably. By the time she turned in that night at ten, Ethan was not yet home and she told herself she really didn't care. He had his life and she had hers and she was just fine with it being that way.

Total lie, yes. But a comforting one, nonetheless.

In the morning, he was dressed in Wranglers, a chambray shirt and rawhide boots, an old bandana tied around his neck, ready to go when she emerged from her rooms at 8:20.

"Chocolate peanut-butter pie *and* raspberry kuchen," he accused. "I came in at eleven and there they were."

She grinned. "I hope you had some of each."

"I did. Keep that up and I'll have to poke a new notch in all of my belts."

She thought how she'd love to wrap her arms around him and claim a nice, long good-morning kiss. And then she wondered if he'd been out with someone last night—someone other than a couple of landmen. Someone pretty and petite, someone with well-behaved hair who didn't dither over saying yes to what she wanted.

He was watching her kind of thoughtfully. "Something bothering you?"

"And you ask that why?"

"You baked bread. And croissants, too. And also double-fudge cookies."

"So?"

"That much baking usually means there's something you're upset about. When your dad died, I gained ten pounds, remember? Took me months of busting my ass at the gym to lose it."

I think I'm in love with you and I also think I want to buy a bakery right here in Thunder Canyon....

No. Really. Not now. It wasn't the time.

If any time ever would be. "We should get going."

He frowned, but then he agreed, "Yeah, you're right."

They took their hats and jackets from the pegs by the door to the garage and headed for the resort.

There were six of them in the group, as it turned out. Lizzie, Ethan, Grant, Connor and Tori McFarlane—and also Grant's wife, Stephanie.

Grant seemed especially pleased to have his wife with them. Steph, as everyone called her, was a Thunder Canyon native, like Grant. She ran the family ranch. They had a four-month-old, Andre John, whom they called AJ. Grant's mom was watching the baby so Steph and Grant could have a day to themselves.

They all had breakfast at the Grubstake, the resort's coffee and sandwich shop. And then they toured the golf course. That took over an hour. Like most golf courses, it was lovely and green with lots of nice trees and a few gorgeous wind-ruffled ponds. But, well, what else was there to say about it? Lizzie had never been much of a golfer.

Ethan, Grant and Connor agreed to meet the next morning at six. They would play all eighteen holes, so Ethan could get a feel for the course.

They went to the stables next, where their horses were already tacked up and waiting for them. Grant had ordered a picnic from one of the resort kitchens. He and Steph carried the food on their mounts in saddle baskets.

It was a beautiful day, the sky as blue as a baby's eyes, dotted here and there with cottony clouds. They took a series of switchbacks, moving upward, past a settlement of pricey-looking resort condos. Some of them, Grant explained, were for renting out to guests who wanted more of a private living situation than that offered in the hotel at the main clubhouse. And some of them were owned by regular resort visitors.

Farther up, spaced wide apart, were a series of one-of-a-kind cabins for big-spending guests who wanted total privacy. These Grant pointed out from the trail at a distance. Lizzie thought each cabin looked so inviting. Each was built of natural stone or logs and surrounded by tall evergreens.

They continued to wind their way up the mountain. Gradually, the trees thinned out as they reached the higher elevations. Abundant wildflowers grew on the windy, open mountainside. It was up there, not far below the rocky, snow-crested peaks, by a bright little stream, that Steph suggested they stop for lunch.

They hobbled the horses. Under a lone, wind-twisted spruce tree, they spread the big blanket Grant had brought, anchoring the corners against the gusty, cold wind with rocks they found on the hillside. They all had their jackets on by then.

But the view was so spectacular that nobody minded the cold. Spread out far below them were wild, overgrown canyons and green rolling pastureland. You could even see the town itself, looking quaint and picturesque in the distance.

They all got comfortable and shared the light meal. There were various excellent cheeses, fresh-baked bread, fruit, summer sausage and sparkling water.

Lizzie spread brie on a slice of crusty bread. "Food always tastes best when you're out in the open."

Ethan, who sat next to her, raised his bottle of sparkling water. "To good food, good company—and the great view."

They all joined in the toast.

A moment later, Ethan leaned close. "Admit it." He pitched his voice for her ears alone. "You love it here. Thunder Canyon is one of those places. You come for a visit and before you know it, you realize that you're already home."

She was all too aware of him, of the lean line of his jaw, of the shape of his lips—lips she had kissed when she shouldn't have.

Lips she longed to kiss again.

She made herself meet his dark, knowing eyes. "Okay, I admit it. I love it here."

His smile was slow and also contagious. "I knew it," he said. And nothing more.

Lizzie spotted the deep-blue flowers growing along the stream bank as they were shaking out the blanket, getting ready to mount up again. They were low-growing flowers, maybe eight inches high, the nodding blossoms in clusters, shaped like tiny thimbles.

Steph saw her admiring them. "Mountain bluebells," she said. "They don't grow tall so high up, but they sure are pretty, aren't they?"

"Yes," Lizzie agreed. "Oh, yes, they are."

It seemed, somehow, an omen. Instead of the Texas Bluebell Bakery, why not the Mountain Bluebell?

An image took form in her mind of a nice wide wooden sign above her bakery door, a sign she would hire Allaire to paint for her. The Mountain Bluebell, it would say in proud, tall block letters, with a sprig of blue thimble-shaped flowers nodding over the words.

She turned to mount up and found Ethan, already on the bay mare he was riding, watching her. Even shadowed by the brim of his hat, it seemed to her he had the strangest expression on his handsome face.

"What?" she demanded.

He laughed. "Not a thing, Lizzie. Not a thing."

Chapter 9

They got back to the house at six. Ethan said he was going out for dinner. She'd have the evening to herself again.

She knew then, with a grim sense of certainty, that there had to be someone else.

Someone else. How ridiculous. How could there be someone else when they'd never been together in the first place?—not in *that* way.

Not in the man-woman way.

She put on a smile. "Have a great time."

He gave her one of those long, unreadable looks he'd been giving her way too often lately. "Thanks, I will." And he went to his rooms to shower and change.

She didn't hang around waiting to watch him go. No way. She headed for her own room, where she picked up the phone to call the broker in Midland and let him know she'd changed her mind about buying a bakery in Texas.

It was a brief conversation. He spent a minute or two trying to convince her not to be hasty. But then he seemed to get that she'd made up her mind. He wished her luck and told her to give him a call if there was any way he could help her again.

After that, she looked up the Realtor's numbers she'd taken from the for-sale sign at the empty bakery. But then she backed out of the contact without dialing.

It didn't seem right to go ahead with her new plans until she'd talked to Ethan about it—and no, not because she would ever let him change her mind.

Uh-uh. She was set on her course now. She was going to live right here in Montana. She had a whole new perspective on the situation now and she could see that she'd been much too hung up on recreating the past. She realized that she needed to move beyond her family's lost bakery. She needed to create something new, something all her own.

And she was going to do exactly that.

But still, she felt that she had to share her plans with Ethan before the fact, before she began to make them a reality. It seemed the least she could do, to forewarn him that she was staying in Thunder Canyon, too.

Should she tell him now?

No, not right this minute but soon. She would choose a moment when he wasn't on his way out the door.

After he left, she made herself a sandwich for dinner and had a big, fat slice of chocolate peanut-butter pie for dessert. She went to her desk and paid some bills. And then she went online to instant banking to see if her paycheck had come through from TOI for the month.

It had. And then some.

That ginormous bonus Ethan had promised she would get if she stuck with him until the end of July?

Already deposited.

Lizzie gaped at the entry. And then she blinked several times in rapid succession, certain she must be having some kind of hallucination.

But no. When she looked again, that giant direct deposit was still there, way before it should have been.

And the only way that could have happened was if Ethan had put it through early.

She logged out of instant banking and shut down her computer.

And then, kind of moving on autopilot, she went to the family room, where she turned on the TV, chose a movie on Showtime and settled in to watch the whole thing. She would not be turning in. Not until after Ethan got home.

There was just no point in putting off the talk she needed to have with him. She was waiting up for him tonight and she was telling him about her change of plans when he got home. She was also asking him why he'd decided to pay her that bonus more than a month ahead of time—well, unless he brought someone home with him.

If he brought someone home with him, he would be much too busy to listen to what Lizzie had to say. Too busy up in the master suite.

With the door closed.

Oh, God. The numb, confused feeling she'd had since she'd seen the bonus in her bank account was suddenly replaced by sheer misery.

It hurt so bad to think that he might show up with

some pretty little thing on his arm. More than once, she almost turned off the TV and went to bed. At least if she went to bed, she wouldn't have to see him with someone else.

But of course, she knew she was being ridiculous. If he came home with company, chances were she would see the woman eventually anyway—probably at breakfast. Now, that would be an experience. Cooking breakfast for Ethan's new girlfriend...

It was too ironic. How many breakfasts had she cooked for Ethan's various lady friends? A lot of them. Before now, she'd been happy to do it. Most of the women he dated were too skinny anyway. They could use a healthy breakfast. She'd enjoyed coddling them, making them feel comfortable. She'd known they wouldn't be around that long and, deep in her heart, she'd felt kind of sorry for each one of them.

Sorry and a little bit superior, too, a little bit smug. She'd been so sure that she would never put herself in a position to get her heart stomped on by a rich player's fancy boots.

Lizzie blew a few wild strands of hair out of her eyes and promised herself she would never feel smug about anything ever again. And as for tonight, well, she wasn't running and hiding in her room. She needed to just stick it out and wait up till he came home.

The movie ended. She started watching a second one.

And then, finally, at a little before eleven, as she dozed in the easy chair, she shook her head to wake herself up—and saw Ethan standing in the doorway to the hall.

Alone.

Or at least, there was no one tiny and adorable anywhere in sight.

His hair was windblown and he wore new jeans and dress boots, a plain dark shirt and a beautifully cut sport jacket. He gave her his trademark slow smile. "You're half-asleep." He shrugged out of the jacket, swung it behind him and let it dangle by a finger. "Why aren't you in bed?"

She blew that persistent curl of hair out of her eyes again. "I need to talk to you. Are you alone?"

"Last time I checked, yeah." He was giving her that steady look he'd given her way too often lately, that look that made her feel he could see inside her head—and maybe under her clothes, as well.

She sat up straighter, smoothed her hair, which she knew was sticking out on the sides and flattened in the back, and pressed her lips together to keep from saying too much. But then she couldn't stand it. She said it anyway. "I thought maybe you were out with, um, someone new."

Another long, unwavering look. "No, I was on my own tonight."

"Well." Relief poured through her, cool and refreshing as a mountain spring. And her heart had set up a racket inside her chest. It pounded so loud that she almost feared he might hear it—though of course she knew he couldn't. "All right, then."

He was looking down now, the jacket still dangling back over his shoulder. He seemed to be studying those fine boots of his. "Dinner was about business. I've bought a three-story brick office building over on State Street, a block from the town square. It will be my new headquarters for TOI, Montana. I made the offer yesterday while you were at lunch. And I accepted the seller's counteroffer this evening. And then, to celebrate, I had dinner with the seller. I liked him. He got caught in the crunch when the market tanked and was only too happy to give me a killer lowball price just to unload it."

A building. He'd bought a building in town. Of course. That made perfect sense.

And she realized she felt a little hurt, even though she knew she had no right to be. In the past, he would always keep her in the loop when he made a deal such as the one he'd just described. He would want to know what she thought of the purchase, and get her impressions of the various people involved. He'd always claimed he appreciated her insights.

But for some reason, he'd seen the building and then signed the papers without letting her know what was happening.

He left the doorway and he came toward her in long, purposeful strides. Her skin kind of tingled just watching him approach. He was so glorious and manly and he looked so good in his jeans.

The TV was still on. She shook herself out of her reverie of inappropriate desire, raised the remote and pressed the power button. The flat-screen went dark as he tossed the jacket on the back of the chair beside her and then sat down.

"All right," he said. "I'm home. What did you want to talk to me about?"

Where to start? "I checked my bank balance after you left."

"Fascinating," he remarked, meaning it wasn't. He swung his boots up onto the ottoman.

"You already paid me that bonus I'm not supposed to get until the end of next month."

He shrugged, a lazy lifting of one hard shoulder. "You were going to get it anyway. Why not now rather than later?"

"Well, that wasn't the deal, though. What if I packed up tomorrow and walked out on you?"

He slanted her a look. "Like you would try and cheat me, Lizzie. Cheating's not in you. We both know that."

Okay, he was right. She would never cheat him. Still… "It's only that I have this feeling that I've taken advantage of you."

"Well, stop it. You haven't."

"Yeah, I kind of have. It was too much money in the first place, just for two extra months. I shouldn't have taken the deal. It wasn't ethical of me, but I was greedy."

He chuckled, a sound that made her body ache somehow. With yearning. With something very close to need. "Lizzie, Lizzie, Lizzie. Don't waste your energy on guilt. There's no call for that. You were worth every penny of that bonus. Even if you got up from that chair right now, walked out of this house and never came back, I'd consider myself way ahead in any cost-benefit analysis of your term of employment, both at TOI and as my housekeeper."

She felt as if she might cry and that thoroughly annoyed her. As a rule, she wasn't the type to turn on the waterworks at the drop of a hat. But lately, her tears always seemed to be lurking way too close to the surface. She swallowed, sniffed, ordered them gone. And she said, "Well, thank you. But since we got back from eastern Montana, I've hardly done any work for you."

"I'll say it again. You haven't taken advantage of

me." His voice was gruff. "Get over it." He held her gaze. His eyes were darker than ever right then, dark and endlessly deep. "If anyone's been taking advantage, it's been me. And not only with my fatheaded campaign to keep you glued to my side until you gave up your own dream to answer my phone and bake my muffins for the rest of your life."

"Oh, Ethan…"

"I've been thinking." He watched her so steadily, so seriously. "About you."

Warmth spread through her. "You have, huh?"

He gave a slow nod. "Thinking that if your goal hadn't been to own a bakery, I'd have lost you as my assistant long ago. You'd have your own office at TOI by now. You know that, don't you?"

She figured he wasn't expecting false modesty from her. "Yeah, but that wasn't what I wanted."

"So, then, let's talk about what you do want, Lizzie Landry."

You, Ethan. I want you. The words echoed in her mind. But right then, she didn't quite have the guts to say them.

And besides, there was something else she wanted, too. She wanted to realize her dream at last. And her dream was the subject at hand right now. "I've changed my mind about going back to Texas. I want to buy a bakery that's for sale on Main Street, right here in Thunder Canyon."

She waited for his shocked reaction.

It didn't come. He asked, "La Boulangerie, you mean?"

Now she was the one with her mouth hanging open. "You already knew?"

He made a low sound in the affirmative. "I had a feeling you were changing your mind about Thunder Canyon, that you were starting to really like it here."

"Oh, Ethan. I have. I do."

"I drove by that bakery on the way to sign the contract for the office building. I noticed the for-sale sign. Bonnie Drake's the Realtor."

"Yes."

"Bonnie's also *my* Realtor. So after I dealt with the papers for the office building, I asked her about the bakery. She says the owner is eager to sell. He wants to return to France, evidently."

"You think I could get a good deal, then?"

"I think you could get a terrific deal."

She let out a soft, disbelieving laugh and covered her face with her hands. "This is so not the way I expected this conversation to go."

He chuckled, too. "You expected me to be an ass?"

She lowered her hands and met his gaze. "I really didn't know how you would react."

"I told you I was through being an ass, didn't I?"

"Yes, Ethan, you did."

"You should start believing in me—at least a little." He held out his hand between their two chairs.

She took it without so much as a second's hesitation. His fingers closed around hers, strong and warm, and the now familiar thrill shivered up her arm. "I do believe in you."

He lifted her hand and he pressed his warm lips to the back of it. The touch of his mouth to her skin felt so good that she had to stifle a sharp gasp of pleasure. He lowered their joined hands but didn't let go. "I have a plan."

"Tell me."

"I'm pretty sure I can start moving into my new building in two weeks, right after Independence Day weekend."

"That's fast."

"It's empty. It should be no problem to close on the property quickly. We'll get right on the inspections, see that any necessary repairs are done. And I'm going to talk to HR down in Midland, see if there's someone clerical, someone on staff now and already trained. Someone who would be willing to relocate here temporarily, with an eye toward staying if everything works out."

"My…replacement, you mean?" Even though his finding someone new was what she wanted, it still caused a twinge of sadness to see it happening, to know that someone else was really going to take her place.

He didn't answer her question—not directly anyway. "I would want my new assistant to start on the fifth of July."

She forced a cheerfulness she didn't exactly feel. "And that way I would have almost a month to train her—or him."

"No, you're going to be much too busy for that. I'll make sure they send me someone with experience, someone who's ready to hit the ground running."

"But I don't… What do you mean, Ethan?"

"I mean, if you meet with Bonnie Drake and you can get as good a deal as I think you can, you should buy that bakery fully equipped ASAP. And I also mean that I would be letting you go early. On the fifth of July."

It wasn't right. She'd promised to stay with him until July 31. "No, that wasn't the deal."

"So what? I'm changing the terms."

"Ethan, it's not right."

"I'm the boss. If I say it's right, there's not a thing wrong with it. And if all goes according to plan, your replacement will be here and ready to take over by the fifth. And you'll have a new full-time job."

"I will?" She almost didn't dare believe what he seemed to be telling her.

But then he said it, right out loud, "You'll be running yourself ragged getting ready for your grand opening."

It was too huge. Too amazing. Too wonderful for words. Lizzie couldn't control herself. With a screech of pure joy, she leaped from her chair. "Oh, Ethan!"

Still stretched out with his feet up, he gave her the slow, lazy once-over, starting at the flip-flops on her feet and ending with her ill-behaved hair. "Whoa, Lizzie. Could you show a little enthusiasm, you think?"

"Get up here. Get up here now." She dragged on his hand until he swung his boots to the floor and rose to stand with her.

"What now?" His mouth kicked up at one corner as he arched a straight dark eyebrow.

She grabbed him by his big shoulders. "I will pay you back the bonus. It isn't fair that you should—"

He stopped her with a finger against her lips. "Shh. Listen. You're keeping that bonus."

"But it's not—"

"Lizzie."

"What?"

"Don't argue with the boss."

"Oh, Ethan."

"Enough about the bonus. Please?"

"You are the best friend I ever had and I don't know

how to tell you how much I… How much it means to me. Not only that you're finally seeing what I need to do in my life, but also that you're…well, you're…" She ran out of words. Because there *were* no words.

He found them, though. "Willing to help you get what you want?"

She clapped her hands in ecstasy, gave him a double thumbs-up. "Yes. That. Exactly that."

He laughed. "You're happy. I like that."

She dropped her hands to her sides, feeling just a little bit foolish. "Yeah. But I know that sometimes I do get carried away."

"It's all right. There's nothing wrong with being happy—and showing it." For a few lovely, breathless seconds, he stared at her and she stared back at him. Finally, he said, "So… I was thinking tomorrow, as soon as I get back from playing golf with Grant and Connor, you'll call Bonnie Drake and say you'd like to see the bakery. I want to go with you, if that's all right."

"Um. Go with me?"

"Yeah—when you see the place, when you meet with Bonnie. Don't worry, I won't interfere. But it never hurts to have backup when you're making an important deal, or to have a sounding board when it gets down to negotiating."

It was so generous of him. She'd been thinking she would need to get her own Realtor for this. But Bonnie Drake had already done business with him and knew he was one of the rich Texas Traubs. If Ethan had her back, well, she felt okay about going directly through the Drake woman.

And suddenly, she just couldn't stop herself. She yanked him close and hard. "Kiss me, Ethan. Kiss me now." She didn't wait to see if he would follow her instructions. No way. She leaned in fast and she pressed her mouth to his.

He made a low noise in his throat, a growly sort of sound, a very...exciting sort of sound, actually.

And then his big arms came around her and he was holding her as hard as she held him and they were kissing and kissing.

Oh, it was wonderful. Lovely. So thrilling.

To have his arms around her again, to feel his hard chest crushing her breasts, and also, well, that other hardness, lower down, the one that proved he really did like her—and not just as a friend.

It was wonderful, fabulous, to kiss him and kiss him some more, with his breath so warm in her mouth and their tongues all tangled up together.

At last! she was thinking. She really didn't care what the future might bring right then. She wanted Ethan. She wanted him *now.*

But then he took her face in his two hands and broke the magical, beautiful kiss. "Lizzie..." He sounded almost regretful.

Huh? What was there to regret? Everything was going along just fine as far as she was concerned. With a groan, she leaned in and tried to capture his lips again.

He didn't let her. "Lizzie." He said her name more insistently that time.

With another groan, a frustrated one, she opened her eyes. "Oh, Ethan. What?"

He looked at her so intently, his dark eyes soft and tender. And she did love it when his lips were red from kissing her. It made her feel limp and yearning and lovely inside.

But then he spoke. “I don’t think we should rush into anything, you know?”

Her desire-fogged mind strove to register the words—and the meaning behind them. “But I don’t get it. I thought you *wanted*…” Ugh. How to go on from there? Why should she even try?

Suddenly, she was feeling much less than limp and yearning. She was starting to feel just slightly rejected.

He spoke gently. “Lizzie…”

“You keep saying my name. It’s not reassuring.” She took his wrists, guided them away from her and stepped back. “Sorry. I got a little carried away, I guess.” All at once, it was hard to look at him. So she didn’t. She stared down at her flip-flops.

“Come on, Lizzie.”

He was being sweet and considerate and she knew that. In fact, he’d been absolutely terrific to her tonight, telling her he was letting her go early, offering to help her get the property she wanted.

She needed to get a grip on herself, to stop acting like a rejected lover. Even if that was exactly how she felt. She lifted her chin and fluffed at her hair. “Don’t tell me. It’s my hair. Or maybe these ancient sweats, huh? I’m not exactly dressed for seduction.”

A grin tried to pull at the side of his mouth. “Your hair is adorable. I love those sweats.”

“Hah. Nothing about me is adorable. I’m more the… sturdy type. The kind of woman you can count on.”

“Yes, you are. But you’re also adorable.”

She couldn’t resist asking, “So how come you don’t drag me up to your room and have your way with me?” He opened his mouth to answer and then apparently changed his mind. "What?" she demanded. "Say it. Please."

He shook his head. "You should be sure, that's all."

"How much more sure can a woman get? I just threw myself at you, in case you didn't notice."

"Oh, I noticed."

"Well, then?"

"It doesn't seem right."

She couldn't help it. She rolled her eyes. "Honestly. *Right?* Now you're worrying about whether it seems right? For over two weeks now, you've made it more than clear that all I have to do is say the word. So finally, I did, I said the word. And all of a sudden, you're into the ethics of the whole thing."

"I've been thinking, that's all."

"Yeah, got that. You've been thinking way too much, if you ask me."

"You're my assistant. How tacky is that, to be sleeping with my assistant? How…predictable, you know?"

She couldn't help it. She laughed. "You won't make love with me because it would be predictable?"

"Don't make fun of me. Please. I'm trying to do the right thing here, in case you didn't notice."

"Well, you're kind of oversharing."

Now he looked glum. "I am?"

"Yeah, a little. And think of it this way, if everything goes according to plan, I won't be your assistant for all that much longer. So maybe this thing with us isn't as tacky and predictable as you seem to think."

"It's not only that."

"Oh, great." She blew hair out of her eyes again. "How did I know there was more?"

"We don't want the same things, Lizzie. I'm not… your kind of guy. We both agree that I'm not."

"So? That didn't seem to bother you before."

"Like I said, I've been thinking. About the consequences of my possible actions."

"Well, that's new and different."

"Could you just not insult me? Please."

"Sorry. Really. Go on."

"You're important to me, Lizzie. I don't want to lose you, you know? And when it ends…"

Okay, that hurt. "*When,* huh? Not *if?* Couldn't there be just a little bit of *if* in this whole situation?"

"Lizzie, I'm thirty-seven years old. I've never once even considered getting married. My relationships with women have the shelf life of an avocado with the skin peeled off."

She hated to hear him say that, mostly because it was true. "But…what if you wanted to change?"

"We've been through this. You know that I really like my life the way it is. There have to be statistics out there on guys like me, statistics that say a woman is more likely to get hit by a runaway train than to make a lasting relationship with someone like me."

She could really start to get annoyed with him about now. "I think you have a few more years before you become a statistic. Give yourself a little credit, will you?"

"I'm just trying to be realistic, that's all. And come on, don't look at me like that."

"I can't help it. You make it all sound so hopeless."

His expression remained painfully somber. "Not hopeless. Just not especially promising."

She hated that he was right. And she did give him credit for holding back, for trying *not* to get something started between them that could ruin their friendship—especially now that they knew they were going to be living in the same small town. He had a point, he truly did. She should be considering how important their friendship was, too.

She gave it up. "You're right. We don't need to go rushing into anything." She reached out and clasped his shoulder, the gesture of a friend. And she studiously ignored the little thrill she got just from putting her hand on him. Because she *was* his friend. And she intended to stay his friend. No matter what. "Thanks in great part to you, I have a big day tomorrow."

He made a low noise in his throat. "Yeah, you do."

"I want to be at the top of my game for it."

And finally, he smiled. "I hear you."

"So I think I'll go to bed now. Alone."

"Good idea." He reached out then, wrapped his big hand gently around the back of her neck and pulled her in close. "Good night, Lizzie." He pressed his warm lips to her forehead.

It felt so good, his hand against her nape, his lips on her skin, the warmth of his fine body so close. She really, really wanted to tip her chin up just enough that his mouth could meet hers.

But no.

They were friends. They weren't rushing into anything. And she had a big day tomorrow.

She stepped back. He let her go. It caused a small ache within her, to lose the press of his lips on her flesh, the lovely clasp of his hand on her nape. "Good night, Ethan."

And she turned and left him there.

Chapter 10

Ethan watched her go, a tall, no-nonsense woman in baggy gray sweats. Her hair was kind of mashed in the back.

He'd never seen anyone so beautiful—going or coming.

He wanted…everything for her. The rich, full life she deserved. In this great little town where she already had about a hundred friends. Now he'd finally realized that he couldn't bear to hold her back, he wanted her to have the bakery of her dreams.

Not only *wanted,* but he was also going to make it happen.

He went over to the wet bar, put some crushed ice in a glass and added two fingers of good scotch. He sipped the drink slowly, feeling pretty good about himself in spite of the ache in his jeans.

Sometimes a guy just did what was right for a really good person. Sometimes a guy chose a great friendship over a hot roll in the sack because there were other things in life that mattered more than sex.

Yeah, there were times when he got a little hazy on that, on what could matter more than sex. But not now, not when it came to Lizzie.

Tomorrow, if no unforeseen issues cropped up, she would buy herself a bakery. And after that, he'd get two last weeks with her—well, twelve days, to be exact. Until the fifth of July.

And when she was no longer working for him, they could still keep their friendship. Because he wasn't going to mess up what he had with her.

He was going to keep his hands off her. Just enjoy her company. And leave it at that.

When Ethan returned from the resort at ten the next morning, Lizzie was sitting at the kitchen table wearing a slim tan skirt and a silk shirt the exact color of her gray-green eyes. Her hair was smooth, tamed-looking. Her makeup was light as always. A little bit of shadow to bring out her eyes, and gloss on her lips that made them look wet.

Wet and much too kissable.

Forget the kissable, he commanded himself. He wasn't going to be thinking about kissing her. He wasn't going to imagine messing up her hair so it got wild the way he liked it best, or think about slowly unbuttoning that silvery-green shirt, spreading it open, unclasping her bra and seeing her breasts for the very first time.

Uh-uh.

That wasn't what they were about, him and Lizzie.

She had a glowing, self-satisfied smile on her face. "So how was the golfing?"

"It's a great course. The fairways are tight."

"Uh. Good to know."

"Spoken like a woman who knows zip about golf. And let me guess, you already called Bonnie."

Her smile widened. "I did. She says she can meet us there at eleven."

"Well, all right."

"Did you get breakfast?"

"Yeah, at the Grubstake. I'll just jump in the shower and be ready in plenty of time."

Everything went as Ethan intended it to.

They met the Realtor in front of the bakery and she let them in. It was an attractive little shop, with high, pressed-tin ceilings and wide plank floors. In the front area, Lizzie spent a lot of time behind the counter, checking out the display cases, the cold cases, the bread slicer, the cash register, the vintage Italian espresso machine.

In the back, she had to open every door and get a close look at each piece of equipment. That took over an hour, after which they went down the hallway to the back exit, pausing to have a look inside both of the restrooms, and then going on outside to see the good-size parking lot that the bakery shared with the gift shop next door.

There was extra storage upstairs, as well as a two-bedroom shotgun-style apartment. The living room of the apartment was in the front, overlooking Main Street, and was roomy and bright with the same wide plank floors as in the shop below. Lizzie seemed charmed by the farm-style sink in the kitchen and the checkerboard linoleum on the kitchen floor. The one bath had an old claw-foot tub with a shower attachment added on.

Throughout the tour of the property, Ethan hung

back as he'd told her he would. It was Lizzie's deal, after all. He was only there to make certain she got what she wanted at a reasonable price. As he watched her turning on faucets, peering into closets and cabinets and even the oven, he tried to picture her living there.

The kitchen was really small, more of a hallway than a room, nothing like the expansive, state-of-the-art kitchens she'd run living with him. How could she be satisfied with such a dinky little space to do her cooking and endless baking in?

But then he had to admit that he was only being negative. She would have the whole bakery downstairs in which to practice her love of cooking. She probably wouldn't need any more of a kitchen in her living space than the apartment provided.

The bedrooms were not especially exciting. One was in the center of the space, with a single window that gave a view of the brick wall next door. But the larger one, in the back, had two windows overlooking the parking lot and a nice view of State Street and beyond.

Bonnie Drake said the French baker, Aubert Pelletier, was willing to sell everything in the place. Lizzie told the Realtor she'd keep that in mind.

Once the tour was finally finished, Bonnie had to rush off to another appointment, but she said she'd be free that afternoon in case Lizzie had more questions for her. Ethan and Lizzie went to lunch at the Hitching Post. He watched her across the table. Her cheeks were pink and her eyes had a definite gleam in them.

"Well?" he asked, once the waitress had served them their burgers.

"I want it." She popped a french fry into her mouth. "I'm buying that bakery."

He laughed. "I kind of had a feeling you were."

They discussed what she should offer and the state of the equipment, which Lizzie said was excellent. "One thing that baker knew, it was equipment. All the best brands and all of it in great condition."

"So you think you're ready to make your offer?"

"Oh, yes, I do."

So at four that afternoon, in Bonnie's office at Thunder Creek Real Estate, Lizzie submitted her offer on Aubert Pelletier's bakery. She would put down a significant amount in cash and she had a letter from a local banker acquired an hour earlier with Ethan's help that guaranteed her a loan for the balance.

Lizzie wanted to take possession on the fifth of July, when she would move into the apartment upstairs and start working furiously toward the day when the Mountain Bluebell Bakery opened for business.

Aubert Pelletier, who was currently staying in New York, would have forty-eight hours to take the offer or to counter. Bonnie assured Lizzie that she was in close contact with the bakery's owner and that Pelletier was eager to settle all his business in the United States and be on his way back home.

When they left Bonnie's office, Ethan suggested they go out to celebrate.

"Uh-uh," said Lizzie. "Not until the deal is done."

"What? You're afraid you might jinx it by celebrating too early?"

She laughed and put her hand against his mouth. "Shh. Don't even say that word."

Her fingers were so cool and soft. He wanted to kiss them, but he didn't. He gently pushed her hand away and teased, "Celebrate? I shouldn't say *celebrate?*"

"Ha-ha." She wrinkled her nose at him. "I want to go home, if you don't mind."

Home. He found himself thinking that in no time at all, she'd be calling that dinky apartment over the bakery her home. He didn't like that much, but he knew he had to get used to it. Lizzie was moving on and his job as her friend was to support her in that.

She added, "I'd like a nice, quiet evening to…come to grips with the huge step I just took."

He knew what she was really saying. "You want to cook. It will relax you."

Her eyes shone, green as spring grass. "You know me so well."

He ached to reach for her, to pull her close, to kiss her, right there on Cedar Street, and not care that anyone driving by might see.

But he didn't. He remembered the objective: to do what was best for Lizzie.

And kissing her was not it.

They went back to the house. Lizzie made lasagna and garlic bread and a fresh green salad. He opened a bottle of Chianti and they toasted to change and a bright, exciting future for each of them.

When dinner was over, he helped her clear the table and then he went to his office to take care of some paperwork. When he came out at ten, the house was quiet, the kitchen dark.

He drank a glass of water from the tap and stood at the counter, staring into the dimness, thinking that it was going to be very strange to live in a house without Lizzie. He wasn't really looking forward to that.

But he would manage. Eventually, he would get used to the new order of things. He would adjust.

* * *

"Come with me to the resort this afternoon."

Lizzie glanced up from her computer at her desk off the kitchen. It was a little after eleven Thursday morning. "Yes. Anything to take my mind off watching the clock, waiting for the phone to ring with Aubert Pelletier's response to my offer…."

"Stop worrying," Ethan said.

"I'm trying, I'm trying."

"We'll leave after lunch. Grant's arranged to have horses waiting for us. I want to take a look at the interior of a few of the condos, just to see the quality of the furnishings, the finishes, that kind of thing. And we'll get a closer look than we did Tuesday at a couple of those cabins higher up, too."

"Will Steph and Tori be coming?"

"Nope. Connor and Tori are out of town until tomorrow. Stephanie's busy at the Clifton ranch. Grant's got meetings. He's going to leave the keys with the stable hand. It will be just the two of us this time."

Just the two of us. It sounded downright romantic. She wished. "Want to go before lunch? I can pack some sandwiches."

"That would work."

She shut down her computer. "Give me twenty minutes. I'll be ready and so will the food."

The horses were waiting at the resort stables as promised. The groom gave them a set of keys and a map of the resort, with the route to the condos and the various cabins marked in red. Because it was the same way they'd gone Tuesday, they probably would have had no trouble finding what they were looking for. Ethan took the map anyway and thanked the groom.

They mounted and set out on the road to the condos, side by side. It was another gorgeous day, warm with a nice breeze. Lizzie was glad to be out in the open, glad to be with Ethan.

He sent her a smile from under the shadow of his hat. Her heart warmed. If she couldn't have it all with him, well, at least he was her friend. The best friend any girl could ever have.

They reached the condos within half an hour and toured two of them, one in the first block of buildings on the ground floor and one deeper into the complex, upstairs.

Ethan seemed pleased with the furnishings, which were all of good quality, in rich jewel colors—vivid reds, deep blues, golds and emerald greens. The small kitchens had granite counters and stainless-steel appliances. Everything was clean and well maintained.

When they left the second condo, they stood on the landing and stared out at the pine-covered mountains all around. "No surprises here," he said.

She nodded. "Just like the rest of the resort. Everything in great condition."

"Grant runs a tight operation all right." He sent her a glance. "And this is probably an unnecessary trip."

She put a finger to her lips. "Shh. Don't say that. It's a gorgeous day and the view is spectacular."

His gaze was warm. Appreciative. She basked in it.

They mounted their horses again and proceeded up the mountain.

"You hungry?" Ethan asked before they reached any of the cabins. He gestured at the open meadows that surrounded them on either side. A stand of cottonwoods at the edge of the meadow directly west of them seemed to indicate a stream nearby. "Great place for a picnic."

They rode out among the tall grasses and wildflowers, and heard the soft rushing sound of the stream as they approached it. Lizzie had brought a blanket, which they spread under a cottonwood tree right at the spot where the bank sloped away toward the creek. She had roast-beef sandwiches, bags of chips, some ripe red apples and a big thermos of iced tea.

She sat close to him on the blanket, munching an apple and indulging herself in a little fantasy of what it might be like if they were lovers. They would share a few kisses certainly, maybe take off their boots and wade in the cool, clear water of the little creek.

They might even go farther. She hadn't seen any other people since they left the settlement of condos. What would it be like to make love here, in the shade of the cottonwood trees on this breezy, sunny day?

It seemed kind of depressing that she would never know.

She glanced his way and found him watching her and she had a feeling that he was thinking more or less what she was thinking.

But she didn't ask him. Because he seemed so determined to be her friend and only her friend, it was probably better not to know.

"Nice here," she said, keeping it neutral. Safe.

He made a low noise of agreement. "Ready to move on?"

She wrapped up the remains of their meal and packed it in her saddlebag as he rolled the blanket. In no time, they were back on the horses and setting off across the meadow toward the road.

It was a little after two when they reached the first

cabin. Ethan had a key to that one, so they rode right up to the front porch, tied the horses on the rail there and went in.

The door opened on a great room with a soaring two-story ceiling furnished in a comfortable rustic style. There were lots of windows letting in the daylight, framing a view of a wide deck and the piney mountains all around. The open kitchen had all the modern conveniences.

"It's beautiful," Lizzie said, as they entered the master suite which shared the deck with the great room and also had the same spectacular views.

Ethan went into the master bath, but Lizzie continued on toward the French doors that opened onto the deck. She flipped the lock and pulled the door wide and went out to stand at the railing and gaze over the canyon that fell away below.

The wind had picked up in the past half hour or so. As she stared out over the crown of trees below, she caught a faint whiff of smoke. She scanned the surrounding hillside for a sign of the source.

There was nothing.

Ethan came out through the open door. "Do you smell smoke?"

Just as he asked the question, she heard the strangest whooshing sound.

And suddenly, the hillside about a hundred yards below her was on fire.

Lizzie gasped. "Oh, my God!" She knew such things could happen, a fire smoldering in the underbrush and then, in an instant, leaping upward into the crowns of the trees.

Still, she had trouble believing her own eyes. She stared at the bright, roiling balls of vivid flame. And as she watched, with another sizzling *whoosh,* the balls of fire leaped closer, setting the tops of more trees ablaze.

It was climbing the hillside, coming straight for the cabin.

Ethan grabbed her hand, his warm fingers closing over her suddenly numb ones. "Time to go, Lizzie."

It just didn't seem real. She hung back as he tugged on her arm. "We should…call someone, shouldn't we?"

"Come on." He pulled her inside and went straight to the phone on the nightstand. "Deader than a hammer." He slammed it back into the cradle. "They must turn it off when there's no one using the place."

"Oh, Ethan…" Now, out through the French doors, she could see the billows of smoke rising from below the deck.

"We can try a cell. As soon as we're out of here." He grabbed her hand again and they made for the front door.

Outside, the horses were snorting, tugging at their leads, agitated by the smell of smoke, which was much stronger now than it had been only moments before out on the deck. Her gray gelding shook his mane and pawed the ground.

"Easy, now, easy…" Lizzie tried to soothe him.

Ethan was already mounted. "Lizzie, need help?"

"He's a little freaked out, but I think I'm okay." She got her boot up into the stirrup and her other leg over, finding her seat. Then she bent forward and whispered more reassurances to the agitated gray. He pranced and tossed his head some more, but then seemed to settle a little.

"Fire moves toward the oxygen," Ethan said.

She patted the gray's powerful neck. "Uphill. And the wind's going that way, too."

"I'm hoping it's just in that area down the canyon and the road is safe—as of now, anyway."

She knew what he was saying. The fire would be

spreading, moving up toward the road at the same time as it burned toward the cabin.

He urged his horse in the direction of the road. She guided the gray along behind him. He was already getting out his cell. "No signal," he told her. "We can try again in a few minutes, farther on. Up here, the signals seem to fade in and out."

The air swiftly thickened with acrid, throat-scratching smoke as they rode down the winding dirt driveway that led to the main road.

They reached the road within minutes and started down the mountain.

Ethan took out his phone again. "I've got a couple of bars and the resort on autodial. I'll try 911 first." He did. And shook his head. "Nothing. I'll call the resort."

That time, when he put the phone to his ear, he gave Lizzie a nod; he'd gotten through. "This is Ethan Traub," he said. And he repeated his cell number and gave their location. "There's a fire burning fast up the mountain from the canyon right below the first cabin. Call for help, please. And tell Grant Clifton… Hello? Hello?" He pulled the phone away from his ear. "That was the switchboard. I lost her."

"You think she understood?"

"I sure hope so." He put the phone away and coughed against the smoke that now filled the air. "Protect your face." He pulled up the bandana he always wore when he rode, covering his mouth and nose.

She did the same. The cloth barrier helped a little against the choking burn of the smoke.

He gave her a nod from behind his makeshift mask. "Let's get a move on."

They started down the road. The horses chuffed and

snorted against the smoke. But so far, they were doing all right. If it got too much thicker, though, they would need to dismount and lead them. It looked clear ahead—lots of smoke rolling up from the canyon, but no flames so far—and Lizzie began to feel more confident that they would make it down the mountain safely.

But then, right ahead of them, a wild-eyed doe burst from the brush, up from canyon, fleeing the fire.

The terrified animal zipped across the dirt road and scrambled up the bank on the other side, spooking the already uneasy horses.

She heard Ethan talking to his mount. "Whoa, whoa, girl. Settle now, settle..." She glanced over and saw that his horse was dancing in circles.

And then her gray reared up on his hind legs. She should have been ready for that, but she wasn't. One moment she was on the back of the gray.

The next, she was flying through the air.

"Lizzie!" Ethan's voice. Calling her name.

And then she hit the ground. Hard.

The breath fled her lungs. Her teeth clanged together hard enough that she wondered if she'd cracked a few of them. She heard the furious pounding of hooves somewhere, moving away. Her horse, maybe running off?

The world had started spinning. Faster and faster. And then slowly, it resolved into a tiny pinpoint of too-bright light.

The light didn't last long. Within a second or two, everything went black.

Chapter 11

"Lizzie. My God. Lizzie..."

She opened her eyes. Ethan loomed above her. He looked like a bandit with the bandana still covering the lower half of his face—an absolutely terrified bandit. She realized she'd never seen him scared before. Not like he was now. Not stark-eyed, life-and-death scared.

"Hey." She blinked. Twice. Her own bandana had slipped down around her neck again. Her head hurt. And so did her teeth. But she knew where she was—flat on the ground in the middle of a dirt road. She knew what had happened. And she could still smell smoke. That smell was getting stronger. "So I'm thinking I'm not dead, after all. Tell me I'm right."

"Don't move." He slid something under her head—his jacket. "Just stay right where you are."

"Ethan, I'm fine. My horse?"

"Bolted." He yanked his own bandana down. And she saw his lips were white with fear. For her. "Don't worry about the damn horse."

She reached up, touched his dear, frightened face. So warm. So real. "I'm okay. I really am. Please believe me. We need to get out of here."

He laid a tender hand on her forehead, stroked her hair back out of her eyes, his touch so light, so full of care. "You hit your head. Oh, God, Lizzie. You were knocked out. You could have been—"

"I said I'm fine. Let me up."

He scowled and put a hand on her shoulder, holding her down. "Lizzie—"

"I mean it. Let me up."

Reluctantly, he released her. She popped to a sitting position, groaning a little, reaching around to probe at the back of her head where there was already one heck of a goose egg taking shape. "Ugh."

He was still scowling. "I don't think you should be sitting up."

"As if we have any choice in the matter. I think we really have to get moving." She brought her hand around to the front. There was blood on her fingers. "Yuck. I'm bleeding."

Ethan swore. "Let me see."

She turned around so he could have a look. "Where's my hat?" As she asked the question, she saw it a few feet away, trampled on the road. Ethan's mare was there, too, patiently waiting beside the crumpled hat. "At least we still have a horse."

"The bleeding's not too bad," he said. "But you've got one hell of a bump back here."

"Ouch." She put her hand to her mouth and coughed

against the black roiling smoke rising up from the bushes on the side of the road where the bank dropped off sharply into the canyon below. "We have to go. Quit poking at it. Help me up."

"Lizzie—"

"I can't sit here in the road all day, not with the smoke getting thicker and the fire coming closer." She pulled up her bandana to cover her nose again and held out her hand to him. "Help me up." He swore some more, but then pulled up his own bandana and gave her his hand. With his strong arm to aid her, she rose unsteadily to her feet.

As soon as she staggered upright, he got hold of her by the shoulders. "Are you dizzy?" He peered hard into her eyes.

"No, I'm not dizzy." Yes, her head hurt, but it could have been worse. "I'm fine. I mean it. My hat?"

"I'll get it." Slowly, as if he feared she might suddenly drop in a dead faint, he released her and bent to grab the hat. She brushed the dust off her jeans and shirt as best she could. "Here you go." He handed it over, bending to retrieve his balled-up, slightly bloodied jacket.

She fisted the hat back into reasonable shape and put it on. "Let's get out of here." She could see the fire now, not ten feet away, eating into the brush at the cliff edge of the road, spreading out to either side in shining red trails, the black smoke billowing, blown right at them by the wind that seemed to gust harder every second. That fire was much too close. Even Ethan's patient mare was starting to snort and circle.

He mounted up. The mare snorted once more, but

seemed to calm as soon as her rider had the reins. He held down his hand and Lizzie swung up behind him.

Whoosh.

Ten yards ahead of them, right before the road turned, the fire jumped to the other side. The bushes on the upper bank burst into flame and the fire licked higher, moving on up the mountain.

Lizzie wrapped her arms around Ethan's waist and buried her face against his broad back. "Let's go—now!"

He urged the horse forward at a walk. It wasn't safe in a danger zone to go above a trot. Ethan played it extra cautious and kept the speed way down. Lizzie held on and formed a silent prayer, that they would make it, get through the fire to safety.

If anyone could get them out of there, Ethan could. She so admired him during that deadly ride. It took nerves of steel to keep the mare going slow and steady in spite of the choking smoke, the constantly increasing heat and the crackling, hissing sounds the fire made.

As if it were a living thing, and hungry, ready to jump at them and eat them alive.

In minutes, they were in the hottest area, with fire surrounding them, on either side of the road. It was like riding through a tunnel in hell.

Ethan kept the horse going steadily forward. She was a champion, that mare. She startled twice, when a jack-rabbit ran directly across their path and then when drifting embers from the fire burned her sleek red-brown coat. Ethan managed to calm the horse both times, and he brushed away the burning ash with his hand.

Lizzie had the easy job. She only had to hold on and not lose her seat.

It didn't take all that long. It only seemed like forever and a day. Within maybe ten minutes of mounting behind Ethan, the smoke was thinning and the fire was mostly above and behind them. A few embers still smoldered on the canyon side of the road.

Ethan urged the mare to a trot then. "Hold on, Lizzie."

"I am. Don't worry about me."

They rode on at a brisk pace for fifteen or twenty minutes. By then, the danger was well behind them. Ethan slowed the horse and then reined her to a stop.

As he got out his phone and tried the resort again, Lizzie dared to look back the way they had come. It wasn't pretty. Thick, black smoke billowed up to the clear, blue sky. Someone surely must have seen it and turned in an alarm by now.

Ethan got through. "This is Ethan Traub— Yes? Okay. Great. Good. We made it, yeah. We're below the fire now, out of danger, on our way to the clubhouse." He ended the call and told Lizzie, "That first switchboard operator was on the ball. She called it in. The forest service is sending up crews."

As he said the words, she heard the planes overhead on their way to dump loads of fire retardant on the blaze.

Ethan clucked his tongue at the mare and she ambled on down the road again.

Lizzie's gray had made it back to the stables ahead of them. He was lathered and winded, but otherwise okay.

Ethan refused to go back to town until she'd visited the infirmary at the resort's clubhouse. The doctor checked out the bump on her head, cleaned it with disinfectant and told her he thought she would be stiff and achy tomorrow but otherwise okay. Just to be on the safe side, he ran down the danger signs to watch for with a head injury. Ethan listened with fierce concentration and promised he'd be keeping his eye on her for any sign of disorientation or sudden confusion.

Grant found them in the infirmary. He reported that the forest service already had the fire under control, thanks to Ethan's early call. The cabin was a burned-out shell, but other than that, the only damage was the torched hillside.

Ethan asked, "Do they know yet what started it?"

Grant grunted in disgust. "A couple of hikers decided to build a fire. The wind came up and the fire got away from them."

Lizzie hoped they'd escaped with their lives. "Are they okay?"

"They're fine—except for the whopping fines they'll be expected to pay. Insurance will cover our losses. But those hikers may be in for another shock if the insurance company decides to sue."

"I don't feel a hell of a lot of sympathy for them," Ethan said darkly.

"I'm just glad you two are okay," Grant told them. He asked Lizzie, "How's your head?"

"I'm fine. Really. Don't worry about me."

"She keeps saying that." Ethan reached out and put his arm around her. The last time he'd done that in front of Grant, she'd thoroughly disapproved and told Ethan so in no uncertain terms.

But now, well, everything was different.

She leaned in closer to his strength and his warmth

and she sent him her most grateful smile. "I'm lucky. You saved me."

"Hardly."

She elbowed him in the ribs. "You did. You know you did. And can we please go home now?"

He was looking in her eyes and for a moment, she thought he might kiss her—right there in the infirmary, in front of the doctor and Grant Clifton.

But then he only said softy, "Sure, Lizzie. Whatever you want."

"A bath," she said, when he pulled the SUV into the garage and the big door rumbled down behind them. "I want a hot bath and I want to soak for about a year. And after that, I want reheated lasagna."

"You got it," Ethan said gruffly. And then he reached across the console and put his hand against her cheek. He seemed, since they'd made it through the fire, to need the reassurance of touching her. She completely understood. His touch made her feel better, too. He asked, "How's your head?"

"Dusty and sore like the rest of me." She gave him what she hoped was a stern look. "And stop worrying about me."

Reluctantly, he dropped his hand away.

They went inside, hung their hats and jackets back on the pegs by the door.

He asked, "You need anything?" as she was turning to go to her rooms.

She winced as she put her hand at the small of her back where she was reasonably certain a big bruise was forming. "I'll keep you posted."

He hovered close. "I'm kind of afraid to let you go off by yourself. What if you pass out or something?"

It seemed as good an excuse as any to put her hand on him. So she did. She pressed her palm to his cheek, which was getting a little sandpapery with his afternoon beard. "I am not going to pass out. I am not dizzy, nor am I confused. Or disoriented. I have none of the symptoms that might indicate approaching unconsciousness or incipient brain damage. So can we just give that a rest now, you think?"

He grumbled, "Yes, ma'am." And then he added, "But leave the door open—to the bathroom *and* the bedroom, will you? I'll be in the kitchen. And I'll be able to hear you if you scream."

She couldn't stop herself. She kissed him.

It wasn't a big deal of a kiss. On the contrary, it was no more than a slight brush of her mouth against his. "Ethan." She breathed his name against his lips.

"What?" He tried to look disapproving. But she thought he mostly just looked so handsome and worried about her and very, very dear.

"If I'm going to pass out in the bathtub, it's unlikely I would scream first."

"Right. Exactly. All the more reason you shouldn't be taking a bath right now anyway."

She frowned at him, but in a good-natured way. "I'm taking a bath. Get used to it."

"Can you do me one favor?"

"Depends. What?"

"Give me ten minutes. I'll grab a quick shower. Then I'll sit in the kitchen and be ready in case you need me."

She shook her head. "Apparently, there is no getting through to you." She took him by those muscular shoulders and turned him around. "Go. Have your shower. Ten minutes. That's all you get."

For once, he didn't argue. He headed for the front foyer and the stairs.

She went to the kitchen, drank a tall glass of iced water and checked her email.

He was back in eight minutes flat, his lean cheeks stubble-free, smelling of soap and aftershave. It was a big improvement over the acrid scent of smoke. "All right," he growled at her. "Your turn. And don't you dare pass out and drown."

She rose from her computer and headed for her rooms before he had a chance to come up with any more objections.

As the tub filled, she got undressed and studied the damage to her poor body in the full-length mirror on the bathroom door. She did have a big bruise on her lower back as well as a few cuts and scrapes, and more bruises on her legs and arms.

But in a week or two, she would be good as new. She wasn't complaining. She'd been bucked off her horse and knocked unconscious. And then she'd ridden through a tunnel of fire. Considering the circumstances, she was in pretty good condition.

She sank into the warm, scented water with a happy sigh and for a while she just drifted, resting her head on a towel, letting the water soak the aches and pains away, smiling happily to herself. And thinking about Ethan.

Ethan. Waiting in the kitchen, worried to distraction that she might not be all right.

Ethan. The best friend she'd ever had.

Ethan. Who had saved her.

And whom she loved.

It all seemed so simple and straightforward really. She wanted Ethan.

And he was trying so hard to do the right thing. But he wanted her, too.

They had eleven days left together in this house. Eleven days they could spend denying the power of this amazing, who-knew-this-could-happen attraction between them.

Or eleven days where they could have it all.

It didn't seem such a difficult choice when she looked at it that way.

He might think otherwise. He was trying to do right by her after all. But she had a pretty strong feeling she could bring him around to her point of view.

Still smiling, she sat up and reached for the shampoo.

Ethan was getting a little bit worried.

Lizzie had disappeared into her rooms over an hour ago. He'd already been down that hallway twice, just to make certain that the door was still open, so if she did happen to call for him he would have a chance of hearing her. Both times, he'd caught the faint scent of vanilla and a hint of moisture in the air that seemed to indicate she was doing exactly what she'd told him she would be doing: taking a long, hot bath.

Both times, he'd almost spoken up, demanded a response from her, just to be certain that she was okay. But then he'd chickened out at the last minute. She'd had a rough time of it up on the mountain. It seemed only fair to let her have her damn bath in peace.

Come on, Lizzie. You're freaking me out here....

He kept picturing her lying at the bottom of the bathtub, staring up through vanilla-scented bathwater with sightless eyes. It was creepy and scary and she'd damn well better get out here within the next five minutes, or he was getting up and marching into the hallway and yelling at her to speak up and let him know that she was all right.

"Ethan." Lizzie's voice.

He swiveled his head around and saw her standing in the kitchen doorway. Her skin was all pink and soft-looking. She had a bruise on her right shoulder, two on her left forearm and one on her long, rather muscular left thigh. Her hair was shining, falling to her shoulders and drooping over her eyes, loose and wild. Just the way he liked it.

She wore a bath towel. And apparently nothing else.

Chapter 12

"Not fair," Ethan said in a voice that was more an animal growl than any noise a man might make. "Go put some clothes on."

She did the opposite of what he told her to do, which really didn't surprise him because she generally did everything *but* what he told her to do. She left the doorway and came toward him, her bare feet making no sound on the limestone tile of the kitchen floor.

He stood up and faced her. Which was probably a mistake, given that his physical reaction to her standing there in that towel had been instantaneous. Now it was obvious—to him, and to her.

She looked down at the ridge in his jeans and then, with a slow smile, back up into his eyes. And she kept coming. Until she was standing right in front of him and he could smell her—vanilla and a hint of something tart. Lemons, maybe—no. Oranges. Ripe, juicy oranges.

"Lizzie, come on." He groaned. He couldn't help it. "Don't do this to me."

She didn't say anything. Only lifted a hand and laid it on his chest. His heart pounded like wild horses set loose on a midnight run. He knew she could feel the pounding.

"Lizzie, don't…" That was as far as he got.

Because she slid that hand up over his shoulder and clasped the back of his neck. The towel dropped into a puddle at her feet.

He couldn't help it, couldn't stop himself. He looked down.

Into heaven.

He saw her pretty breasts with their hard pink nipples. He saw all of her, all of that soft, firm, smooth flesh. And then she did worse.

She pressed herself against him—those warm, amazing curves of hers, touching him all along the front of him. The hardness in his pants got harder.

It hurt to want her that much.

And then she leaned that fraction closer. She kissed him, her soft mouth opening beneath his.

What did she expect? A man could only go so far in trying to do the right thing. After a point, the woman he wanted and was trying desperately to protect from his bad self had to meet him halfway.

Lizzie wasn't helping him. Lizzie refused to meet him halfway.

Lizzie was blatantly, shamelessly leading him into temptation.

And temptation was just too fine of a place to be.

He gave in.

With a low, angry, frustrated growl, he reached out and hauled her hard against him.

Heaven. Oh, yeah. Lizzie, naked, in his arms. He ran his hungry hands across the silky skin of her long, strong back. He cupped the sweet twin curves of her bottom in his palms.

She gave a little moan into his mouth. He drank that sound. It tasted of her eagerness, of her warmth and her breath. Her sounds were his—*she* was his. Her body, her mouth, that annoying, too-quick brain of hers, her big heart, her goodness. All the things that were Lizzie.

For now, at least, they were his. *She* was his.

A bed, he thought. *We really need a bed.*

Hers was closest. So, still kissing her, still holding on tight, he bent enough to get one arm under her knees. The other, he used to hold her shoulders.

He straightened, lifting her high in his arms. She let out a strangled little squeak of surprise. He smiled against her parted lips.

And then, with a happy little sigh, she wrapped her arms around his neck and went on kissing him. She was no lightweight, his Lizzie, but he knew he could make it down the hall to her bed.

He started walking. She kissed him harder, deeper. He lost track of where he was going and collided with the door frame on the way through. She groaned.

He groaned, too. “Sorry…”

“I’ll live,” she muttered against his mouth. “Keep walking.”

And he did.

At least she’d left her bedroom door wide-open. He carried her through, turning that time, so she went in feetfirst and they could fit without running into anything.

Her bed was waiting, wide and inviting, the covers already turned back. He set her down on the white sheets. She held on. Probably afraid that if she let go of him, he would start telling her why they shouldn't do this.

She didn't have to worry. He had no arguments left. He wanted this and she did, too.

So be it.

They were doing it.

Gently, he took her hands and peeled them off his neck.

She moaned as he broke the never-ending kiss. "Ethan, don't go..." She tipped her face up to him longingly, offering those soft, tempting lips.

He took her shoulders. "Lizzie. Lizzie, open your eyes."

With great reluctance, she did. They were so soft right then, her eyes, soft and moss-green. "Don't you dare turn me down," she said in a whisper that promised everything and threatened some, too.

He laughed then, low and huskily. "I'm not turning you down."

"I mean it. This is what I want. This is..." She blinked and blew several strands of hair out of those beautiful eyes. "Uh. What did you say?"

He kissed her, quick and hard. "I said, I'm here. I'm staying. All I'm trying to do right now is take off my clothes."

Her eyes somehow got brighter. Slowly, she grinned. "You're serious. You surrender?"

"I do, yes. You win, Lizzie."

"Well, then." She blew the hair out of her eyes again. "By all means. Go right ahead and take off your clothes." She released him and scooted back among the pillows, gathering her long, bare legs up under her chin, looking about as cute as he'd ever seen her.

Plus, she was naked. That definitely added to her considerable appeal. He straightened and started stripping. He had his shirt off, his belt undone, his zipper down in seconds. He kicked off the mocs he liked to wear around the house. All that was left was to shove down his jeans and his boxers and step out of them.

She licked her lips. "Oh, Ethan…"

He started to go down to her, but then he remembered. "We need condoms."

And just like that, she reached over and pulled open the bedside drawer. "Got 'em," she said. "Plus, I'm on the Pill."

He should have known. It was so like her, to take care of her own protection. Lizzie was not the kind of woman who left things to chance. Especially not something so important as a new life—or as dangerous as an STD.

Well, all right. That problem solved. He took the box from the drawer, set a couple of packets on the nightstand and then put the box back. She slid the drawer closed.

And then, finally, there was nothing else—no questions unanswered, no necessities unattended to. There was only the two of them.

Him and Lizzie. At last. Naked.

He went down to her, gathered her close in his arms. She sighed as she eagerly accepted his kiss.

She was…a miracle, in his arms. Nothing like the small, fragile women he'd always chosen. There was so much more of her, and all of it womanly and smooth and strong and sweet-smelling.

So good.

She filled his arms.

And his senses.

She rolled him over until she was on top of him and then she kissed him until he hardly knew where he was or how he'd gotten there. He only hoped he would never have to leave.

He rolled them both again, so she was on her back. He cupped her breasts in his hands. They were full and so beautiful. He kissed them. He took her nipple into his mouth and sucked on it, teasing it with his tongue, drawing on it deeply, while she wove her fingers in his hair and held him close and lifted her body toward his mouth, offering herself up.

Giving him all of her. Every glorious, long, sturdy inch.

He touched her all over, molding the inward curve of her waist, dipping his index finger into her navel and then his tongue after that. He eased his hand over her lower belly, which was smooth and slightly rounded, begging for his caress.

She lifted her hips to his hand, letting her long, strong thighs fall open. He touched her there, at the womanly heart of her. And she moved against his hand, her hips rocking, her soft mouth sighing. She said his name. She said it more than once.

As if she meant it. As if he was someone so special. The only one for her.

He kissed her. Right there, where it counted. He parted the vanilla-and-orange-scented dark gold curls and he put his mouth on her. She was wet and soft and slick and hot. He drank her in. She tasted so sweet. Sweet as heaven.

His Lizzie—and yeah, okay. She wasn't his. Not really. But that evening, together with her in that way he never had been before, it felt as if she was his.

And he was hers.

And this thing they had, this way of being that was open and true and, yeah, about sex, but also about so much more…

It was like nothing he'd ever known before with any other person. It was so special.

It meant everything to him. More than he knew how to say in words. More than he even really understood.

She reached down and she held his head as he pleasured her, her fingers splayed in his hair. She lifted toward his secret kiss, open, ready, her body rising toward the finish so easily, so freely.

Strange. To think of Lizzie as a lover. *His* lover.

Strange. But *right,* too. Just exactly right.

"There," she whispered. "Oh, Ethan. Just…there…"

And he felt the butterfly wing fluttering against his tongue, felt her as she came, as the finish took her and rippled through her, as she cried his name yet again.

And then again.

He stayed with her. He kissed her through the soft explosions of her climax. He went on kissing her until, with a final long sigh, she lay limp under his touch.

Then he lifted his head enough to rest on her belly. She stroked his hair and traced the shape of his eyebrows, one and then the other.

And then she urged him up her body, one slim, strong arm reaching out to take a packet from the nightstand. She tore it open with her teeth.

He found that unbelievably sexy for no reason he really understood: Lizzie, placing her neat white teeth on the edge of that wrapper, tearing it open.

She eased a hand down between them. And she encircled him.

He almost choked with the thrill of that, of her cool and capable hand surrounding him.

And then she kissed him. She caught his mouth with her soft lips, and below, she was stroking him....

He knew he was going to explode. Just lose it, right then, without having felt the ultimate, longed-for, dreamed-about heat of her body surrounding him.

But somehow, he held on. Held out.

And after a long, wet kiss and numberless glorious and almost unbearable slow strokes with her clever hand, she finally lowered the condom between them, positioned it and rolled it carefully down over him.

He knew then that he would make it. He could hold out long enough to be inside her at last.

"Lizzie." He whispered her name.

She opened her eyes and met his gaze. She looked dazed, gone, lost in this impossible moment. She looked like *he* felt.

He smiled. And she responded with a slight lifting at the corners of her red, wet mouth.

"Now?" he asked.

She nodded. And she held his gaze as she wrapped her legs around him and guided him home.

He sank into her with a low groan. She welcomed him, lifting herself, opening.

Nothing like it. Ever. In bed with Lizzie, her slim arms and her long legs around him.

He gave it up to her. He buried his face in the curve

of her sweet-scented throat. He rocked his hips against her in a slow, perfect glide.

She went with him. She took his every thrust and gave it back to him. She was like no other woman he had ever known.

She was all the good things, the strong things, the *real* things.

She was everything.

And more.

Later, he kissed every bruise on her body, lingering over the really big, angry-looking one at the base of her spine.

Then they got up and went upstairs to his rooms—and the master bath, where the jetted tub was big enough for two and then some. They soaked for a while.

And they made love again.

And then, around eight-thirty, they both decided they were starving. He gave her a flannel shirt to wear and he pulled on some old sweats. They went down to the kitchen where they ate leftover lasagna.

They talked a little, sitting at the kitchen table. They agreed that they would just enjoy these last days together, really *be* together in every way.

There would be no worrying about the future.

He still felt a little guilty, though. Lizzie was his friend. He knew her goals included a good marriage and eventually babies. He was not going to be the guy who put a ring on her finger.

He admitted, "I really feel like I'm taking advantage of you."

And Lizzie threw back her head and laughed. "No, you are not. You are showing me how to live in the now and I plan to love every moment of it. So shut up and stop trying to be noble."

He felt vaguely offended. "Trying? I'm only *trying?*"

"Well, if you were really going to *be* noble, you wouldn't have let me seduce you today."

He found that totally unfair. "Lizzie, you came out into the kitchen, all pink and sweet from a bath, with your hair curling and wild-looking just the way I know you know I like it. You were wearing only a *towel.*"

"Yes, I was, wasn't I?" She looked downright proud of herself.

"And then you dropped the towel."

"You liked that, did you?"

"Lizzie, I'm only a man."

"Yes, you are." She raised her water glass. "And a very good man, I must say. A wonderful man."

He grunted. "How can I get annoyed with you when you call me wonderful?"

"You can't." She set her glass down. "Let it be, Ethan. It is what it is. Let's enjoy the time we have together."

It was good advice. *Great* advice.

So why couldn't he shake the feeling that in the end, when it was over, she wasn't going to just give it up and walk away? Why couldn't he shake the feeling that she wanted more from him than to be her lover for the next eleven days, that she wanted more than he had it in him to give?

She shoved back her chair and started unbuttoning the shirt she'd borrowed from him. "Ethan." Slowly, she peeled the shirt wide. He saw her pretty breasts and her soft belly and that little patch of curly, tempting hair down low.

"That's not fair," he said darkly.

"Stop thinking. Enjoy." She shrugged the shirt off her shoulders and let it fall to the floor.

He swore. And then he got up and went around the table and took her in his arms.

They were still in bed the next morning when Bonnie Drake called. Lizzie lay back on the pillow next to Ethan and listened to the Realtor tell her that Aubert Pelletier had accepted her offer.

Lizzie's mind started spinning. It was happening! It was real. She owned a bakery!

Bonnie said something else about the inspections and all they had to get done before the closing on July fifth. As if Lizzie could think of anything else right that moment but the one, shining fact that her cherished dream was finally coming true.

She thanked Bonnie politely.

"I'll need your earnest-money check right away," Bonnie reminded her. Earnest money was a good-faith deposit on her down payment.

"Of course," Lizzie said. "I'll bring it by. Um, say, one this afternoon?"

"That will work. I'll be here at the office then."

She thanked Bonnie again. They said goodbye. Lizzie turned off the phone and, staring dazedly at the ceiling, reached out and dropped it on the nightstand.

"Well?" Ethan rose on an elbow and leaned over her. His hair was rumpled and his eyes were lazy. His bare chest and shoulders were big and broad and tempting as the rest of him.

She reached up, slid her hand around his neck and pulled him down for a long, wet kiss.

When she finally let him go, she said it out loud for the first time. "I just bought myself a bakery."

They got up eventually, had a very late breakfast and then drove to Thunder Creek Realty to deliver the earnest-money check.

After that, they went to Bozeman, where Ethan met with some ranchers about more oil-shale leases. They got back to the house after six.

She had her girls' night out with Erin and the group at seven. She rushed to get ready while Ethan called Dillon and Corey and the other men whose wives would be out with Lizzie that evening. He invited them all over to play poker.

DJ, Dax and Dillon had babysitting duty. Ethan said they should bring the little ones over. He would make them popcorn and they could watch Disney movies on the DVR.

Lizzie kissed him goodbye at the door, a very long kiss, one that left her giddy and yearning. She found herself kind of wondering why she was going out when she could be home with him.

But then she met all her Thunder Canyon girlfriends at the Hitching Post and she totally got it. A surprise love affair with Ethan was a very special thing, but girlfriends mattered, too. They mattered a lot.

Every one of those wonderful women hooted and hollered and clapped and jumped up and down when she told them that she'd bought La Boulangerie.

Allaire said, "I knew it."

And Tori just grinned.

Steph Clifton asked, "Are you changing the name—and when are you opening?"

"It will be the Mountain Bluebell Bakery," Lizzie announced. She could tell by the gleam in Steph's eyes that she remembered that moment up on Thunder Mountain, when Lizzie had seen the blue thimble-shaped flowers and Steph had told her what they were called.

"I like it," said Steph, with feeling. She raised her tall glass of tonic with lime high. "To Lizzie and the Mountain Bluebell Bakery. Much success."

"To Lizzie," the others echoed. "To Lizzie and her bakery..."

"And what about your grand opening?" Allaire wanted to know. "You didn't say when."

Lizzie hardly dared to admit her plan. She knew she was probably being unrealistic, so she started hedging. "I know this will sound impossible, but the equipment is all in place. If there are no surprises, we're pretty much ready to go. I know there will be a mountain of permits to get, some kind of a promotional campaign to plan. And I'll have to hire and train at least a couple of employees, just to get the doors open. But I did practically grow up in a bakery. I know what needs doing and I know how to do it. I have all my mother's time-tested recipes and they are fantastic. And I've had my basic business plan worked out and ready to go for years now."

"But when?" Erin demanded. "We want to know *when*."

Lizzie confessed, "I'm shooting for the last Saturday in July."

There was more applause, more stomping and fist pumping and excited whistles. They all told her she could make it, and they promised to help any way they could.

It was a great evening, Lizzie thought, one she would always remember. It meant so much, not only to have actually bought her bakery at last, but also to have friends who believed in her, who offered unstinting encouragement and a boatload of support.

She had so much fun that she stayed out until well after midnight with the diehards of the party for that evening: Shandie Traub, Hayley Cates and Erin and Tori. Erin wouldn't let Lizzie buy a round or even a plate of nachos the whole night. "This is my tiny little payback," she insisted. "For my beautiful, perfect wedding cake."

The house was dark when Lizzie got back. The poker game must have ended, the players and the little ones they'd brought with them all gone home.

When she came through the inner door of the garage, she could see the faint glow from the kitchen, the under-counter lights that they always left on during the night. But everything was very quiet.

Ethan must be in bed. She seriously considered tiptoeing up the stairs and joining him. But really, the poor man probably needed his sleep. She'd kept him up most of the night last night—and before that, there'd been all the excitement up on Thunder Mountain during the day.

Uh-uh. He deserved a break. She went on down the hall to her own room, where she quietly shut the door and got undressed.

The soft knock came when she stood by the bed in her panties and matching camisole. She felt a definite rising sensation under her breastbone and her pulse sped up.

So he wasn't asleep, after all.

She padded over and pulled open the door and there he was, barefoot and bare-chested in a pair of frayed sweats that rode low on his hips.

"I heard the garage door open," he said, his eyes full of promises she fully intended to see that he kept.

"I didn't want to wake you…" She was whispering, moving in nice and close. He drew her like a magnet. She wanted his touch, his kiss, his body heat.

He did touch her. He ran the back of his index finger down her cheek, setting off sparks of desire, making her breath catch. "I wasn't asleep. I was waiting for you."

"Ah." It was more a sigh than an actual word.

He slipped his warm fingers under her hair and wrapped them around the back of her neck. "Did you have fun with the girls?"

"I did. So much fun." She couldn't have resisted if she'd wanted to. She leaned in, brushed a kiss across his lips.

Electric. Amazing. Every nerve in her body seemed to be purring.

He settled his mouth more firmly over hers. "Lizzie," he said against her lips. Just that. Just her name. So softly. So intently.

And then his tongue was there, tracing the shape of her mouth, leaving a trail of wet and heat. She opened. He slipped his tongue in as he gathered her closer.

They kissed, standing there in the open doorway. They kissed for a long, sweet time.

And then he undressed her. That didn't take long. He slid down the panties, pulled up the camisole and tossed it to the floor. She helped, too. She pushed down those sweats he was wearing. He kicked them away.

And she thought, as he sank to his knees before her,

that she didn't want to lose him. She couldn't stand the thought of that, even though she knew that too soon, she *would* lose him.

Too soon, she would move out. And he would move on. She had accepted that. Or so she kept telling herself, so she had told him last night when he tried to get her to talk about it.

No, she didn't want to talk about it. Talking would ruin everything. As soon as they started talking, it would all become too clear. That she *did* want his ring on her finger.

She wanted it a lot. She wanted Ethan for a lifetime.

And Ethan for a lifetime was something no other woman had managed to get. A lifetime was something he just didn't want to share.

She sighed and she gazed down through half-closed eyes at his dark head. He parted her with those clever fingers. He kissed her there, at the heart of her sex. It felt so good. So right.

Good enough that she moaned and speared her fingers in his hair and let her head fall back. Good enough that she forgot everything but the moment, everything but the silky feel of his dark hair between her fingers, everything but his hot mouth against her, and the fire building within.

A few minutes later, he scooped her up and carried her, limp and satisfied and yet longing for more, to the bed. As he gently lowered her to the sheets, she told herself that whatever happened later, it was worth it. To be with him like this, just the two of them. For a little while.

As a man and a woman.

In the middle of the night.

Chapter 13

Each day was a treasure.

Every night like a sweet, naughty dream.

It all fled by much too fast. In the last week of June, they spent Monday morning dealing with inspections—both for Ethan's new office building and for Lizzie's bakery. Both buildings required some minor repairs and those were scheduled to be handled within that week.

Monday afternoon, at a local car lot, Lizzie bought a barely used Chevy cargo van with all-wheel drive. It had only ten thousand miles on it. She was thrilled to have found it, because she was not only going to need her own vehicle, but she was also going to need one with plenty of space for hauling goods to and from the bakery. Ethan had the rental place pick up the economy car she'd been using and she parked the van in the garage.

Tuesday and Wednesday they were on the road meeting face-to-face with more ranchers and landowners, following new leads Ethan had turned up. Thursday, Ethan's mom and stepdad flew in. They spent the rest of that day and Friday, too, at the resort finalizing the investment that TOI had decided to make. To represent TOI's interest, Ethan assumed a seat on the Thunder Canyon Resort Group board.

Saturday, Rose arrived in town for a monthlong vacation. She took a luxury suite in the clubhouse at the resort, confiding to Lizzie that she liked to be where the action was. Allaire had a family party out at her and DJ's ranch that night. Ethan and Lizzie went together—and the strangest thing happened: nothing.

No one seemed to notice that they were together in a different way than before. Probably because it wasn't anything all that new in a social setting for him to spend a lot of time talking with her, or to throw his arm around her shoulders in a companionable sort of way. Over the years, she'd often stood in as his "date" for parties and family gatherings. He'd always said he liked going out with her. She was fun, he said. And he felt relaxed around her. Plus, she never clung or acted needy, unlike some of his girlfriends.

At home in his bed that night they joked about it, that they were having a hot affair, and no one had a clue.

But in her heart, Lizzie was starting to wonder if it might have been the two of them who didn't have a clue. They had never realized what they actually were to each other, that they were more than just friends, more even, than lovers.

And they'd both been blind to the truth for too long.

Now, she had the blinders off. She knew that she loved him. But he had never once so much as hinted that he might love her.

So did that mean he was hiding his true feelings from her?

She wanted to think so. But then again, what would be the point? He knew that she wanted a home and a family. If he wanted that, too, and with her, well, why not just ask her? Some men were shy about going after what they wanted.

But not Ethan. No way.

Which led her right back to the original problem, to the most likely truth: she loved him and she'd started picturing a life with him.

And he just wanted what he'd always wanted: to have a good time and to be free.

She told herself not to think about it. She promised herself she would enjoy what they had right now. And then she would let him go. She told herself it was good for her, to just go for it for once in her life, to live in the moment and not always be thinking ahead, always worrying about what was going to happen next.

And then she realized that she was doing just what she'd told herself this one time she wouldn't—worrying about the future.

Monday, Independence Day, the day before the fifth of July, came much too soon.

It was a big day in Thunder Canyon, with a parade down Main Street and a Fourth of July rodeo out at the fairgrounds. And then, that evening, there was the Independence Day dance upstairs in the ballroom of the town hall.

Ethan insisted they do it all. They watched the parade, went to the rodeo, had dinner at the Rib Shack with half of the town. And then, in the evening, they went to the dance.

It was a casual kind of thing, the women in summer dresses and the men in jeans, Western shirts and boots. Lizzie and Ethan danced to the six-piece band up on the stage at the far end of the rustic, wood-paneled ballroom. She also found time to hang out with her friends. Everyone wanted to know about her progress with the bakery. She told them that she was closing the sale the next day. And she'd be moving into the apartment above the shop before the end of the week.

They were all so sweet and encouraging. Anything she needed, they reminded her, she only had to let them know.

At ten, out on Main Street, the town merchants put on a fireworks display. Everyone piled out onto the ballroom balcony or down the stairs and outside to watch the show. She and Ethan managed to squeeze into a corner of the balcony. There were fountains and spinners and those rockets that rose with a high, screaming sound and exploded into huge, varicolored pinwheels of light high in the clear night sky.

Ethan whispered in her ear, "Now aren't you glad you gave in and came with me to Montana?"

She answered without hesitation. "Oh, yeah." No matter what happened—or didn't happen—between the two of them, she was happy she had come here, happy to be calling Thunder Canyon her home.

"Let's dance," he said a few minutes later, after the last bright fountain of flame had lit up the night. He led her back inside and took her in his arms.

She surrendered to the moment then. To the feel of his big body pressed close to hers, to the touch of his hand at the small of her back. She thought of the years she had been with him and how fast, in retrospect, they had flown by.

Too soon, the night was over.

They went home to his house, to his bed. They made love and it was sweet and hot and perfect. Then he pulled her close.

They slept. Together. For the last time.

In the morning, they each had a closing to go to. His was at ten and hers at eleven, both in the same title company's conference room. Ethan stayed on after he closed on his office building to be there for Lizzie when she signed the endless series of papers finalizing her sale.

By noon that day, she owned her bakery.

Ethan had agreed to meet some business associates for a late lunch in Bozeman. He wanted her to come with him. She said she couldn't. She had a million things to do.

"I'll see you around five or so, then?" he asked so easily. As if he'd totally forgotten that today was the last day, the day they'd agreed to say goodbye.

So, had the fact that it was ending between them just slipped his mind? That seemed impossible. But then again, Ethan could be oblivious when it came to personal relationships, especially when he didn't want to face what was happening.

Or maybe he did remember. And he was fine with it.

They were standing on the sidewalk outside the title company offices. It was neither the time nor the place to ask him if he happened to remember that she was leaving him that day.

So she forced a smile and leaned close to brush a quick kiss against his warm lips. "See you at five."

At the house, she longed to head for the kitchen and

start baking. She felt so awful about leaving him and baking would have soothed her.

But no. She really was going. Today, as she'd planned.

She started packing. It didn't take all that long. Most of her stuff was still in Midland, in storage, and at Ethan's house there. She'd already made arrangements to have it all shipped to the shop. The apartment upstairs was fully furnished. Aubert Pelletier had given her a great price on not only the shop, all its contents and the building, but also the contents of the living quarters. She would have no problem getting by until the bulk of her things arrived next week.

Because she knew that Ethan wouldn't be back for hours yet, she put everything in her van and drove on over to Main Street, where she lugged her suitcases up the stairs and put all her clothes away in the larger bedroom at the back of the building.

So strange to imagine herself living here. She felt kind of numb at the prospect. Her dream was finally coming true and it felt just a little *too* much like a dream—meaning slightly unreal.

But it was going to happen. She *would* be sleeping here. Tonight, as a matter of fact.

She stood at the window that looked out over Main Street and thought again how charming and homey Thunder Canyon was. It was going to be fine. It was all going to work out perfectly.

And for right now, it was best to keep moving. To do what needed doing. To leave no time for wishing that certain things could be different, no time for brooding over the fact that tonight was not only her first night in the apartment, but it was also the night she would have to find a way to say goodbye to the man she loved.

She went into the kitchen where she plugged in the refrigerator and went through all the cabinets. Thanks to Aubert Pelletier's willingness to leave so much behind, she had all the basics: dishes, flatware, utensils, pots and pans.

She had no linens, though. She should have thought of that. And she would also need food. So she grabbed her keys and headed over to the JCPenney in the New Town Mall, where she loaded up a shopping cart with a mattress cover, pillows, sheets and blankets in addition to towels and washcloths and the like. After Penney's, she stopped in at a supermarket to stock up on food and sundries.

At the apartment, she lugged the linens to the small service porch off the kitchen. She stuck the sheets in the washer half of the stacked washer/dryer and started the cycle. Then she made three more trips up and down the stairs, hauling in the groceries. She put everything away, transferred the sheets to the dryer and stuck the towels in the washer.

By then it was almost five and she knew that Ethan would be back at the house anytime now. She wanted to be there when he arrived. To thank him for everything.

To maybe, just possibly, try to get up the courage to say what was in her heart—yes, she knew he was a total commitment-phobe. But still, it didn't seem right to walk away without telling him exactly how she felt about him.

And then, if telling him she loved him changed nothing, to wish him well. And say goodbye.

She returned to the house.

When the garage door rumbled up, she saw that his SUV was already inside. Her heart lurched at the sight.

One big fat moment of truth, coming right up.

As she jumped down from the van, the inside door to the house opened. "Don't you ever answer your cell?" Ethan demanded in a tone that wasn't exactly angry, but close. "I got home at four. And I called you twice."

She shut the door to the van and fumbled in her purse until she found her cell. *Two missed calls.* "I'm sorry. I just didn't hear it ringing. And you know, sometimes, with all the mountains around, there are dead spots. The calls don't get through when you make them. It's possible that the phone never did ring and I..." Sheesh. She was babbling. She needed to stop that.

"You what?" He stepped back so she could enter.

"Never mind. I'm sorry, all right? I'm just...sorry."

For that, she got nothing. He waited for her to come in.

She did. She crossed the threshold and then she hesitated. Where to go? After all, she didn't live there anymore.

And he was not helping. All he did was shut the door and stand there some more. So she turned and started walking until she reached her favorite place in any house.

The kitchen.

She went to the table, pulled out her usual chair and sat down.

He hung back in the doorway, looking distinctly suspicious. "Okay, Lizzie," he said finally. "What's going on?"

She bit her lip. "Ethan, I..." The words just wouldn't come.

"Your apron," he accused. "It's missing." He marched over, opened the pantry door and pointed at the empty hook on the back of it. "And I went to your room. Everything of yours is gone."

She gave a wimpy little sweep of her hand toward the chair across from her. "Come on, sit down. Please."

He looked at her as if he wouldn't mind strangling her. "You moved out. Just like that. While I was in Bozeman."

"Ethan, we agreed that—"

He put up a hand. "Uh-uh. Don't give me that. We talked about it almost two weeks ago. Once. Nothing specific was said."

"That's not so. We agreed—"

"—today would be your last day working for me, yeah. But that's all. You never once mentioned you were just going to pack your stuff and go."

Softly, she asked, "What exactly did you think I would do?"

"Not this." He shut the pantry door. Hard. "Not this, that's for damn sure."

She had no idea where to go from there. Nothing she might have said seemed right or appropriate. So she just sat there, mute, wondering if maybe the thing to do was to simply get up and go.

Finally, he came toward her in long strides. Her pulse accelerated. She really had no idea where this was going.

But then he only yanked out his chair and dropped into it. "All right. I'm sitting. Talk."

"Ethan, come on..."

He only glared at her. "Talk."

"I just... I'm sorry. I truly am. I didn't want it to turn out like this. But it's only that I, well, I can't..." Lord, she was making a hash of this.

Apparently, he thought so, too. He made a scoffing sound. "You can't what?"

Say it, a brave voice in her head commanded. *Just tell him. Get it over with.* "I… Look. I've tried, okay? I've really tried. To…live in the moment. To just be with you and not think about where what we have is going. Because I know you. I know what you want out of life and it's not what I want."

He braced both forearms on the table and loomed closer, still glaring. "You're not telling me anything I don't already know."

"Ethan, you're acting really strange. Huffing around. Slamming doors. It's not like you at all."

He sat back in the chair and let out a slow, careful breath. He looked away, then back at her again. Now, in his eyes she saw hurt. He was hurt that she was leaving him.

The last thing she'd wanted was to hurt him.

He said, "You know it's not over with us." Now his voice was low and soft. Too soft. "Everything's been going great. I don't get it, that's all. Why walk out on a good thing?"

Tell him. Do it. Say it now. "I love you, Ethan." She said the words and she instantly wanted to take them back, but she didn't. She pushed ahead, eager to finish it, to get it all out there, to give him the truth as she knew it. "I'm *in* love with you. Yes, I've had a great time these past couple of weeks, but I want a lot more from you than a really good time. I want to marry you. I want you for the rest of our lives."

"Oh." He gulped. Yes, he did. He actually gulped. She watched in despair as his Adam's apple bounced up and then down. And then he coughed into his hand.

Lizzie didn't know whether to burst into hysterical laughter or break down in tears. Somehow, she managed to do neither. She held it together. "I don't want to be just your girlfriend for a little while longer. Until you get tired of me. Until you're ready to move on. I'd rather have it end now, when it's still good between us. I'd rather walk away with a little dignity. I'd rather spare us both all the crap that happens later, when it's finally just too painfully obvious that I want more than you want and we can't deny that anymore. So I'm just telling you right out that I'm in love with you and I've had such a beautiful, magical time, living in the moment with you. But you know, I've learned that I just can't go on with this anymore, that living in the moment doesn't work for me. Not unless the moment is connected to an endless chain of moments. A lifetime of moments of you and me, together, building a future, making a family."

He spoke in a ragged voice. "Married. My God. It's not like I didn't know it. I did know it." He rubbed the bridge of his nose between his thumb and forefinger.

Was she giving him a headache? It sure looked as if she was.

She felt a little insulted. And a little sorry for him. But mostly, she just loved him and wished that this could be over. Or that there had been some better, more graceful way to do this.

"Well?" he demanded. "Just tell me. If I said right now that I would marry you, would you stay?"

"No," she said simply. Because she *didn't* want marriage. Not like this. No way.

"But you just said—"

"Ethan. Stop."

"But I don't—"

"Seriously, stop. Remember that night I told you that you were being an ass?"

His eyes narrowed. He muttered, "Yeah. I remember."

"Well, you're doing it again, okay? Stop."

He raked his fingers back through his hair and said a few bad words in quick succession. "I would do it. All right? I would marry you. That's how I feel right now. I would marry you to keep you with me. I would do anything. Just about any damn thing you said I had to do. Because…you do it for me, Lizzie. You do it for me in every way. And if marriage is what you need to make it work for you, well, okay. Marriage it will be, then."

Lizzie only stared at him. How strange. He was offering her what she wanted most, and yet there was no way, under these circumstances, that she could accept his proposition.

He shot her a hot, fuming glance. "Well? Don't sit there looking at me like I just shot your dog. What do you say?"

She held his eyes. She refused to look away. "I already said it. No. No way. I happen to believe in marriage, Ethan. I believe in two people, together, making the best life they can. I believe in love and commitment and a white dress and a diamond ring. I believe in *you,* and that's the God's truth. And I believe you're better than this."

Her tears clogged her throat now. They couldn't be stopped. Her nose was hot and her eyes were burning. The salty wetness broke the dam of her lower eyelids and trailed slowly down her cheek. She swiped them away. And then she shoved back her chair, went to the counter and whipped a few tissues from the box waiting there.

He was still sitting where she'd left him, watching her, his eyes dark and haunted. And then he started to rise. "Don't cry, Lizzie. Damn it. Don't cry."

"No!" She stuck out a hand. "Don't, okay? Just… don't."

He sank back into the chair.

She blew her nose, dried her cheeks, turned to toss the soggy tissues in the trash bin under the sink. Finally, when she turned to him again, she brought up her hands and pressed the cool tips of her fingers against her eyelids.

He said, "It's only… I came home and you weren't here. And I *knew,* you know? I knew that you were moving out. I wasn't surprised, but I was pissed off all of a sudden. I was just really mad. Lizzie, I don't get this. You. Me. This whole thing. I, well, I like my life the way it is. But then, I think of my life without you and I hate it. You know?"

She did know. She knew too well.

Slowly, she lowered her hands from her face and met his gaze. And then she told him, her voice barely above a whisper, "I can't say yes to you when you don't even know if my saying yes is what you really want. That would be wrong, all wrong, for both of us. There has to be…joy in it, Ethan. You have to come to me with your mind and your heart wide-open."

All his previous anger was gone now. He only looked hurt and confused. And in his eyes she saw his longing. For her. For what they had together. For the years of true friendship. And for the last few brief, glorious days when there had been so much more. "I…don't know how to give you what you want, Lizzie. I don't know how to be that guy. Not everybody's like you. Not everybody wants to settle down and live happily ever after."

Her eyes were dry by then. She understood what she had to do.

She went to him. He watched her approach, his gaze wary and yet somehow tender, too. When she stood above him, she took his handsome face in her two hands and she bent down close. She pressed her lips to his.

He sighed against her mouth. "Lizzie…" But at least he didn't reach for her.

She made herself straighten to her height again. She made herself step back from him, moving over to the chair she had left, dipping to grab her bag and settle it over her shoulder. "Goodbye, Ethan."

He said nothing.

She passed in front of him to get to the door. He didn't try to stop her.

And that, she told herself, was for the best. She went out the way she had come in, through the garage, opening the outer door with the button on the wall, taking the remote opener out of her van and leaving it on the front passenger seat of his SUV, where he would see it the next time he used the car.

She got in the van, started it up, backed down the driveway and headed for Old Town. Her new life was waiting for her.

Too bad her chest felt hollow, echoing with emptiness. As if she'd torn out her heart and left it behind.

Chapter 14

The next day, Ethan's new assistant arrived from Midland. Her name was Kay Bausch. Kay was fifty-two and had been with TOI for over two decades, assisting several different executives in various departments. She was smart and efficient, a widow who'd wanted a new start in a different town. She took an apartment in a complex in New Town and went to work right away, setting up shop in the new office building on State Street.

Ethan didn't look for a housekeeper at first. He couldn't bear the thought of having to see some other woman in the kitchen, doing what Lizzie had always done, the cooking. The cleaning up.

But within a week, the house started looking really bad. He kept thinking he would clean the damn place up himself. But he was working long hours, getting TOI Montana going, and traveling around the state a lot. Eventually, he had to accept that he possessed neither the time nor the inclination to whip the place back into shape.

He lucked out when he went to dinner at Tori and Connor McFarlane's on the second Wednesday of the month. Tori told him that her housekeeper had a sister who was looking for a steady housekeeping job. The woman's children were grown, but there was a husband. She didn't want to live in, which was fine with Ethan. He didn't want some stranger living in Lizzie's rooms anyway.

Her name was Norma Stahl. She came the next morning. She was quiet and she worked fast. When she left that evening, the house was spotless and there was meat loaf in the oven.

It was nine days since Lizzie had left him. And he'd already succeeded in finding her replacements both at home and on the job. He had a very capable assistant and a pleasant, hardworking housekeeper. Things could have been worse.

Or so he kept trying to tell himself.

If only he didn't miss Lizzie every moment of every day. If only he didn't feel so damn lonely. If only life without Lizzie hadn't turned out even worse than he'd thought it was going to be.

Allaire had him over for dinner that Friday. Casually, his cousin's wife mentioned that she'd seen Lizzie several times in the past few days. Lizzie had hired Allaire to paint the new sign that would go over the bakery door. And the place was really coming together—new paint, new light fixtures, that sort of thing. Lizzie had hired someone to help on the counter and was training someone else to assist her with the baking.

"She's an amazing woman," Allaire added.

As if he didn't damn well know that. As if he even needed to hear all that stuff about how well she was doing, how everyone in town just couldn't wait until her grand opening.

Had he seen the ads she'd put in the *Thunder Canyon Nugget?* Cute, weren't they? Really eye-catching.

Allaire modestly admitted that she had designed them.

He left his cousin's house at nine that night, earlier than he should have, he knew. Leaving so early was borderline rude, but he had to get out of there.

Lizzie this. Lizzie that.

It was driving him crazy.

He headed for the Hitching Post, thinking maybe he'd meet someone, a pretty, big-eyed woman, someone delicate and sweet. But when he got there, he couldn't go in. He sat in the parking lot for a while, feeling like a wuss, wondering what had happened to him. And then he started up the SUV again and got out of there.

It didn't seem right to try to forget Lizzie in some strange woman's arms. If that made him a wuss, so be it.

The bakery just happened to be on his way home. He drove right on by, not slowing or stopping. He wasn't that bad off, he told himself. No so bad off that he would hang around her place, just hoping for a glimpse of her. But still, he couldn't help glancing up at the second story as he passed.

The lights were on in the apartment. He thought he saw her shadow move behind the drawn shades. Was she alone?

It hurt bad to think that she might not be. But then, he was already hurting. Hurting with missing her. He was beginning to see that she had filled a hole he hadn't even known was there in his world. In his life.

A hole he only recognized as an emptiness now that she was gone.

He went back to the house, where it hurt to go inside and smell nothing but a faint hint of lemon wax, which Norma used when she dusted. No muffins, blueberry or otherwise. No butter-pecan sugar cookies. No strawberry-rhubarb pie.

No Lizzie in her old blue robe, her hair wild on the sides and flattened at the back of her head, offering a drink or a hot cup of decaf.

He poured his own drink. A big one. And he sat in the easy chair in the family room. He sipped and he brooded.

He considered certain facts that he'd been avoiding admitting. Like how Lizzie provided everything a man could ever want from a woman; she created a place to call home where otherwise there was nothing but a lonely house. She gave him muffins in the morning—or whenever he wanted them. From her, he got straight talk and a few laughs, too. She told him the truth always. Nothing less.

And then there was the sex. It was terrific with Lizzie. Better than just good. She made love like she baked—with her whole heart.

He shook his head. Come on, what was he doing?

The point was to get over her. To get over her and get on with his life. He couldn't do that if he kept looking back, kept going over all the things he missed about her now that she was gone.

Right then and there, he made a silent vow not to

think about Lizzie anymore. It wasn't the first time he'd made such a vow.

They never lasted, those particular vows, because seriously, how does a man make himself *not* think about a woman?

He only ended up thinking about how he *wasn't* going to think about her. Which, when you came right down to it, still counted as thinking about her.

Ethan dropped his head to the chair back and glared at the ceiling. What a damn mess.

None of this was working out the way he'd planned.

The next day, Saturday, he drove to Great Falls. He had dinner with a landowner who had agreed to lease him mineral rights. And he had a reservation at the same motel he and Lizzie had stayed in back in June.

He ended up getting back in his SUV and driving home because the motel reminded him of Lizzie.

Which was downright pitiful, if he really thought about it.

He kept good and busy through the third week in July. He flew down to Midland Monday for a series of meetings at TOI. He had dinner with his mom and Pete twice during the three-day visit. They each made a point to get him aside and ask him if he was all right.

He told them both that he was fine. Great. Perfect. He had it all. The resort investment was a solid one. TOI Montana was a go. Things couldn't be better.

Did either of them believe him? He had no clue. He told himself it was nice that they cared, but he wished they would just mind their own damn business.

He got back to Thunder Canyon Thursday and there

were a million things to do at the office. He got on top of that as best he could.

Sunday, he went with Corey and Erin to the same church they'd been married in. Afterward, Erin fixed them a big lunch at her and Corey's new house.

Erin, like most of the women in town, had become good friends with Lizzie. Ethan felt a little edgy the whole afternoon, waiting for Erin to start in about how wonderful Lizzie was.

But Erin didn't even mention Lizzie's name.

For some reason, his sister-in-law's silence on the subject of the woman he couldn't stop thinking about irked him even more than if she'd gone ahead and babbled about Lizzie constantly.

After lunch, Corey suggested the two of them retreat to his study. They refilled their coffee cups and went into Corey's office at the front of the house.

Corey gestured at one of the leather easy chairs in a grouping near the tall front windows. "I gotta ask. You all right?"

Ethan sat down and put his coffee on a waiting coaster. "What the hell kind of question is that?"

Corey went over and shut the door before taking the other chair. "You seem edgy. Like any minute you're going to bite someone's head off."

"I'm fine, got it? Fine." He grabbed his coffee, took another sip.

Corey shook his head. "Whatever you say."

"I mean, why shouldn't I be fine? I've got it all."

"You certainly have."

"I should be happy as a bull in high clover."

Corey just looked at him.

"What?" he demanded.

And Corey did it. He said it out loud. "Well, yeah. You've got it all—except for Lizzie. You let *her* go."

Ethan considered how satisfying it would be to jump up, haul his brother out of that fat leather chair and bust him a good one right in the chops.

Corey knew it, too. "Think about it. What good is it going to do you to hit me?"

Ethan waved a hand and mumbled, "None. No good at all, but it's still tempting."

"You're in love with Lizzie, aren't you?" Corey asked the question gently.

For several seconds, Ethan refused to answer. He scowled at the far wall. But in the end, he came out with it. "Yeah."

"So why did you let her go?"

He blew out a hard breath. "She really wants that bakery. I tried to hold her back at first, for my own selfish reasons. But the more I found out how much she means to me, the more I wanted her to have it, to have everything she ever wanted."

Corey made a snorting sound. "I'm not talking about the bakery, you idiot. I'm talking about you and her and what you've got together. The whole family—the whole *town*—knows how you feel about her. *And* how she feels about you. What you two have together is a rare thing. I'm asking you why you wanted to let that go."

Ethan groaned. "You're serious? The whole town knows?"

Corey only gave him a long, patient look.

Finally, Ethan told him, "Lizzie's a forever kind of woman. And you know me, I get nervous when a woman starts getting serious."

"You keep telling yourself that long enough, you're bound to make it true no matter what."

"What the hell is that supposed to mean?"

"It means that you and Lizzie have it all. You started out working together, then you became the best of friends. And then, over time…more. How long has it been since you were with another woman?"

Ethan shot his brother a lowering glance. "What kind of question is that?"

"Just answer it. How long?"

"I don't know. Six months, maybe—no, wait. Seven."

"There's been no one else in the last seven months."

"Didn't I just say that?"

"I was only making sure."

Ethan muttered darkly, "I hope you're going somewhere important with this."

"Have you been *thinking* about going out with someone else since you and Lizzie called it quits?"

Ethan picked up his coffee cup and plunked it down without drinking from it. "No, all right? No, I don't feel like going out with anyone else. And is there a point you're getting to here?"

"Well, I'm only saying that it seems to me that you're not acting like the player you keep insisting you are. Not anymore. You're acting like a man who is serious over one particular woman. A man in love, which you have just admitted to me you are. A man who's finally found someone so right for him that he doesn't need to keep looking anymore. You've got all you want in Lizzie. But you're so thickheaded that you went and sent her away."

Ethan opened his mouth to argue but then he shut it without a word. Why fight the truth? Corey had him nailed. He'd finally found the woman for him and Lizzie was that woman. It had taken him five years of knowing her to realize what he really wanted from her.

Not someone to run his office. Not someone to keep his house. Not someone to bake his muffins or make sure his dinner was in the oven.

What he wanted from Lizzie was… Lizzie. Just Lizzie.

He wanted to spend his life with her.

And yet he had turned her down when she'd offered him everything.

He asked his brother in a voice rough with emotions he was only now starting to face, "You think she might take me back?"

Corey grunted. "You'll never know unless you try."

At eight o'clock Monday morning, the twenty-fifth of July, one week before her grand opening, Lizzie stood at the window in her living room and gazed down on Main Street. She sipped her morning coffee and felt a definite flutter of excitement in the pit of her stomach.

Five days from now. On Saturday morning, I'll be opening the doors. It will be my first day, my grand-opening day...

It seemed like a miracle, that it was really happening. There had been a thousand things to accomplish, and swiftly. Just getting all the necessary inspections and permits had been close to impossible, but she had done it. By driving herself relentlessly, every day, dawn to dark, she was making it happen. She would be ready on time.

Yeah, okay. Her heart might be hurting. Every day without Ethan was a day with a sad little empty spot in the middle of it. But sometimes a woman just had to move on. And she was doing that. She had a lot to be grateful for: good friends, a beautiful little town to live in and her dream of her bakery at last coming true. She was determined to focus on the good things, of which there were plenty.

Lizzie sniffed. With the heel of her hand, she brushed off the two lonely tears that had slid down her cheeks. It was okay, she told herself. Okay to cry a little. Sometimes a few tears helped to ease the pain.

And then she gasped.

A big SUV was driving by on the street below. Her heart bounced to her throat and her pulse started racing: Ethan.

She said the beloved name aloud. "Oh, Ethan…"

But he didn't stop. He drove on by. From her angle at the window above him, she couldn't tell if he glanced up toward where she stood, if he noticed the beautiful sign Allaire had made for her, hung just as she'd pictured it, by iron-lace hooks above the shop door.

She leaned close to the window so she could watch until the SUV turned a corner and disappeared. And when it was gone, she rested her forehead against the glass. More tears fell. She wiped them away and was just about to go grab a tissue when she saw the small, black-haired woman coming up the street from Pine. The woman was not familiar. Lizzie couldn't recall ever seeing her before.

She stopped in front of the shop. She stared up at the sign over the door, a strange, stricken look on her heart-shaped face.

After a moment or two, she started to walk away. But then she stopped, turned decisively on her delicate high heels and marched to the shop door.

The door buzzer sounded in the apartment.

Lizzie frowned. She wasn't expecting anyone. And the sign in the window made it clear she wasn't open for business yet.

The buzzer went off again. Lizzie turned, set down her coffee and headed for the door that led out to the stairs, grabbing a tissue from the box on a side table as she flew by.

She pulled open the shop door. "Yes?"

The tiny woman—she couldn't have been more than four-foot-six or seven—gaped up at her. "*Excusez-moi.* I am wanting to speak with Aubert. Aubert Pelletier?"

Lizzie realized who the woman reminded her of: her own darling *maman.* She had similar delicate features and dark, curly hair. "I'm sorry. He…well, he sold me this place a month ago. He doesn't live here anymore."

"But…where has he gone?"

"Back to France, I think his real estate agent said."

"Back to France…" The woman's huge eyes seemed to get even bigger as tears welled up in them. She put her hand over her soft rosebud of a mouth.

Lizzie made a snap decision. "Come in. Please."

"Oh, *non,* I am not here to bother you…"

"Please." Lizzie stepped back.

The woman gave her a wobbly smile. She brushed a tear from her eye. "You have been crying, too, eh?"

Lizzie drew in a shaky breath. "I'm Lizzie."

"And I am Colette."

Upstairs in the living room, Lizzie served coffee and fresh-baked croissants. And she kept the box of tissues handy.

"I…left Aubert two months ago." Colette dabbed at her wet eyes.

"You were living with him here?"

Colette nodded. "We met here. At the Hitching Post, down the street. I was staying at the resort, a little trip to America, to see the Wild West after a very messy divorce. That was in September of last year. He was a sad man. Trying to build a business here, longing for home. Aubert is from Paris. I'm from Lyon. Still, it was like magic with us, finding someone from home in this faraway place."

"You fell in love?"

Colette nodded. "I moved in here, with him, above his bakery. For a while, we were so happy. He wanted me to marry him. I was…reluctant. I'd just broken free of a bad relationship. I wanted to remain free."

"Oh, I know how that goes…"

Colette's big eyes were so wise right then. "You have left someone, too, I think."

"Yeah. *He* was the one who wanted to be free. But still, same result, huh?"

Colette seemed to draw herself up. "Oh, I hope not." She set down her coffee cup. "Wonderful croissants."

"Thank you."

"As good as Aubert's."

"I'm flattered. I understand he's a very talented baker."

"He is." Colette blew her delicate little nose. "And I love him. I want him. I want to *be* with him. To marry him."

Lizzie gave her a sideways look. "What about being free?"

Colette tucked the tissue into her purse and made a

flicking movement of her hand, a gesture that seemed to Lizzie to be supremely French. "I don't want to be free of Aubert. I know that now. I came here today to tell him so."

"So…what will you do next?" Lizzie asked, although she'd already guessed the answer.

"Go home," said Colette. "Fly to Paris and find the man I love."

Lizzie sighed and pressed her palms to her cheeks. "Oh, now *that* is what I needed to hear."

"I *will,*" said Colette, rising. "I will go, I will find my love. And I will tell him that yes, I will marry him, I *want* to marry him." Her slim shoulders drooped a little. "I only hope I am not too late."

Lizzie stood up, too. "Don't even think it," she commanded. "It's all going to work out beautifully. You'll see."

"Ah, Lizzie. You give me hope."

"He's going to be so thrilled to see you, so glad you've come back to him. I just know it. You're going to be so happy together."

They went back down the stairs. Lizzie pressed a newly printed business card into Colette's delicate hand. "Call me. Anytime you need encouragement. Don't give up."

"*Merci,* Lizzie. You, too, must keep courage in your heart. May your lover realize what a fool he's been and find his way back to you."

In the hectic days that followed, Lizzie often found herself thinking of Colette, hoping that the Frenchwoman had found her man, that Colette and Aubert were together in the city of love.

Wednesday morning, as she sipped her coffee and stood at the front window, she saw Ethan's SUV go by again. Her heart lifted—for a moment anyway.

Until he drove on past just like before, without stopping, without even slowing down.

She had started hoping. She couldn't help it. Hoping Colette's last words to her might come true. That he would see he'd been all wrong to let her go and find his way back to her. She even considered going to him, trying again to make it work between them…

But what good would that do in the end? The basic problem remained. They simply did not want the same things out of life. She'd told him she loved him, told him exactly what she wanted from him. If he changed his mind, if he decided he wanted more than just a love affair, well, he knew where to find her.

She turned from the window and went downstairs and got to work.

Working helped. It helped a lot. By the end of the day, she was worn-out. She slept deeply and without dreaming. That was a blessing. If she couldn't have Ethan, at least she didn't have to dream of him at night.

Friday morning, Colette called. It was Friday afternoon in Paris and she and Aubert were together and staying that way. Lizzie congratulated them both and thanked her for calling and letting her know.

Before they said goodbye, Colette asked if Lizzie's love had come to his senses yet. Lizzie confessed that he hadn't.

Colette said, "I know he will. I feel it in my heart."

* * *

Saturday morning, Lizzie was up at three and downstairs working. The air of the shop was filled with the sweet smell of baking.

One of her employees arrived at five and the other at six-thirty.

By eight, when they opened the doors, there was a line down the street. Lizzie stood by the door and greeted her customers. Many of them she knew. Allaire, Tori, Hayley, Shandie, Steph, Erin and Erika were all there, along with their husbands. Allaire brought her little boy and Hayley's brothers came, too. Steph and Grant brought their son and Erika brought her daughter.

There were a whole lot of Traubs. Besides Allaire and her family, Corey and Erin, Dax and Shandie and Shandie's little one, Kayla, there was also Rose. And Jackson Traub. Jackson said he was following in his brothers' and sister's footsteps, planning on moving to town.

Along with Grant and Steph, there was Elise Clifton Cates and her husband, Matt.

And more. So many more. People Lizzie recognized, some of whose names she remembered, some not. And a whole bunch of other people she'd never met before.

It seemed to Lizzie as though the whole town had turned out. Many had clipped the free-muffin coupon she'd offered in the newspaper. They got their free muffins and they bought more. They also bought bagels, fruit and cheese Danish, breads and fruit kuchen. They ordered coffee to go and coffee to stay. They filled the tables and when there were no more chairs, they took their orders and stood around the big, high-ceilinged room sipping and chatting.

Lizzie got compliments. So many. She beamed in satisfaction. Everyone loved the muffins, of course. But they all loved what she'd done to the place, too. They admired the new café lights with their blown-glass shades of swirling orange, yellow and blue, which echoed the color scheme. She'd painted two walls in sunny yellow and one in orange. And the long one behind the counter was a rich, deep burnt umber.

At waist level along each wall flowed an endless chain of mountain bluebells, hand-stenciled by Allaire. Lizzie promised everyone who asked that yes, within the week there would be Wi-Fi. They could bring their laptops, eat Mountain Bluebell muffins, drink espresso and surf the web to their hearts' content. Everyone said it was charming and homey, the kind of place you wanted to come and sit and chat for hours.

And most of her friends did just that. A lot of folks came and went, clutching bags of goodies as they rushed out the door. But Lizzie's girlfriends and their families hung around. So did Rose and Jackson. They all had second and third cups of coffee and most had more than one muffin or cinnamon roll.

By nine-fifteen, the mad rush had been handled. There was still business coming in, but the line down the street had been dealt with. Lizzie left her two employees, Rhea and Giselle, to handle the counter on their own, grabbed a vanilla latte and went to sit with her friends.

She'd just taken the chair between Allaire and Tori when Allaire elbowed her in the ribs. "Guess who?"

Corey, across the table next to Erin, said loud enough that Lizzie heard him, "And about time, too."

The little bell over the door jingled. Lizzie heard it only vaguely, like a faint echo from the real world.

She herself was somewhere else.

She was…transported. To some dreamy, impossible place.

A place where only two people existed.

Lizzie. And the tall, dark, irresistible Texan who had just come in the door.

She heard herself whisper in a voice suitable for praying, "Ethan. Oh, Ethan…"

And then he saw her—but then, how could he miss her?

She was a tall woman, after all. And somehow, without realizing she was doing it, she had risen to her feet. She kind of floated away from the table. And everyone else had moved aside—silently, it seemed to Lizzie.

There was a clear path between her and the man at the door.

"Lizzie," he said. Just that. Just her name, rough and low, with passionate intent.

And she knew then. She had no doubts. None. Not a one.

He wasn't here to wish her well, or to order his favorite strawberry-rhubarb pie. He wasn't here to support her on her opening day.

He was here for her in the truest, simplest, most basic way.

She knew it. She could feel it in her bones.

He crossed the wide plank floor in long, swift strides, stopping only inches away from her. His eyes were dark as midnight. And they were focused only on her. He spoke, his voice as husky and rough and low as it had been when he said her name at the door. "I've been by this place every day for the past week—and more than once before that."

She swallowed. Hard. "I…saw you, twice. Both times in the morning. You didn't stop. You didn't slow down."

His dark gaze searched her face. "I couldn't. I wanted…" He seemed to run out of words. But then he muttered, gruffly, "Lizzie, I was afraid…"

"Oh, Ethan…"

"I've been such a damn idiot."

As if she could deny that. "Oh, yeah, you have."

"I'm so sorry. You can't know. I'm usually smarter than this, but I guess I just got locked into a certain idea of myself. It took me way too long to see that I'm not that guy anymore. It's no fun being single, not anymore. I've been so stupid, not seeing how I love you, not admitting the truth to myself. But I know what I want now, Lizzie. I want you and me, together. I want you for my wife."

His wife. He wanted her for his wife. That was beyond huge. She really needed to say something, but all that would come out was, "Ethan…"

"Lizzie. Oh, God. Don't say it's too late."

"Ethan, I…" How to say it? How to tell him?

And right then, in the middle of her bakery on her opening day, he dropped to his knees.

Somebody gasped.

And from over near the cash register, she clearly heard Jackson Traub let out a groan. "I don't believe it." Jackson said a bad word. "He took a knee."

And he had. Right there in front of everybody, Ethan Traub was on his knee. Lizzie stared down at him and he put a hand over his heart and gazed up at her with a world of passion and longing in his eyes. It was the most perfect, beautiful, *right* moment of her life—so far.

Ethan said, "I love you, Lizzie Landry. There is no woman in the world for me but you. You're it. My answer to the big question I didn't even know I'd been asking myself until you finally got fed up with me and moved out of my house. You are the only one. I've been a fool. I know it. But if you'll only give me one more chance, I'll never be a fool again—not about what matters anyway. Not about you and me. I swear it, Lizzie. I love you and only you. And I'm willing to come here to your bakery every day for the rest of my life to get my muffins in the morning—if you'll only promise to come home to me every night."

She put her hands against her burning cheeks. "Is this…really happening?"

"Lizzie." He reached up, caught her left wrist, brought it down to him. And…there was something in his other hand. Something sparkly. "Marry me, Lizzie." He slipped a huge, gorgeous diamond onto her ring finger.

"Oh, Ethan…"

"Say yes," he pleaded.

And somehow, she did it, she managed to whisper the word that mattered most. "Yes."

"Lizzie!" He swept to his feet and he reached for her, gathering her close to him. "Aw, Lizzie…"

And he kissed her then. A beautiful, perfect, tender kiss.

And everyone in the bakery burst into wild applause.

When he lifted his head, she opened her eyes and gazed at him. And he looked…so happy. So sure. So full of joy.

She said, “I can’t believe you just asked me to marry you right here in front of everyone.”

He pulled her close and he whispered so only she could hear, “Remember that night you told me that someday I’d find someone special and I’d *want* to settle down?”

She sighed. “And you said you didn’t do serious, that you never would.”

“And then you punched me in the arm.”

“Yeah, I remember that, too.”

“It was a good punch. Hurt like hell. And I deserved it. I was so wrong. Because it was you, Lizzie. Even then, when I didn’t have a clue. It was always you.” He wrapped an arm across her shoulder and turned to all their friends and his various relatives with a big, broad smile. “Ladies and gentlemen, she said yes!”

Everyone started clapping again, even the little kids. There was whistling and a few catcalls and some more groaning from Jackson as he came to grips with the idea that another of his brothers had voluntarily surrendered to love.

Lizzie pushed Ethan into the empty seat next to Allaire. And then all her friends were up and crowding around to see the ring, to wish her well.

A few minutes later, she bent close to him and whispered, “How about a blueberry muffin?”

He gazed up at her, a killer smile curving his mouth and all the love in his heart shining in his eyes. “Blueberry. Yeah. I thought you’d never ask.”

* * * * *

MAROONED WITH THE MAVERICK

For my dad.
I love you, Dad.
And miss you so much!

Chapter 1

At 2:10 in the afternoon on the Fourth of July, Collin Traub glanced out the great room window of his house on Falls Mountain and could not believe what he saw in the town down below.

He stopped stock-still and swore under his breath. How could the situation have gotten so bad so fast? He probably should have been keeping an eye on it.

But he'd been busy, his mind on work. And it was later than usual when he stopped for lunch and came upstairs.

To *this*.

He could kick his own ass for not paying more attention. It had to be about the wettest day on record in Rust Creek Falls, Montana. The rain had been coming down in buckets since yesterday morning. And Rust Creek, which ran northeast to southwest through the center of town, had been steadily rising.

Collin had told himself it was no big deal. The creek had good, high levees on either side, levees that had held without a break for more than a hundred years. He'd never doubted that they would hold for another hundred.

And yet somehow, impossibly, sections of the levee on the south bank were crumbling. Through the thick, steady veil of rain that streamed down the windows, he watched it happen.

The levee just…dissolved, sending foaming, silvery swaths of water pouring through more than one breach. It was a lot of water and it was flowing fast and furious onto the lower-elevation south side of town.

People were going to lose their homes. Or worse.

And the water wouldn't be stopping on the edge of town, either. South of town lay Rust Creek Falls Valley, a fertile, rolling landscape of small farms and ranches—and any number of smaller creeks and streams that would no doubt also be overflowing their banks.

The Triple T, his family's ranch, was down there in the path of all that water.

He grabbed the phone off the table.

Deader than a hammer.

He dug his cell from his pocket. No signal.

The useless cell still clutched in his hand, Collin grabbed his hat and his keys and headed out into the downpour.

It was a hell of a ride down the mountain.

One-third of the way down, the road skirted close to the falls for which the mountain was named. The roar was deafening, and the pounding silver width of the falling water was twice what he was used to seeing. He made it past without incident. But if the rain kept on like this, the road could easily be washed out. He'd have himself a real adventure getting back home.

But now was not the time to worry over coming back. He needed to get down there and do what he could to help. He focused his mind on that, keeping his boot light on the brake, giving the steering wheel a workout, as he dodged his 4x4 F-150 around mudslides and uprooted trees, with the rain coming down so thick and fast he could hardly see through the windshield. Now and then, lightning lit up the gray sky and thunder boomed out, the sound echoing off in the distance, over the valley below.

Lightning could be damned dangerous on a mountain thick with tall trees. But with the rain coming down like the end of the world and everything drenched and dripping, a lightning strike causing a forest fire was probably the last thing he needed to get anxious over today.

Water. Rivers of it. That was the problem.

There were way too many spots where the streams and overflowing ditches had shed their contents across the narrow, twisty mountain road. He was lucky to make it through a few of those spots. But he did it.

Fifteen endless minutes after sliding in behind the wheel, he reached Sawmill Street on the north edge of town. He debated: go right to North Main and see what he could do in town, or go left over the Sawmill Street Bridge, skirt the east side of town and make tracks for the Triple T.

The rest of his family was three hundred miles away for the holiday, down in Thunder Canyon attending a wedding and a reunion. That made him the only Traub around.

His obligation to the family holdings won out. He

swung left and crossed the Sawmill Street Bridge, which was still several feet above the raging water. With a little luck and the Almighty in a generous mood, that bridge might hold.

The Triple T was southeast of town, so he turned south at Falls Street until he caught sight of the miniature lake that had formed at Commercial and Falls. He saw a couple of swamped vehicles, but they were empty. He swung left again. Having been raised in the valley, he knew every rutted dirt road like he knew the face he saw when he looked in the mirror to shave. Collin used that knowledge now, taking the higher roads, the ones less likely to be flooded in the troughs and dips, working his way steadily toward the ranch.

About a mile from the long driveway that led to the barns and houses on the Triple T, he crested a rise and, through the heavy curtain of pouring rain, saw another vehicle on the road ahead of him: a red Subaru Forester moving at a dead crawl.

He knew that Subaru. And he knew who was behind the wheel: Willa Christensen, the kindergarten teacher.

In spite of everything, the pounding, relentless rain and the flooded road and the pretty-damned-imminent danger, Collin grinned. Since a certain evening a little more than four years before, Willa had been running away from him—and no, he hadn't been chasing her.

Yeah, he had something of a reputation. People called him a skirt chaser, a player, the Traub family bad boy. But come on. He had better things to do with his time than sniff around after a woman who wanted nothing to do with him. And since that night four years ago, Willa took off like a shot whenever she saw him coming. Collin found her frantic efforts to get away from him pretty comical, if the truth were known.

His grin faded. She shouldn't be out in this mess. The way she drove—so cautious, like some nervous old lady—she was way too likely to misjudge a flooded spot, to get all flustered and stomp the brake and end up trapped in the waters that swamped the low sections of the road.

He knew where she was headed. The turnoff to the Christensen Ranch wasn't far past the one to the Triple T. But the way she was handling her vehicle, he didn't like her odds for getting there in one piece.

Collin readjusted his priorities, skipping the turn to the Triple T, staying on her tail.

The rain came down harder—if that was possible. He had the wipers on high, beating fast and hard across the windshield. *Thwack thwack thwack thwack.* Even on high, they could hardly keep up with the sheer volume of water falling out of the gunmetal-gray sky.

Lightning flashed, a jagged spear of it striking a twisted oak on a rise up ahead. The red Subaru in front of him lurched to a stop as the old oak crashed to the ground, smoke trailing up in a shower of sparks. Thunder boomed across the valley as the Subaru inched forward once again.

Every dip in the road held a churning miniflood. Each time Willa drove that little red station wagon down into a trough, Collin held his breath, sure she wouldn't make it through the swirling waters streaming across the road. But each time, she surprised him. She drove steadily forward at a safe, even crawl. And each time, the swirling water had to surrender her to higher ground. He went through in her wake, gritting his teeth, letting out a long breath of relief when he made it clear, too.

The sick ball of dread in his gut tightened to a knot when she suddenly hit the gas—no doubt because she'd finally realized that he was the guy in the pickup behind her. Instead of taking it slow and steady as she had been, watching the bad spots on the streaming, rutted road in front of her, suddenly she was all about getting the hell away from him.

"Damn it, Willa," he muttered under his breath, as if she might actually hear him. "Slow the hell down...." He leaned on the horn to get her to ease off the accelerator and watch the next dip. It looked pretty deep down there.

But the honking only seemed to freak her out all the more. She must have lead-footed it right to the floorboards. The Forester shot forward—and then took a nosedive into the water rushing across the low spot in the road.

It was bad. Deeper than he'd realized. As the vehicle leveled out, she was up to her side windows in churning brown floodwater.

And going nowhere. She'd swamped it.

Collin hit the brakes. The pickup came to a stop several feet above the flood. He shoved it into Park, turned off the engine, kicked down the parking brake and jumped out, hitting the rain-slick road at a run. Instantly drenched to the skin, with the rain beating down like it wanted to flatten him, he reached the churning water and waded in.

The Subaru was already drifting, picked up by the current and, half-floating, pushed toward the lower side of the road. The water was too high to see the danger there, but Collin knew that the bank at that spot dropped off into a ditch. A deep ditch. If the Subaru went over the edge, he'd have a hell of a time getting Willa out before she drowned.

She'd been raised in the valley, too. She knew what waited at the edge of the road. Inside the station wagon, she was working the door latch, trying to get it to open. She shouted something at him and beat on the window.

He kept slogging toward her, though the water seemed to grab at him, to drag him back. It was like those dreams you have where you have to get somewhere fast and suddenly your legs are made of lead. It seemed to be getting deeper, the pull of the swirling current more powerful, second by second.

Half stumbling, half swimming, while the Subaru slowly rotated away from him as it drifted ever closer to the shoulder and the ditch beyond, Collin bent at the knees and launched himself at the driver's door.

He made it. His fingers closed around the door handle. He used it to pull his feet under him again.

"You push, I'll pull!" he yelled good and loud.

She just kept pounding on the window, her brown eyes wide with fright.

He hollered even louder than before, "Push, Willa! Count of three."

She must have heard him, must have finally understood. Because she pressed her lips together and nodded, her dark, pulled-back hair coming loose, the soft curls bouncing around her fear-white cheeks. She put her shoulder into the door.

"One, two, three!" He pulled. She pushed. The door didn't budge.

"Again! One, two, three!"

The miracle happened. The Subaru rotated just enough that the current caught the door as he yanked the handle and she threw her shoulder against it. The damn thing came open with such force it knocked him over.

He went under. The door hit him in the side of the head. Not all that hard. But still.

Trying to be a hero? Not the most fun he'd ever had.

Somehow, he managed to get his waterlogged boots under him and pushed himself upright, breaking the surface in time to see his hat spinning away on the current and Willa flailing, still inside the Subaru as the water poured in on her through the now-open driver's door.

Wonderful.

He went for her, diving through the open door, grabbing for her and catching her arm. He heard her scream—or she tried to. The water cut off most of the high-pitched sound. It kept pouring in, beating at them as it filled the cab.

They had to get out and get out now.

He pulled on her arm until he'd turned her, faceup, and then he caught her in a headlock. Okay, it wasn't delicate. It wasn't nice and it sure wasn't gentle. But with his arm around her neck, at least he could turn and throw himself out the door. She grabbed his arm in both her hands, but by then, she seemed to have caught on to what he was trying to do. She wasn't fighting him anymore. She was only holding on as tight as he was.

He squirmed around to face the open door. The water shoved him back, but at least the rotation of the vehicle kept the door from swinging shut and trapping them inside. He got his free hand on the door frame, knees bent, boots braced on the side of the seat. Another hard push and they were out just as the Subaru went over the bank into the ditch.

The weight of the vehicle going under sucked at them, but Willa slipped free of his hold and started swimming. Since she seemed to be making it on her own steam, he concentrated on doing the same.

Side by side, they swam for the place where the road rose up out of the ditch. His boots touched ground. Beside him, she found her footing, too—for an instant. Then she staggered and went under.

He grabbed her again, hauling her up, getting one arm around her waist. Lightning tore another hole in the sky and thunder boomed as he half carried, half dragged her up and out of the racing water.

She coughed and sputtered, but she kept her feet moving. The woman had grit. He had to give her that. He kept hold of her, half-supporting her, urging her to the high side of the road and up the hill far enough that they were well above the water and reasonably safe.

They collapsed side by side onto the streaming ground as the rain continued to beat down on them, hard and heavy, never ending. She turned over, got up on her hands and knees and started hacking and coughing, spitting up water. He dragged in one long, hungry breath after another and pounded her back for her, helping her clear her airways so she could breathe. When she was finally doing more breathing than hacking, he fell back on the ground and concentrated on catching his own breath.

Lucky for him, he just happened to turn his head and glance in the direction of his truck about then. The water *had* risen. Considerably. It was maybe two feet from his front wheels now.

He turned to the waterlogged woman gasping beside him. “Stay here. Do not move. I’ll be right back.”

Swearing low and with feeling, he lurched upright and beat feet on a parallel track with the road. When he got even with his truck, he half ran, half slid down the hill, raced around the rear of the pickup and hauled himself up into the cab. The key was still in the ignition—and the water was lapping around his front wheel wells by then.

He turned it over, released the brake, put it in Reverse and backed to the top of the last rise. Once there, he slammed it in Park again and jumped out to see how things looked behind him.

Not good. The road was flooded in the previous trough. Water in front of him, water behind. The truck was going nowhere until the water receded.

Fair enough. He got back in and parked on the shoulder. Taking his keys with him that time, he left the truck and locked it up.

Then he looked for Willa.

She was gone.

Chapter 2

A moment later, Collin spotted her.

She was on her feet and slogging up the long slope of the hill. He knew then where she was headed. There was a big, weathered, rambling structure way at the top—the Christensen barn.

"Willa, what the hell?" he yelled good and loud. "Hold on a minute!"

She didn't pause, she didn't turn. Her hair plastered to her head, and her little white T-shirt and snug jeans covered with mud and debris, she just kept on putting one boot in front of the other, heading up that hill.

He was powerfully tempted to let her go.

But who knew what trouble she'd get herself into next? If something happened to her, he'd end up with a guilty conscience for leaving her all by her lonesome. Plus, well, he didn't have a lot of options himself, at the moment. The floodwaters were all around.

And it might be July, but the rain was a cold rain and the wind was up, too. He needed shelter to wait out the storm and the barn had walls and a roof. It was better than nothing. Willa was going to have to get over her aversion to him, at least until there was somewhere else he could go.

With a grunt of resignation, he climbed the hill after her, tucking his head down, putting one foot in front of the other, as the water streamed over him and his boots made sucking sounds with each step he took.

He caught up to her maybe twenty yards from the barn. She must have heard the sloshing of his boots at last.

She stopped, her arms wrapped around herself to control the shivers that racked her, and whirled to confront him. "Collin." She tipped her head up and drew her slim shoulders back. Water ran down her cheeks, into her wide mouth and over her chin.

He could see her nipples, hard as rocks, right through her T-shirt and her bra. "What, Willa?"

"Thank you for saving my life."

"Hey." He swiped water off his nose. Not that it did any good. "No problem. Can we move it along? It's pretty damn wet out here. I'd like to get in that barn."

She gripped her arms tighter around herself. "I would like for you to go away and leave me alone."

"Oh, you would, would you?"

"Yes. Please."

He raised his arms out wide, indicating all of it—the never-ending storm, the floodwaters surrounding them, the cold wind and the flash of bright lightning that lit up the sky again right at that moment. The thunder rumbled. He waited for the sound to die away. "Exactly where do you suggest I go, Willa?"

She flung out a hand. "What about your truck?"

He folded his arms across his chest and simply looked at her.

Her shoulders sagged and she let out a low cry. "Oh, fine. All right. You can come in the barn. Just...fine. Okay." And she turned around again and continued walking.

He fell in behind her.

The barn loomed ahead. When they reached it, she undid the latch and slipped in. He went in after her, pulling the door to, latching it from within.

The barn had another door on the far wall. Someone must have left the latch undone, because that door stood wide-open. It was probably not a bad thing in this situation. The Christensen livestock needed more than a run-in shed on a day like today and the animals had found what they needed through that wide-open door.

The rambling space was wall-to-wall critters. There were cattle, goats, some chickens and several cooing pigeons. Carping blackbirds perched in the rafters. A couple of pigs snorted beneath one of the two windows and somewhere nearby a barn cat hissed and then yowled.

A dog barked. Collin spotted a muddy white Labrador retriever. The dog was headed for Willa.

She let out a happy little cry. "Buster! There you are!" She dropped to a crouch and opened her arms. The dog reared up and put his front paws on her shoulders. Whining with excitement, he licked her face with his sloppy pink tongue. "You are such a bad, bad dog," she crooned in a tone that communicated no criticism whatsoever. "Hey, now. Eww." She turned her head away from Buster's slobbery attentions and saw Collin watching her.

"Nice dog." He'd had a great dog named Libby who'd died the winter before. She'd been sixteen, with him since he was eleven and she was an ugly pup, the runt of the litter wanted by no one—but him.

"Down, Buster." She rose again and tried to brush the mud and water off her soaking wet shirt and muddy jeans. It did zero good. "Technically, he's my dog," she explained, "but he's always loved it here on the ranch, so he lives here more than with me. He was supposed to be staying with me in town, though, while my parents and Gage are in Livingston for the big rodeo." Gage Christensen, her brother, was the town sheriff. "That dog just will not stay put. He keeps running off to get back here." A shiver went through her. She wrapped her arms around herself again.

"You're freezing," he said. It came out sounding like an accusation, though he didn't mean it that way.

"I am fine." She shivered some more. Her hair was plastered on her cheeks and down her neck. She swiped at a soggy hunk of it, shoving it back behind her ear. "Just fine." She scowled at him.

Whoa. For a minute there, she'd almost seemed friendly—but then she must have remembered that she hated his ass. She turned her back on him and started weaving her way through the crush of horses and cattle. The Lab followed her, panting happily, wagging his muddy tail.

It should have been warmer in there, with all the steaming, milling livestock. But it really wasn't. How could it be, with that far door wide-open and both of them soaking wet? He slapped the bony butt of a little red heifer who'd backed in too close. She let out a cranky "moo," and ambled away—not far, though. There wasn't really anywhere to go.

He found a hay bale against the wall and sat on it as he pondered what he ought to do to make things a little more comfortable. He hesitated to go over and shut the other door. The smell of wet livestock and manure would get pretty strong if he did that.

As he considered what to do next, he watched the dripping brown-haired woman who had spent the past four years avoiding him and now happened to be stuck with him until the rain ended and the floodwaters receded.

Willa was keeping busy shivering and ignoring him, wandering from steer to goat to barn cat to bay mare, petting them all and talking to them low and soft, as though she had a personal relationship with each and every four-legged creature on her family's place. And maybe she did.

She'd always been a fanciful type, even way back when they were kids. He knew this from actual observation.

Collin had run wild as a kid. He was the youngest, sixth of six boys, and his mom was worn-out by the time he came along. She didn't have the energy to keep after him. He went where he wanted and came home when he felt like it. He wandered far and wide. Often, he found himself on Christensen land. Now and then, he'd run into Willa. She would be singing little songs to herself, or making crowns out of wildflowers, or reading fairy-tale books.

She'd never seemed to like him much, even then. Once she'd yelled at him to stop spying on her.

He hadn't been spying. A kid wasn't spying just because he stretched out in the tall grass and watched a neighbor girl talking to herself as she walked her big-haired brunette Barbie doll around in a circle.

Collin tried to get more comfortable on the hay bale. He scooted to the wall, leaned his head back against the rough boards, closed his eyes and tried not to think how cold he was, tried not to wish he'd grabbed a snack to take with him when he'd run out of the house. His stomach grumbled. He ignored it.

It would have been nice if he could drop off to sleep for a little and forget everything. But no such luck. He would just start to doze when a fit of shivering would snap him awake and he would realize anew that they were smack-dab in the middle of one hell of a disaster. He hoped that no one in town had drowned, that the hands and the animals on the Triple T were safe. He couldn't help wondering how much of both the town or his family's ranch would be left standing when the floodwaters receded.

And how much of the state was affected? What about Thunder Canyon, where his family had gone? Were they underwater, too?

Eventually, he gave up trying to sleep and opened his eyes. Willa stood at the window that faced southwest, the one not far from where two spotted pigs were snorting over an upturned bucket of feed. With the white Lab at her feet, she stared out through the endless curtain of the rain. He rubbed his arms to try and warm up a little and knew she must be staring at her parents' place. The Christensen house was about level with the barn, on high ground, atop the next hill over.

He knew he was asking for more rejection to try and

talk to her, but he was just tired and dejected enough to do it anyway. "The house should be safe," he said. He didn't mention her brother Gage's house, which was down the slope of the hill behind her parents' place. It wouldn't be visible from Willa's vantage point, which was just as well. As Collin remembered, it was a ways down the hill and probably already below the rising waterline.

She surprised him by replying. "Yes. I can see it. It's okay, for now…." She sounded strange, he thought. Kind of dreamy and far away. She had a few scratches on her arms. And a bruise on her cheekbone. But like him, no serious injuries. They'd been very fortunate. So far. She added, "It's all so unbelievable, don't you think? Like maybe this isn't even actually happening. Maybe I'm just dreaming it."

"Sorry, Willa." He meant that. He *was* sorry. "I think it's really happening."

She sent him a glance. For once, her mouth didn't pinch up at the sight of him. "I lost my phone." A shiver went through her and her teeth chattered together. "Do you happen to have yours with you?"

"It's in my truck, I think. But there must be towers down. I was getting no signal when I tried using it at a little after two."

Willa sighed and turned back to the window. "Life is so…fragile, really, isn't it? I mean, you go along, doing what you need to do, thinking you're taking care of business, that you're in control. But you're not in control, not really." Outside, lightning flared. Thunder rolled out. "Anything could happen," she said. "It could rain and rain and never stop…." Her lips looked kind of blue, he thought.

He really needed to come up with a way to warm her up a little. Rising, he began to work his way around the barn, looking for a blanket or a tarp or something.

Willa kept talking. "Oh, Collin. I keep thinking of the children in my class last year. And the ones in our summer school program. I can just close my eyes and see each one of their sweet, smiling faces. I hope they're all safe and dry. Our school, the elementary school? It's on the south side of town. That's not good news. And my house is on the south side, too…."

He pushed a goat out of the way as he came to a spot where the wall jogged at a ninety-degree angle. Around that corner was a door. He opened it. "Willa, there's a tack room here."

She sighed again. "Yes. That's right. And a feed room over there." She put out a hand in the general direction of the other shut door farther down the wall. And then she started in again, about life and the flood and the safety of her friends, her neighbors and her students.

Collin took a look around the tack room. There were the usual rows of hooks holding ropes and bridles and bits. He was a saddle maker by trade and he grinned at the sight of one of his own saddles racked nice and neat, lined up with several others on the wall. There was a window. And another door, allowing outside access.

The floor in there was wood, not mixed clay and sand as it was out in the main part of the barn. And the walls were paneled in pine.

And then he saw the stack of saddle blankets atop a big cedar storage trunk. He went over and grabbed one. Shooing out the goat that had followed him in there, he shut the door and made his way through the milling animals to Willa.

She didn't even flinch when he wrapped the blanket around her. "Thank you."

He took her by the shoulders. "Come on. Let's go…." She went where he guided her, back through the cattle and horses and goats, with the dog right behind them. He let the dog in the tack room with them, and then shut the door to keep the rest of the animals out. There were a few hay bales. He sat her down on one and knelt in front of her.

She frowned down at him. "What are you doing?"

He held her gaze. "Don't get freaky on me, okay?"

She looked at him in that pinched, suspicious way again. "Why not?"

"You need to get out of those wet clothes. There are plenty of blankets. You can wrap yourself up in them and get dry."

"But…my clothes won't dry."

"It doesn't matter. Right now, *you* need to get dry."

She considered that idea—and shook her head. "I'll take off my boots and socks. I'll be all right."

He decided not to argue with her. "Fine. You need help?"

"No, thank you." All prim and proper and so polite. "I'll manage."

"Are you thirsty?"

She gaped at him. "Thirsty?" And then she let out a wild little laugh. "In this?" She stuck out a hand toward the water streaming down the lone window.

"Are you?"

And she frowned again. "Well, yes. Now that you mention it, I suppose I am."

He rose. "I'll see if I can find some clean containers

in the barn. We can catch some of the rainwater, so we won't get dehydrated."

She blinked up at him. "Yes. That makes sense. I'll help." She started to rise.

He took her shoulders again and gently pushed her back down. "Get out of your boots and shoes—and wrap this around your feet." He held out another blanket.

She took it, her gaze colliding with his. Holding. "What about you?"

"Let me see about setting out containers for water. Then I'll grab a few blankets and try and warm up a little, too."

Half an hour later, he had his boots and socks off. They'd pushed four hay bales together and spread a blanket over them. Side by side, wrapped in more blankets, they passed a bucket of water back and forth.

When they'd both drunk their fill, there was still plenty left in the bucket. He set it on the floor, where Buster promptly stuck his nose in it and started lapping. "You don't happen to have a nice T-bone handy, do you, Willa?"

She chuckled. There wasn't a lot of humor in the sound, but he took heart that at least she wasn't staring blindly into space anymore. "Plenty on the hoof right outside that door." She pointed her thumb over her shoulder at the door that led into the barn.

He scooted back to the wall for something to lean against. "Not that hungry yet."

"I didn't think so." She scooted back, too, settling alongside him, and then spent a moment readjusting the blanket she'd wrapped around her feet. "There."

She leaned back and let out a long breath. "I believe I am actually beginning to thaw out."

"That was the plan." Outside, the rain kept falling. The sky remained that same dim gray it had been all day. "Got any idea what time it is?"

"I don't know. Six, maybe? Seven?" She sounded… softer. A little sleepy. That was good. Rest wouldn't hurt either of them. "Won't be dark for hours yet…."

He was feeling kind of drowsy, too, now that he wasn't chilled to the bone anymore and most of the adrenaline rush from the various near-death events of the day had faded a little. He let his eyelids droop shut.

But then she spoke again. "It's really very strange, Collin, being here with you like this."

He grunted. "This whole day has been pretty strange."

"Yes, it has. And scary. And awful. But, well, that's not what I meant."

He knew exactly what she meant. And why was it women always had to dig up stuff that was better left alone? He kept nice and quiet and hoped she wasn't going there.

But she was. "Maybe this is a good chance to clear the air a little between us."

"The air is plenty clear from where I'm sitting."

"Well, Collin, for me, it's just not."

"Willa, I—"

"No. Wait. I would like a chance to say what's on my mind."

He didn't let out a groan of protest, but he wanted to.

And she kept right on. "It was very…humiliating for me, that night at the Ace in the Hole." The Ace was on Sawmill Street. It was the only bar in town. People went there to forget their troubles and usually only ended up creating a whole new set of them. "It was my first time there, did you know? My twenty-first birthday." She sounded all sad and wistful.

He'd known. "I think you mentioned that at the time, yeah."

"Derek had just dumped me for a Delta Gamma." Straight-arrow Derek Andrews was her high school sweetheart. They'd graduated the same year and headed off to the University of Idaho together. "Collin, did you *hear* me?"

"Every word," he muttered.

"Did you *know* it was over between me and Derek?"

"Well, Willa, I kinda had a feeling something might have gone wrong with your love life, yeah."

"You led me on," she accused. "You know that you did." He'd seen her coming a mile away. Good-girl Willa Christensen, out to find a bad boy just for the night. "And then you…" Her voice got all wobbly. "You turned me down flat."

"Come on, Willa. It wasn't a good idea. You know that as well as I do."

"Then why did you dance with me all those times? Why did you flirt with me and buy me two beers? You acted like you were interested. More than interested. And then, when I tried to kiss you, you laughed at me. You said I wasn't your type. You said I should go home and behave myself."

He'd had some crazy idea at the time that he was doing her a favor, keeping her from doing something she wouldn't be happy about later. But with Willa, no good deed of his ever went unpunished. And was she going to start crying? He hated it when a woman started crying.

She sniffled in her blankets, a small, lost little sound. "I still can't believe I did that—made a pass at *you.* I mean, you never liked me and I never cared much for you and we both know that." That wasn't true—not on his part anyway. Far from it. But he wasn't in the mood to dispute the point at the moment. He only wanted her not to start crying—and he thought maybe he was getting his wish when she squirmed in her blankets and grumbled, "Everyone knows how you are. You'll sleep with anyone—except *me,* apparently."

Mad. Now she was getting mad. As far as he was concerned, mad was good. Mad was great. Anything but weepy worked for him.

She huffed, "I just don't know what got into me that night."

He couldn't resist. "Well, Willa, we both know it wasn't me."

She made another huffing sound. "Oh, you think you're so funny. And you're not. You're very annoying and you always have been."

"Always?" he taunted.

"Always," she humphed.

He scoffed at her. "How would you know a thing about me the last four years? Since that night at the Ace, all I see is the backside of you. I come in a room—and you turn tail and run."

"And why shouldn't I? You are a complete tool and you never cared about anything or anyone in your whole life but yourself."

"Which is girl talk for 'You didn't sleep with me,'" he said in his slowest, laziest, most insolent tone.

"You are not the least bit clever, you know that?"

"You don't think so, huh?"

"No, I do not. And it just so happens that I'm *glad* we never hooked up that night. You're the last person in the world I should ever be sleeping with."

He tried not to grin. "No argument there. Because I'm not having sex with you no matter how hard you beg me."

"Oh, please. I mean just, simply, *please*." She sat up straight then. Dragging her blankets along with her, she scooted to the edge of the hay bales, as far from him as she could get without swinging her bare feet to the floor. Once there, she snapped, "You do not have worry. I want nothing to do with you."

He freed a hand from his blankets and made a show of wiping his brow—even though she wasn't looking at him. "Whew."

"In case you didn't know, it just so happens that I have a fiancé, thank you very much."

"A fiancé?" That *was* news to Collin. The information bothered him. A lot—and that it bothered him bugged him to no end.

"Yes," she said. "Well. Sort of."

"Willa, get real. You do or you don't."

"His name is Dane Everhart and he's an assistant coach at the University of Colorado. We met at UI. We've been dating on and off for three years. Dane loves me and knows I'm the one for him and wants only to marry me and, er, give me the world."

"Hold on just a minute. Answer the question. You're saying you're engaged?"

She fiddled with her blankets and refused to turn around and look at him. "Well, no. Not exactly. But I *could* be. I promised to give Dane an answer by the end of the summer."

He stared at the back of her head. Her hair was a tangle of wild, muddy curls from her dip in the floodwaters. It should have looked like crap. But it didn't. It looked like she'd been having crazy good sex with someone—and then fallen asleep all loose and soft and satisfied.

And why the hell was he thinking about sex right now? Was he losing his mind? Probably. A few hours trapped in a barn with Willa Christensen could do that to a man, could drive him clean out of his head.

He sat up, too, then, and sneered, "You're in love with this guy, and you're not going to see him until *September?*"

"So? What's wrong with that?"

"Well, I mean, if you're in *love* with him, how can you *stand* to be apart from him? How can *he* stand to be away from you?"

"You wouldn't understand."

"Are you in love with him, Willa?"

She squared her slim shoulders. "I just *told* you that you wouldn't understand."

"That's right. I wouldn't. If I loved a woman, I'd want her with me. Where I could touch her and be with her and hold her all night long."

Willa gasped. She tried to hide the small, sharp sound, but he heard it. "Oh, please. As if you know anything about being in love, Collin Traub."

"I said if I *was* in love."

"Well. Humph. As it happens, Dane has gone to Australia until the end of the month. He gets only a short summer break before practice begins again. And do you know how he's spending his limited free time? I will tell you how he's spending it. At a special sports camp. He's helping Australian children learn about American football. Because he's a good man, a man who *cares* about other people. That's how he is. That's *who* he is…"

There was more. Lots more.

Collin let her heated words wash over him. The point, as far as he saw it, was that she hadn't answered the main question. She hadn't come out and said, "Yes. I'm in love with Dane Everhart."

He felt absurdly satisfied with what she *hadn't* said. She could rant all night about the wonderfulness of this Dane character while talking trash about *him.* At least she was acting like the Willa he'd always known. At least she was full of fire and vinegar and not shaking with cold, shock and fear anymore.

Collin smiled to himself, settled back against the wall and closed his eyes.

Chapter 3

Willa felt Collin's presence behind her acutely.

But she didn't turn to him. She sat on the edge of the pushed-together hay bales and stared resolutely out the tack room's one window as waves of never-ending rain flowed down the glass.

She finished what she had to say about Dane. "It just so happens that Dane would have liked to have taken me with him. But he was going to be very busy with the Australian children and I had things I could be doing here at home. We have summer school at Rust Creek Falls Elementary, in case you didn't know and I…" Her voice trailed off.

Collin hadn't said a word for a couple of minutes, maybe more. Had he fallen *asleep,* for heaven's sake?

She wouldn't put it past him. He was such an exasperating, impossible man. Always had been. And no doubt always would be.

So why am I starting to feel ashamed of myself?

Willa's cheeks were flaming. She tucked her chin down into the scratchy saddle blanket he'd wrapped around her. At least he couldn't see her embarrassment at her own behavior—not as long as she didn't turn and face him.

Which she was not going to do right now, thank you very much.

Stretched out on the floor by the hay bales, Buster huffed out a long sigh. Willa bent down and scratched him on the head. His tail bounced happily against the rough plank floor.

She gathered her blankets close again. All right, she probably shouldn't have gone off on Collin like that. No matter how humiliating her history with the guy, he'd been there when she desperately needed him. He'd saved her life a few hours ago, at no small risk to himself.

Plus, well, she hadn't really been honest while she was getting all up in his face just now, had she? She hadn't bothered to mention that she had serious reservations about her and Dane. Dane was the greatest guy in the world and he did want to marry her, very much. But Rust Creek Falls was her home and he wasn't about to give up his wonderful career at CU. And more important than geography, Dane somehow didn't quite *feel* like her guy.

Whatever her guy *should* feel like. She wasn't sure. She just had a certain intuition that Dane wasn't it.

And worse than her doubts about her future with an ideal man like Dane, well, there was that longtime *thing* she'd had for Collin—oh, not anymore. Of course not. That night at the Ace in the Hole had put an end to her ridiculous schoolgirl crush on the town bad boy.

But before that night she used to fantasize about him now and then.

Or maybe even more often than now and then.

She used to wonder what it would be like if bad-boy Collin were to kiss her. Or do more than kiss her…

Not that it mattered now. None of her past silliness over Collin mattered to anyone. It had been a fantasy, that was all. *Her* fantasy. He'd never been the least interested in her. He'd made that painfully clear on the night he led her on and then laughed in her face.

And really, after all that had happened today, her four-year grudge against him for not having sex with her was beginning to seem nothing short of petty. She really needed to let the past go. She needed to be…a bigger person than she'd been so far about this. She needed to be a *better* person.

And she needed to start doing that now.

Willa cleared her throat. "Um. Collin?"

He shifted a little, back there against the wall. "What now, Willa?" His voice was scratchy and deep. Lazy. What was it about him? He just always made her think of wrinkled sheets and forbidden passion.

In a purely impersonal, objective way, of course.

"I, um, well…"

"Come on. Spit it out."

She made herself say it. "I'm sorry, okay?" She hauled her blanket-wrapped legs back up on the hay bales and wiggled around until she was facing him again. He lay sprawled under his blankets, his head propped against the wall, his eyes shut, his eyelashes black as coal, thicker than any girl's, his full mouth lax and lazy, just like his voice had been, the shadow of a beard on his cheeks. A curl of that impossibly thick black hair of his hung over his forehead. She clutched her blankets tighter to keep from reaching out and smoothing it back. "I shouldn't have jumped all over you like that. I shouldn't have called you a tool. That was…small-minded and mean-spirited of me, especially after all you've done for me today."

He didn't say anything for a minute. And he didn't open his eyes. Again, she wondered if he'd dropped off to sleep and she had to resist the urge to reach out and shake him. But then those bad-boy lips curved upward in a slow smile. "So you don't think I'm a tool, then?"

"Um. No. No, of course not. I shouldn't have said that. I'm sorry. I am."

"And you think maybe you could stop racing off like your hair's on fire every time you see me coming?"

A fresh wave of embarrassment had her cheeks flaming all over again. But what did it matter? He couldn't see her blush. His eyes were shut. Also, she truly wanted to make amends. "Ahem. Yes. Fair enough. I will do that. I will stop avoiding you."

"Well, all right then. I accept your apology." He patted the empty space beside him. "Stretch out. Try and get some sleep. I'm thinking we're going to be busy when the rain stops and the water goes down."

His words brought reality crashing back down on her. She hung her head. "Oh, Collin. It seems like it's never going to stop. I know my brother's house is already underwater. And what if it just keeps rising, what if we—?"

"Shh." He reached out and clasped her arm through the thick wool of the blanket. His grip was strong. Sure. It made her so very glad that he was here with her, that she wasn't huddled in the family barn all alone, waiting out the endless storm. "Don't go there." His voice was calm and firm. "There's no point."

She lifted her head. His eyes were open now, steady on hers. Shamelessly, she pleaded, "Tell me that we're going to be okay, that Rust Creek Falls will be okay, that we'll make it through this, come back better and stronger than ever."

He didn't even hesitate. He told her what she needed to hear. "We will. Just watch. Now come here. Come on..." He lifted the blanket that covered him.

She didn't think twice. She went down into the shelter of his offered arm, resting her head on his shoulder. He was so warm and big and solid. He smelled of mud and man, which at that moment she found wonderfully reassuring. He fiddled with the blankets, smoothing them over both of them.

Willa smiled to herself. All those crazy teenage dreams she'd had about him. And here she was, damp and dirty, bruised and scratched up, lying practically on top of him, grateful beyond measure to share a pile of saddle blankets with him. The world seemed to have gone crazy in the space of a day. But right now, in Collin's arms, she felt safe.

Protected.

She closed her eyes. "I didn't realize until now how tired I am...."

He touched her hair, gently. Lightly. "Rest, then."

She started to answer him, but then she found she didn't have the energy to make a sound. Sleep closed over her. She surrendered to it with a grateful sigh.

When she woke, the light was different.

Sun. It was sun slanting in the window—and the

window faced east. That meant it had to be morning, didn't it?

Also…

She was lying on a man. Collin. He had both arms wrapped around her and his cheek against her dirty, snarled hair. Her head was on his shoulder, one arm tucked in against her side.

Her other arm rested on Collin, which was perfectly acceptable, given the circumstances. But the hand that was attached to that arm? That hand was exactly where it shouldn't be.

And where it shouldn't be was hard.

Blinking, not quite putting it all together as reality yet, Willa lifted her head from his shoulder and blearily squinted at the morning light. Outside, faintly, she could hear birds singing.

Without moving her hand away from his very definite, very thick and large hardness, she looked down at him. Because, seriously. Could this actually be happening?

It was.

And he was awake. He gazed up at her with the strangest, laziest, *sexiest* expression. "Mornin'."

She puffed out her cheeks as she blew out a slow breath. And then, with great care, she removed her hand from his private parts and whispered, "The sun's out."

He nodded. "The rain's stopped. It stopped hours ago." He was playing along with her, pretending the contact between her hand and his fly had not occurred. Which was great. Perfect. Wonderful of him.

She backed off him onto her knees, dragging the blankets with her, and shoved her hair out of her eyes. "You, uh, should have woken me."

"Uh-uh." He reached out and clasped her shoulder, a companionable, reassuring sort of gesture that made tears clog her throat. She swallowed them down. And he said, "You needed your sleep and so did I. I woke up in the middle of the night and it was quiet. I knew the rain had finally stopped. I thought about getting up, but then I just closed my eyes and went back to sleep."

Buster was up, making whining noises, scratching at the door that led outside. "I should let him out…." He took his hand from her shoulder. She wished he hadn't, that he would touch her again, hold on tight and never, ever let go. But he didn't. And she pushed the blankets aside, swung her legs over the edge of the hay bales and stood up. Barefoot, she went and pulled the door open. Buster went out and she scolded, "Don't run off, now." And then she lingered in the open doorway, staring up at the sky. Blue as a newborn baby's eyes. She glanced back over her shoulder at Collin.

He was sitting up, bare feet on the floor. He had a case of bed head every bit as bad as hers, and he was kind of hunched over, his elbows on his knees. "Come on," he said gruffly. "Put your boots on," He raked his fingers back through all that thick, every-which-way hair. "We'll see if the water's gone down enough that we can get across the ravine to your folks' house."

They put on their damp socks and boots and pulled open the door that led into the main part of the barn.

"Needs a good mucking out in here," Collin said. Did it ever. Most of the animals had wandered off, out into the morning sunshine, leaving a whole lot of fresh manure behind. "You supposed to be taking care of the place all by your lonesome while your folks and your brother are off at the rodeo?"

She shook her head and named off the neighbors who'd agreed to look after things and feed the stock until the family returned. "But I'm guessing they probably all have their own problems about now." At least it was summer and grazing was good. The animals wouldn't starve if left to their own devices for a few days.

Instead of slogging through the mess on the barn floor to one of the outer doors, they ducked back into the tack room and went out through the exterior door there. Buster was waiting for them, sitting right outside the door, acting as though he'd actually listened when she told him not to wander off.

Willa scratched his head and called him a good dog and tried to tell herself that the jittery feeling in her stomach was because she hadn't eaten since lunch the day before—not rising dread at the prospect of how bad the damage was behind the barn on the next rise over, and along the roads that crisscrossed the valley. And in town…

"It's a beautiful day," she said, tipping her head up again to the clear sky. "You'd almost think yesterday never even happened."

"Hey."

She lowered her gaze to him. Even with his hair sticking up on one side and a smudge of dirt at his temple, he still looked like every well-behaved girl's naughty, forbidden fantasy. "Hmm?"

His dark eyes searched hers. "You okay?"

And she nodded and forced her mouth to form a smile.

On the other side of the barn, the two pigs from the night before were rooting around near the water trough. A rooster stood on a section of busted-down fence and crowed as Willa stared across the ravine at her parents' house.

The house was untouched by the flood, though the water had gotten halfway up the front walk that was lined with her mother's prized roses. Her dad's mini-tractor lay on its side at the base of that walk. And a couple of steers had somehow gotten through the fence and were snacking on the vegetable garden in the side yard.

Below, in the ravine, the water had receded, leaving debris strewn down the sides of the hill and up the one on which the house sat. There were tree trunks and lawn chairs down there, boulders and a bicycle, a shade umbrella and any number of other items that looked bizarre, scary and all wrong, soggy and busted up, trailing across the pasture. Willa turned her eyes away, toward the road.

And saw her red Subaru. It had drifted past the ditch and lay on its side in the pasture there. It was covered in mud.

"Guess I'll be needing a new car." She tried to sound philosophical about it, but knew that she didn't exactly succeed.

"Come on," he said. "Let's go check out the house. Watch where you put your feet in that ravine."

Buster and the two pigs followed them down there. They picked their way with care through all the soggy junk and knotted tree roots. It was going to be quite a job, cleaning up. And she knew that all the other ranches in the valley had to be in a similar state, if not worse. Her family still had a barn and the house, at least. And as far as she could see, there were no animals or—God forbid—people lying broken amid the wreckage down there.

When they reached the house, they skirted the downed tractor and went up the front steps. She'd lost her keys. They were probably still stuck in the ignition of her poor Subaru. But her mom had left a house key where she always did, in the mouth of the ceramic frog by the porch swing.

They went inside. The power and phone were both out, but still, it all looked just as it had the last time she'd been there, the white refrigerator covered with those silly smiling-flower magnets her mother liked, some of them holding reminders to pick up this or that at the store. There were also pictures of her and her brother and a few recipes her mom was meaning to try. In the living room, the remote sat on the magazine table by her dad's recliner and her mother's knitting bag waited in its usual place at the end of the fat blue sofa.

Her childhood home. Intact. It seemed a miracle to her right then. And she wanted to cry all over again—with a desperate, hot sort of joy.

Collin turned on the water in the kitchen. It ran clear, but they both knew that the flood could have caused contamination of any wells in its path.

She said, "We have wells for the stock. But for this house and Gage's place, we have a water tank that taps an underground spring higher up on this hill. The floodwaters wouldn't have reached that far. So the water here, in the house, is safe."

"That's good. A lot of valley wells are going to need disinfecting. Any source of clean water is great news."

She nodded. "And in town, they get water from above the falls. So they should be all right, too, shouldn't they, at least on the north side of the creek?" He shrugged. She knew what he was thinking. Who could say what they would find in town? And what about his family's place? "I know you probably want to head over to the Triple T…."

"Yeah. But let's check out your brother's house first, and then see about getting something to eat."

Gage's house. She realized she didn't want to go there.

But she did it anyway. And she was glad, again, for Collin's presence at her side. The house was locked up. They looked in the windows. It was bad. The waterline went three feet up the walls, but the moisture had wicked higher still in ugly, muddy little spikes. Gage's furniture was beyond saving, soggy and stained, the stuffing popping out.

"Can we get to the propane tank?" Collin asked. "Better to be safe than sorry when it comes to a possible gas leak." She showed him the way. They were able to turn it off from outside. Then he said, "Come on. There's nothing more we can do here right now."

They went back to her parents' house and found plenty to eat in the pantry. She filled Buster's food bowl and the hungry dog quickly emptied it. After the meal, she took the perishables out of the fridge and put them in a bucket in the front yard. The two pigs went right to work on the treat.

By then it was still early, a little after seven. Collin suggested they make use of the safe water source and take showers before they left. There was just no way to guess the next time they'd have a chance to clean up a little. As at Gage's place, the tank was heated by propane, so they even had hot water.

Willa chose from some of her own old clothes that her mom had stored for her in a box under the stairs.

She got clean jeans, a fresh T-shirt and a pair of worn but sturdy lace-up work boots to wear. For Collin, she found an ancient purple Jimi Hendrix Experience shirt that belonged to her dad, a pair of her dad's boots that were a pretty decent fit, and some trusty bib overalls. She also gave him a towel, a toothbrush, shave cream and a disposable razor. He took the guest bathroom. She used the master bath, and she made it quick.

Still, as she stood before the steamy bathroom mirror wrapped in one of her mother's fluffy towels, combing the tangles out of her wet hair, she couldn't help but think that Collin was just down the hall in the other bathroom, possibly naked.

Or if he wasn't by now, he *had* been a few minutes ago.

She caught her lower lip between her teeth and glared at her own reflection. "Get your mind off Collin naked," she told her steamy image in an angry whisper. "Seriously. You should get help, Willa Christensen."

And that struck her as funny, for some reason. The idea that she needed counseling over Collin Traub. She laughed. And then she pulled herself together and pinned her still-wet hair into a knot at the back of her head.

A few minutes later, they were out in the kitchen again, deciding what to take with them when they left.

She didn't tell him so, but he looked sexy even in overalls. He'd used the razor she'd given him and his dark stubble was gone, his hair still wet, but minus the dried mud from the flood.

Before they left, they filled a couple of gallon-size plastic containers with water. She stuffed a backpack with a few personal items. Her mom had a key to Willa's house in town and she took that, since hers was lost somewhere in her mud-filled car. She also grabbed a leash and a plastic container of food for Buster. She would have grabbed her dad's first aid kit, but Collin said he had one in his pickup.

"You want to wade out to your car?" Collin asked her. "See if maybe we can find your purse or your keys?"

It was way out there in the middle of that muddy field. And it didn't look promising to her. "We just got dry boots," she reminded him. "Let it go."

Collin didn't argue. She figured he was probably anxious to get to the Triple T.

They locked up the house again and headed for his truck, which waited at the top of the road where he'd left it. Buster hopped in the back and they climbed in the cab.

His cell was stuck in one of the cup holders. He tried it. "Still no signal."

Willa hooked her seat belt. He started the engine, pulled a U-turn and off they went.

It took them over an hour to get to the Triple T. The roads were washed out in several places and they had to find a way around the trouble spots. There was soggy, broken stuff strewn randomly wherever the water had risen, not to mention swamped, abandoned vehicles. Willa tried to take heart that they were all only *things*.

Collin played the truck's radio for news. Roads and bridges were out everywhere. Any number of small towns on the western side of the state from Butte north had sustained serious damage. A third of the state had been designated a disaster area and there were constant warnings—about staying off the roads as much as possible, about exercising caution in flooded buildings, about the danger of snakes and the hazards of rats. About steering clear of downed power lines.

At the Triple T, all the buildings were above the waterline and undamaged, but there would still be one heck of a cleanup to deal with. The hands who'd been taking care of the place were there and safe. Willa told them how to get into her parents' house to get fresh water for the next day or so, until they could disinfect the wells. They said they would check the stock for her as soon as they'd dealt with the animals on the Triple T.

Once Collin seemed satisfied that the hands had things under control, he said, "We should get going, go on into town."

She caught his arm before they got in the cab.

He stopped and turned to look at her. "Yeah?" His skin was so warm under her hand. Smooth flesh, hard muscles beneath. She felt suddenly shy with him and jerked her hand away. He frowned. "What's the matter?"

"I, well, I was just thinking that I'll bet you really want to go back up the mountain to check on things at your place. You could just drop me off when we get to Falls Street and I can hitch a ride in."

He stuck his fists into the front pockets of her dad's overalls and tipped his head to the side. "What the hell, Willa? I'm not leaving you alone on the street."

His words warmed her. But still. She really did need to stop taking advantage of his kindness to her.

Kindness.

Incredible. She'd been so busy judging him as a heartless, undisciplined sex maniac for all these years, she'd never had a clue what a softy he really was. She shook her head. "Oh, come on now. It's Rust Creek Falls. We both know I'll be perfectly safe."

"We don't know what's going on since last night. And I don't want you wandering around alone."

"Collin, I would hardly *wander.* And I know everyone in town, so I won't by any stretch of the imagination be alone."

"I'm coming with you. I want to be with you when you check on your house." He said the words in a cautious tone. They both knew where her house was: directly in the path of the water. She was already resigned to the fact that it had to be flooded and was hoping that at least some of her clothing and furniture might be salvageable.

"Honestly, I can handle it. I was pretty shell-shocked yesterday, I know. But I'm over that. I'm ready to face whatever comes. You don't have to worry about me."

He was scowling now. "Why are you trying to get rid of me?"

She fell back a step. "But I'm not. I just thought…"

He caught her arm with his calloused hand. It felt so good, his touch. And his grip was so strong. "What?" he demanded. "You thought what?"

She looked up at him, at his smoldering dark eyes and those lips that seemed like they were made for kissing a woman and she wondered what he would do if *she* kissed *him*. The idea made her feel both embarrassed and giddy. She almost giggled.

"Willa," he demanded. "What is going on with you all of a sudden?"

Now she was thinking about earlier that morning. About waking up with her hand where it shouldn't have been—about how he'd been turned on.

Get real, Willa. Just because he became aroused didn't mean he was dying to have sex with her in particular. It was simple biology, and she needed to remember that.

And if he wanted to keep on being kind to her, well, maybe she'd just let him. Maybe she'd just go right on taking advantage of Collin Traub and enjoying every minute of it. "Nothing is 'going on' with me. I just wanted to make sure I wasn't taking advantage of you."

"You're not."

"So…you don't mind going into town, then?"

"It's not about minding. It's what I planned to do. People will need help. They'll need every able-bodied man."

"And woman," she reminded him.

"Right." He had the good sense to agree.

She pressed her lips together to keep from grinning up at him like some addled fool and said, "Well, fair enough, then. I was just, um, checking."

He seemed to realize suddenly that he was gripping her arm—and let go. "Checking." Now he looked suspicious.

She put on her most innocent expression. "Uh-huh. Nothing wrong with checking, making sure you're okay with what's going on."

"If I'm not okay, you'll know it."

"Well, then, I'll stop checking."

"Good. Can we go now?"

She had that silly urge to grin again. Must be the stress of all she'd been through since yesterday. Yeah. Right. That must be it.

The trip into Rust Creek Falls was as booby-trapped with obstacles as the ride to the Triple T had been.

There was the smell of smoke in the air. It wasn't just from wood fires in stoves and fireplaces. They heard the sirens, saw the roiling smoke in the distance. On the south side of town, some homes had caught fire. Willa prayed her house wasn't one of them—and then she put her house out of her mind and prayed that no lives were endangered by the fires.

Other travelers were on the road by then, most of whom they recognized. Everyone seemed to have somewhere important to go. People waved and honked, but nobody pulled over to talk about what they'd been through or exchange information about the disaster. Collin had the radio on. All the way there, they listened to advice on how to deal with the aftermath of the Great Independence Day Flood.

When they finally got to Falls Street on the southeastern edge of town, they had to circle around and take other roads farther east and then work their way back in. It was nothing but mud, pools of water, swamped, abandoned vehicles and way too much debris south of the creek. The buildings they saw before they turned east were still standing, but bore the telltale signs of water damage within.

Eventually, they reached Sawmill Street and turned west again. The water level was way down from flood stage and the bridge appeared intact. Collin pulled the pickup to the shoulder before they crossed it. They both got out to have a look, to make sure that crossing would be safe. Buster jumped out to follow them.

But then a couple of pickups came rolling across from the town side. Behind the wheel of the second truck was a rancher they both recognized, Hank Garmond. Hank owned a nice little spread at the southwestern edge of the valley.

He pulled to a stop. "Willa. Collin. I see you're both in one piece and still breathing. Could be worse, eh? I'm headin' back to my place. We still got a house, but we lost the barn and sheds. Haven't started counting cattle yet. I just stopped in at Crawford's to try and get a few supplies to tide us over." Crawford's General Store, on North Main, was a town landmark. The store sold everything from basic foodstuffs to farm supplies, hardware and clothing. "Shelves are already lookin' pretty bare in there."

Collin asked, "How bad is it?"

"In town? Power's out, and all the phones. North of the creek is okay, from what I heard. No flooding, the water supply unaffected. South is not lookin' good. Commercial Street Bridge is washed out. There's damage to the Main Street Bridge. People are bypassing it. We still got this bridge though." He pointed a thumb back over his shoulder. "Praise the Lord for small favors." *Very small favors,* Willa couldn't help thinking. True, it was pretty much what she and Collin had thought it would be, but somehow, to hear Hank confirm their suspicions made it all the more horribly real. "And then there's what happened to Hunter McGee." Hunter McGee was the mayor.

"What?" Willa demanded.

"Tree fell on that old SUV of his. So happened he was in the SUV at the time."

Willa respected Mayor McGee. He was a born leader, a real booster of education and had planned and promoted several school-related fund-raising events. "My Lord," she cried. "Was he hurt?"

"The tree fell on the hood. Not a scratch on him." Hank resettled his hat on his head and Willa felt relief. But then Hank added, "Must have scared the you-know-what right out of him. He had a heart attack."

Willa put her hand over her mouth. "Oh, no…"

"Oh, yeah. It was over real quick for Mayor McGee."

"Over?" Willa's heart sank. "You—you mean he's…?"

Hank nodded. An SUV and another pickup came across the bridge. The occupants waved as they drove by. Hank said somberly, "They took him to Emmet's house. Emmet pronounced him DOA." Emmet dePaulo, a nurse-practitioner, ran the town clinic. "Clinic's flooded, in case you were wondering."

Willa and Collin exchanged grim glances. They weren't surprised. The clinic was south of Main. "Emmet and a couple of his neighbors waded in there and saved what equipment and supplies they could first thing this morning. Luckily, Emmet had a lot of his medical stuff stored on the second floor and the water didn't make it that high. He's set up an emergency clinic at his house, for now."

"They got the volunteer fire guys out on search and rescue?" Collin asked.

Hank shrugged. "Can't say. I ain't heard of anybody dead, hurt bad or stranded…'ceptin' Mayor McGee, I mean. Rest his soul. But I did hear that some county trucks brought in salvage-and-rescue equipment and sandbags yesterday before the levee broke. This morning, the town council put together an emergency crew to patch up the places where the water got through. So that's taken care of for now. And you can just have a look at the creek. Water level's back to normal range."

Collin gave a humorless chuckle. "Yeah, one good

thing about breaks in the levee. They tend to bring the water level way down."

"That they do," Hank concurred. "Plus, there's no rain in the forecast for at least the next week. So we're unlikely to have a repeat of what happened yesterday—oh, and the town council called a meeting at noon in the town hall to talk cleanup and such. Wish I could be there, but I got way too much cleanup of my own out at my place and I need to get after it. Bought the bleach I needed, at least. I can disinfect my well." Hank tipped his hat.

"You stay safe and take it slow on the road, Hank," Collin said.

"Will do. You keep the faith, now." The rancher rolled on by.

Collin put his arm around her. "You're lookin' kind of stricken, Willa."

She leaned into him, because she could. She needed someone to lean on at that moment. And Collin was so solid. So warm. So very much alive. "I'd been letting myself hope that at least no one had died—and I really liked Mayor McGee."

"I hear you. Hunter was a good man and this town could sure use him about now." He pulled her a little closer in the shelter of his arm and turned them both back to the pickup, Buster at their heels. The dog jumped in back again and they got in the cab.

As they drove across the bridge, Willa tried not to dread what might be waiting for them on the other side.

Chapter 4

It didn't look so awfully bad, Willa told herself as they drove along Sawmill Street. In fact, there on the northern edge of town, things seemed almost normal. Willa spotted a couple of downed trees and some flattened fences, but nothing like the devastation they'd witnessed coming in.

When they turned onto Main Street going south, they saw that the Crawford store parking lot was packed, people going in—and coming out mostly empty-handed. She supposed she shouldn't be all that surprised. It wouldn't take long to clear out the shelves of emergency supplies if everyone in town and most of the valley's ranchers showed up all at once and grabbed whatever they could fit in a cart.

The Community Church had its doors wide open. People sat on the steps there or stood out under the trees in front. Most of them looked confused. And lost.

"Shouldn't the Red Cross be showing up any minute?" she asked hopefully. "And what about FEMA and the National Guard?"

Collin grunted. "With a lot of the state in this condition, the phones out and the roads blocked, we'll be real lucky if a few supply trucks get to us in the next day or two." And then he swore low. "Isn't that the mayor's SUV?" The old brown 4x4 was half in, half out of the town hall parking lot. It had definitely come out the loser in the encounter with the downed elm tree. The tree lay square across what was left of the hood. The driver's door gaped open. A couple of boys in their early teens were peering in the windows.

"That's just too sad," Willa said low. "You'd think they'd want it off the street."

"Damn right." Collin muttered. "A sight like that is not encouraging." He hit the brake—and then swung a U-turn in front of the library, pulling in at the curb.

"Collin!" Willa cried, surprised. "What in the...?"

He shouted out the window at the two boys. "Hey, you two. Get over here."

Both boys froze. They wore guilty expressions. But then they put on their best tough-guy scowls and sauntered to Collin's side of the truck. They were the older brothers of a couple of Willa's former students and when they spotted her in the passenger seat, they dropped some of the attitude and mumbled in unison, "'Lo, Ms. Christensen."

She gave them both a slow nod.

One of them raked his shaggy hair off his forehead and met Collin's eyes. "Yeah?"

As he'd already done several times in the past eighteen hours or so, Collin surprised her. He knew their names. "Jesse. Franklin. Show a little respect, huh?"

Jesse, who was fourteen if Willa remembered correctly, cleared his throat. "We are, Mr. Traub." *Mr. Traub.* So strange. To hear anybody call the youngest, wildest Traub *mister.* But then again, well, the Traubs were pillars of the Rust Creek Falls community. Some of that probably rubbed off, even on the family bad boy—especially to a couple of impressionable teenagers.

Franklin, who was thirteen, added, "We were just, you know, checkin' things out."

Collin leaned out the window and suggested in a just-between-us-men kind of voice, "You two could make yourselves useful, do this town a real big favor…."

The two boys perked up considerably. "Well, yeah. Sure," said Jesse.

"How?" asked Franklin.

"Head on up to the garage. See if Clovis has a tow truck he can spare." Clovis Hart had owned and run the garage and gas station at Sawmill and North Buckskin for as long as Willa could remember. "Tell him the mayor's SUV is still sitting in the middle of Main Street with a tree trunk buried in its hood and lots of folks would appreciate it if Clovis could tow it away."

The boys shared a wide-eyed look. And then Franklin said, "Yeah. We could do that."

"You want me to take you up there?"

"Naw," said Jesse, puffing out his skinny chest. "We can handle it ourselves."

"Good enough, then. Thanks, boys—and tell Clovis he probably ought to bring a chain saw for that tree."

"We will." The two took off up Main at a run.

"That was well done," Willa said, and didn't even bother to try and hide the admiration in her voice.

Collin grunted. "Maybe, but do you think they'll make it happen?"

"You know, I kind of do. They're good kids. And this is a way for them to help. And you know Clovis."

"Yes, I do. Clovis Hart respected Hunter McGee and he won't like it that the car Hunter died in is sitting on Main with the hood smashed in for everyone to stare and point at."

She glanced toward the dashboard clock. It was 10:45 a.m. "So what do we do now?"

"I was thinking we could go and see how your house made out…."

She glanced over her shoulder, out the back window, past a happily panting Buster, at the Main Street Bridge. Someone had put a row of orange traffic cones in front of it to warn people off trying to use it. And one of her brother's deputies was standing, arms folded, in front of the pedestrian walk that spanned one side. "It doesn't look like they're letting folks cross the bridge."

Connor glanced over his shoulder, too. "We could try heading back to the Sawmill Street Bridge, then going on foot along the top of the levee until we get to your street."

"That could be dangerous… I mean, with the breaks in the levee and all. We would have to go carefully, and we don't know what we'll find if we manage to get to my house. It could take hours and we would miss the noon meeting Hank mentioned. I do think we should go to that."

Collin faced front again, his big shoulders slumping, and stared broodingly out the windshield back the way they had come. “You know who’ll be running that meeting now Hunter’s gone, don’t you?”

She did. “Nathan Crawford.” Nathan was in his early thirties, a member of the town council. Everyone expected him to be mayor himself someday. He and Collin had never liked each other. It was as if the two had been born to be enemies. Nathan was as handsome and dynamic as Collin was brooding and magnetic. Collin had always been a rebel and Nathan considered himself a community leader.

Rumor had it that five or six years back, Nathan’s girlfriend, Anita, had gone out on him—with Collin. Word was Anita had told Collin that she and Nathan were through. But apparently, she’d failed to inform Nathan of that fact. There’d been a fight, a nasty one, between the two men. Some claimed Collin had won, others insisted Nathan had come out the victor. After that, the two had hated each other more than ever.

Plus, there was the old rivalry between their two families. Nathan was a Crawford to the core. The Crawfords not only owned the general store, they were also as influential in the community as the Traubs. And for as long as anyone could remember, Crawfords and Traubs had been at odds. Willa didn’t really know the origin of the feud, but it seemed to be bred in the bone now between the town’s two most important families. Traubs didn’t think much of Crawfords. And the Crawfords returned the favor.

She spoke gently, but with firmness. “I really think it’s important that everyone who can possibly be there attends that meeting.”

He put his arm along the back of the seat and touched her shoulder, a gentle brush of a touch. She felt that touch acutely. His dark eyes sought hers—and held them. "So you want to go to the meeting first and then decide what to do about getting to your place?"

She smiled at him. "I do. Yes." Right then, a Rust Creek Garage tow truck came rumbling toward them down the street.

"I've got a chain saw in my toolbox in the back." Collin got out to give Clovis a hand.

At ten past two that afternoon the town hall meeting was still going on.

Collin sat next to Willa and wished he was anywhere but there. He was getting hungry, for one thing. And he figured the rest of the crowd had to be hungry, too.

The big multipurpose meeting room was packed. They had a generator for the lights, but there was no air-conditioning, never had been in the town hall. As a rule, it didn't get that hot in Rust Creek Falls. But with all the bodies packed in that room, it was hot now.

Tired, frightened, stressed-out townsfolk had taken every chair. More people stood at the back or along the side walls. There were children, too. People didn't want to let their kids out of their sight at a time like this. And kids got restless when forced to sit or stand in one place for too long.

Babies were wailing and small voices kept asking, "Daddy, when can we go?" and "Mommy, is this over yet?"

There were a lot of big talkers in town and every one of them was insisting on being heard. Plus, that jerk Nathan sat up there on the hall stage with the other useless members of the council and kept banging the mayor's big hand-carved oak gavel for order.

All right, it was true. A lot of people thought the world of Nathan Crawford. And maybe, if Collin were being fair about it, he'd admit that Nathan had a few good qualities. However, when it came to most Crawfords, and Nathan in particular, Collin just plain didn't feel like being fair.

Nathan had the council in his pocket, naturally. They all looked at him like he was wearing a damn halo or something, like he was the one sent down from heaven to single-handedly fix everything that had gone so completely wrong since the day before.

"Everyone, your attention!" Nathan boomed in that smooth baritone that made people think he knew what he was talking about. "We all have to work together here. As I've said before, though phone, internet and TV are temporarily out of commission, we have the radio system at the sheriff's office and we are in communication with DES—that is the state office of Disaster and Emergency Services. They are well aware of what is going on in Rust Creek Falls and the valley. And, unfortunately, in far too many other communities in western Montana. The good news, however, is that everything is under control and moving along."

Somebody in the crowd made a rude noise.

Nathan banged the mayor's gavel some more. "If we could all just be patient for a little bit longer, we will get these teams firmed up, so we can all get going on the cleanup right away."

Collin knew he should keep his mouth shut. His plan had been to get through the meeting, help Willa deal with the probable ruin of her home and then pitch in wherever he was needed. But Nathan and the council had their priorities turned around. And while there were plenty of people willing to go on and on about the difficulty of the situation and how much they wanted to help, nobody else seemed ready to tell the council they were putting the cart before the horse.

He got to his feet. Beside him, Willa startled and looked up at him, wide-eyed. She did amuse him, the way she always looked so worried about what he might do next. He sent her a glance that he meant to be reassuring. Her eyes only got wider. So much for soothing her. He faced front and waded in.

"I'm sorry. Nobody's speaking up about the real issue here and so I suppose I'm going to have to be the one. Nathan, cleanup is not the issue yet," he said good and loud. "First, we need to get teams into the flooded areas and see who needs help there. We need search and rescue and we needed it hours ago."

A chorus of agreement rose from the crowd. Apparently, others thought there should be a rescue effort. It was only that no one had been willing to stand up and say it out loud.

Nathan banged his gavel. He looked at Collin the way he always did: as though he'd just crawled out from under a rock. "Order. Please, everyone. I already explained. We have the volunteer firefighters out searching for trapped or injured survivors."

"One team, you're saying? With how many men on it?"

Nathan didn't answer either question. Instead, he went right on with his argument. "Those men are trained for this and know what they're doing. We don't think it's a big problem. No one has reported anyone missing."

"And how're you going to know if someone's missing?" Collin demanded. "People can't call. The phones are out. There can't be more than a third of the people in the valley here at this meeting or hanging around Main Street. Where are the rest of them? Trying to clean up what's theirs? Off to Livingston for the rodeo, or down in Thunder Canyon with the rest of my family? Or trapped on the upper floors of their houses, wondering why no one's come looking for them?"

"But we *are* looking. And I honestly do not believe—"

Collin didn't even let him get started. "And you didn't answer my first question. How many men are out on search and rescue, Nathan?"

Others spoke up then. "Yeah! How many?" someone demanded.

"Not enough, that's how many!" answered another.

Nathan's face had gone a deep shade of red. "People, please. Order!"

Collin stuck his hands into the pockets of Wayne Christensen's overalls and waited for Nathan to stop pounding that gavel. Once he did, Collin answered the question himself. "I'm guessing about nine. Nine men to cover the whole of this town and the valley. Have I got that right?"

"Nine strong, able men who are trained in effective search and rescue," Nathan insisted, his face even redder than before.

Collin kept after him. "It doesn't matter how good they are. Nine men are not enough. We need to put every able-bodied adult on the search until we've made a circuit of all the homes and ranches in town and in the valley. It shouldn't take more than the rest of today and tomorrow, if we get a move on. After that, we can change our focus to salvage and cleanup."

Down the row from him and Willa, one of the Crawford men called out, "Sit down and shut up, why don't you, Traub? Let them that knows what they're doing make the decisions here."

"Yeah," said another voice. "We don't need the likes of *you* tellin' us what to do first."

And that was when Willa shot to her feet beside him. At first, Collin thought she would grab his arm and beg him to stay out of it.

But it turned out he'd misjudged her. "I feel I must add my voice to Collin's," she said in that prim schoolmarm way of hers that never failed to get him kind of hot. "We have no idea how many people might be trapped in their homes or their barns. There are bound to be collapsed buildings. People could be buried in the rubble, praying they'll be rescued before it's too late. We've already lost Mayor McGee."

"Bless his soul," said a woman's voice.

"Amen," said another.

Willa wasn't finished. "Search and rescue is the first job. And we need to give it everything. We can't afford to lose one more precious life in Rust Creek Falls or the valley."

And Collin added his voice to hers. "We've got to save our *people* before we worry about our property."

The room erupted in whistles and applause. People shouted, "By God, he's right!" and "Search and rescue!" and "Collin's said it!" and "Listen to the schoolteacher!"

By the time the clapping finally stopped, even Nathan had seen the writing on the wall. He did what he had to do and went along. "The council, as always, seeks to understand and take action according to the wishes of our citizens. We will call in the nine trained men and reassign them as team leaders."

Willa leaned close and asked softly, "Call? The phones are out...."

He whispered back, "They'll have handheld radios—walkie-talkies."

"Oh. Right..."

Nathan was still talking. "For today and tomorrow—and as long as is needed—those nine leaders will head the teams in our search-and-rescue efforts. Volunteers, seek out a leader. Marjorie?"

Marjorie Hanke, the council member to Nathan's right, stood, picked up a pointer and smacked it against the map of the county that hung behind the council table. The map had already been divided into sections for the proposed cleanup teams. "Team one, section one—and so on," Marjorie announced. "We've been fortunate in that rubber boots, heavy rubber gloves and necessary tools have already been trucked in and will be provided to each of you. Please wear the boots and gloves at all times when searching in mud or standing water. Be on careful lookout, everyone, for vermin of all persuasions. Floods bring out the rats and displace the snakes. Thank you, Nathan." With a nod, she set down the pointer and took her seat again.

Nathan wrapped it up. At last. "Getting around in the flood areas isn't easy, but we are able to truck in supplies from Kalispell for those in need. The Ladies Auxiliary of the Community Church has set out a meal on the church lawn while we've been busy with our meeting here. If everyone will file outside in an orderly manner, Pastor Alderson will lead us in a prayer, after which we will share a late lunch. By then, your team leaders will have returned—and the search for missing survivors can commence."

Chapter 5

Buster, leashed to a railing outside the town hall, whined and wiggled in greeting when Willa went to collect him. She took a minute to pet him and praise him for being such a good dog.

Collin got her pack from his pickup for her and then he walked across the street to the church at her side. When her friend and fellow teacher, Paige Dalton, waved and called her name, Willa quickly looked away and pretended she didn't hear.

No, it wasn't nice of her to treat a friend that way. But she wanted a few more minutes with Collin. Soon, he would be off with one of the search teams. And then he would probably want to go up the mountain, to check on his house. There would be no reason, once he left with the searchers, for them to be together anymore. The time had come when they would go their separate ways.

She would always be grateful to him—for saving her life in the flood, for helping her make it through those awful first hours trapped in the barn. But she felt a bit wistful, too. For most of that day, it had almost seemed as though she and Collin were a team, ready and able to do what needed doing, fully capable, between them, of handling whatever challenges might arise. It had been a strangely heady feeling.

She wished she didn't feel so sad suddenly. But already, she was looking back longingly on the afternoon and evening before, and at the morning just passed. In retrospect now, it seemed hard to believe that she'd held a grudge against him for four long years. Her recent ill will toward him seemed something from another lifetime—from someone *else's* lifetime. She simply didn't have it in her to feel bitterness toward him now.

Now, she could almost view the flood and its immediate aftermath as some sort of lovely, exciting adventure story come to life, an adventure starring the two of them—which was way too self-absorbed of her and she knew it. This was no adventure story. This was a bona fide real-life disaster. People she cared about were losing everything.

Including herself, if you came right down to it. She wasn't holding out a lot of hope for the condition of her house. And what about all of her stuff? She had so many treasures—her favorite velvet sofa pillow, the fairy-tale books she'd collected since childhood, that spindly inlaid table she proudly displayed in the front hall…

The list was endless. What would be left of the things that she loved?

She ordered herself not to go there. Her belongings

might be precious to her, but they *were* only things and she needed to remember that now.

At least she had flood insurance, as did Gage, thank God. Whatever condition her house might be in, there would eventually be money to repair or rebuild. Many people in town and in the valley couldn't afford flood insurance. They could end up with nothing.

Collin nudged her arm. "You're wrinkling up your forehead. What's the matter?"

She tugged on Buster's leash as he dawdled, sniffing at the curb. "Just worrying, I guess."

"Stop." He gave her one of those sexy bad-boy grins of his. "We're going to get fed. It's something to be happy about."

At the church, the ladies auxiliary had been busy. They'd set up rows of tables out on the lawn. And they'd even thought of people's pets. Thelma, Hunter McGee's mother, gave her a bowl of water for Buster and a couple of dog biscuits. The older woman looked pale, Willa thought, and her eyes were swollen and red-rimmed.

Willa wrapped her in a hug and whispered, "He will be greatly missed."

Thelma sniffed and forced a brave smile. "We must soldier on," she said, and bent to give Buster a pat on the head.

Everyone remained standing while the pastor said a short prayer. He praised the stalwart heart and fine leadership of their lost mayor and asked that the people of Rust Creek Falls might find the strength they needed to endure this difficult time. At the last, he blessed the food.

"Amen," they all said softly, in unison.

It wasn't a fancy meal, but when you're hungry, the simplest food can be so satisfying. They had chicken salad sandwiches, chips, apples, oatmeal cookies and all the water they could drink. Collin sat next to her. They didn't talk. They were too busy filling their empty stomachs.

The volunteer firemen started coming in, muddy and looking tired. They washed up in the church restrooms and grabbed sandwiches, which they ate standing up. People rose from the tables and surrounded them, eager to join their teams.

Collin leaned close to her. He smelled faintly of her dad's shaving cream, which made her smile. He muttered, "I meant what I said before. Finish eating and we'll find a way to get to your house. I can join a team after that."

She set down her cup of water. "Thank you, but no. You said it yourself in the town hall just now. The search for survivors has to come first."

He looked at her, a probing sort of look. That dark lock of hair had fallen over his forehead again the way it tended to do. More than ever, she wanted to smooth it back.

But she didn't. Instead, she took a bite of her cookie and downed her last sip of water.

"You sure?" He looked doubtful.

"I am, yes. First things first."

Willa assumed she would end up watching the little ones while their mothers and fathers went out on the search-and-rescue teams. People knew she was good with their kids and trusted her with them.

While Collin went to join a search team, she asked

Mrs. McGee about pitching in with child care. Thelma told her to check in with the church nursery. The older woman also volunteered to look after Buster for the rest of the day.

"He's a nice dog," Thelma said, her tone bright and cheerful, endless sadness in her eyes. "Taking care of him will be no trouble at all."

Willa thanked her, gave her another quick hug and ran up the steps into the church, headed for the nursery in back.

Paige caught up with her in the sanctuary. "Willa. I've been so worried about you. The whole south side is flooded. Your house, is it…?"

"I don't know. I haven't been there since it happened. I left to check on the ranch and track Buster down before the levee broke. On the way, my car got swamped."

"Oh, my Lord. But you got out all right…."

"Thanks to Collin Traub." Willa brought her friend up to speed on how Collin had saved her from the flood. "My car's a total loss. And we ended up waiting out the rest of the storm in the barn."

"I don't know what to say. It's awful. But I'm so glad you're okay."

"Yeah. Still breathing and all in one piece—and the barn and my parents' house are fine."

Paige asked hopefully. "Gage's place?"

Willa bit her lip and shook her head. "Bad."

"Oh, Willa." Paige held out her arms.

Willa went into them and held on tight. "It's all so scary…"

"Oh, I know, I know." Paige pulled back, took Willa by the shoulders and gazed at her through solemn, worried brown eyes. "Collin, huh?" she asked gently.

Willa wasn't surprised at her friend's cryptic question. Paige was one of the few people in town who knew about that awful night at the Ace in the Hole *and* about Willa's longtime crush on the Traub bad boy. Willa had told her friend everything on one of those Friday nights they shared now and then—just the two of them, watching a romantic comedy on DVD, a big bowl of popcorn between them. Paige could keep a secret. She would never tell a soul.

Willa realized it was time to admit that she'd let injured pride cloud her judgment in a very big way. "I was all wrong about him." There was no one else nearby, but she kept her voice low just in case. "I mean, so what if he turned me down once? It's not that big of a deal. He's a good guy, someone anyone would want at their back in a crisis."

"Well, I can see that, but still…" Paige let the sentence die unfinished.

Willa reminded her friend, "Paige, seriously. The man saved my life yesterday and he was right there, sticking by me all night and this morning, too, when we had to face all the damage."

Paige put up both hands. "All right. He's a hero. You've convinced me." And then she shrugged. "I'm not surprised, really. I always believed there was a good guy underneath all that swagger." Like Willa, Paige knew the Traub family well. She'd even been in love with a Traub once—Collin's brother Sutter. It hadn't worked out for them. Now Sutter owned a stable in the Seattle area. He didn't come home often, and when he did, he never stayed long. "So…" Paige hesitated.

Willa tried not to roll her eyes. "Go ahead."

"Are you and Collin together now?"

Together. With Collin. The thought made her cheeks grow warm. She hastened to clarify, "No. It's not like that. He helped me out when I needed a hand, that's all. He helped me a lot and I'm grateful to him."

"Right." Paige gave her a knowing look. "And there *is* still Dane to consider."

Willa felt instantly guilty. She hadn't given Dane Everhart a thought since last night, when she'd made a big show of throwing the poor guy in Collin's face. "I told you. I really don't think it's going anywhere with Dane—and yes, when he proposed marriage, I should have said no right then and there. But Dane is so sure that he and I are a good match. And he's so charming and confident and… I don't know. We get along, but it's never been anything romantic."

Her friend said softly, "But Dane would like it to be."

Willa gulped and nodded. "It's so completely… *Dane,* to decide to marry me and refuse to take no for an answer. But in the end, he'll have to face facts. He's just not the guy for me."

Page coaxed, "But Collin is?"

"No. Really. Come on, Paige. I said it was nothing like that with Collin."

"But you *always* liked him—and not in that friends-only way that you seem to feel about Dane."

Willa lowered her voice even more. "It was a crush that I had on Collin, a teenage crush, that's all—and stop looking at me like that."

"Like what?"

"Like you think I'm lying to myself."

"Did I say that?" Now Paige was looking way too innocent.

"You didn't have to. And you've got it all wrong.

It's just that Collin and I have patched up our differences and we're on good terms now." Okay, she'd spent the previous night in his arms, but only because it had helped them keep warm. And she wasn't even going to *think* about that moment in the morning when they first woke up. Uh-uh. She was just wiping that moment clean out of her head.

"So you and Collin are friends, then?"

Friends? With Collin? It kind of felt that way, but maybe it was just the flood and all they'd been through since yesterday. She had to be careful not to read too much into it. He was off helping with the rescue effort now. When he returned, there would be no reason for him to seek her out. Their future contact with each other would be casual: saying hi when they passed each other on the street, stopping to chat now and then when they ran into each other at the store or the donut shop. "I don't know. We're…friendly, okay? We're getting along."

Paige's soft mouth tipped up in that warm smile that always made Willa so glad to be *her* friend. She chuckled. "Honey, you sound confused."

Why not just admit it? "Okay. Yeah. I am, a little…"

"You come and stay at my house tonight." Paige lived on North Pine, well north of the flooded area. "We'll have a nice glass of wine and I'll set you straight."

Willa laughed, too. "Uh-oh."

"Seriously. I want you staying with me as long as you need to. And don't you dare go out and stay at the ranch alone now. You need to be with a friend."

Willa felt suddenly misty-eyed. "Thanks, Paige."

Paige leaned closer. "And I have to say, I like it that Collin stood up in the meeting and got everyone to see that we need to put all our effort on searching for survivors first."

"Yes—and that reminds me. Are you helping with child care? I was just going to the nursery to see if they need me."

Paige caught her arm again. "I guess you didn't hear. The older ladies are taking care of the kids. Women our age in good shape, they want pitching in with the rescue effort. Come on. We'll get ourselves on a team."

Three people were rescued that day: two disabled shut-ins marooned upstairs in their flooded houses, and a rancher, Barton Derby, who lived alone and whose barn had collapsed on top of him. The team leaders kept in communication on their handheld radios and passed on the news when someone was found.

Barton Derby had compound fractures to both legs and had to be taken to the hospital in Kalispell, a long drive with so many of the roads badly damaged or still flooded. The word was that Derby survived the trip without incident.

The two shut-ins were physically unhurt, just very hungry and frantic over the damage to their homes. Willa and Paige's team leader told them that Thelma McGee, who owned a big house on Cedar Street, had taken them both to stay with her until other arrangements could be made.

For Willa and Paige's team, the triumphs were small. They pulled two foundering heifers from a pond, contacted old Barrett Smith, the local vet, to treat an injured horse and brought a frightened cat down from up a tree. Mostly, though, they made the circuit of the houses and outbuildings in their section of the search map and found the owners in residence doing their best to deal with the thousand and one challenges the flood had dumped in their laps.

The teams began returning to Main Street at dusk. The phones and electricity were still out, but there was food in the church multiuse room for anyone who needed it. Makeshift dormitories had been set up in the town hall and Masonic Hall for those who had nowhere else to go.

Paige came with Willa to the church, where they ate with their team by the light of kerosene and battery-powered lanterns. Once they had food in their stomachs, she nudged Willa. "Come on. Let's go to my place and get some rest..."

Willa hesitated. She would have loved a shower and to settle into that nice, big bed in Paige's guest room. But somehow, she couldn't do it. "I think I'll just get a cot in the town hall."

"Willa. Why? I want you to come and stay with me."

"And I love you for that. But I just can't..." It seemed important right then to stick with the other people who had been dispossessed. She wanted to stay close to the center of things, at least for the first night or two, until the search for survivors was finished and she could be certain that everyone in town and in the valley was safe and whole, with food in their bellies.

"You're sure?" Paige brushed her arm, a companionable touch.

Willa nodded. "Yeah. It just...feels right, to stay with the others for now."

So Paige gave her a hug and promised to be back for breakfast before the search began again in the morning. Then she asked around to see who needed lodging.

She took Buck and Bella McAnder and their two little girls home with her. The McAnders lived a few houses down from Willa, on South Broomtail Road. All over the north side of town, people were doing that, taking in families who lived south of the creek.

So far, Collin had yet to appear for dinner. Once Paige was gone, Willa checked out the team sign-up sheets that were posted on the wall right there in the church multiuse room. He'd joined Team Three, headed by Jerry Dobbs. It was the team that had rescued Barton Derby.

Team Three came in a few minutes later. Collin wasn't with them. She knew she ought to leave it alone. If he'd been injured in the search, she would have heard about it. There was nothing to worry over.

But then, well, she just *had* to know for sure that everything was okay with him. She approached Jerry Dobbs and asked if he knew where Collin might be.

"A real asset to our team, that Collin," Jerry said. "Without him, we might not have gotten Bart out from under his barn. People can't help but get scared around piles of unstable materials. Some held back, afraid to pitch in. Or worse, some were *too* brave and not careful enough. Collin reassured the scared ones and kept an eye on the chance-takers. The man's a born leader, levelheaded and calm and encouraging to others in a crisis. Plus, he's in top shape and light on his feet."

Willa didn't especially like the sound of all that. Had Collin put himself in danger to get Barton out? It would be just like him, after all. "Yes," she said, and tried to sound cheerful. "Collin Traub has no fear."

Jerry nodded. "And I think he mentioned something

about stopping over at the Triple T to see how they were getting along out there."

She should have known. Of course he would have to go see how the hands at the family ranch were managing. She thanked Jerry, shouldered the pack she'd been dragging around with her all afternoon and walked over to Thelma's to get Buster.

By then, Thelma had a houseful of visitors. She'd made room not only for the two rescued shut-ins, but also for a couple of young families who owned houses on the south side of the creek.

"I'll be over at the church for breakfast tomorrow," Thelma said, as Buster sat on the step, cheerfully panting, cocking one ear and then the other, glancing from Thelma to Willa and back again. "I'll be happy to take Buster then. He's been a comfort, I have to tell you. He likes to stick close to me, but he's not in the way."

"He's a good dog," Willa said fondly. Buster made an eager little whining sound in response. "Just don't let him out unsupervised or you never know where he'll head off to."

"I won't," Thelma promised. "I'll keep him close."

Willa thanked her again and said good-night.

In the town hall, the generator was still going strong. It seemed so bright in there compared to the lantern light at Thelma's and in the church. The chairs in the meeting room had been folded up and stacked against the walls. Rows of narrow cots waited for her and about fifty other people whose houses were in the still-restricted area south of the creek. She was a little anxious that Buster might not be allowed in. But it wasn't a problem. Marjorie Hanke, the councilwoman assigned to supervise sleeping arrangements in the hall, told her that as long as he behaved himself he could sleep beside Willa's cot.

Collin wasn't there. Disappointment tried to drag her down, which was ridiculous. The man had his own life, after all. He had things he needed to do. He could be staying at the Triple T for the night, or over at the church getting something to eat, or possibly bedding down in the other makeshift dormitory in the Masonic Hall. He might even have headed up the mountain to his house.

She truly hoped he hadn't been foolish enough to do that. Not in the dark. After the storm, there was no telling what condition that road would be in.

It was very annoying. He was so unpredictable. A person hardly knew what he might do next.

And really, she needed to stop thinking about him. She needed to be grateful that he'd saved her life and glad that she'd gotten past her issues with him—and let it go at that.

She leashed Buster to a leg of the cot and took her turn in the bathroom, washing up as best she could in the sink. Marjorie was passing out baggies containing personal grooming supplies to those without, but Willa had her own. She'd raided her mother's medicine cabinet for soap, deodorant and a toothbrush, and she'd also thought to grab an old pair of lightweight pink sweatpants, flip-flops and a clean T-shirt from the box under the stairs.

Back in the meeting room, people were settling in, getting as comfortable as possible for the night. When everyone had finished in the restrooms, Marjorie turned off all the lights, save one. She left it on low, for a night-light.

Willa lay back, stared at the dark ceiling overhead

and felt certain she'd be awake half the night, worrying about her parents and Gage, who were probably going nuts, wondering what was happening at home. She knew she would end up lying there, eyes wide-open, obsessing over the extent of the damage of her house. She was positive that she would have to firmly remind herself not to get all worked up over the tragic death of the mayor, and not to think about Collin, who surely would not have been so foolish as to head up the mountain in the dark of night.

But strangely, within minutes of zipping up her borrowed sleeping bag, her eyes had drifted shut. With a sigh, she turned on her side, tucked her hand under her cheek, and let sleep steal all her worries away.

The double doors to the town hall meeting room were shut when Collin arrived. He eased through them soundlessly.

Marjorie Hanke, in a cot by the door, sat up and pointed to an empty one a few feet away. Collin whispered a thank-you and tiptoed to the unoccupied cot. It wasn't that far from the door, which was great. He had a big plastic bag full of stuff for Willa and a pack for himself. Both of those, he stowed under the cot.

A couple of rows over, he heard a low, familiar whine. A tail thumped the floor: Buster. So Willa *was* sleeping here. He considered going over there and making sure she was all right.

But come on. His creeping close and peering down at her wouldn't help her in the least.

Uh-uh. If he went to her, he wouldn't be doing it because she needed him right now. It would be because he wanted to see her, plain and simple. In the space of one night and the morning after, he'd found it all too easy to get used to having her around. All too easy to wish she might *stay* around.

He liked her.

Always had, though he knew she used to think he didn't.

Maybe he liked her too much. He needed to keep a rein on himself because he knew that nothing was going to come of his liking Willa Christensen more than he should. She was a nice girl. She had a college-graduate Mr. Good-Guy boyfriend off in Australia, a boyfriend who'd asked her to marry him.

There was no way Collin fit into that picture.

Someone coughed. A cot squeaked as someone else turned over. At the other end of the room near the stage, somebody was snoring. Collin should shuck off his boots, stretch out on the cot and try to get a little sleep. Morning would come way before he was ready for it.

Too bad he didn't feel all that much like sleeping. He moved silently back to the doors and slipped through again. Swiftly, he crossed the dark front hall and let himself out into the cool of the night.

On the steps, he sat down, drew his legs up and wrapped his arms around his knees. It was a clear night, a sliver of the waning moon hanging above the distant mountains way across the valley. He stared up at that moon and tried not to think about the woman sleeping in the dark hall behind him, tried not to think about that morning, when he'd woken up with her soft, pretty little hand on his fly. A bad, bad idea, to think about that. Thinking about that would only get him all worked up all over again.

He heard a faint sound at his back, the squeak of

heavy hinges as the door opened behind him. Buster nuzzled his shoulder. He threw an arm over the dog and scratched him behind the ear as the door squeaked shut. The latch clicked.

Willa. He could feel her, hovering there behind him in front of the door. He was way too glad she'd come out to find him.

"Go back to bed, Willa," he said lazily, not turning to look at her, keeping his gaze front, on that sliver of moon. "How many times do I have to tell you? I'm not having sex with you."

Willa laughed, a low, slightly husky sound, one that seemed to skim the surface of his skin, raising goose bumps as it went. Raising more than goose bumps if he was going to be honest about it. He drew his knees up a little tighter so she wouldn't see how she affected him.

"You are impossible," she said in a voice as low and husky and full of good humor as her laugh.

He shrugged. "So I've been told."

And then she came and sat on his other side, so he was sandwiched between her and her dog. It wasn't a bad place to be. Not bad at all.

She said, "Buster's happy to see you. He woke me up when you came in."

"Sorry."

She leaned toward him a little, nudging him with her shoulder in a way that felt downright companionable. "Don't be."

He stroked the dog's big white head. "He's a great guy." The dog turned, tongue lolling, and gazed at him adoringly. "And so good lookin'."

Willa chuckled again. "Oh, yes, he is."

He still hadn't looked at her. Mostly because when

he did, he knew he wouldn't want to look away. "What about you, Willa? You happy to see me, too?"

"I am," she answered in a near whisper. "Yes." She was quiet. He could feel the warmth of her along his side. She smelled of soap and toothpaste—and something else. Something that was simply Willa. Kind of green and fresh and a little bit lemony. Who knew the smell of soap and lemons could get a man worked up? She spoke again. "I was kind of worried you'd tried to go up the mountain to your place."

"Not in the dark."

"Good."

"I went to the Triple T. They got the wells disinfected and are hoping to be using the water by tomorrow or Sunday. Most of the stock survived. And they're busy with cleanup. I stopped in at Clay's house and borrowed a few things—clean jeans and boots, a couple of shirts." Third-born of his five brothers, Clay had recently married. He lived down in Thunder Canyon now, but he still owned a house on the Triple T. "Then I went over to your family's place, just to see if things were okay there."

"You didn't have to do that."

"Willa. I wanted to."

A silence from her, then, "Thank you."

"I used the guest-room shower again. And I left your dad's clothes in the hamper. Hope you don't mind."

"I don't mind at all. How was it there?"

"Better."

"Really?"

"Yeah. The neighbors and the hands from the Triple T had been there. The pigs are back in their pen and the chickens are in the coop. Looked like they even made a start on the cleanup."

"That's good," she said. "Really good. I'm grateful."

He did look at her then. She was staring out toward the moon, the curve of her cheek so smooth in the dim light, her pretty lips slightly parted. She wore a different T-shirt from the one she'd had on earlier, pink sweatpants with white trim and a worn-down pair of flip-flops.

She kept her gaze on the moon, and that was fine with him. Gave him more time to look at her. He took in everything about her. Her toenails were painted. In the dark, it was hard to be sure of the exact color. Maybe purple. Like plums. He stared at them for a time. When he looked up, she was watching him. "Did you get something to eat?"

He nodded. "I had some stew at the Triple T."

Those cute dimples of hers tucked themselves in at the sides of her mouth as she smiled. "Jerry Dobbs says you're a natural leader, that they might not have saved Bart Derby if not for you."

"Well. You know Jerry, heavy on the 'go, team, go.'"

"I think you're being modest, Collin." Her big brown eyes gleamed at him.

He felt an odd little pinch, a heated tightness in his chest. Also, in his borrowed jeans. "Modest? Me? Not a chance."

Buster got up and wandered down the steps to lift his leg on a tree trunk. When he started sniffing the ground, moving toward the street, Willa called to him. "Buster. Come." He came right back and plopped down where he'd been before.

Collin said, "I filled a bag with clothes from that box

under the stairs at your folks' house, in case you need them. I left it back in the hall, under my cot. I brought jeans and shirts and underwear, too." There had been little lace panties and a bra and several pair of socks. "Not that I noticed the underwear or anything..."

"As I recall, it was pretty frayed, that underwear. But I'm grateful to have it at this point." She groaned, lowered her head and put her hand over her eyes. "I can't believe I'm sitting here discussing my old underwear with you."

"Hey." It was his turn to bump her shoulder with his. "What are friends for?"

She looked up and into his eyes, all earnest and hopeful, suddenly. "We are, aren't we? Friends, I mean."

He wanted to kiss her. But he knew that would be a very bad idea. "You want to be my friend, Willa?" His voice sounded a little rough, a little too hungry.

But she didn't look away. "I do, yes. Very much."

That pinch in his chest got even tighter. It was a good feeling, really. In a scary sort of way. "Well, all right then. Friends." He offered his hand. It seemed the thing to do.

Her lower lip quivered a little as she took it. Her palm was smooth and cool in his. He never wanted to let go. "You better watch it," she warned. "I'll start thinking that you're a really nice guy."

"I'm not." He kept catching himself staring at that mouth of hers. It looked so soft. Wide. Full. He said, "I'm wild and undisciplined. I have an attitude and I'll never settle down. Ask anyone. Ask my own mother. She'll give you an earful."

"Are you trying to scare me, Collin Traub? Because it's not working."

He took his hand back. Safer that way. "Never say I didn't warn you."

She gave him a look from the corner of her eye. "I'm onto you now. You're a good guy."

"See? Now I've got you fooled."

"No, you don't. And I'm glad that we're friends. Just be straight with me and we'll get along fine."

"I am being straight." Well, more or less. He didn't really want to be her friend. Or at least, not *only* her friend. He wanted to be *more* than her friend. But sometimes a man never got what he wanted. He understood that, always had. Sweet Willa Christensen was not for the likes of him. But right now, he just needed to look out for her, take care of her a little. Make sure she got through this hard time all right. He added, "And I've been thinking."

"About what?"

"The things that need doing."

She braced an elbow on her knee and dropped her chin in her hand. "Such as?"

"I'm guessing we'll finish up the search for survivors by around noon tomorrow. Meet me at the church when your team comes in. One way or another, we're going to get to your house tomorrow."

Her smooth brow furrowed. "What if they won't let us into the area?"

"You worry too much. They'll let us in. They pretty much have to."

"Not if they don't think it's safe."

"At some point, people are just going to go in anyway. The whole town has pitched in, put their own problems aside to search for survivors. It's not right to expect them to wait forever to get to their homes. Nathan and the rest of them have to take that into account or they'll have trouble on their hands."

"Collin..."

"Your face is all scrunched up again. Relax."

"It's only that I feel kind of bad, to keep on taking advantage of you like this."

"Don't," he commanded gruffly.

She just couldn't let it go. "But I know you need to get up to *your* place."

"My place is fine."

"But you can't be sure."

"Willa. We're going to your house and we're going tomorrow."

"I'm only saying that you don't have to—"

He put up a hand. "I know I don't have to. And you don't have to worry. It's pretty much impossible to take advantage of me. If I say I'll do a thing, it's because I *want* to do it." And when it came to the woman beside him, well, what he wanted was to do whatever she needed. He added, just to make himself sound tough and uncompromising, "I don't do anything because I think I *have* to. Life is too damn short for that."

Chapter 6

It all went as Collin had predicted, which only made Willa more aware of how completely she had once underestimated him. He understood so much, really. About people. About the way things worked.

The nine teams searched for four hours the next day, covering the rest of the valley and the flooded area south of the creek in town. They found a couple of stranded pets and more cattle that had to be pulled from muddy ponds, but no people in need of rescue.

Willa's team was out at the far western reaches of the valley. They finished up the search of their section by a little past noon and returned to town, where everyone had gathered at the church for the midday meal. Willa sat with Paige and the rest of their team.

Collin sat at another table, his team around him. He glanced up and saw her and gave her a nod that she took to mean he still intended to take her to her house.

Her heart kind of stuttered in her chest and then recommenced beating a little too fast. Partly because trading meaningful glances with Collin excited her more than it should. And partly because it was happening at last: she would see her house again. She sent a little prayer to heaven that it wouldn't be too bad.

While they ate, Nathan Crawford got up and gave a speech. He thanked everyone for the great job they were doing. He praised Rust Creek Garage for having plenty of gas to share with the searchers and the foresight to own a generator so that the pumps were still working. He said that state and county workers were on the job around-the-clock, trying to get services back online and roads and bridges repaired.

He advised, "If you have family members who were out of town for the holiday and you're wondering why they haven't returned—please don't be overly concerned. The governor has declared a state of emergency and asked that people try and stay off the roads, many of which are badly damaged. Bridges are out all over the western half of the state. It's just going to take a while to get all our services back up and running and for people to get back home."

Nathan also reminded them that the next phase was cleanup. "I hope many of you will pitch in with the community effort, that you'll donate your time if you can spare some. But we're suspending our teams for the rest of the day and all day Sunday so that everyone can handle personal business. Those who live south of the creek will have a chance to visit their homes." The floodwaters had sufficiently receded, he added, and gas and water mains to the damaged areas had been shut off for the time being. The town council realized that people had to be allowed back in to begin to assess the condition of their property. "Please use the Sawmill Street Bridge only. Follow the newly posted signs for the safest route to your property."

Next, he got to the hazards, which were many. "Please, please, be extra careful about entering buildings. Proceed with caution. If you see a downed wire or pole, keep clear and remember to report it." He reminded them all to wear boots and gloves and watch out for dangerous animals displaced by the flood. "Also, take note. Any buildings roped off with yellow tape have already been determined to be unsafe for entry. We've done our best to personally warn all of you whose houses are in that condition, but the priority until now has been rescuing the stranded. There are assuredly buildings that should have been roped off but haven't yet. Please. Don't approach any houses that are taped off. Search-and-Rescue Team One reports that our elementary school is badly damaged and possibly structurally unsound. So, also, we ask that you stay away from the school and the school grounds."

Willa's heart sank at that news. Beside her, Paige made a low sound of distress. Were they going to lose the school?

That would hit hard. If they had to rebuild, how long would it take? They only had two months until the start of the next school year.

Nathan ended by saying that dinner would be served at six and thanking the charitable organizations that had come through with donations of food and supplies. Then Pastor Alderson got up and invited them all to a brief Sunday service after breakfast the next morning, a service that would include a final farewell to Mayor McGee.

A funeral. Willa sighed. Lately, life was just packed with

sad and difficult events. But then again, it was important to give people a chance to pay their respects and to grieve.

She glanced toward Collin again. But he'd already left his table. She thought of last night, of sitting out on the front steps of the town hall with him. That had been so nice. Just the two of them and Buster, alone under the sliver of moon.

She almost wished she could go back there now, just run away from reality and all the everyday grimness of surviving the worst flood in the history of Rust Creek Falls. Run away and sit out under the moon with Collin, forever.

Even if they were just friends.

"You ready, Willa?" His voice, behind her. A little thrill pulsed through her.

Beside her, Paige frowned. "Ready for what?"

She pushed back her folding chair and gathered up the remains of her meal to carry to the trash and recycle stations. "Collin's taking me to see my house."

Paige looked at Collin. He gazed coolly back at her. "How are you, Collin?"

"Just fine, Paige. You?"

"Wonderful," Paige said in a tone that could have meant anything. She turned her gaze to Willa. "Shall I come with you?"

Willa shook her head.

"Are you certain?"

"Yes. But thank you. I'll be fine."

"You be careful."

"I will. Don't worry."

They got into Collin's truck and he paused before he started the engine. "Where's Buster?"

"Thelma's keeping an eye on him."

"Good. Safer for him if he stays at Thelma's until this is done."

She nodded her agreement and he pulled the truck out into the flow of traffic, most of which was going where they were going. Her neighbors were as eager as she was to see firsthand how their homes had fared.

They followed the signs across the Sawmill Street Bridge, down Falls Street and then west on Commercial. They had to move at a crawl, even though road crews had already been hard at work. Fallen trees, utility poles and flooded vehicles had been cleared from the roadway. But the streets themselves were badly damaged, the pavement erupted and broken apart in places, pools of standing water and puddles of mud everywhere, some as big as ponds. The buildings that lined the street had not fared well. Some were partially collapsed and roped off with yellow tape. Yards were still cluttered with household items and who knew what all.

Fires had taken out a whole row of houses on South Pine. A few of them were burned all the way to the ground.

At Main, they passed the elementary school. It was still standing, at least, though sections of the roof had fallen in. There was no way to tell from the street how bad the damage might be.

For Willa personally, the moment of truth came much too soon. They turned onto South Broomtail and pulled to a stop at what was left of the curb in front of her one-story bungalow.

She had to stifle a gasp of dismay at what she saw. Like all the other yards on the street, hers was a mess, strewn with a bunch of mud-caked stuff she couldn't even identify. The roof on one side of her front porch sagged alarmingly. The porch itself was empty. Her white wicker chairs and cute little spray-painted metal folding tables topped with potted geraniums were nowhere to be seen. And the cosmos and columbines, the boxwood hedge and the rows of mums and Shasta daisies she'd so lovingly planted along her front walk? If they were still there, she couldn't recognize them under the layer of mud and trash.

Collin reached over and took her hand. She wove her fingers good and tight with his. It helped—his warm, strong grip, the calloused flesh of his palm pressed to hers. The contact centered her down, reminded her again that she *could* get through this, that she wasn't alone.

He said, "You can wait for the insurance people, let them tell you what can be saved. I can turn this truck around and get us the hell outta here. You don't have to try and go in there."

She gripped his hand tighter. "What was that you said last night? About not wasting any part of your life doing what you think you *have* to do?"

"So don't. We'll go." He tried to pull his hand from hers.

She held on. "I mean, I *want* to go in. I…need to go in, Collin."

"Look at that porch roof. It could be dangerous. Someone on one of the county crews should have roped it off."

"I'm going in."

"Willa, it's not safe."

She hitched up her chin and stared straight in his eyes. "I have to. I do. I don't agree with what you said last night. Some things, well, a person does just *have* to do."

* * *

Collin tried to think of a way to talk her out of it. But she had that look—so solemn and determined. When Willa got that look, there was no changing her mind.

Maybe he could bargain with her a little. "Just let me go in first, okay? Let me make sure that it's safe."

She still had his hand in a death grip. "Great idea. You can get killed instead of me."

"Willa. I'm not going to get killed—and if you think that it's too dangerous, well, why are we even talking about going in?"

"It was a figure of speech, that's all. I'm sure it's all right. We can go in together. But you're not leading the way. I won't have it. Do you understand?"

In spite of the very real danger in the situation, he wanted to smile. "You know you sound like an angry schoolmarm, don't you?"

"Well, I *am* an angry schoolmarm. And you'd better not cross me right now, Collin Traub."

He put on his most solemn expression. "No, ma'am. I wouldn't dare."

She let go of his hand and he wished that she hadn't. "Here." She passed him his heavy black rubber gloves. He put them on and she put on hers. They were both still wearing their waterproof search-and-rescue boots. "All right," she said. "Let's get it over with."

They got out and picked their way through the piles of broken, muddy junk in the yard. The smell was pretty bad—like spoiled food and smelly socks and other things he decided not to concentrate too hard on.

"Look," she said, and pointed. "One of my wicker porch chairs. Right there—and look over there. Isn't that a slow cooker?"

He only shrugged. The things she pointed to were unrecognizable to him.

The mud-caked porch creaked in an ominous way when they went up the steps. But it held. One front window was busted out, the other crisscrossed with cracks.

She reached for the door—and then she dropped her hand and laughed. "The key…"

For a moment, he knew relief. She'd forgotten the key. Good. But then she reached into her pocket and came out with it. She stuck it in the lock and gave it a turn.

The door swung inward.

It wasn't anything he hadn't expected. Mud everywhere and water wicking halfway up the walls. The same rotting, moldy smell as in the yard.

They went through the small entry hall and into the living room, where he doubted that any of the furniture could be saved. The large picture window on the side wall had cracked from corner to corner. The fireplace was full of mud.

"My grandmother's clock," Willa said in a tone of hope and wonder. It was on the mantel, a brass carriage clock, untouched. She went over to it, and gathered it into her arms. "It's an antique. A mercury pendulum clock." She glanced up and met his eyes. Hers were suspiciously misty. "Hey. It's *something....*"

They moved on, first to the kitchen and then down the short hallway to the bedrooms and the single bath. It was bad, all of it, every room full of mud. There wasn't much worth saving.

But there were some pictures on the walls that were good as new, and some stuff in the kitchen, dishes and such in the higher-up cabinets. And the things on the counter, too: a red toaster, cutting boards, some glass figurines on the windowsill. He suggested that they try and see if they could scare up some boxes to put the stuff in.

Willa shook her head. "And put the boxes where?"

He wanted to offer his house, but he hadn't made it up the mountain yet, and he knew she'd only argue that she couldn't impose on him. He thought of Paige. He didn't like what had gone down with Paige and his brother Sutter, but he knew Paige was a good woman at heart and a true friend to Willa. She would store Willa's stuff for her in a heartbeat. But then Willa would only give him some other excuse as to why that wouldn't work. "We'll haul them out to your parents' place. How's that?"

She clutched the brass clock like a lifeline and said primly, "That would take the rest of the day. And they are just *things,* after all."

"They're *your* things. And you need to get them out of here." He asked gently, "And what else are we gonna do with the rest of the day?"

"Other people might need our help and we should—"

He didn't let her get rolling. "Need our help doing what? Saving *their* things? We're doing this. Deal with it."

Her lower lip was trembling and her eyes were more than misty now. "I can't… I don't…" He felt a tightness in his chest at seeing her cry. She sniffed and turned her head away. "Oh, this is ridiculous. I have so much to be grateful for. There is no point in my crying over this. My crying will not change a thing…." A tight little sob escaped her.

"Come on. Come here." He reached out his rubber-gloved hands and pulled her close. "It's all right."

"No. No, it's not. I loved this house. I loved my little red Subaru."

"I know," he soothed. "I understand."

"I… I keep telling myself how it doesn't matter, that what matters is I'm alive and in one piece and so is most everyone else in town. But then I think of my…my treasures. My fairy-tale books, my favorite velvet pillow… I want them back, Collin. I want my *things* back."

"Shh, now. I know you do. There's nothing wrong with that. It's natural. Don't be so hard on yourself…."

"Oh, I am being such a big baby…." Sobs shook her slim frame.

He held her. He stroked her back. She curved into him, fitting against him as though she was made to be in his arms. For that moment, he forgot about everything. It all just…receded: her ruined house, the smell of mud and mildew, her grandmother's clock poking into his belly. There was only the woman in his arms. He held her and rested his cheek on her soft hair and waited.

Eventually, she pulled back enough to gaze up at him. Her nose was red and her eyes were puffy and she was so beautiful that his chest got tight all over again. He wished that…

But no. It was never happening. He wasn't going there. No way.

She sniffed. "Well. This is embarrassing."

He took her lightly by the upper arms. "You okay now?"

She sniffed again. "My nose is red, isn't it?"

"Your nose is beautiful."

"Liar."

It all seemed…strange and scary, suddenly. For a moment there…no. *Uh-uh. Not going there,* he reminded himself for the second time. He put on a big, fake smile and asked, “What do you say we go find those boxes?”

It took the rest of the day to scare up the crates and boxes, pack up what was salvageable and drive it out to the Christensen place. Her dad had a storage area off his work shed. They put it all in there.

By then, it was past time for the community meal back in town. They’d planned ahead and brought clean clothes with them so they could take advantage of the chance for hot showers. As before, he took the hall bath and she took the one off her parents’ room.

She came out of her parents’ bathroom, her brown hair still wet, smoothed back into a knot at the nape of her neck, smelling like flowers and rain and lemons, better than any woman he’d ever known.

And he’d known a lot of them—well, not in the past couple of years. After he hit twenty-five or so, all that chasing around had begun to seem kind of pointless. But back when he was younger, he’d lived up to his rep as a player. Then he’d been out to have himself a good time every night of the week.

And not one other woman back in the day had ever smelled as good as Willa did right then.

They raided the pantry. As they ate canned stew, crackers and peaches, Willa said how happy she was with the cleanup around the ranch.

“They’ve done a lot,” she said, “in just a couple of days.”

Her car was still out there on its side in the pasture and probably would be until she could call her insurance guy or the FEMA people and have it towed away, but the animals were back in their proper pastures and pens. The neighbors were making sure the stock got fed.

They headed back to town at a little after eight, stopping off at the Triple T for a few minutes on the way, just to check on things. In Rust Creek Falls, they went to Thelma's to get Buster, and then they returned to the town hall for the night. There were several empty cots. Some people had found neighbors to stay with and some had gone to live with out-of-town relatives for a while.

Marjorie Hanke turned out the lights at eleven. Collin still felt wide-awake, so he got up and went outside to sit on the steps under the sliver of moon.

What do you know? He wasn't out there five minutes before Buster was nudging up against him on one side and Willa was dropping to the steps on the other.

He almost teased her about how he wasn't having sex with her. But no. Sex seemed a little dangerous to speak of now, something he couldn't afford to joke about.

And then she kind of leaned against him and said, "Aren't you going to tell me to keep my hot little hands to myself?"

There was nothing he would like better than her hot little hands all over him. However, that was not going to happen, as he knew damn well and kept constantly reminding himself.

He kept it light, meeting her eyes, teasing, "I know I can count on you to do the right thing."

She didn't reply. There was one of those moments. They looked at each other and neither looked away. He would only have to lean in a few inches to capture that mouth of hers, to feel her lips against his.

Finally.

At last.

But he didn't. Apparently, he had some small amount of self-control left.

He thought of the boyfriend, the one who had asked her to marry him. He reminded himself that it was only an accident of fate that had her sitting next to him on the town hall steps at a quarter of midnight on July 6. And somehow, he managed to turn his head and stare at the moon again.

She said, very softly, "Remember when we were kids? You used to spy on me…."

He chuckled. "I had a lot of free time on my hands. And I never thought of it as spying."

"You would watch me when I had no idea you were there. That's spying, Collin Traub. I would look up—and there you would be, staring at me."

He gave her a grin. "You're getting mad about it all over again."

She frowned—and then her brow smoothed out. "You're right. I am. And that's silly. It was years ago. It's like that night at the Ace in the Hole. Better to just let it go." She tipped her head sideways and studied him. "You were so different from your brothers…."

"Yeah, well. My mom was tired when I came along. She had five boys already. Boys are exhausting. They need discipline and supervision. Mom did a good job of that with the rest of them. But she kind of gave up on me. I ran wild."

"I remember," she said wryly.

He elaborated with some pride, "I broke every rule and climbed every fence and spied on you when I knew it would freak you out. I also used to like to tease the bulls."

"Well, that's just plain asking for it."

"Yeah, it is. I guess I had an angel on my shoulder, though. Because somehow, every time I got in the pasture with one of the bulls and danced around shouting and waving my arms, I managed to jump the fence before I got gored."

She was shaking her head. "What were you thinking?"

"That it was fun! I mean, I liked it, being known as big trouble just waiting to happen. I got blamed for everything, sometimes for things I didn't even do. And it kind of got to be a point of pride for me that not a day went by I didn't get grief for some crazy, dumb-ass behavior or other."

She was looking at him again, her eyes shining brighter than the stars in the clear night sky overhead. "So you became known as the family troublemaker, the one no one could ever depend on."

"Because I *am* the family troublemaker that no one could depend on."

"But you're not," she argued. "Just look at you lately, standing up for what's right in the town meeting, getting a couple of kids to make sure the mayor's car was towed off Main Street the day after he died, saving Barton Derby from under the wreckage of his barn…."

"My *team* saved Bart Derby, the mayor's car was not a big thing—and you stood up in that meeting, too."

"What about rescuing me when I would have drowned, and then looking after me during the storm? And what about afterwards, too? What about today, at my house, when you held me while I cried and promised me it was going to be all right?"

"It was what you needed to hear right then."

"Exactly. Honestly, Collin. I don't know what I would

have done without you since the flood." She'd better stop looking at him like that. If she didn't, well, he was going to grab her and plant one on her.

"Don't make a big thing out of it, okay?" he heard himself mutter.

"But it *is* a big thing."

"No, it's not…."

"Yes, it is!" She got that bossy schoolteacher look. "And that does it. I'm not sitting still while you minimize all the good you've done. I'm going to tell you how I see it."

"Uh-oh."

"You listen to me, now…."

He tried not to groan. "What will you do if I don't?"

She put her hand on his arm, apparently to hold him there by force. He felt that touch from the top of his head to the tips of his toes—and everywhere in between. "You are a born leader, Collin. This town is going to need a new mayor and I keep thinking that you could be the right man for that job."

Mayor? She thought he should be *mayor?* He couldn't help it. He threw back his head and laughed out loud. "Willa, okay. We're friends now and everything. But you don't know what you're talking about."

"Oh, yes, I do. I am onto you, in a big way."

He grunted. "No, you're not. You're making something out of nothing."

She pursed up her mouth at him. "When you're finished blowing me off, you just tell me. And then I will share my insights with you."

There were a whole bunch of sarcastic comebacks to that one. But for some unknown reason, he didn't use any of them. Probably because he did kind of want to hear what she had to say. "Okay, fair enough. Hit me with it."

"I will. Ahem. So you grew up a wild child, undependable. And as it so often happens in a small town like ours, people get it in their heads what a person is like and that's it, that's just the way it is. No one ever thinks to look at that person differently, to take a chance on depending on him, to expect more than misbehavior. There's a local perception and no one ever tests it. The perception becomes the reality."

"Took psychology at UI, did you, Willa?"

She gave him her sweetest smile. "And I'm not even at the good part yet.... Where was I? Oh, yes. So in the meantime, you're keeping busy fulfilling everyone's low expectations of you. And, as you said yourself, you find that not having anyone expect much of you is actually kind of fun. Because you can do what you want. You're not stuck like all your brothers, bearing up under the weight of everyone's high estimation of your sterling character. You actually have the freedom to live exactly as you please and you never have to worry about letting anyone down."

He could easily become annoyed with her. "Think you got me all figured out, don't you, Willa?"

She didn't back off. "To a degree, yes. You are adventurous and bold, with no desire to settle down. So naturally, in your teens, you become the town heartbreaker. You do a lot of experimenting with women. Because, as you said, it's fun."

He'd heard about enough. "Come on. You're getting into dangerous territory here. You know that, right? Next you'll be digging up that night at the Ace again, getting all up in my face for not taking you up on what you were offering."

She put her hand on his arm again. He wanted to jerk away—and also to grab her and kiss her senseless. "No. Honestly. I'm over that." And then she smiled. So sweet and open, that smile. He realized that he definitely wanted to kiss her more than he wanted to get away from her. "Even if I am probably the only woman you ever turned down."

He almost told her that wasn't true, but then she'd just say he was bragging. "Seriously. Where are you going with this?"

She tipped her head to the side, frowning a little the way she did when she was thinking something over. "Hmm. I guess I'm just trying to make you see that being defined by other people's low expectations of you isn't really working for you anymore."

"And you know this, how?"

"I'm not blind, you know. I've been around you a lot the past few days. And what has been a tragedy for Rust Creek Falls has brought out the best in you. After all that's happened and all the good you've done—all the good you *will* do in the coming days, you're not going to be able to go back."

"Go back where?"

"To the way things were before the levee broke."

"Believe it or not, I happen to like the way things were."

"Maybe you did. Before. But it won't be enough for you now."

"You have no idea what's enough for me, Willa." He ached to reach for her. Reach for her and pull her close and kiss her until her head spun and she let him do whatever he wanted with her, until he finally got a taste of what she'd been tempting him with since before he was even old enough to know what temptation was.

She just wouldn't stop. "You've started to expect more of yourself and that is a wonderful thing. Why can't you admit that?"

It was the tipping point. He couldn't stop himself. He reached out and grabbed her by the shoulders good and tight. And then he growled at her with all the frustrated heat and hunger he was trying so hard to deny. "I don't need you telling me how I feel or where I'm going."

She blinked at him and her big eyes got bigger and her mouth looked so soft and surprised he only wanted to cover it with his and stick his tongue inside. "But, Collin. I was only—"

"*Don't,* all right? Just don't." With great care, he straightened his arms, pushing her away from him. Then he let her go.

"Collin, I..."

He stood up. That was pretty damn stupid. He was as hard as a teenage kid caught thumbing through *Playboy.* All she had to do was look and she would see it.

Too bad. He wasn't hanging around to watch her reaction. He mounted the top step, hauled the door wide and went in, pulling it firmly shut behind him.

Chapter 7

Willa had trouble getting to sleep that night. She felt awful. She knew that she'd gone too far. Yes, she did honestly believe she'd only told Collin the truth about himself.

And really, not a thing she'd said to him had been bad. Some men wouldn't mind being called a born leader. Some men would be pleased to hear how wonderful they were.

But not Collin, apparently.

And all right, well, maybe she'd laid it on a bit heavy. She'd turned her inner schoolmarm loose on him—and not the good, patient, understanding and gentle schoolmarm.

The other one. The bossy one who knew what was good for you and was bound to tell you all about yourself whether you wanted to hear it or not.

Had she wrecked their new friendship?

Oh, she did hope not. Because she really, really liked being his friend. She liked it more than she should, probably. With a guy like Collin, well, a girl could get really confused as to where she stood with him.

On the floor by her cot, Buster whined in his sleep. She reached her hand down to him, ran her fingers over the smooth, warm crown of his big head. He woke enough to press his wet nose against her palm and then settled back to sleep with a sweet chuffing sound.

She thought of all the good things Collin had done for her since the flood, of the way he'd held her that afternoon, so tenderly, so kindly, in the muddy ruin that had once been her home.

No. He was a real friend to her now. Too good a friend for her to lose him just because she'd presumed to lecture him about his life.

In the morning, she would apologize. And everything would be all right.

He wasn't there for the community breakfast in the morning and he didn't come to the church service after the meal.

Willa sat with Paige and wished he was there. She worried that he *wasn't* there because she had pushed his buttons and made it necessary, somehow, for him to prove what a tough, bad guy he was—too bad to show up for Sunday services and give Willa a chance to say she was sorry.

The choir sang of sweet comfort and the pastor quoted inspirational sections of scripture, verses meant to be uplifting in hard times. He gave a sermon on sacrifice and the meaning of community. He talked about how the Lord was with them and that each and every one of them was proving their worth and their goodness by their deeds in this time of trial.

And finally, when the sermon was over, Pastor Alderson led them in a prayer for Mayor McGee and the service became a farewell for Thelma's only son.

People stepped up with vases full of flowers, picked wild or from their own gardens. The choir sang the songs that Hunter had liked best, a couple of country-and-western love songs, "Red River Valley," a Bob Dylan ballad and some other songs Willa hadn't heard before.

It was during one of those other songs that she sensed movement at the end of the pew. She glanced that way.

Collin.

He wore clean jeans and a white shirt and his face was smooth from a recent shave. Had he made it up to his house on the mountain, then? He caught her eye, just for a moment. He didn't smile. But he wasn't scowling, either. She could have stared at him forever.

But she didn't. She forced her eyes front again while he made his way along the pew toward her. He muttered soft apologies as their neighbors slid their legs to the side, giving room for him to pass. Shelby Jenkins, a friend who sometimes worked as a substitute teacher at the elementary school, was sitting on her left.

She heard Collin whisper, "S'cuse me, Shelby..."

Shelby slid over and he took the empty space next to Willa. He smelled of soap and aftershave and her heart just lifted up when he settled in beside her. She couldn't even look at him right then, there were so many strange and powerful emotions chasing themselves around inside her. She had a dopey smile on her face, she just knew it, a totally inappropriate expression for a funeral.

He did that thing—that thing they'd started when they sat out on the town hall steps in the evening—leaning to the side in her direction, nudging her so gently with his shoulder.

She had to press her lips together to keep from letting out a silly squeak of pure joy. Because he wasn't all that mad at her, after all, evidently.

Because now she knew that everything between them would be all right.

The service continued. Pastor Alderson invited folks to stand and say a word or two, to speak their testimony on the life of Hunter McGee.

In the front pew, Thelma stood first. Her voice only shook a little as she spoke of how proud she was to be Hunter's mom, as she told a little story about his boyhood, about his dreams for Rust Creek Falls, about how his one true love had died too young and he'd never known the joy of fatherhood, but he had loved Rust Creek Falls. It had meant the world to him that the people of his town had elected him their mayor.

When Thelma was finished, others stood, one at a time, taking turns, telling about growing up with Hunter, about the many ways that he'd helped them or made their lives richer, somehow. Each of the town council members took a turn, with Nathan Crawford going first. Willa had thought she might speak, but then it turned out that the things she would have shared were already said. She felt content to let it be.

The testimonies went on for over an hour. Until finally, one of the older Daltons sat back down after speaking of how Hunter had pitched in to help repair the Masonic Hall. There was a silence in the chapel. Willa thought that the sharing was done.

But then Collin shifted at her side. She blinked and looked over at him as he rose to his feet. He looked a little nervous, she thought, and so very handsome and dear.

Everyone turned and watched him expectantly. As a rule, Collin Traub didn't speak out in public, but Willa knew they all had to be remembering his impassioned arguments in the town hall the other day and eager to hear whatever he might contribute now.

Collin cleared his throat. "I just want to say that Hunter McGee was a man we all thought of as a friend. He had a way about him. He was wise and he was patient, too. But he had a killer sense of humor and that gleam in his eye that let you know he didn't judge you and he wanted only the best for you, no matter how big a troublemaker you might happen to be." Collin paused then, and glanced around with an abashed sort of expression.

People grinned and a few even chuckled.

Collin continued, "Somehow, Hunter always managed to get to the heart of an issue without ever choosing sides. He had a rare sort of fairness in him and a willingness to help. Yes, he's gone to a better place now. But at the same time, it seems to me that he's still here with us in spirit, that he's working beside us now, in this tough time when we need men like him the most. We haven't really lost him." Collin fisted his hand and laid it against his heart. "He's right here." He raised his hand and touched his temple. "And he's in here, too, in all of us. We can remember all he showed us about how to live and work together. And we can be grateful that we have his fine example to carry us forward as we work side by side to rebuild this town."

Collin sat back down.

There was a silence. Somebody murmured, "Oh, yeah."

And someone else said, "Tell it, Collin."

Several more "Oh, yeahs" and one or two "Praise Gods" followed.

Collin turned and looked at Willa, which was when she realized she was staring at him. He gave her a scowl, mouthed, *What?*

She only shrugged and faced front again and tried not to feel smug that he had just proved the truth in what she'd said to him the night before.

Outside after the service, Thelma embraced Collin and laid her hand gently on the side of his face. "Such a fine young man," she told him softly. And then she raised her lacy handkerchief to dab at her wet eyes.

A couple of the Dalton men clasped his shoulder as they filed out of the chapel. Willa observed all this and tried really hard not to feel too self-righteous about the things she'd said the night before. He really was a born leader, but what he did with that talent had to be of his own choosing.

Paige touched her arm. "I'd ask you to come sit with me for lunch, but I have a feeling you've got plans."

Willa gave her a hug and they parted. Buster whined at her, eager to be released from the iron bench where she'd leashed him. She went over and got him, crouching to pet him and make a fuss over him for being so good during the long church service.

"Rumor has it the church ladies are serving pizza for lunch today," Collin said from behind her.

Buster whined and wagged his tail in greeting and Willa's heart seemed to do a sort of forward roll under her breastbone. She asked, without turning, "Does the rumor mention pepperoni?"

"Yeah. Pepperoni and sausage, too." He dropped to a crouch at her side. Buster wiggled closer to him and head-butted his hand. Collin scratched the dog behind both ears and Buster lolled his tongue in doggy bliss.

Willa felt terribly shy suddenly. She stared at his hands as he petted her dog. "I, um, should walk Buster first…."

"Hey."

Her throat had a big lump in it. She gulped it down and made herself meet those low-lidded black eyes. "Hmm?"

"We okay, you and me?"

She remembered that she was going to apologize. "I lectured you. I shouldn't have done that. I'm sorry."

"You got nothing to be sorry for." His voice was low and more than a little rough. The sound of it sent a warm, lovely shiver running underneath her skin. He added, "You got a right to your opinion."

"But, well, you did get mad."

He smiled then, one of those slow smiles of his, the kind that used to make all the girls back in high school sigh and fan themselves. "So then, *I'm* sorry. I had no right at all to jump all over you for telling the truth as you see it." He kept on looking at her, a deep look that made her whole body feel sensitized, excited. Wonderfully alive. "Forgive me?"

That lump was back in her throat again. She gulped a second time to clear it. "I do. And yes. We're okay."

"Whew."

She felt her mouth tremble into a smile that answered his. "Did you go up to your house, then?"

"No. I'm hoping I'll get to that tomorrow. This morning, I went out to the Triple T and had breakfast with the hands. They got the wells in working order, so I had a shower, too." He swept upward and she stood, too. "Let's walk this dog," he said.

"Good idea."

"The park? We can let him run."

"Perfect."

After lunch, the governor dropped in—literally—in a helicopter.

The chopper landed in the middle of Main Street and the governor emerged, waving and smiling, trailed by a guy in a FEMA vest and another, more muscular fellow in dark glasses. Waving as he went, the governor ran up and stood on the town hall steps, where the town council members waited. He shook hands with each of them.

And then he gave a little speech—more of a pep talk, really. He said the same things Nathan was always saying: that road crews and the power and telephone companies were working around-the-clock to get the roads open and services back online. He asked everyone to sit tight until services were restored and, whenever possible, to stay in the Rust Creek Falls Valley until the roads were declared safe for travel.

He praised their spirit of independence, their ability to roll up their sleeves and do for themselves. Since the good people of Rust Creek Falls seemed to be managing better than most in the stricken areas, he could see that the Red Cross and the National Guard wouldn't be needed there—not at that point anyway.

After the governor spoke, the FEMA guy talked about the services FEMA offered and the progress of the cleanup. And then, with more smiling and waving, the three visitors ran back and boarded the helicopter and off they went.

Collin leaned close and said in her ear, "Wasn't that inspiring?" She gave him a look and left it at that. And then he said, "I was thinking we could try and see what we can salvage from Gage's house."

She wanted to grab him and hug him—for being so generous, for thinking of her poor brother, who had to be worried sick about now and was no doubt moving heaven and earth to get back to town. "Yes. Please. Let's do that."

The church ladies had several boxes they could spare. So she and Collin put them in the back of his pickup and headed for the ranch, where they worked until after five packing up things at Gage's and putting them with Willa's boxes in her father's work shed.

They made it back to town in time for dinner at the church. As they ate beans and rice with ham, Nathan got up and proudly announced that cell phone service was restored. He reminded them of the places that had generators where they might charge their batteries. People applauded the news—and then hurried off to find the phones they'd stopped carrying around with them for the past three days.

In the pickup, Collin called his mother first. Willa had run out with him and ended up sitting in the passenger seat beside him as he nodded and listened, and seemed to be having trouble getting a word in edgewise. He kept trying to tell his mom what had happened there at home, but Ellie Traub had never been the quiet type. As soon as he started talking, she would get going again and he ended up mostly saying, "Yeah. Okay. All right. That's good, Mom. Really..."

When he finally said goodbye, he reported to Willa that his mom, his dad and his brothers were fine. "They got the rain down there in Thunder Canyon," he said, "but flooding was minimal. Mom says they're willing to wait a few more days until the governor gives the go-ahead. But if the okay doesn't come soon, they're heading for home." He added that the people of Thunder Canyon were already talking about ways to help Rust Creek Falls with flood cleanup and the rebuilding that would follow.

And then he handed her the phone. "Go on. Call your folks."

Again, she had a really strong urge to hug him. But instead she started dialing.

Lavinia Christensen cried when Willa said hello. "We've been calling and calling," she sobbed. And then she wanted to know why Willa wasn't calling from her own cell.

Willa explained that she'd lost it in the flood. "This is Collin's cell."

Her mother sniffled. "Collin *Traub?*"

"Yes." She cast Collin a warm glance. "He's been great to me, Mom. Wonderful." Collin sent her one of those *knock-it-off* looks when he heard her praising him. She pretended not to notice.

Her mom was kind of sputtering. "Well, I, ahem. The Traubs are good people."

"They certainly are—and if you need to reach me, just call this number. Collin will make sure I get back to you until I can get a phone of my own."

"I… I will. Yes. Of course."

Willa assured her mom that she was all right and that the ranch house was fine and so was the barn. She said that most of the stock had survived the flood and the neighbors had all pitched in to keep the animals fed and to clean up the mess. Her mom cried some more when she heard the bad news about Willa's house and Gage's place.

It turned out her folks were still in Livingston, waiting for news that the roads were clear. Gage, however, had set out for home.

When Willa called him, she had to explain all over again that he should call her on Collin's phone for the time being. He started quizzing her about Collin.

She cut him short. "What about you? Where are you now?"

He said he'd been held up three times so far with washed-out bridges and roads, but he wasn't giving up and had spent each night since the flood in a different town. Willa got teary eyed then and told him about the condition of his house—and hers. Her brother said he loved her and not to cry and he would be there as soon as he could. He said he'd visited the sheriff's stations in the towns where he'd stayed and used their radio systems to contact his office. So he'd known that she was all right and he'd been told of the death of Hunter McGee.

When he mentioned Mayor McGee, Willa started crying all over again. She'd been dry-eyed at the funeral, but there was something about her brother's voice.

She could tell that the mayor's death had hit him hard. Collin hauled a box of tissues from the glove box and passed it to her. She grabbed one and wiped at her streaming eyes.

When she hung up with Gage, she gave the phone back to Collin. He turned on the pickup so he could hook up his car charger and then, with the phone plugged in, he called a couple of his brothers in Thunder Canyon and then his brother Sutter, in Washington State.

When he hung up, he said in a tone that dared her to argue, "I think a lot of Sutter. He's a damn good man."

Willa only nodded. There were people in town who didn't approve of the stand Sutter had taken when their older brother Forrest went off to fight in Iraq. And then there was the way he'd broken Paige's heart. But still. Willa had always liked Sutter and if he and Collin were on good terms, well, that was just fine with her.

Collin narrowed those almost-black eyes at her and his full mouth curved down at the corners. "You got something on your mind, Willa, you ought to just go ahead and say it."

Willa answered sweetly, "You love your brother. There is nothing wrong with that."

That evening, the number of citizens requiring emergency shelter was a third what it had been the first night. FEMA had brought in some trailers that day for people to stay in temporarily. And more people had either left town to stay with relatives or moved in with friends. A lucky few had discovered that the damage to their homes wasn't bad enough to keep them from moving back in.

Willa and Collin stayed in the town hall again that night. After the lights were out, she took Buster and went to join Collin under the stars.

"Been waiting for you," he said when she dropped down beside him.

A little thrill shivered through her at his words and she had to remind herself not to be an idiot. It wasn't a man-woman kind of thing between them. They were friends. Good friends, amazingly. But that was all. He wasn't interested in her in *that* way and he never had been.

She wrapped her arms around her knees and rested her chin on them. "Are you still planning to go up the mountain tomorrow?"

"Yeah. In the afternoon. It should be fine up there. The generator automatically kicks in when the power goes out, so what's in the fridge and the freezer stays cold. I've got a freezer full of food I'll bring down and donate to the church kitchen."

She stared at him, thinking how smoking hot he was—because, hey, even if they were just friends, there was no law that said a girl couldn't look. She could get lost in those eyes of his. And even in the darkness, his hair had a shine to it. And it was so thick.

That night four years ago, at the Ace in the Hole, before he laughed at her and told her to get lost, they'd danced to a couple of slow numbers together. She remembered so clearly the feel of his hard, hot shoulder beneath her hand. His lips had looked soft and dangerous, both at once. And the scent of him: incomparable, a heady mix of aftershave, man and something temptingly wild. The rush of blood through her veins had been dizzying. And she would never forget her powerful desire to slide her fingers upward, over the hot flesh of his neck and into that thick, crow-black hair of his.

He asked, "Do I have dirt on my nose?"

She chuckled, the sound surprisingly husky to her own ears. "No. Why?"

He held her gaze as though he never planned to look away. "You're staring at me."

Right. She supposed that she was. She went on staring and told him way too dreamily, "Buster and I are going with you."

"Going with me where?"

"Up to your house tomorrow."

Those thick inky brows drew together. "It's not a good idea."

Too bad. He wasn't talking her out of it. But for now, she played along. "Why not?"

"The road up there is bound to be a mess. It could be dangerous."

"All the more reason you shouldn't go alone."

"You're going to protect me, are you?"

She braced her chin on her hand. "I am. Absolutely. You're a big, tough guy and all, I know. But even tough guys sometimes need a little help."

The way he was looking at her now, she could almost imagine that he did think of her *that* way. Which probably meant she was being an idiot again. But so what? There were a lot worse things than being an idiot. A girl could live her whole life without ever getting her fingers into Collin's black hair. That would be sad. Immeasurably so.

Now he was looking stern. "It's not a good idea."

"You already said that."

"I'll probably end up staying up there overnight."

"So? I'll take the sleeping bag from my cot. It will be fine."

He seemed a little insulted. "I have a guest room—and believe it or not, it has a bed in it, complete with sheets and blankets and pillows."

"Wonderful. So it's settled."

He wasn't going for it. "I told you. You need to stay here."

"We'll see…."

"I mean it, Willa. You are not going up the mountain with me."

The next morning, Collin rejoined his team.

Before he left to help with cleanup down in the area around the flooded clinic, Willa told him that she and Paige and some of the other teachers had been asked to reconvene summer school. Since the day would be a clear one, they would hold their classes in Rust Creek Falls Park. On rainy days, classes would be hosted by some of the parents—and a few of the teachers, as well.

When he came in for lunch in the church, he returned a call from his mom, one from his brother Clay and another from Sutter. Then he made calls to a few top CT Saddles customers. He apologized for the fact that he would be filling their orders late. They'd all heard about the flood and told him not to worry, to stay safe and take his time.

Willa wasn't there at the church for lunch. He ignored the little curl of disappointment in his chest when he didn't see her. Every day he was with her, it got easier to let himself think that there was more going on between them than friendship.

There wasn't. Once things got back to normal, her

big-shot boyfriend would show up. She would realize what that other guy could offer her and she would end up with his ring on her finger. Which was the way it should be. Willa deserved the best.

Dolly Tabor, one of his teammates on the rescue-turned-cleanup crew, had kids in summer school. She mentioned that the church ladies were delivering the school lunches to the park.

So, great, he thought. Willa was having lunch with the kids in the park.

He asked Dolly, real casual-like, when summer school would be over for the day. Dolly said at three.

Collin made his plans accordingly. He knew Willa and he knew her ways. She thought she was going up the mountain with him. And there was more than one good reason why he couldn't let that happen. For one thing, the trip up there was likely to be hazardous. He wasn't putting Willa in danger. And then, if they ended up stuck at his place for the night, well, that would present a whole other kind of danger.

It was one thing to be alone with her for an hour out on the town hall steps at night, or while they worked side by side hauling stuff out of her brother's flooded house. It was another thing altogether to spend the night with her at his place, just the two of them, alone on Falls Mountain.

Uh-uh. That would be asking for the kind of trouble they weren't going to get into together. He had to face reality here. He'd done what he could to help her through the worst of it after the flood. Her family would be back in town any day now. From what she'd said about Gage working his way north, her brother could be home already.

Collin needed to start getting a little distance from her. He had to stop spending so much time with her, had to give up those nighttime talks out on the town hall steps. He needed to stop kidding himself that it was innocent, that they were just hanging out, joking around a little before turning in.

It wasn't innocent—not for him anyway. Every night it got harder to keep his hands to himself. If he didn't get some distance, he would end up making a move on her.

He knew she really wanted to be his friend and all that. But he wanted more than friendship and where was that going to go? He liked his relationships with women to be simple—and short.

Nothing with Willa was simple. So he would put an end to it, make sure it never even had a chance to get started. She would be hurt and probably angry with him for taking off up the mountain without a word to her. But too bad.

It was for the best.

He got Jerry Dobbs aside and said he was heading up to his place. Jerry clapped him on the back and told him to be careful on the road up there.

Across the street at the town hall, he collected the plastic bag full of clothes and personal items he'd left under his cot. Marjorie Hanke was there, so he told her he wouldn't be needing the cot anymore.

And that was it. He was free to get the hell outta town.

He shouldered the bag and headed for his truck in the parking lot in the back, feeling more down than he should have, wishing things could be different and calling himself ten kinds of fool to want a thing he was never going to have—and wouldn't know what to do with anyway.

He almost tripped over his own boots when he caught sight of Willa. She was leaning against his rear wheel well, Buster on one side, her bag of stuff and backpack on the other.

Chapter 8

She had her arms folded across her middle and her head tipped to the side. The early-afternoon sun brought out bronze highlights in her coffee-colored hair. She gave him a slow once-over. "I knew it."

He glared at her, trying his best to look pissed off. "You knew what?"

"You were just going to sneak away without even telling me. That's not very nice, Collin."

"I did tell you. I told you last night."

She tightened her arms around herself and pressed her lips together. "And I told you that I was going with you." She pushed off the wheel well and stood up straight. "So here I am."

His bag of clothes rustled as he let it slide to the pavement. He was actively ignoring the rapid beating of his heart, the ridiculous surge of happiness that was blasting all through him.

She really did want to go with him. She wasn't letting him get away without a fight.

But so what? He needed to focus on the goal: to get her to give up this insanity and go back to the park. "No. It's a bad idea. And aren't you supposed to be over at the park teaching summer school?"

"Shelby Jenkins is helping out. She took over for me."

"But you—"

"I'm going, Collin. Don't mess with me on this."

How in hell could he do the right thing if she kept pushing him to screw up? A voice in the back of his mind kept chanting, *She wants to come, she wants to come.* And the bad-acting idiot inside him kept whispering, *Man, if it's what she wants, why not?*

He ground his teeth together. "I wasn't planning to come back until tomorrow."

"That's okay. I've got my stuff. And you've got a guest room. It's all good."

"I thought you had summer school."

"I told you, Shelby's helping out. I explained to her that I was going up the mountain with you and we might not make it back until later tomorrow. She'll take my kids for me. I'm covered."

"Get real, Willa. You go up the mountain with me and spend the night, the whole town will be talking when you come back down. The Traub bad boy and the kindergarten teacher. I can hear them all now."

She laughed. Like it was funny. He watched the dimples flash in her pink cheeks and he thought about licking them. "I'm sure they're already talking. We've practically been joined at the hip since the flood. And in case you've forgotten, we spent a whole night together in my dad's barn and the world didn't come to an end."

In case he'd forgotten? He would never forget. Especially not what had happened in the morning. His fly. Her hand. Sitting there on the edge of that hay bale, willing the humiliating bulge in his pants to go down. He strove for calmness and reasonableness. "We had no choice then. It was the barn or drowning. This—you and me, up the mountain together? That's a clear choice."

Her mouth had pinched up tight. "What is going on with you? Suddenly you're acting like it's 1955 or something. Like you're worried about my reputation, which is excellent and unimpeachable, thank you very much."

Unimpeachable? She really did talk like a schoolteacher sometimes. Which got him hot. Real hot. But he wasn't going to think about that. "It's a very small town, Willa. People here are conservative. You know that as well as I do."

She just wouldn't back down. "You're making way too much of this. Everyone in town knows me and respects me. No one has—or will—judge me for being your friend." In her excitement, she unfolded her arms and waved them around. "In fact, Crawfords aside, this town happens to think the world of *you,* in case you haven't been paying attention."

"That doesn't mean they won't gossip."

"Oh, please. You never cared about people talking before."

"I care now."

"I don't believe you. Here's the way I see it. If you really don't want me along, if you're sick of having me around and you want to get rid of me, that's one thing.

If you just *have* to have a little time to yourself, well, okay. I can accept that. But all this other stuff you've been handing me about my reputation and how it's 'a bad idea,' how I should be over at the park instead of with you, well, you can just stop that, Collin Traub. You can just...get a little bit straight with me. Please." And with that, she blew out a hard breath and flopped back against the wheel well again, folding her arms across her chest once more.

"Crap, Willa." He folded his own arms. He told himself that this argument was over and he'd won it. Because she'd just given him the out that he needed. He only had to say he didn't want her with him, that he preferred to be alone. He only had to lie to her.

Which he had no problem doing, under the circumstances. After all, it was for her own good.

Buster whined and stared up at him hopefully. And Willa simply waited.

He opened his mouth and said, "Fine. Get in the truck."

Willa had always loved the drive up Falls Mountain. It was paved only a part of the way up, but when the pavement ran out, the dirt surface was well tended and the ride reasonably smooth—or at least, it always had been until the flood.

The narrow road proceeded in a series of switchbacks under the tall evergreens. Now and then a switchback would lead out onto a rocky point before doubling back. You could park your vehicle and stroll to the edge and gaze out over the whole of the Rust Creek Falls Valley below, a beautiful sight that never failed to steal her breath away.

And then, two-thirds of the way to the summit, you would round a sharp turn—and see the falls up ahead, hear their splendid, endless roar. The air would turn misty and the sun would slip through the spaces between the trees and light up the falling water with a million pinpricks of shining light.

This trip, however, wasn't so much about the scenery. This was about getting safely to Collin's place and dealing with whatever obstacles the big storm might have left in its wake.

As they set out, you could cut the tension between them with a knife. He was pretty steamed at her. He seethed where he sat, strong hands viselike on the wheel, staring out the windshield with fierce concentration, never once glancing in her direction.

And frankly, well, she was annoyed with him, too. She only wanted to help. And he could have gotten rid of her just by honestly saying he didn't want her around.

But no. It had to be all about protecting her good name. Please. She wasn't buying that silliness and he should give her more credit than to imagine she would.

So she spent the first part of the ride until the pavement ran out keeping very quiet, not pushing her luck with him. Buster was in the back and they'd taken their bags of stuff up front with them. She had them both on her side, his on the floor, hers tucked in next to her with her pack against the console. She leaned on the door armrest and stared intently out at the trees and the occasional glimpses of blue Montana sky and told herself that when they got to his place, they would talk it out.

She was so busy staring out her side window she didn't see the first downed tree until he stopped the truck.

"This'll take a while," he said sourly. "Hope you brought a book or maybe a little knitting." He leaned on his door and got out.

Oh, for crying out loud. As if she hadn't helped her father and brother clear any number of fallen trees off the ranch in her lifetime. She'd come ready to work. She had on her old lace-up work boots from the box at her mother's. Her jeans were sturdy and her sleeves were long. She dug around in her plastic bag until she found the pair of work gloves she'd borrowed from Thelma.

Collin's chain saw roared out as she left the truck. Buster was already down from the bed and sniffing around on the side of the road. He would probably take off if she didn't put him on his leash, but he looked so happy and free, she didn't have the heart to tie him up.

So she decided to leave him free, but keep an eye on him. If he started ranging too far, she'd call him back.

She went to join Collin at the fallen tree.

Willa hauled and Collin expertly stripped the branches from the log, then cut the log into sections. When he was done with the saw, he helped her drag off the brush.

As they cleared the brush, he finally started speaking to her again.

"I hate to waste firewood," he said. "But I've got more than enough up at my place."

They left the stove-size logs and the cleanest parts of the branches stacked on the side of the road for anyone in need to collect. It wasn't that big of a tree. In an hour, they had the roadway clear.

She took off her gloves. With her sleeve, she wiped sweat from her brow. And then she remembered to check on the dog. Wouldn't you know? "Buster's run off again."

He put two fingers between his lips and let loose with a whistle so high and piercing, she put her hands over her ears. As soon as he stopped, Buster came bounding out of the trees. He ran straight to Collin and dropped to his haunches in front of him.

"Good dog," Collin said. "Stay."

Willa blinked in admiration. "Wow."

"I used to call Libby that way. Never failed."

She remembered his dog. A sweet-natured brown-spotted white mutt that followed him everywhere. "What happened to Libby?"

"Lost her last winter. She was pretty old."

"I'm sorry. She always seemed so devoted to you."

"Yeah. I guess she was." He made a low, thoughtful sound. "I still miss her. Now and then I think I see her out of the corner of my eye. I forget for a split second that she's gone and I turn to call her to me…."

Willa was nodding, thinking of Mr. Puffy, the barn kitten she'd claimed as her own when she was five. Puffs had become a house cat and lived to be seventeen. "Oh, I know the feeling. It's like they're still with you, somehow, even though you know that they're gone…."

"That's right." He regarded her for a moment that seemed to stretch out into forever. He didn't seem angry anymore and she realized that neither was she.

"Thirsty?" he asked at last.

At her nod, he turned and started walking, pausing only to signal her with a wave of his powerful arm.

"Come on, Buster." She fell in behind him.

A trail took off below the road. They followed it,

pine needles crunching under their feet, Buster taking up the rear.

Maybe two hundred yards later, they came to a ditch full of rushing, clear water. They both got down on their bellies to drink. Buster tried to join them, but she shooed him downstream a ways.

It was so good, that water. Fresh and cold and perfect. When they'd both drunk their fill, they scrambled upright and returned to the pickup. They got in, Buster hopped in the back and off they went.

After that, it was stop and go. There were three more downed trees to clear and any number of rutted, rough places scattered with rock, where instant streams had formed during the storm, destroying the road surface, dragging debris. Often they would have to get out and clear away the biggest of the boulders. It was dusty, thirsty work. But there were plenty of ditches to drink from once the road was passable again.

At one of the outlook points, they found that the road had fallen away at the edge of the cliff. It was just wide enough for the pickup to proceed. Twice on that narrow spot, she felt the back wheel on her side slip over the edge.

But Collin had done a lot of driving on narrow, treacherous mountain roads. He knew when to change gears and when to hit the gas. Both times, there was only a split second of falling and then the truck gained purchase again and they went on.

They didn't reach the falls until a little after seven. More than two hours of daylight remained to them, so they stopped the truck. Buster following behind them, they walked close to admire the view.

"It was twice as wide when I came down on the

Fourth," he told her, as they stared at the wall of shining water.

"So beautiful." She stood near the edge, looking over, entranced by the plumes of mist that rose from the rocks below. A prayerful kind of feeling came over her. It happened every time she visited the falls.

When they turned for the truck, he said, "It's not that far now." He put down the gate long enough for Buster to hop in the back again. Then he joined her in the cab.

Around the next sharp curve another tree lay, uprooted, across the road. They got out and got to work. By the time that one was out of the way and he was starting up the truck again, it was nine-thirty and the sky was steadily darkening.

He sent her a glance across the console. "We're there in five minutes, barring more crap in the road."

She grinned. "I will pray for an absence of crap."

"Good thinking." He started to shift into gear—and then stopped. "I would be sleeping in this truck tonight, three fallen trees back, if not for you."

"If more crap happens, you could still end up sleeping in this truck."

He arched a brow. "That was a thank-you."

She felt hugely gratified. "Well, all right. You're welcome."

"And an apology."

"Which is accepted."

They did that thing, the eye-contact thing. The moment stretched out. Finally, he said, "I'm glad you're with me."

"That is so nice to hear." She said it softly, a little bit breathlessly. "Because I'm glad to be with you."

They shared another endless glance. The world

seemed a fine place, exciting, a place where anything might happen. A place where a girl's lifelong forbidden fantasies might just come true.

Friends, she reminded herself. *We are friends and that's all.*

But the way he was looking at her, well, a girl could definitely get ideas.

"We should get going," he said.

"Yeah," she whispered, as though there was some kind of secret they were sharing.

He buckled his seat belt and put it in gear.

The headlights were on, the powerful twin beams cutting the thickening shadows. Everything looked clear up ahead. The road was very steep, though, there at the last. Gravel spun out from under the tires as they kept losing traction. But Collin held it in low, with an even pressure on the gas. They climbed steadily upward, almost there.

"One more switchback," he said. The sharp turn loomed ahead. Tires spinning, gravel flying, the truck slipping to one side and then the other, Collin guided them around it.

They'd made it without having to sleep in the cab. Through the tall, thick trees, she could see the shadowed form of his house up ahead. A light shone in the window, one he must have left on when he raced down the mountain four days ago, a light that still burned because he had a generator.

Lights that wouldn't be turned off promptly at 11:00 p.m. How wonderful. She had a couple of bestsellers she'd borrowed from Paige in the bottom of her bag. Why, she might read late into the night if she felt like it. She might blow-dry her hair—well, if only she'd thought to scare up a blow-dryer.

And not only would there be light that was hers to control, she would sleep on a real bed, in a real bedroom, without all those other people nearby snoring or mumbling in their sleep….

The truck slid, snapping her back to reality, and she felt a stomach-turning lurch as the rear wheels lost contact with the road. Collin swore under his breath.

The truck—and the world—hung suspended by two front wheels.

It was bad. She knew it. She tasted copper in her suddenly dry mouth. Her heart boomed, the sound a roar in her ears.

It took her a second or two to realize what had happened. As they came around the turn, the road had collapsed on the cliff side, just dropped off and fallen away under the back wheels.

"Oh, dear Lord," she whispered, and nothing more. Words were lost to her.

The truck was sliding backward, the bed dropping, dragging. They were going to go over the cliff, tail first….

But Collin hit the gas then. The front wheels grabbed and held. Praise heaven for four-wheel drive. He eased the throttle even higher.

The truck lurched again, jumping forward this time, grabbing at the road. The front wheels had good purchase. Gravel flew every which way, grinding grooves in the dirt, but they did move forward. The truck leveled out as the rear wheels reached the road again.

He had done it. He had all four tires on solid ground

again. She heard him suck in a long breath and realized that she was doing the same thing.

"We're okay," she whispered, as though to say it too loudly would somehow send them rolling backward over the cliff once more.

But then she glanced through the rear window. Buster wasn't there.

Chapter 9

"Collin, Buster's gone!"

Collin hit the brake as Willa's door flew open. "Willa. Wait..." But she didn't wait. She was out the door before the truck came to a full stop. "Be careful at the cliff edge!" he shouted.

Not that she heard him. She was already out and running back to that last almost-deadly turn.

He slammed it in Park, turned off the engine, and shoved in the parking brake, grabbing a flashlight from the glove box before he jumped out and ran after her. "Stay back from the edge, damn it, Willa!"

She was already there, craning to see over, calling the dog. "Buster! Buster, here, boy!"

He went to her, grabbed her arm and hauled her back a few feet. She tried to shake him off, but he held on. "Don't," he warned. "It could be dangerous."

"But Buster..." Frantic tears clogged her voice.

He shone the light on the ground at the edge he'd dragged her back from. Hard to tell, but it looked pretty solid. "Careful, okay?" Reluctantly, he let her go. "Just take it easy...slow."

Together they moved toward the cliff again. He shone the flashlight down into the darkness, spotted the small ledge created by two joined sets of tree roots maybe thirty feet down. Buster was young and agile. All he would have needed was something to break his fall and chances were he would have been okay.

No sign of him on that ledge, though.

"Buster!" Willa called again, more frantic than before. "Buster!"

Not knowing what else to do, Collin put his fingers between his teeth and let out with the whistle that always brought the dogs running. He glanced over at Willa, at the tears already streaming down her soft cheeks.

He was just about to start blaming himself, when he heard the scrabbling sounds over the side, up the road a little, near where he'd stopped the truck.

Willa whipped around toward the noise. "Buster!" Collin turned the light on her, so she wouldn't trip on the uneven road surface as she took off again in the direction of the sounds.

About then, the white dog scrambled up over the bank, apparently unhurt. He got to the road and shook himself.

"Buster!" Willa dropped to a crouch and threw her arms around him. The dog whined and swiped his sloppy tongue all over her face and wagged his tail as though he'd just done something pretty spectacular.

And maybe he had.

Collin went to them. With another happy cry, Willa jumped up and threw her arms around *him*. "He's fine. He's okay. Oh, thank God." She buried her face against his neck.

He held her close and tried not to let himself think about how right she always felt in his arms.

Buster rode the last short stretch inside the cab, sandwiched between Willa's feet.

Collin didn't much care for dogs in the front. But he wasn't complaining. A couple of minutes after they'd piled in the truck again, Collin parked in the flat space not far from the front door to his house.

"We made it," Willa said softly. "I can hardly believe it."

He reached over and grabbed his bag out from under Buster's big feet. "I'm starving. Let's scare up something to eat."

Inside, he got Libby's bowl down from a cupboard and filled it with kibble leftover from last winter. Buster went right to work on the food.

Willa stood holding her black plastic bag, her pack slung on one shoulder, staring out the wall of windows that faced the valley. With the lamps on and the antler chandelier overhead casting its warm glow, there was nothing to see but her reflection in the glass. "This is so beautiful, Collin."

He left the open kitchen area and went to stand beside her. "Pretty dark down there tonight. Usually, even with the great room all lit up, you can see the lights of town."

She turned to him, her eyes so soft and bright. "You'll be seeing them again before you know it."

He took her arm and tried not to feel too happy to have her there, in his house, alone. "Come on. I'll show you the guest room and the spare bath."

Her face lit up. "A shower? You mean it?"

"Right this way."

Willa pushed her empty plate away. "Steak. A baked potato. Even a salad." She sent him a mock glare. "And to think, if I hadn't made you bring me along, it would have been macaroni and canned ham all over again."

He gave her one of those grins that always made her pulse speed up. "Is that what the church ladies are serving tonight?"

"I believe so, yes." She sat back and looked around her. The living area was all one room, with a comfy-looking sofa and chairs grouped around a rustic fireplace. He'd built a small fire that crackled cheerfully. Up on the mountain, even summer nights had a bite to them.

The galley-type kitchen had butcher-block counters, the cabinets painted a woodsy green.

She asked, "This place was your uncle's?"

"That's right." He polished off his beer. "Uncle Casper was an independent old coot—and he was always good to me."

She remembered Casper Traub. He had a handlebar mustache and he always wore a white Resistol hat. "A confirmed bachelor."

"Damn straight. Uncle Casper and I got along. We just seemed to understand each other—but I've made a lot of changes to the house since he passed. This area had a wall down the middle before, the kitchen separate from the living room. I like it open. And I had bigger windows put in to take advantage of the view."

"You did a great job." She stared up at all the lights strung on the antler chandelier. "It's comfortable and homey. Inviting, but not cluttered."

"That's good." He gestured with his empty beer bottle. "It's pretty much what I was going for."

"You got it right."

He was watching her. "But not what you expected." It wasn't a question.

She confessed, "Not really. I was thinking you would have more of a woodsy man-cave, to tell the truth."

Twin creases formed between his brows. "It's not a woodsy man-cave?"

"Collin. You can't have a man-cave with all those windows. With a man-cave, there would be stacks of girlie magazines. And the decor would focus on empty liquor bottles lining the walls."

He pretended to look wounded. "You're serious. You see me saving empty liquor bottles to use for decoration, surrounded by girlie magazines…."

"Oh, come on. You know I'm just kidding."

He shrugged and pointed the beer bottle at the big-screen TV. "Well, I've got the right TV anyway. And I get cable up here now, believe it or not—or I do when the cable service isn't down. Even my cell phone works most of the time." He grinned that wicked grin of his. "Admit it. You're impressed."

"Bowled over." She took a small sip of the beer he'd given her. "You miss your uncle?"

He gave her a slow nod. "Every day. He taught me all

I know about the business and he left it to me with the house when we lost him. My shop's in the basement."

"*You* make the saddles now?"

He sent her a wounded glance. "Who would if I didn't? You think I keep a bunch of elves down there?"

"Of course not." But she *was* surprised. She'd known that Casper Traub had left everything to his favorite nephew, but somehow she hadn't really thought about what exactly that would mean—and that made her feel a little ashamed. The past few years, she'd been so busy judging him, she'd never stopped to think about who he was as a person, how he might have changed and grown from the wild, rude boy who used to spy on her out in the back pasture.

He got up, got a second beer from the fridge and twisted the top off. "You want one?"

She still had half of hers. "I'm good."

He came back to her and dropped into his chair again. "What? You're having trouble believing that I work for a living?" He took a drink, his Adam's apple sliding up and down in his strong brown throat. "You have one of my saddles in the tack room of your dad's barn."

Yet another surprise. "My dad's precious CT Saddle? *You* made it?"

"I did."

"But he got that saddle three years ago."

"I've been making saddles since before high school. Uncle Casper had me working with him as soon as I was tall enough to stand at a workbench."

"Oh. I…didn't know."

He grunted and shook his head. And she felt really bad. He seemed to sense her distress, and leaned across the table toward her. "What'd I do? Willa, come on. You look like you're about to cry."

She waved a hand. And then she sighed. "You didn't do anything. Honestly. It's only that I'm disappointed in myself, I guess."

"Why?" He asked it so quietly. Like he didn't want to push her, but he really did want an answer.

She gave him the truth. "We live in a very small town, where everyone knows everything about everyone else. Yet, I didn't know you made the most beautiful saddles in Montana. I didn't know much at all about you. In high school, I never wanted anyone to know that I was..." Her throat clutched. She gulped to loosen it. "Um, attracted to you. So I made real sure that I acted like I couldn't care less whenever anyone mentioned your name. That meant I never learned anything about you—about who you really are. Except that everyone said half the girls had been with you and the other half wished they might."

"Willa..." His voice was husky and his eyes were so soft.

She suddenly felt all warm and quivery inside and she had to force herself to say the rest. "And then, well, after that night at the Ace in the Hole, I was just so... bitter. So angry at you. And that meant I kept on not letting myself know anything about you, kept on judging you without even knowing you. It was all just so narrow-minded and, well, *small* of me, you know? And I like to think of myself as an open-minded and fair person. But maybe I'm not. Maybe I'm already just an old busybody, listening to rumors, believing the worst about people. Never stopping to find out what's really going on."

"You're too young to be an old busybody."

She wanted to smile—but he was letting her off too easy. "Don't be nice to me about this. I don't deserve it."

He set down his beer, got up and came around the table to her, dropping to a crouch beside her chair. "Hey." He took her hand. Heat flowed up her arm, into her heart. And lower down, too. "And I have to tell you, I kind of got a kick out of you avoiding me for four years."

She groaned. "You didn't."

"Oh, yeah. You were so determined. I'd walk in a room—and out you went through the other door."

"But still. Be honest. It did hurt your feelings a little, didn't it?"

"I survived."

She looked down at their joined hands and then back up into those beautiful deep-set eyes of his. "So you forgive me?"

"There's nothing to forgive." He seemed so earnest right then, his face tipped up to her, that lock of hair falling over his forehead the way it always seemed to do.

She couldn't stop herself—she didn't *want* to stop herself. She dared to smooth it back. It was just as she'd always imagined it might be—thick and warm and so very silky, a little bit damp from his recent shower. "I don't know what I would have done in these past few days without you."

"You would have been fine."

She grew bolder. She pressed her palm to his cheek. It was smooth, freshly shaved. "I would have drowned that first day. You know it as well as I do."

"Uh-uh. You're too ornery to drown."

"You think so?"

"Oh, yeah. You would have gotten that door open and made it to safety." His voice was rough and tender, both at once.

Her breath caught in her throat. *A kiss,* she thought. What could a kiss hurt?

Just one. No harm in that.

His gaze seemed to burn her and his sensual mouth was slightly parted. He smelled so good, clean and fresh and manly.

"Oh, Collin…" She dared to bend closer—and then blinked in surprise when he caught her wrist and gently guided her hand away from his face.

He swept to his feet, grabbed up his empty plate and the salad bowl and carried them to the sink. Without turning back to look at her, he said, "You want to watch a movie or something? I've got a bookcase full of DVDs."

Her face was flaming. Talk about making a fool of herself.

What was her problem anyway? The poor guy couldn't be nice to her without her trying to jump his bones.

She reminded herself, as she'd reminded herself about a hundred times in the past few days, that he liked her and he was her friend. But he was not interested in her in *that* way and she needed to get that in her head and keep it there.

His friendship mattered to her. She was not going to lose him because she couldn't stop throwing herself at him.

He still had his back to her as he rinsed out the salad bowl and then scraped off his plate in the garbage and stuck it in the dishwasher.

She picked up her plate and carried it over there.

He took it from her. "So. Movie?"

"As long as I get to choose which one."

He did let her choose. His taste ranged from horror to Western and action/adventure to raunchy guy comedies. Not a tender romance to be found.

She chose a Jason Statham shoot-'em-up. It was fast-paced and entertaining. When it was over, she let Buster out and waited on the step for him to take care of business. Back inside, she told Collin good-night and headed for the guest room, Buster at her heels.

The bed was big and comfortable and she'd worked hard all afternoon. She should have gone right to sleep.

But, no. She kept thinking about what an idiot she'd been at the dinner table, kept wondering if she should have done something other than pretend for the rest of the evening that nothing had happened.

Then again, if not that, what? Certainly they didn't have to discuss the fact that she regretted throwing herself at him and would try really, really hard not to do it again.

Sheesh. How pathetic. That was a conversation she just didn't need to have.

Willa plumped her pillow and turned over. Then she turned over again. Then she sat up and pushed back all the covers but the sheet.

Then she pulled the covers back over herself again.

It was hopeless. Sleep was not in the offing. She turned on the lamp and got her book from the bag and tried to read.

But she couldn't concentrate. The clock by the bed said ten after one.

Maybe she could find some cocoa in the kitchen. Or just some milk to heat up. Or *something.*

She threw back the covers. On the rug by the bed, Buster lifted his head—and then settled back to sleep with a soft doggy sigh. She yanked on a worn plaid shirt over the camisole and knit shorts she'd worn to sleep in and decided to just go barefoot. Flip-flops made too much noise anyway. She didn't want to take the chance of disturbing Collin. At least one of them should be allowed to get a decent night's sleep.

His bedroom was down at the far end of the hall. The door was open, but there was no light on in there.

Not that it mattered. She had no intention of bothering him. Willa went the other way, out to the great room and into the kitchen.

She flicked on the light and was heading for the fridge when Collin said, "Go back to bed, Willa. How many times do I have to tell you? I'm not having sex with you."

With a cry of surprise, she whirled toward the sound of his voice. He stood over in the living area, wearing his jeans and nothing else, his strong legs planted wide apart, hands linked behind him, staring out the wall of windows on the dark town below.

She didn't know whether to laugh or throw something at him…but wait.

On second thought, she did know. The latter. Definitely.

Okay, she'd tried to kiss him and she shouldn't have. But he didn't have to be mean about it. In fact, the more she thought about it, the more she realized how sick and tired she was of hearing him say he wouldn't have sex with her. It had been funny, for a while—but tonight, well, it was downright hurtful.

She zipped around the island counter that separated the living area from the kitchen and marched right for him. "Oh, please. Will you give that up? I couldn't sleep, that's all." She halted a few feet from him and glared at his broad back. "Nobody here is thinking about sex."

"Speak for yourself." Slowly, he turned and faced her. She gasped at the yearning she saw in his eyes.

Chapter 10

Collin couldn't take it anymore.

The sight of her, in those little purple velour shorts and that skimpy, lacy top…well, it was too much. Even if she did have on an old plaid shirt over the top. That old shirt wasn't hiding anything. She hadn't even bothered to button it up.

He could see her nipples very clearly, poking at him through the thin fabric, could make out the tempting, ripe curves of her breasts. She was driving him crazy, that was what she was doing. He'd held out for years, done the right thing by her, even though she'd ended up hating him for it.

But tonight, well, it was too much.

And hadn't he known that it would be? She shouldn't have kept after him until he brought her up here with him. She shouldn't have tried to kiss him. Shouldn't have come out of her room dressed in those soft purple shorts and that skimpy silky top that didn't hide a damn thing.

He burned. He was on fire—to take her breasts in his two hands. To touch the skin of her thighs, to rub his rough palms along all that smooth softness, to inch his fingers upward, under the hem of those shorts, to touch her at last where he knew she would be hot and wet and waiting for him.

He wanted her, wanted sweet Willa Christensen, probably always had, from way back. From before he even realized what he was wanting. Oh, yeah. He wanted her.

And to hell with what was best for her. She wanted him, too. She'd made that more than clear on more than one occasion.

Tonight, he was going to give her exactly what she wanted.

Reaching out, he took her by the arms and hauled her up close to him, reveling in the feel of her body brushing along the front him, making him ache all the harder for her.

He brought his face good and close to hers, so close he could taste the heat of her breath. "You should have stayed in town tonight like I told you to, you know that, don't you?"

She licked her lips and gulped. "Um. I…" Her eyes were so wide. Wide and soft and wanting.

Those eyes of hers called to him. They always had. Those eyes said she knew him, was waiting for him to finally reach out and take her. Those eyes said she would do anything he wanted.

Truth to tell, those eyes had always scared the crap

out of him. They seemed to hint of things a guy like him didn't deserve to know.

Things like forever. Things like a lifetime.

Things he wasn't planning for. He lived his life alone.

Which led back around to the basic issue: he shouldn't be doing this.

But too bad. He *was* doing this.

He was through making jokes about it, through trying to discourage her from wanting a little hot fun with the town troublemaker. If she wanted him so much, who was he to tell her no?

"Oh, Collin..." She said it so softly. So willingly. And then her eyes changed. All at once, they weren't so open and sweet anymore. They'd gone determined. They were sparking fire. "No. Uh-uh. I should *not* have stayed down in town. I'm here with you and I'm *glad* I'm here."

Some final scrap of that protectiveness he'd always felt for her prompted him to give her one last out. He met those eyes of hers. He didn't look away. "What I'm saying is, just tell me no, Willa. Just do it. Do it now."

She let out a strangled sound. It might have been a laugh. Or a sob. "Are you kidding? Don't try and pretend that you don't get it. All I've ever wanted was the chance to tell you yes."

It was the last straw.

"Tell me yes, then. You go ahead. You say it right out loud to me."

She didn't even hesitate. "Yes, oh, yes. Please, please make love to me."

So much for her last out. She'd refused to take it. So be it.

He closed that small distance between her mouth and his. He kissed her.

For the very first time.

He touched her mouth with his and it was…everything. A forbidden dream realized.

A promise so long denied, finally kept.

She kissed him back, sighing so sweetly. She melted into him, all that pride and orneriness and softness. Everything that was Willa.

Right there. In his arms.

Her breasts flattened against his bare chest, the way they'd only done in his dreams up till then. Through the flimsy material of that lacy top, he could feel her nipples, hot. Hard. She opened her mouth to him. He swept his hungry tongue inside and the kiss became something more than a dream. Deeper than a promise.

She moaned as he kissed her, and she ran her slim hands up over his shoulders, into his hair.

He needed…more of her. *All* of her. He had his arms good and tight around her, his aching hardness pressed into her belly. He let his hands roam freely, over the slim, smooth shape of her back, up under that cotton shirt, and then down to the cove at the base of her spine.

Her hair was loose. It brushed his forearms and the backs of his hands. Like feathers. Like a cloud of silk. He speared his fingers up into it, fisted them, pulling her head back so he could scrape his teeth along the slim, pure curve of her white throat.

She cried his name. He covered her mouth again and drank the sound.

He needed…more. More of her.

He had to have the feel of her bare skin under his hands. The plaid shirt was in the way. He fisted it by the sides and peeled it back over her slim shoulders. She moaned a little, as though in protest at having to let go of him, but she let him guide her arms down so he could push the shirt off. He whipped it away and tossed it in the general direction of a chair.

Then he clasped her bare shoulders. So smooth and tender, her skin. White, but with a pink flush on it. Beautiful.

He cupped her shoulders, pressed his palms against her upper chest—and lower, until he had her sweet breasts in his two hands with only the thin fabric of that clingy silky thing to protect her from his hungry touch.

She lifted up to him, sighing, offering him whatever he wanted from her.

And he knew what he wanted. To taste her.

He kissed his way down her slim throat again, scattered more kisses along the ridge of her collarbone, down the sweet-smelling skin of her upper chest and lower, over the tender swell of her breast.

He reached the goal at last and latched onto her nipple, sucking it through the silky fabric, flicking it with his tongue.

She clutched at him, holding him to her, whispering, "Yes. Oh, Collin, yes..."

He couldn't have agreed with her more. She smelled like flowers and lemons and a little bit musky, too. All woman, his Willa.

His? Well, fine, maybe not. Not forever. But at least for tonight.

The lacy thing—what did women call those things?—a cami. Yeah. The cami had to go. He grabbed the hem of it...and then got lost in the feel of her skin again. He eased his fingers up under it, stroking the tender flesh of her back, and then bringing both hands around to the front of her, caressing her flat, smooth belly.

She was breathing so frantically. He lifted his head and kissed her again. She moaned into his mouth.

And he moved his hands higher. He cupped her bare breasts under the cami. They were so perfect, so firm and round—not too big, not small, either. They fit just right in his hands.

He thought about seeing her naked.

He wanted to do that. Right away.

Now.

She made no objections, only moaned eagerly and whispered "yes," and "yes" again, as he pulled off the cami and took down the little shorts.

There.

At last.

He had everything off her. She was silk and fire and magic, all he'd ever wanted. Right there in his arms.

He bent enough to wrap his hands around the twin globes of her bottom. She moaned again and he went on kissing her as he lifted her up, dragging all that softness against him. He moaned, too.

It felt so good. *She* felt so good.

She wrapped those soft, smooth thighs around him and hooked her ankles behind his back.

Now he could feel her, feel the womanly heart of her, right there, pressed tight to his fly. He was so hard it hurt. Hurt in the best, most extreme, most perfect kind of way.

And then, still kissing her, her hair a froth of silk and shadows sliding across his skin, her mouth to his mouth, his breath to hers, he started walking.

Well, reeling was more like it.

He reeled across the great room and down the hall to his room at the end. She held on. She went on kissing him. She wrapped those soft, long arms and slim, strong legs around him like she would never, ever let him go.

In the doorway, he paused. Or more like staggered. He braced his back against the door frame and indulged in just kissing her. She didn't seem to mind that he'd stopped moving toward the bed. She just went on kissing him, went on rocking her hips against him, went on making him want to get out of his jeans and into her softness, pronto.

But then again…

No.

He didn't want to rush it. How many times in his life did a man hold a dream in his arms? Once, if he was lucky. A man would be a fool to rush something like that.

Yeah, okay, he had a whole boatload of faults. And maybe he was a fool in some ways. But not when it came to holding Willa in his arms. He was taking his time about this.

He was making it last if it killed him.

And he was kind of afraid it just might.

She framed his face in her two slim hands. "Collin…"

He opened his eyes, stared into hers, which were shining so bright, even in the dim light from all the way back in the kitchen. "Willa."

She wrapped her legs tighter around him. He groaned at the perfect friction as all that willowy softness slid along the front of him. "You do have protection?"

He nodded on another groan.

"Oh, good." And she sighed and kissed him again.

Paradise. They went on kissing, there in the darkened doorway. Endlessly.

Until a terrible thought occurred to him. He broke the kiss so suddenly that his head bounced against the door frame.

She cried out, "Oh! I'll bet that hurt." And she clucked her tongue and fussed over him, rubbing the bumped spot in a gentle, soothing way. "Be careful…."

Gruffly, he reassured her. "I'll live—Willa, look at me."

She blinked at him owlishly, adorably. In the faint glow of light from up the hallway, her dark hair was a wild tangle all around her sweet, flushed face. A dream. No doubt. This had to be a dream. "What?" she demanded. "What's the matter now?"

"I need you to tell me. Is this your first time?" He did not have sex with virgins.

She pressed those amazing lips together, nervous. Unsure. And then she buried her face against his neck. "No." She said it softly.

"Good." Relief was coursing through him. That fatheaded idiot from high school, Derek Andrews, no doubt. And probably Mr. Wonderful, who wanted to marry her.

Mr. Wonderful, who was another reason Collin shouldn't be seducing Willa. She deserved a bright future with the right kind of guy.

But somehow, at that moment, he wasn't feeling all that guilty about Mr. Wonderful. What guy in his right mind proposed marriage and then went to Australia? Mr. Wonderful deserved a little competition for leaving her on her own at the mercy of a guy like him.

She pressed her plump lips to the side of his throat

and he felt her tongue slide along his skin. He groaned and wrapped his arms tighter around her and was very, very glad that she wasn't a virgin.

He supposed he should have known she wasn't. She didn't act like a virgin. She acted like a woman who knew what she wanted.

"Willa," he whispered, and then again, "Willa…" He'd always loved the feel of her name in his mouth.

"I'm right here." She lifted her head from his shoulder and nuzzled his ear as he kissed his way across her cheek to take her mouth once more.

Then he gathered her tighter, closer, and launched them from the doorway, making it to the bed in four long strides. He laid her gently down and turned on the lamp, and then he just stood there above her, looking down at her, so slim and pretty, naked to his sight.

At last.

"So beautiful…" The words came out of him on a bare husk of sound.

She met his eyes—or at least she did at first. But then she grew shy. She did that thing that women do—an arm across her pink-tipped breasts, a hand to cover the shining brown curls in the cove of her silky thighs.

"Don't…" His voice sounded desperate, ragged to his own ears.

And she reached out. She put a hand against his belly, palm flat. A groan escaped him when she did that. Her touch felt so good, so exactly right. Like the scent of her that seemed to call to him, to beckon him to her.

She said, gently, politely, "Take off your jeans, please."

He couldn't do what she wanted fast enough. Two

of the buttons were undone anyway. He undid the rest and shucked them off and away.

"Oh, Collin, you're so…you're beautiful, you are."

"Men aren't beautiful," he argued gruffly.

"Oh, yes. They are." She held out her arms to him. "I'm so happy. After all this time, I never thought… never imagined…" She seemed to run out of words. It was all right. He understood, he knew exactly what she meant. "Come down here. With me…."

He pulled open the bedside drawer and got a condom from the box in there. And then he went down to her. He stretched out beside her, covered her mouth with his and let his hands wander.

Her body moved beneath his touch, so tempting, so soft. He kissed her as he stroked her hair, her throat, the smooth roundness of her shoulder.

So much to explore, all of her. Beautiful and willing and pliant and tender. The slim curve of her waist called to him. He stroked his hand from her rib cage to the swell of her hip and lower, down the long sweep of her thigh.

He palmed her knee and gently guided it open. Then he did what he'd dreamed of doing, sliding his palm up the inside of her thigh as she rolled her hips and tossed her head and moaned his name in hungry encouragement.

The dark curls were already wet with her excitement. He parted them. She cried his name out good and loud then.

He kissed her slow and deep. He whispered against her lips, "Like this, Willa?"

She gasped. "Yes, oh! Yes…"

He slipped a finger in. Two. Wet silk inside, warm

and slick, welcoming him. Her hips moved rhythmically now, her thighs open, offering him everything. So much. All she had to give.

"Collin…" She said his name against his mouth. And then she gave him her tongue to suck. He kissed her endlessly as he stroked her.

And by then, touching her in that most intimate place wasn't enough. He had to taste her there.

He kissed his way down the center of her. She clutched his shoulders, murmured his name over and over, like she couldn't get enough of saying it. He just kept kissing her, all of her, as he lifted up and slid over and settled between her open thighs. She shifted, adjusting herself with a long, slow sigh, bracing her heels on his shoulders.

The scent of her was so sweet, lemons and musk. And the taste? Exactly as he'd dreamed it. Only better. Endlessly better…

He used his fingers and his mouth and she moved against him, sighing, her hands in his hair, her head tossing on the pillow. She was rising, reaching for the peak, and he stayed with her, all the way. Until at last she went over, crying his name as the soft explosion of her climax pulsed against his tongue.

The condom had been lost somewhere in the tangle of bedclothes. He felt around for it—and got lucky. His fingers closed around it as she sighed once more and went all loose and lazy.

He didn't stop kissing her. She tasted so good.

She moaned his name. And finally, she pleaded, "Oh, please. Oh, my. I can't…it's too much…"

With a low chuckle, he relented, backing off a little, resting his head on her thigh. She stroked his hair, traced the shape of his ear. He was aching to continue. He'd been hard and getting harder forever, it felt like right then.

But at the same time, he was satisfied just to lie with her that way, naked. Together. Unashamed.

A few minutes later, he sat back on his knees. She followed him, sitting up, brushing her wild hair out of her eyes, laughing. "Here. Let me..."

So he gave her the pouch. She tore the end off with her teeth. Hottest thing he ever saw. A guy didn't need those girlie magazines she'd teased him about having in his man-cave. Not with Willa Christensen naked in his bed.

She peeled away the wrapper and set it neatly on the bedside table. Then she bent close to him. She rolled it down over him.

He shut his eyes and tipped his head back and tried not to lose it just from the feel of her sliding it down over him.

"Collin?"

He let a low groan be his answer.

And then the bed shifted as she rose up on her knees and bent close to him, all tart and sweet and womanly. Her hair brushed his shoulder and her mouth touched his, lightly, teasing him.

It was too much. He rose up and took her shoulders and rolled her under him.

She let out a little cry and a soft laugh. And then he was on top of her, his elbows braced on either side of her, framing her sweet face in his hands, her hair all around them. He stared down at her and she looked up at him.

"Willa..."

"Collin."

"Willa, I..." There were no words. And it didn't matter. He was right where he'd never dared dream he would be.

"I'm so glad," she whispered.

He had her arms trapped at her sides. But she could move her legs.

And she did, lifting them, hooking them around the backs of his thighs. He was positioned just right, nudging her where she was so soft and wet and open.

She felt like heaven. Like some lost paradise, found at last, after he'd given up believing he would ever get there.

He entered her slowly, by aching degrees. And he held her gaze the whole time. He needed the sight of her face as he claimed her, so beautifully flushed. Lips softly parted.

Completely willing, with nothing held back from him.

She moaned as he went deeper. He made an answering sound and kept pressing, filling her.

Finally, he couldn't go slowly anymore. With a forceful thrust, he was all the way in.

She gasped. Her eyes widened. Her sweet lips invited.

He lowered his mouth to her and kissed her as he began to move.

After that, time folded in on itself. He lost control and rocked wildly against her. She held him closer, tighter than before.

She made soft, willing sounds that only drove him higher. Deeper. Harder.

His mind was gone, shattered. There was only her

body and his body inside her, the feel of her soft, willing mouth pressed to his.

He hit the peak and sailed over, knowing a faint echo of regret that he couldn't hold out for her—and then, all at once, learning he hadn't left her behind, after all. Her body pulsed around him, drawing him deeper. Pushing him higher.

Hurling him outward through a midnight-blue universe of fast-spinning stars.

Chapter 11

Faintly, far away, Willa heard music playing. It was that Joe Nichols song, "Tequila Makes Her Clothes Fall Off."

She smiled. She'd always thought that song was kind of cute.

The song stopped. And the bed shifted. She remembered.

It was Collin's bed....

"My cell," said a groggy, very masculine voice not far from her ear. He nuzzled her hair. "I left it charging in the kitchen...."

"Um." She cuddled closer to his big, hard, naked body. He wrapped a muscular arm around her and drew her closer, tucking her into him, spoon style, settling the covers more snugly around them.

She smiled some more and opened her eyes to morning light.

Amazing. It really had happened with Collin. Just

like in all her forbidden fantasies. It had been incredible and it had lasted all night long.

He smoothed her hair away from her neck and kissed her there. "You smell good…." Down the hallway, the phone beeped.

"Voice mail," she said on a lazy yawn.

His lips brushed her neck again. "It's after eight. I'd better go see if it's anything important."

She grabbed the arm he had wrapped around her and pretended to sulk. "Oh, no…"

But he only kissed her hair and pushed back the covers, pausing to tuck them around her again. "I'll be right back."

She rolled over and watched him get up. He looked so good without his clothes on. He had a cute little happy trail and a real, true six-pack.

And a beautiful tattoo on the hard bulge of his right shoulder, one of those tribal designs. She'd spent a while the night before studying it, tracing its curves and angles with her fingers. It looked a little like a mask, with horns and a pair of eyes that also seemed to resemble sharks, somehow. She'd asked him what it was supposed to represent and in typical Collin fashion, he'd answered, "Whatever you want it to represent."

He put on his jeans and buttoned them partway, which somehow only made him look manlier and more naked. "Keep the bed warm."

"Will do. Let the dog out?" Buster, who'd ended up on the rug by the bed, was already up and wagging his tail.

He nodded. "C'mon, Buster."

She watched him go, Buster close behind. The view of him walking away was every bit as inspiring as the one from the front.

She heard the outside door open and shut as he let Buster out. And then he came back.

He held out the phone to her. "Your brother."

She sat up, pulling the sheet with her to cover her breasts, and took the phone from him. "Um. Thanks." She hit the icon for voice mail.

Gage's voice said, "Collin, this is Gage. I'm in town. And looking for my sister. Could you have her call me?" He didn't sound especially cordial.

Collin was watching her. "Good old Gage. Finally made it into town and he's wondering where the hell his baby sister's gotten off to."

Willa hitched up her chin and put on a smile. "Oh, I doubt he's wondering. I'm sure someone in town has already told him exactly where I am."

His dark gaze ran over her. She thought of the night before and a hot shiver went through her. "Not feelin' quite so *unimpeachable* now, are you, Willa?"

She pursed up her mouth at him and narrowed her eyes. "Don't start. I do not regret a thing. Last night was beautiful. I mean that. Do you understand?"

He gave her a slow, insolent once-over. "Yes, ma'am."

She puffed out her cheeks with a frustrated breath. And then she whispered, "Come here. Please?"

His fine mouth curled. "You should call your brother back."

She reached out her hand.

He looked at it for a count of five. Her heart sank. She was certain he would turn and walk away.

But then he reached out, too. Their hands met, fingers lacing together. Relief, sweet and good as a long drink of cool water, washed through her.

He dropped down onto the bed at her side. "I feel

bad, okay? I don't want to cause you problems with your family."

She dropped the phone onto the sheet and wrapped her other hand around their joined ones. "You're not. You couldn't."

He leaned closer. She tipped her mouth up to him and their lips met. "Call him," he said against her lips. "I'll let Buster back inside and put the coffee on." He lifted their hands and kissed the back of hers.

Reluctantly, she let him go, picked up the phone again and called her brother back. He answered on the first ring.

"Gage, it's me."

"Willa. Where are you?"

She could tell by his tone that he already knew. "I'm up at Collin's. We drove up yesterday. The road's a mess. I helped him clear the way."

A silence on Gage's end, then, "I don't get it. You never even liked Collin Traub, and all of a sudden, you two are—what? What's going on, Willa? What about you and Dane?"

Dane. Oh, Lord. She'd really messed up with Dane. She never should have let him talk her into taking time to think things over. She'd put off the inevitable and now she felt like a two-timer.

"Willa, are you still there?"

"Yes. Right here." And no way was she getting into all this on the phone. "Listen. I'll call you as soon as we get back down into town. We can talk then—or, whenever you can get a minute."

"*When* will you be back in town?"

"I don't know for sure yet. Collin may have things he has to do up here. And we cleared the road as best we could, but there are some rough spots and some places where the cliff side collapsed. It could take a while to get down."

"Buster okay?"

"He's fine. Yes."

"And you?" He sounded worried. "You…okay?"

Love washed through her. Her brother was such a great guy. "I am just fine. I promise you. And I'm glad you're here. So glad." Rust Creek Falls really needed him now. But she didn't say that. She knew him, knew he had to be beating himself up that he hadn't been there when the levee broke. Telling him how much he was needed would only make him feel worse about everything.

"Call me," he said. "As soon as you're back in town."

When she entered the kitchen, Buster was in the corner, his nose buried in Libby's old food bowl. The coffee was brewing. And Collin stood at the stove, laying strips of bacon in a pan.

She leaned a hip against the counter and stuck her hands in the pockets of the flannel robe she'd found on the back of his bathroom door. "I hope you don't mind. I stole your robe." Her purple shorts, cami and plaid shirt were strewn around the living room.

He glanced over. "Looks better on you than on me anyway."

She wanted to go to him, brush his hair back off his forehead, tell him…

What?

She wasn't quite sure. "That bacon smells so good."

He tipped his head toward the open shelves with the dishes on them. "Put the plates on the table?"

She nodded and then got busy setting the table. He

cooked the bacon and scrambled some eggs. She made the toast and poured the coffee.

They sat down to eat, the silence between them both sharp-edged and a little too deep.

She made herself break it. "Gage is fine. I said I would call him when we got back down into town."

"You need to get going right away, then?"

She sipped her coffee. "No. There's no hurry."

"You sure about that, Willa?"

The question seemed to hang heavy in the air between them.

Willa pushed back her chair. He watched her, dark eyes wary, as she went around the table to his side and did what she'd wanted to do since she entered the kitchen. She smoothed his hair back off his forehead. "I'm sure. No hurry."

He caught her hand. But he didn't push it away. Instead, he brought her fingers to his lips and kissed the tips of them. "Your food will get cold…"

"Um. Can't have that." She bent and he tipped his head up. They shared a quick kiss and she returned to her chair.

After that, the silence didn't seem so oppressive. But the romantic and sensual mood of the night before, of that morning before the phone rang, was definitely absent.

She wanted to talk—about everything. About how she was never going to marry Dane Everhart and she'd been wrong not to simply say no when Dane proposed, about how her brother would be fine with her and Collin being together, once she had a chance to talk with him. About how beautiful last night had been and how she was looking forward to more nights just like it.

But somehow, she didn't know where to begin. And that had her looking back wistfully at their recent nights on the front steps of the town hall, when talking with Collin had been as simple and easy as breathing.

And now, here they were. Lovers, at last. And it was suddenly neither easy nor simple. She had so much to say—and yet she feared she might mess things up if she started talking. She might end up blurting out something that would turn him off.

Was it true then, what they said about sex ruining a perfectly good friendship? She did hope not.

Collin knew he had to get her back to town as soon as possible. Her brother's call had been like a bucket of icy water in the face. It had snapped him back to reality hard and fast.

He shouldn't have taken her to bed. He knew that. Really, where was it going to go with them?

Nowhere. Things were crazy now, after the flood. Their whole world had been turned pretty much upside down. He knew that was all it was with the two of them: one of those things that happen when a man and a woman were thrown together by necessity in a crisis, with emotions running high.

It could never be anything permanent. She was a nice girl with a certain kind of life ahead of her. And his life suited him fine as it was. He liked his independence, always had. And she was going to marry a big shot from Colorado. She would remember that soon enough.

Probably already had. She'd been pretty damn quiet ever since she'd talked to Gage. Collin figured that just the sound of her brother's voice had gotten her to thinking twice. She'd realized it was a bad idea, what they'd done last night, that it never should have happened and it needed to stop now.

They loaded the contents of his freezer into coolers, strapped them into the pickup bed, and left for town.

The trip down went smoothly, all things considered. Collin knew the places to be extra careful—and they'd cleared away the worst of the storm debris on the way up.

He handed her his cell when they reached the base of the mountain. "Call Gage."

She made the call.

It was, "Hi, it's me… Yes… All right, I will… A few minutes… Okay." She handed him back his phone and asked him to let her off at the sheriff's office.

He pulled up to the curb.

She hooked Buster's leash to his collar and turned a dewy smile his way. "I…well, I can't tell you to call me, since I don't have a phone." She really did sound like she *wanted* him to call her.

But that had to be wishful thinking on his part. His chest was tight and his throat felt like it had a log stuck in it. "I'll see you." It came out way too gruff and low.

She searched his face. Whatever she was looking for, he didn't think she found it. He reminded himself how that was for the best. "Um. Okay, then. Have a good one."

"Yeah. Say hi to Gage."

"Will do." Another blinding, too-wide smile. And then she shouldered her pack, grabbed her big plastic bag of stuff and got out. Buster jumped down after her.

He didn't allow himself to watch her walk away. As soon as she shut the door, he put it in gear and got the hell out of there.

* * *

Gage was waiting for Willa in his office. He was on a cell phone arguing with someone about roadblocks or something, but he cut it short when he looked up and saw her in the doorway.

"Willa." He gave her a tired smile and ended the call. Then he got up and came around the desk to her. She ran to him and he hugged her close. He said in a voice rough with emotion, "I'm so glad you're all right." She let her bag and pack drop to the floor and hugged him back, hard. He'd always made her feel safe and protected. And right then, after the way Collin had seemed so eager to get rid of her, well, it felt good to have her big brother's arms around her.

When he let her go, she asked, "Have you been out to the ranch?"

His mouth formed a grim line. "Yeah. What a mess. I'll be staying down the street, in a FEMA trailer for a while."

"Why not stay at Mom and Dad's?"

"It's better if I'm right here in town, where I need to be." There was a tap on the door. He went over and opened it and said to the dispatcher, "I need a few minutes here. Won't be long." Then he shut the door again and turned to her. "Buster?"

"He's good. I tied him out in front."

He came back to her, clasped her shoulder and glanced down at the pile of belongings she'd dropped at her feet. "I heard you've been staying over at the town hall on a cot—until last night anyway."

She nodded, her gaze on his handsome face. He looked so weary, the faint lines around his eyes etched deeper than before. "It worked out."

He took charge, the way he always did. "So, then. You need a car, a phone and a place to stay."

She *had* a place to stay—with Collin. Or at least, she'd thought she did until a couple of hours ago. "A car and a phone would really help." She was going to have a long talk with Collin that evening, whether he liked it or not. And then, if that didn't go well, she'd find somewhere else to stay. "I need to get hold of the insurance people—for the house and for the Subaru."

"Have a seat." Gage gestured at one of the guest chairs and then went back to sit behind his desk, where he pulled open a drawer and took out another cell phone, a charger and the key to his pickup. "I've got cells I can use and the county provides me with a vehicle. For now, you take my cell and the pickup."

"Oh, Gage. I can't take your truck."

"Oh, yes, you can. And you will." He shoved it all across at her. "I programmed the number of the cell I'll be using into this phone. So you know where to reach me whenever you need me. Get a hold of your insurance agent. And call Mom. She's been asking about you."

"I will. Thanks."

"And with the truck, you can get around. Got money?"

She admitted, "I lost my wallet in the Forester."

He passed her some cash and a credit card. "You should get over to Kalispell and replace your license. And you need to call about your credit cards…."

She granted him a patient glance. "Yes, big brother."

He went right on. "There's gas available, too. The garage just got its tanks refilled. With the truck, you'll be able to stay at the ranch."

She wasn't committing to that. At least not until she'd had it out with Collin. "I'll be okay. Please don't worry."

He was looking way too bleak. She knew what was coming next. And she was right. "So…you spent the night at Collin Traub's." He practically winced when he said Collin's name.

She sat up straighter. "Yes, I did—and you can just stop giving me that pained look. Collin's not what I always thought, Gage. I'm ashamed of how completely I misjudged him. He's a great guy."

He had a one-word response to that. "Dane?"

"Dane is not the issue here."

"Willa." He used her name as a rebuke. "The man asked you to marry him. I thought you were considering it."

"I blew it, all right? I never should have told Dane I would think it over when he proposed. There's nothing to think over. Dane is not the man for me."

"You say that now…."

"Yes. And I should have said it from the first. As soon as Dane's back in the country, I will apologize to him for keeping him hanging."

"Dane's a good man. Are you sure you want to just cut him loose?"

"I am absolutely certain."

"Well, even if that's so, it doesn't make the Traub wild man right for you. Willa, come on. You know about Collin Traub. He's not a man to hang your hopes on. The guy never met a heart he didn't break. And he's spent more than one night cooling his heels in the jail cell out there for being drunk and disorderly and picking a fight."

She refused to waver. "People mature. They change. Collin grew up without a lot of supervision. Yes, he went a little wild."

"A *little?*"

"He's just not like that anymore. I… I care for him and I respect him." Gage started to speak, but she didn't let him get a word in. "Listen. I know you only want to protect me and I love you for it. But I don't want or need protecting. I'm an adult and I know what I'm doing." *I hope.*

"Well, I don't like it."

"Gage…"

He surprised her and admitted, "All right. I know that he's made a go of his uncle's saddle-making business. I give him credit for that." Willa started to relax a little. At least Gage realized that Collin had created a productive life for himself. But then he went on, "However, when it comes to women, Collin Traub is bad news. I want you to stay away from him. Can you just do that, just stay away from him for my sake? Please."

"I'm sorry. No. You're the best brother any girl could have. But being the best doesn't give you the right to tell me how to run my life."

He started to rise. "Now, you listen here—"

"Sit down, Gage," she instructed in her best schoolteacher tone. Surprisingly, he sank back to his chair. And she pressed her advantage. "I'm a grown woman. And I am fully capable of making my own decisions about my life—and the men in it. I want you to give Collin a chance."

"A chance to what?" he demanded. "To hurt you and mess you over?"

"No. A chance to make you see that there's more to him than your old ideas about him. All you have to do is ask around town and you'll learn a thing or two about everything he's done for Rust Creek Falls since the flood. He saved my life, Gage. He's been at the front line of the rescue efforts and the cleanup. He's a natural leader and he's right there when he's needed—and no, I can't say if what's happening with Collin and me is going to last forever. But I do know that, however it ends up with us, I will never regret being with him."

Gage gave her a long, dark look. And then he grabbed a pencil, pulled open his pencil drawer and tossed it in. He shut the drawer good and hard. "I'm not happy about this."

"That's your prerogative."

"But what can I say?"

She gazed at him coaxingly. "That you'll give Collin a chance."

He blew out a breath. "Fine. I'll stay out of it. For now. I'll just knock myself out being open-minded about Collin Traub."

She beamed him her fondest smile. "Thank you."

"But if that wild man breaks your heart, you can be damn sure I'll be first in line to break *his* face."

Willa spent the day taking care of personal business.

She used the cell Gage had loaned her to call her insurance agent and the FEMA flood insurance number. The clerks she talked to took her number and promised she'd get calls back from adjusters within twenty-four hours—for the car and for the house and for her separate government-run flood insurance policy. Next, she made calls about her credit cards. That took a while, since she no longer had the cards, she was calling from someone else's phone and her records had been turned to mush in the flood. But in the end, she gave the ranch as a temporary address and was promised that new cards would arrive there within the week. After that, she decided to go ahead and drive to Kalispell to visit her bank and her cell phone provider, and to get a new driver's license.

As soon as she got her new phone in her hand, she called everyone back and told them she had her own phone now. Then she called her mom in Livingston.

"You got your phone back," her mother said when she answered. "Oh, honey. We miss you…."

"I miss you, too, Mom."

"I talked to Gage just today…"

"Yeah. He finally made it back. He loaned me his truck."

"Good. There are still a lot of problems with the roads, so we thought we'd just stay here in Livingston a little longer."

"That sounds wise, Mom."

"Gage says they're giving him a trailer so he can stay in town."

"Yes. You know him. He needs to be where the action is."

"Honey, I've been meaning to ask. You *are* staying at the ranch, aren't you?"

"Uh, no."

"But why not?"

Willa didn't want to go into her relationship with Collin. Not now. Not on the phone—and not after last night and the awkwardness of that morning. It was all too new and exciting and scary. Not to mention, up in the air. And evidently, Gage had stayed out of it and said nothing to their parents about where she'd slept last night.

Thank you, big brother.

"Willa? Are you there?"

"Right here. And I've been staying in the town hall." It was true. She had been. Until last night. "They have cots set up for people whose homes were flooded."

"But surely you should be out at the ranch. Even with the power out, it seems to me that you would be so much more comfortable there than sleeping on a hard, narrow cot in a public building…."

"Mom. I'm managing. It's working out fine."

"Just think about it, won't you? Consider it."

"I'll manage, Mom."

Her mother muttered something under her breath. "Always so independent."

"I love you, Mom. Give my love to Daddy. I have to go…."

"And we love you. You're eating right, aren't you? Taking care of yourself…?"

"I'm perfectly healthy and I'm getting plenty to eat. And I do have to go."

With a sigh, her mother said goodbye.

Willa and Buster got back to Rust Creek Falls at a little past three in the afternoon. She stopped in at Gage's office and returned his cell phone. Then she visited the town hall and the Community Church in hopes that Collin might be at one or the other.

He wasn't. She tried not to feel too disappointed. The man could be back up on the mountain working in his shop, or out on flood cleanup—or just about anywhere.

She considered calling him, but decided to wait. Tonight, one way or another, she would track him down.

Summer school was out by then, so she went to Paige's house. Shelby was there with her little girl, Caitlin, who would be in Willa's class next year. Willa got a full report on the day's activities at the park. Shelby said the day had gone well and volunteered to fill in again for Willa whenever she needed a hand.

Willa thanked her. She really liked Shelby, who was a wonderful mother and a talented teacher. Shelby wasn't having an easy time of it raising her little girl alone. A blonde, blue-eyed beauty who had once been the most popular girl at Rust Creek Falls High, now Shelby made ends meet tending bar at the Ace in the Hole. Willa had been encouraging her to apply for a full-time teaching position with the district.

When Shelby and Caitlin left, Willa stayed to brainstorm with Paige on new projects for their summer school kids—projects that would lend themselves to an outdoor classroom setting.

At five-thirty, Willa put Buster on his leash and Paige walked with them to the church for dinner. The gas had never stopped working on the north side of town, but the power was still out. Paige had no generator, which meant she couldn't keep food refrigerated. The church, with the help of donations from a number of sources, would continue to provide meals for the community as long as people needed them. Refrigerated trucks brought in food daily.

Halfway there, Paige asked gingerly, "Are things okay with you and Collin?"

Willa sent her a sideways glance. "Ask me in a day or two."

"I'm here and ready to listen anytime you need me."

Willa hooked an arm around her friend's slim shoulders. "I know. It's just another reason why I'm so glad you're my friend."

At the church, Willa spotted Jerry Dobbs sitting at

a table with three other members of Collin's cleanup team. Collin wasn't with them.

Willa told Paige she'd join her in a moment. She got a bowl of dog food from one of the church ladies and took it outside to Buster. As the dog wolfed down his dinner, she gave Collin a call.

He didn't answer.

She left a message. "Hey. It's Willa. Note this number. It's mine. I went to Kalispell and replaced my cell phone today, along with my driver's license. I also dealt with replacing my credit cards, insurance adjusters and with my bank..." And really, did he need a blow-by-blow? She realized she was nervous because he hadn't picked up when she called. She tried again. "Right now, I'm down at the church for dinner. No sign of you. Give me a call...." She couldn't think of anything else to say, so she left it at that.

Back inside, she went through the serving line and sat down with Paige. Throughout the meal, she kept waiting for the phone to ring.

Didn't happen.

She couldn't help but feel a little bit dumped. Which was ridiculous, and she knew it. How could she be dumped? To be dumped implied that you'd shared some sort of at least semi-committed relationship with a guy. She and Collin? They were friends who'd slept together. One time.

So then, did that make her just another of Collin Traub's one-night stands?

Oh, dear Lord. She did hope not. Collin couldn't be that disappointing and hurtful. Could he?

She wished she could stop remembering her argument with Gage that morning.

Was Collin going to go and prove her big brother right?

No.

She needed to stop this. She was not going to think like this. If she kept on in this vein, she'd be right back where she started before the flood: racing out of rooms just because Collin Traub entered them.

That morning, she'd argued fervently with Gage on Collin's behalf. She'd said how Collin had grown and changed from the no-strings wild boy he used to be. And she had absolutely believed what she'd said.

Collin *had* changed. And if he could do it, so could she.

The friendship they'd found since the flood meant a lot to her. And last night had been beautiful—no matter what happened next. One way or another, she was working this out with him. If he didn't want to be with her in a man-woman way, well, that would hurt.

A lot.

But she would get over it.

Right now, what she needed to do was talk this out with him. And to do that, she had to *find* him.

Jerry Dobbs had finished his meal. He was busy putting his tray away, tossing his trash and separating his dishes from his flatware.

Willa told Paige she'd see her tomorrow, picked up her tray and went to ask Jerry if he might know where Collin had gone.

Collin tried to concentrate on the intricate pattern of leaves and vines, on the good, clean smell of veg tan top-grain leather, on the slow, exacting process of stamping the custom design with his stylus and mallet.

But his mind was not cooperating. His mind was on a certain brown-eyed woman. On the scent of lemons, on the way it had felt to have her tucked up against him naked all night long.

She had called over an hour ago. He hadn't answered and he hadn't called her back, though he *had* played her message. Three times. So far.

Yeah, he was being a real jerk and he knew it.

Still, he kept thinking it was better this way. Let her be completely disappointed in him, start avoiding him again.

Better for everyone.

Being her friend was one thing. But taking it further…

Bad idea. He'd blown it and he knew it. He shouldn't have given in to that thing he'd always had for her. He'd seriously stepped over the line and he wasn't going to let it happen again.

The sound from upstairs stopped his thoughts in midramble and his mallet in midair.

Someone was knocking on his front door.

He dropped the mallet and stylus and headed for the stairs as fast as his boots would carry him.

"Why do I get the feeling you're avoiding me?" she asked when he pulled open the door. She stood there in old jeans and a frayed T-shirt, her hair loose on her shoulders, Buster at her feet. He'd never in his life seen a sight quite so beautiful. She tapped her booted foot. "Do I get to come in or not?"

Chapter 12

Collin glanced past her shoulder, saw her brother's pickup parked next to his. Of course, Gage would have seen to it that she had transportation.

He accused, "The road up here is still dangerous."

"You'll be happy to know that Buster and I made it just fine." She stuck out her chin at him. "Ahem. May I come in?"

It was a bad idea. And he was way too crazy happy to see her.

"Collin. *Hello?*"

He stepped back automatically. She moved forward, the dog right behind her. He edged around her, shut the door and turned to her. "What?"

She squared her shoulders, kind of bracing herself. "Look. If you regret last night, that's fine. I can deal with that. I would rather you *didn't* regret it. I would rather be, um…" She paused, swallowed. He watched the warm color flood upward over her sweet, soft cheeks. "I would rather be your lover. But if you don't want that, well, okay. If you think it was a big mistake, what we did last night, okay. I won't like it and it…hurts me. But I *will* get over it. Because what I really want, most of all, Collin Traub, is to still be your friend."

He drank in the sight of her. It occurred to him that he would never get tired of seeing her pretty, clean-scrubbed, earnest face. "My friend." It came out low and kind of threatening, though he didn't really mean it that way. "You want to be my friend."

She hitched her chin higher. "Yes. I do. I want to *remain* your friend, above all."

"What about that guy you're going to marry?"

"Collin. I'm not marrying Dane. And I will tell him that as soon as I get a chance to talk to him."

He wasn't sure he believed her. "Why keep the guy hanging if you're only going to say no?"

"I'm not keeping him hanging. He asked me to think it over. I said I would. I *have* thought it over and I'm not going to marry him."

Collin still wasn't really buying it, still had that feeling that this thing between them was only temporary, something born out of the chaos caused by the flood. Not the kind of thing that lasted.

Which should have been fine with him. He'd never been a guy who worried about whether or not what he had with a woman was going to last.

Because for him, it never did.

Three steps separated them. He took the first one. Couldn't help himself. Looking at her was like drowning in a whirlpool, the spinning current dizzying, sucking him down.

And then, when he was only two steps away, well, he had to get even closer. He took the second step.

And the scent of her came to him: sweet and tart and way too womanly.

That did it.

To hell with trying to do the right thing here. She wanted him and he wanted her and why shouldn't they both have what they wanted?

He snaked out a hand and caught her wrist.

She gasped. "Collin! What…?"

He pulled her to him, wrapped an arm around her. How could she be so perfect, so slim and soft and way too exciting, bringing the scent of lemons and Ivory soap to drive him wild? She stared up at him, her eyes so wide. Heat flared in his groin. "Right now, Willa, I'm not really thinking about being your friend."

That full mouth formed a round O. "Well." Breathless. Hopeful. "It's all…workable. Don't you think?"

"Thinking," he said roughly. "Who's thinking?"

And then she lifted a hand and cradled the side of his face. "Don't be afraid…."

Another wave of heat blasted through him. He put on a scowl. "I'm not afraid."

"Right." Soft. Indulgent. Way too knowing. Her eyes had that gleam in them now.

He still couldn't really believe she was here, in his house. In his arms. "You shouldn't have come up here."

"Yes. Yes, I should have."

"Your brother warned you about me, right?"

"Gage is willing to be open-minded."

"You mean he warned you and you argued with him."

"And now he's willing to be open-minded."

"I know how you are, Willa. So damn determined."

She smiled then, dimples flashing. "I am, yes. It's one of my most sterling qualities."

He bent his head closer, nuzzled her hair, breathed her in. Nothing. No one. Ever. Not like her. "Willa..." It came out harsh, low. Hungry.

She clung to him. She felt like heaven. She closed her eyes and pressed her lips to his throat. "Yes." She kissed the word into his skin, once. And then again. "Yes."

He put a finger under that stubborn chin of hers. With a sigh, she opened her eyes. He advised, "I should send you back down the mountain right now."

"Oh, but you won't." She clucked her tongue. Softly. "It's much too dangerous, remember?"

He pulled her even closer. "*This* is what's dangerous." There were a thousand reasons they should stop right now. He tried to remember at least a few of them, but it wasn't happening. "I'm not the right guy for you."

"That's for me to decide. All you have to figure out is whether *I'm* the right girl for *you*."

"I don't—"

"Shh." She put two fingers against his mouth. It took all his will not to close his teeth around them and suck them inside. "We don't have to decide anything now," she whispered. "We can just...be together, you and me. Just enjoy every minute we have, for now. Just kind of wing it and see where it takes us."

"It's not a good idea, Willa." He formed the words against the soft pads of her fingers.

"Your mouth says one thing, but the rest of you is sending another message altogether." She pressed herself against him, snugger. Tighter.

He caught her fingers, touched his lips to them. Somehow, he couldn't help it—couldn't help holding her, touching her. Wanting her. "You're getting pretty bold lately…."

She lifted her mouth higher, offering it to him. "Must be the company I'm keeping."

That did it. He dipped his head and settled his lips on hers.

She sighed in welcome.

He wrapped his arms tighter around her and kissed her slowly. With care and attention and longing and heat.

She responded by sliding her hands up his chest to his shoulders, by sifting those soft fingers up into his hair. By sighing her willingness against his parted lips.

And by then, he'd pretty much forgotten all the reasons they shouldn't be doing this.

If she wanted to be with him, he could only put up so much resistance. After all, *he* wanted to be with her.

He burned to be with her.

And now, tonight, again, at last, he *would* be with her.

He started undressing her, right there in the entryway.

She didn't object—on the contrary, she started undressing *him*. He got rid of her T-shirt and she returned the favor. He unhooked her bra. She undid his jeans.

And then he lifted her high and carried her down the hall to his bedroom. He set her on the bed and knelt to unlace her boots. He got one off, and the sock beneath it, and he was starting on the other one when she reached out and laid her palm on his hair.

He looked up.

She gazed down at him, her eyes and her mouth so soft. So tender. "Collin…."

He kind of lost it then. He got her other boot off, ripped away the sock. And then she was clasping his shoulder, pulling him up to her.

It all happened so fast. He got the condom from the drawer as she pulled down her jeans and panties and kicked them away.

Her hands were on him again, pushing his jeans down. He still had his boots on. Neither of them cared.

He rolled the condom on and then went down to her. He tried to take it slow, to make sure she was ready.

But she tugged at him. She was so insistent, making tender sounds of need and encouragement, wrapping her arms and her long legs around him and pressing herself up to him, inviting him.

What could he do, given an invitation like that?

Accept. With enthusiasm.

And he did. He kissed her deeply as she slid her arm down between their bodies. She closed her soft fingers around him and guided him home.

After that, he was lost. Lost in the best, sweetest, hottest way.

She was all around him, all woman and softness and heat.

He surrendered. She moved against him, calling him down.

He was lost in her. As his climax rolled through him, he couldn't help hoping he might never be found.

When he could move again, he took off the rest of his clothes and pulled the covers up over them.

They made love again, more slowly that time.

And then, for a while, they just lay there, arms around each other, watching the shadows lengthen out the window across from his bed. He started talking about his Thunder Canyon relatives, about the wedding of his long-lost cousin that had taken place over the Fourth of July.

She asked, "Why didn't you go to the wedding with the rest of your family?"

He stroked her hair. "I had work that needed doing. And anyway, weddings have never been my kind of good time. They're like family reunions—there was one of those going on down in Thunder Canyon, too, over the Fourth—both are just excuses for the old folks to ask me when I'm getting married and how come I'm such a troublemaker."

She laughed. "Well, when *are* you getting married? And why are you such a troublemaker?"

"I'm not getting married. And troublemaking's fun."

She wrapped her leg across him, ran a soft finger down his arm in a slow, teasing caress and whispered, "I think you've put a big dent in your troublemaker reputation lately."

"Naw."

"Yeah. Jerry Dobbs told me you talked old Mrs. Lathrop into putting her shotgun away and relocating to a FEMA trailer today."

He traced the wings of her eyebrows, one and then the other. "You know Mrs. Lathrop. She's so, so proud. She moved back into her house, even though it's not safe in there since the flood. We had to talk her into leaving."

"Jerry said *you* talked her into leaving—and that she had her shotgun on you while you did it."

"Jerry exaggerates. And is he the one who told you I'd gone on up the mountain?"

"Mmm-hmm."

"Jerry's also got a big mouth."

"Oh, now. You like Jerry. You and Jerry get along."

He pressed his nose against her throat. He loved the texture of her skin almost as much as the way she smelled. He also cupped her breast. Because he could. Because it felt so good. Because it fit his hand just right. "Stop trying to make a hero out of me."

She laughed again, husky and low. "Oh, I'm not trying anything. You're being a hero all by yourself."

Willa had decided to take the advice she'd given Collin that Tuesday evening.

She was going to take it day by day. Enjoy being with him.

And she wasn't expecting anything. She was letting this beautiful, exciting thing between them unfold in its own way.

She taught summer school both Wednesday and Thursday. In the afternoons, she met with insurance adjusters.

She and Gage, as it turned out, were two of the "lucky" ones. Their houses would have to be taken down to the studs and rebuilt—but at least they had flood insurance. Too many didn't.

In the evenings, Willa and Buster went up the mountain, where Collin was waiting. Those two nights were glorious, perfect. Just Willa and Collin all wrapped up tight in each other's arms.

Friday, Willa got a call from her insurance company. They would provide her a rental car until the replacement check came through. After summer school was done for the day, she gave Gage back his truck and Collin drove her to Kalispell, where she got the keys to a green Forester.

By then it was after six, so they stopped in at a little Italian place Collin liked. It was wonderful, to sit in a restaurant lit by actual electricity and be served crisp salads, fragrant garlic bread and piping-hot lasagna. She was feeling so festive she even had a glass of red wine while Collin enjoyed a cold beer.

"I could sit here forever," she confided when her plate was empty and the waitress had whisked it away. "It's funny how easy it is to take simple things like restaurants and electricity for granted. I keep telling myself that I'll never consider basic services as a given again."

He was looking at her so…intimately. A look that curled her toes and made her think of the night to come. "How 'bout dessert?"

They ordered gelato with yummy waffle biscuits. Willa took her time savoring the cool, creamy treat.

It was almost nine when they started back to Rust Creek Falls. The plan was to skip stopping in town and caravan up the mountain, but when Willa saw that the Sawmill Street Bridge lights were on, she honked at Collin, who was in the lead.

He pulled over and she swung in behind him, jumping out to run to his side window. He rolled it down. "Looks like the power's back on."

She felt like a little kid at Christmas. "I can't believe it. I sat in that restaurant fantasizing about all the lights coming on. And what do you know?"

"Let's go into town. See what's going on." His eyes had a gleam to them, one she completely understood.

He had that troublemaker image he sometimes hid behind, but she wasn't fooled, not anymore, not since the flood. He loved Rust Creek Falls as much as she did. Every step toward recovery from the disaster that had wiped out half the town mattered. To both of them.

She glanced across the bridge. It wasn't fully dark yet, but the streetlights were on. "Yes!" She ran back to her rental car and followed him across the bridge.

Main was blocked off between Sawmill and Cedar. They parked in the Masonic Hall parking lot. Willa left the windows down partway for Buster and they went to investigate.

It was a street dance.

They ran into Thelma on the corner. She told them that not only was the power back on, the landline phones were operational again, too. People had decided to celebrate by throwing a party.

At least half the town was there. Several local musicians had grabbed their instruments and formed an impromptu band. They were set up on the sidewalk midway between the two roadblocks. Folks stood around, clapping and laughing. And the street was full of dancers, everyone spinning and whirling under the streetlights. Willa spotted Paige dancing with her dad and Shelby and little Caitlin dancing together. Gage stood over by Nathan Crawford across the street from the musicians. He spotted Willa and gave her a wave.

Collin grabbed her hand. "Come on." He led her out into the crowd and they danced a couple of fast ones. And then came a slow one. He pulled her against him. She went into his arms and closed her eyes and swayed with him beneath the streetlights, thinking how the moment was about the most perfect that ever could be:

dancing with Collin in the middle of Main Street on the night the lights came back on.

The next day, Saturday, Collin's parents and brothers returned at last from Thunder Canyon. They all rolled in to the Triple T in the early afternoon.

Collin was in his workshop up on the mountain when his mother called.

Ellie had a lot to tell him. She and his dad and his brothers and Dallas's three kids hadn't come home alone. They'd brought friends from Thunder Canyon, people who wanted to help and who had the kinds of skills that would be needed to begin to rebuild the south side of town. There were several members of the Pritchett family, who owned a carpentry business. And there were also Matt Cates and his dad, Frank, of Cates Construction, among others. Lots of others.

"You come on down to the ranch for dinner tonight," his mom commanded.

He thought of Willa. He'd been indulging himself in a big way with her, spending every spare moment at her side. She'd gone down the mountain to help with a food drive at the church that morning, but she would be back around five. He'd been looking forward to that—to a quiet dinner, just the two of them.

To another whole night with her in his bed.

On the floor by his feet, Buster raised his head from his paws and twitched an ear at him. Collin bent and gave the dog a pat. It had just seemed a natural thing that Buster would stay on the mountain with him while Willa went to help out down in town.

They were getting real…settled in together, him and Willa. He probably needed to dial it back a notch with her.

But somehow, every time he thought about that, about putting a little space between the two of them, he got this ache in the center of his chest. It was the kind of ache a man gets when he's making himself do something he doesn't want to do.

Because he didn't want to dial it back with Willa. He only thought it would be better for her if he did.

But not for him. Uh-uh. He liked it with her.

He liked everything about being with her.

He liked it too much.

"Collin?" His mother's voice sent his dark thoughts scattering. "You're too quiet. What's going on?"

"Not a thing. I'm right here."

"You come home for dinner."

"Tomorrow, okay? Tonight, I have plans."

"I said, tonight. Your family's home and we want to see you. Bring that sweet Willa Christensen. I'm so glad you're seeing her. I always did like that girl."

Swear words scrolled through his mind. His mom already knew about Willa.

Was he surprised?

Not particularly. His mom knew everyone and he had no illusions that he was the only one in town she'd been talking to while she was away.

"Who told you about me and Willa?" He knew he shouldn't ask. But he was kind of curious.

"Are you kidding me? Who didn't? She's a prize, that girl. I never dared to hope. My own Last Straw and the dear little Christensen girl." *The Last Straw.* It was his mom's pet name for him. She always claimed it was only because he was the last of her children. He knew better and so did everyone else. She called him the Last Straw because he'd given her so much grief with his bad behavior and untamed ways. "I'm very pleased," she added. "Very. Don't you blow it with her, now. Hear me?"

"S'cuse me, Mom. But what's going on between Willa and me has got nothing to do with you."

Ellie sighed. Deeply. "Dear Lord in heaven, you are a trial to me. I only asked you to come to dinner tonight and bring Willa. Please. Six o'clock. Don't be late."

"Mom, I..." He let the objection die unfinished. He was talking to dead air anyway.

Willa's cell rang as she carried a case of baked beans into the church's multiuse room.

She passed the beans to Mindy Krebs and took the phone from her pocket. The display read "Collin." Her heart did a happy dance and she was grinning like a love-struck fool as she answered. "What?"

"My mom, my brothers and about half of Thunder Canyon just arrived in town. Mom knows about you and me. And she wants us both to come to the ranch for dinner."

Willa couldn't help laughing. "Collin. You should hear yourself. You sound like a covert operative passing state secrets."

"She drives me nuts."

Willa had a hard time believing that. "But your mom's so thoughtful and generous and smart and perceptive. I just love her."

He made a low, growling sound. "So does everyone else in town. And she's a good mom, don't get me wrong. She's just way too damn pushy sometimes, that's all. At least when she's dealing with me."

"Because you never did do what she told you to do."

"That's right. It's kind of a point of pride with me never to do what my mother says."

"You know that's childish, right?"

A silence on his end, then, in a surly tone, "Will you come to dinner at the Triple T with me tonight?"

She smiled widely. "Of course. Dinner at the Triple T would be lovely."

Ellie and Bob Traub knew how to throw a barbecue.

Their house was packed with people. Neighbors, friends, ranch hands, Thunder Canyon visitors and a whole lot of family spilled out onto the wide front porch and into the yard, where Bob had two smokers going along with a grill.

Gage was there. Willa spotted him on the front porch when she and Collin arrived. She worked her way through the groups of people to give him a hug.

He offered his hand to Collin. The two men shook.

And Gage said, "Been hearing good things about you lately."

Willa felt a wash of love and appreciation for her brother. He'd done what he'd promised, kept an open mind about Collin and been willing to listen when people told him all Collin had done for their town since the flood.

Collin grunted. "But you know not to believe everything you hear, right?"

Gage chuckled. "Word is you have good ideas, you don't lose your head and you're willing to pitch in." He grew serious. "So I'm asking you for what Rust Creek Falls needs from you. I'm asking for your help with the big job ahead of us."

Willa hid her smile at Collin's wary expression. "Sure," he said at last. "What can I do?"

"Come to the town hall Monday morning at ten? We're putting a group together. We'll start figuring out ways to get funding and volunteers to rebuild south-side homes for folks who had no flood insurance. Also, there's the clinic. We want to get it operational again. And most important, the elementary school. The high school isn't big enough to hold the younger kids, too. We have to do something so the K through eighth graders have a place to go in the fall."

Willa was nodding. "Good. September is just around the corner."

Gage asked, "So what do you say, Collin?"

He didn't hesitate. "I'll be there."

"Willa, dear." Ellie Traub descended on them, all smiles. "I'm so glad to see you!" She grabbed Willa in a bear hug.

Willa laughed in surprise at being clutched so close by Collin's mom. "Good to see you, too, Ellie."

Ellie took her by the shoulders. "I heard you were flooded out—and Gage, too." She sent Willa's brother a sympathetic frown. "It's horrible. Awful…."

"We'll survive," Willa said. "And we'll rebuild."

"Lavinia and Wayne…?" Ellie asked about Willa and Gage's parents.

"They're fine," Gage assured her. "I talked to them just an hour or so ago. They should be back at the ranch sometime tomorrow."

Collin said, "They were in Livingston, at the big rodeo, when the storm hit."

"So was I," Gage told Ellie, regret in his voice. "Mom wouldn't leave me alone until I agreed to go with them.

She had some idea I was working too hard and needed to take a break and forget everything for the holiday."

"She knows what you need better than you do, huh?" Collin sent his mother a meaningful glance.

"Yes, she does," Gage confirmed, sounding weary. "Just ask her."

Ellie grabbed Collin. "We only do it because we love you. Now, give me a hug," she demanded fondly.

"Aw, Mom..." Collin embraced her with obvious affection.

Then Ellie hooked one arm with Collin's and the other with Willa's. "Gage, there's beer in the cooler out on the lawn."

"Thanks, Ellie."

Eyes shining, Ellie commanded, "You two come with me. I want everyone to know how pleased and happy I am that you're both here—together."

"It was embarrassing," Collin grumbled much later that night, when they were alone in his bed. "Dragging us all over the yard, announcing over and over again that you were with *me.*"

Willa lay with her head on his broad chest. She could hear his heartbeat, so strong and steady. There was no place in the world she would rather be than right there, held close in Collin's strong arms. "She loves you. She's proud of you."

He made one of those low, growly sounds. "She can't believe that someone as amazing as you would be hanging around with me."

"That's not so."

"Yeah, it is." He pressed his lips to her hair.

"No."

"Yeah—and what do you want to bet that Nathan Crawford will be at that meeting your brother talked me into going to Monday morning?"

She tipped her head back and kissed his beard-scratchy chin. "Probably. But you can handle him."

He looked down into her eyes and said gruffly, "You realize my mom is right, don't you? You're much too fine a woman to be wasting your time with me."

"I am not wasting my time. And I really get annoyed with you when you put yourself down."

"It's only the truth."

"No, it isn't." She tried to look stern. "Will you stop it? Please?"

He smoothed her hair and answered grudgingly, "Yes, ma'am."

She gave him a slow smile. "Actually, I'm a lot like your mother."

He widened his eyes in a comical way and faked a gasp of shock. "Don't say that. Anything but that."

"Oh, but I *am* like Ellie. I'm pushy. And determined. And very sure of what's good for the people I love…."

Love. She'd said the word so casually.

But then, as soon as it was out, she didn't feel casual at all.

Love. Once the word had escaped her lips, it seemed to hang by a thread inside her mind, slowly swinging. Tempting her to grab it and run with it.

Love.

The big word, the one that mattered. The word that changed everything.

She dared for the first time to admit to herself what was happening to her, how her life had become something new and fresh and beautiful. The world had a glow to it now.

Because of him.

I love you, Collin Traub.

Buoyant light seemed to fill her. All at once, she was weightless, defying gravity through pure joy.

I love you, Collin Traub.

She opened her mouth to say it—and then she shut it without making a sound.

Saying it out loud would be dangerous. Risky.

He was frowning down at her. "Hey."

She kissed his chin again. "Umm?"

"You okay?" Cautious. A little worried. "You seemed a thousand miles away just now."

"I'm right here." She took his arm, wrapped it snugly around her and settled herself more comfortably against his warm, broad chest. "And I'm fine. Better than fine."

He chuckled then. "You certainly are—and never admit you're like my mother, unless you're purposely trying to creep me out."

She laughed and promised, "Never again," as her heart cried, *I love you, Collin. I love you, I do.* The simple phrases seemed to tickle the back of her throat, working themselves closer to being said.

But she didn't say them.

Not yet. It had only been nine days since the flood, and only five since that first night she'd spent in his arms.

Yes, to her, what they had together now wasn't all that surprising. It felt like a simple progression, a natural unfolding of something that had been there all along. She'd known him all her life, wanted him for so long, been waiting, even when she thought that she hated him, for a chance with him.

She was more than ready to talk about that. About their lives, about their future.

About love.

But she was no fool. She knew that *he* wasn't ready.

So, then, she could wait.

She had a feeling it wouldn't be long.

The time wasn't right yet.

But it would be.

Soon....

Chapter 13

Collin had an ever-growing backlog of work he needed to get going on down in his shop. The next morning, as they were finishing breakfast, he told Willa he would have to spend the whole day at it.

She pushed her empty plate away and rose slowly from her chair.

He stared at her, feeling suddenly wary. "I'm not sure I trust that look in your eye."

She gave him one of those sweet, innocent schoolteacher smiles of hers as she came around to his side of the table. He gazed up at her, narrow eyed. He knew she was up to something. She sat on his lap.

He growled her name in warning.

She only brushed his hair back from his forehead with her soft, cool fingers and then kissed his cheek. "Come to church with me."

"Willa..."

"Please. It'll only take a couple of hours, total, including the drive up and down the mountain. After church, I promise I'll leave you alone to work in peace for the rest of the day."

The problem with her sitting on him was that the feel of her only made him want to touch her. To kiss her. And then to kiss her some more.

He caught her earlobe between his teeth and worried it lightly, because he couldn't quite stop himself. She trembled and let out one of those reluctant little moans that always drove him crazy.

"Shame on you, Willa Christensen," he scolded. "Talking about church while you're sitting on my lap. You know very well what happens when you sit on my lap...."

She wiggled her bottom against him and then he was the one trying not to moan. "Church," she whispered way too damn seductively. "It'll be over before you know it and then you can come right back up here and work all day and half the night if you want to...."

"Wiggle like that again and I won't be getting any work done. We won't be going to church, either. We won't be going anywhere but back down the hall to bed."

"Church. You take your truck and I'll take the Forester. That way, as soon as the service is over, you can head right back up the mountain." She kissed him. And then she slid to the floor and stood above him.

He grabbed her hand. "Get back down here...."

She bent close and kissed him again. "I'll be ready in twenty minutes."

They went to church.

It was kind of nice, really, Collin thought. His family was there, his mom all smiles at the sight of him and

Willa together. Pastor Alderson gave a sermon about finding joy in simple things.

Collin could relate to that, especially lately. Just being around Willa all the time, that was a pretty damn joyful thing for him.

Yeah, it was partly the sex, which was amazing… and which he probably shouldn't be thinking about in church.

But the thing was, the sex wasn't everything.

It wasn't even the most important thing.

Willa herself. *She* was the important thing. The way she would laugh, kind of husky and happy both at once. The way she cuddled up close to him, her ear against his chest like she only wanted to listen to the sound of his heart beating. The way she listened so close when he talked, but then had no problem speaking up if she didn't like something he'd said.

The way she could be so kind and gentle—and then turn right around and be tough as nails when something mattered to her. The way she could pull on a pair of work gloves and keep up with him clearing storm debris all the way up the mountain. The way she wasn't ashamed to be with him in front of everyone. Even if she *was* a schoolteacher with a certain reputation she really ought to be looking out for.

He'd thought he was happy before Willa.

But the past few days, he'd started thinking that before Willa, he hadn't even known what happiness was.

He was living in a dream, and he knew it. This thing with her, well, it couldn't last. He was who he was and he'd always seen himself in an honest light. He'd grown up wild and he hadn't been to college. He could change some, but not completely.

Not enough to be with a woman like Willa in a forever kind of way.

The pastor told them all to rise. They sang an old hymn that Collin had known since childhood.

Out of the corner of his eye, in the pew across the center aisle, he caught sight of Nathan Crawford, standing so tall and proud, singing good and loud. Nathan saw him looking and shot back a narrow-eyed glare. Nathan would probably be ticked off that Gage had asked him to the meeting about flood relief tomorrow.

Well, too bad. Collin was going. He had a few ideas for raising money and getting folks together to rebuild what they'd lost. And he wanted to help in any way he could.

There were other Crawfords in church that day. He got a few scowls from more than one of them. They'd always looked down on him. Not only was he a Traub, he was the no-good, skirt-chasing, *troublemaking* Traub.

Since he and Willa started in together, he'd worried that the Crawfords might come after her for being with him, might smear her good name. So far, that hadn't happened. But it still nagged at him. In a little town like Rust Creek Falls, people had certain standards. They didn't like to think of their schoolteachers living in sin. Especially not with the local bad boy.

Willa nudged him with her elbow. He sent her a glance. She sang even louder, brown eyes full of teasing laughter.

He forgot his worries and let himself enjoy just being with her. It couldn't last forever, but as long as it did, he intended to enjoy himself.

After church, Willa longed to ask Collin to take her to the donut shop for a Sunday snack. The shop had re-opened the day before and it was a Sunday tradition in town. Folks went to church and then to the Wings to Go or Daisy's Donuts over on North Broomtail Road.

But he did need to work and she'd already made her deal with him. So she kept her word and sent him back up the mountain.

When he got in his pickup, Buster whined to go with him. Collin shot her a questioning look.

"Go ahead," she said indulgently. "Take him." So Collin got out and let the dog in—ever since the day Buster fell from the pickup bed on the way up the mountain, they'd been letting him ride in front. "I'll be back by five or six," she promised. Thelma was expecting her to help sort donated clothing for flooded-out families.

Collin kissed her, a warm brush of his lips against her cheek—and then he climbed back up behind the wheel and headed for Sawmill Street.

Willa's mother called her from the ranch at a little past two. "We're home," she announced, then, "Where are you? We've missed you."

"I'm at Thelma McGee's, helping out."

"Honey, we would love to see you. Can you come on over?"

"I'll check with Thelma..."

The older woman made a shooing gesture. "Go on, now. Go see your mother. Give her my best."

When Willa arrived, her dad was out in the northeast pasture somewhere, repairing a fence.

Her mom had the coffee ready and a box of bakery sweet rolls she'd picked up in Kalispell. After hugs and greetings, they sat at the table together, each with a steaming mug and a treat from the bakery box.

Willa knew her mother. She could tell by the way her mom sipped her coffee thoughtfully and then said nothing for a moment, her head tipped to the side, that she was working up to broaching an uncomfortable subject.

"Ellie Traub came by," Lavinia said at last.

Willa got the message then. Ellie must have mentioned her and Collin. Willa picked up her fork and ate a bite of cheese Danish. "I'm sure she's happy to have you home safe and sound."

Lavinia took a big sip of coffee and set the mug down a little too firmly. "Ellie's *happy* because she's always liked you so much. She's always hoped that you might end up with one of her boys."

"I like Ellie, too, Mom. But then, you know that."

Her mom gave up on subtlety. She leaned across the table. "Oh, honey. *Collin?*"

Willa drew in a slow, calming breath and reminded herself that she'd gotten through to Gage about Collin and she could get through to her mom, too. "I care for Collin. I care for him a lot. Since the flood, I've gotten to know him—really know him. He's strong and good and brave. And he doesn't give himself enough credit, but I'm working on getting him to see that he's a much better man than he's willing to admit. And I've been staying with him, up at his house, since last Monday night."

Her mother winced and sipped more coffee. "Staying."

"Yes."

"But is that wise?"

"I'm proud to be with him, Mom. He's a wonderful man. He's done a lot to help people, to keep people's spirits up, since the flood. Ask around town. Please. Ask Gage. *He'll* tell you."

Her mother frowned. "Gage hasn't said a word to me about you and Collin Traub."

"I'm sure Gage was waiting for me to talk to you first. I appreciate his staying out of it."

"But you never even seemed to *like* Collin. And what about Dane Everhart?"

"I *always* liked Collin. A lot more than I ever wanted to admit."

"But—"

"And as for Dane, it was never going to work with him and me." Lord, she was tired of explaining about Dane. It was her own fault, though, and she had to remember that. She should have had the courage to say no when she meant no. "Dane's a great guy. He's just not the guy for me."

"But Collin is?"

Willa sat back in her chair and folded her arms across her chest. "I love you, Mom. A lot. I will always be there if you need me. But I'm twenty-five years old and perfectly capable of managing my own life. I can't say what the future will bring, but I am with Collin now and I am proud to be with him."

Her mother tipped her head to the side again. Willa braced herself for another onslaught. But her mom surprised her and slowly smiled. "I always did kind of wonder about you and Collin. I had a feeling there might be a spark or two between you…"

A burst of relieved laughter escaped Willa. Her mom was going to be all right with Collin, after all. She teased, "No way."

Lavinia nodded, looking smug. "Yes." And then she scolded, "But you really must clear things up with Dane as soon as possible."

"You're right. And I plan to. I'll be going to see him as soon as he gets back from Australia."

Her mom got up, brought the coffeepot over and refilled their mugs. "Collin has done well with the saddle-making business. He made your dad's CT Saddle, did you know?"

"I didn't know. Until Collin told me."

"And I hear that he's turned that old cabin of Casper's into something quite beautiful."

"Yes, he has. You and Daddy will have to come up for dinner. Maybe next weekend."

"We would enjoy that, honey. Very much."

Willa got back to Collin's at five. The main floor was deserted.

She called down the stairs. "I'm here!"

Buster came bounding up. As she scratched his ears in greeting, Collin called from below, "Half an hour?"

"Take your time!"

She fed Buster. There was leftover meat loaf and several servings of browned potatoes in the fridge. She put them in the oven to reheat and cut up a salad. Then she set the table.

By then, fifteen minutes had passed. The oven was on a timer, so she felt safe grabbing a quick shower.

She was rinsing off when the shower door opened and Collin stepped in.

"S'cuse me," he said with that slow smile that seemed to fire all her circuits at once. "Just need to freshen up a little…."

She laughed as he grabbed her close. "Don't get my hair wet!"

Of course, he took that as a challenge, turning her

beneath the spray so the water poured down directly over her head. "Oops."

"Collin!" she sputtered, trying to wiggle free.

But she didn't try too hard.

And then he kissed her again. She realized it didn't matter that her hair was soaking wet.

All that mattered was that his mouth was pressed to hers and his arms were nice and tight around her.

The meat loaf was a little dry when they finally sat down to eat.

"Delicious," he said, and poured on the ketchup.

She asked him how the work was going. He said he'd made progress, but there was still a lot to catch up on. Tomorrow he had that morning meeting in the town hall, but after that, he would come right back up the mountain and work for the rest of the day.

"I've been thinking I'm going to need to hire someone to work with me," he said. "Not right now. But it's coming. I know a couple talented saddle makers in Kalispell. I'm going to contact them, see if they have any interest in joining forces with CT Saddles. They could work in their own shops, but put in some of their time on projects I bring them."

"Growing the business. Excellent. And you can't do everything yourself—especially when you also want to help out with the rebuilding effort."

"There should be more hours in a day."

"No argument there." She ate a bite of potato. "Thelma told me today that she thinks you should run for mayor. She thinks you're the one to carry on, to build on what Hunter started."

He sent her a look from under his thick eyelashes. "Don't."

"Don't what?" She widened her eyes at him.

"Don't start in about me running for mayor. It's not going to happen."

She cut off a bite of meat loaf neatly. "I think it is."

"You don't know what you're talking about."

She set down her fork and put up a hand. "All right. Subject closed." She pressed her lips together to keep from smiling. "For now."

He made a low, grumbling sound, but let it go at that.

She ate the bite of meat loaf. And then she said, "My parents got back today. I went out to the ranch and had a nice visit with my mom."

He studied her for a moment, his grumpy expression softening. "Sometimes I don't believe you're actually here, in my place, heating up the meat loaf, naked in my shower, harassing me over dinner…."

Tenderness filled her. "I like it, being here with you. I like it a lot." For a moment or two, they simply gazed at each other. They were both smiling by then. She remembered what she'd been about to tell him. "*Your* mother got to *my* mom before I did."

He forked up more meat loaf. "That doesn't sound good."

"Well, it was kind of scary when Mom started in on me, I'll admit."

"Started in on you about being with me?"

"She was surprised, that's all."

"Your mother knows you're too good for me," he said in that voice that seemed to be joking—but really wasn't.

She set down her fork. "No. She doesn't think that. She doesn't think that at all."

"Yeah, right."

"And neither do I, which you really ought to know by now."

He grabbed the big glass of milk he'd poured himself and guzzled about half of it. "This is a dumb thing to argue about."

"I agree. As soon as you admit what a great guy you are, we can *stop* arguing about this."

He actually rolled his eyes. "Okay, okay. I'm great. I'm terrific."

She raised her own glass of milk in a toast. "Yes, you are." She drank. When she set the glass down, she asked, "Would you mind if we had my parents up here for dinner? Maybe Friday or Saturday night? I was thinking we could have your folks, too. And maybe Gage and any of your brothers who wanted to come."

He was silent. A definite hesitation. "I have a lot of work I need to be doing, Willa."

"I understand. But I would do the dinner. You only have to come upstairs when everyone gets here."

"The road is still iffy."

"I go up and down it every day. As long as you know the spots to watch for, it's fine. I'll just tell them all where to be extra careful." She waited. He said nothing. Finally, she said, "If you don't want to have the family here, I think you ought to just say so."

He looked away. "It's not that."

"Then what is it?"

He pushed his plate away. "Come on, Willa. People get…expectations. Especially in this town. You saw how my mom was last night, dragging us all over the yard, making sure everyone got that you and me are together."

She had a sad, sinking feeling—at the same time as she told herself not to be in such a hurry about everything. She needed to let him adjust to what they shared in his own way, in his own time. She reminded herself that it had only been six days since they became more than friends, and that only a few minutes ago, he'd told her how happy he was just to be with her.

"So." She made an effort to keep her voice calm and reasonable. "You don't want to have the family up here for dinner this weekend. Am I right?"

He gave it to her straight, at least. "That's right."

Something shifted within her. Something died just a little. For the first time since they became lovers, she found herself thinking that it was simply not going to work out with them.

And then she told herself to stop. Just stop.

Maybe it was pushing it a little, to have the whole family over for dinner so soon. He did have a lot of work to do. And he was also unaccustomed to being half of a couple.

In fact, from things he'd said in the past, she had a sense that he'd never planned to be part of a couple. She needed to let him deal, give him the time and the space to start to see himself in a new light.

"You're mad," he said softly. Sadly.

She swallowed and shook her head. "No. It's okay. Really. It's fine."

The rest of the evening was lovely, Willa thought.

Collin was tender and attentive. He was passionate

in bed. They talked for over an hour before they fell asleep. There was laughter. He held her close.

He honestly did seem happy just to be with her. More than happy.

Still, Willa couldn't shake the feeling that he'd drawn a line between them when he told her he didn't want the family over. An invisible but uncrossable line, a line that cut them off from a future together.

For him, they were lovers. The best of friends.

But no more than that.

Never more than that.

On Monday, Willa told her mother that she would have to put the family dinner on hold for a bit. Her mom didn't push. She said she understood. Everyone was scrambling since the flood, trying to catch up with their lives, to get things back to normal. Of course, Collin needed to focus on his work. They would all get together for an evening soon enough.

Willa smiled and nodded. But she was thinking, *I love him. I love him so much.*

And she was starting to get the feeling that loving him wasn't enough, that he would never want to hear her say what was in her heart for him.

That she would never wear his ring.

Collin knew that he'd hurt Willa when he'd dug in his heels about having the family over.

He was trying not to think about that, about how he'd hurt her. He was trying to keep her with him, even though he knew that in the end, what she wanted and what he wanted were two different things.

Tuesday afternoon he sat through a second endless meeting with Gage, Nathan, Thelma and the rest of the group of community leaders they'd put together to come up with ways to speed flood recovery. When he finally left the town hall, he spotted Dallas, his oldest brother, coming toward him on the sidewalk, looking bleak.

But then, who wouldn't be bleak in Dallas's position? His wife, Laurel, had left him and their children last year. He was a single dad raising three boys on his own.

The brothers shook hands and clapped each other on the back. Dallas said he'd driven into town to pick the boys up from summer school.

"You got a little time to kill?" Collin asked him. "We could grab a beer at the Ace…." It was one of those invitations made only for form's sake. Collin had work waiting on the mountain and didn't really expect Dallas to say yes.

But his glum-faced brother surprised him. "Sure. I got about a half an hour until they turn the boys loose. Let's go."

They sat at the bar and ordered a couple of longnecks.

Collin asked how things were going and his brother said, "I'm proud of my boys and I'm getting by—and what's going on with you and Willa Christensen?"

Great. Getting grilled about Willa by his gloomy big brother. That hadn't really been in the plan. Collin sipped his beer and tried to decide how to answer.

Dallas kept after him. "You've made Mom happy for once. I'll say that. But come on. Everyone knows Willa's living up at your place. Yeah, you're the hero of the day and all. You definitely manned up when the flood hit. But do you really think moving Willa in with you was such a great idea?"

By then, Collin just wanted to cut through the crap. "Dallas. What are you getting at?"

"Willa's a great person. And you're not so bad yourself. But she's the marrying kind and we both know it. The big question is, are you?"

Collin wanted to tell his brother to mind his own business. Unfortunately, Dallas had a point. "I'm nuts over her," he said low, so only his brother would hear him. "I've got it bad."

"I kind of noticed that. But let me point out the obvious. You don't move a nice girl like Willa into your place unless you're putting a ring on her finger real soon. Especially not when she's the kindergarten teacher. That's not a thing a man should do—well, maybe in New York City. But not in Rust Creek Falls."

Collin thought about what his brother had said. He thought about it a lot—constantly, as a matter of fact.

He felt bad. Rotten. Low.

He never should have let Willa move in with him. It wasn't good for her. He should have thought of her first, instead of how much he wanted to be with her, instead of indulging himself just because he couldn't shake the hold of needing her so bad.

Wednesday night, she asked him if something was bothering him.

He didn't know how to answer. If he told her that he was feeling like a low-down loser for living with her when he never intended to marry her, well, where would that lead?

To her moving out.

He knew her. There was no way she was going to

hang around if he told her to her face that it was going nowhere between them.

And he couldn't let her move out. Everyone would say that he'd dumped her. She would be shamed in front of the whole town. He couldn't ever let that happen to her.

Plus, he didn't *want* her to move out. He just wanted to be with her. And not to have to think about what was going to happen next.

But then, he *did* think. He thought way too much. His mind was like a hamster on a wheel. A hamster on speed, thoughts going nowhere fast, endlessly chasing themselves in a circle.

He thought about that other guy, that guy from Colorado, the one who'd asked her to marry him. The other guy was a stand-up guy, she'd said.

She'd also said she was telling him no.

But *should* she be telling him no?

It made Collin feel sick in the pit of his stomach to think of her with that other guy. But what if the other guy was the *better* guy?

Collin wanted her. A lot. But he also wanted the best for her. And if the best for her was that other guy, well, Collin ought to step aside and give her some space to make the right decision.

He could do that much for her, at least.

But he did nothing.

Every day, every hour, his thoughts got more and more tangled up and confused. He didn't know how to talk to her about all of it. So he didn't talk to her.

He lied and acted oblivious and said there was nothing wrong—and that only made him more disgusted with himself. He started thinking how he really had a problem with seeing ahead to the consequences of his own actions. He had a part missing, emotionwise. He'd always been that way, chasing the thrill, hungry for excitement. Not thinking who would be hurt or damaged by his doing exactly what he wanted to do when he wanted to do it.

All day Thursday and half of Friday, as he worked in his shop to catch up on his orders, he tried to figure out what he was going to do to make things right with Willa. By three in the afternoon on Friday, he finally came to an actual decision. He realized there was only one choice for him now, only one thing to do.

He took a quick shower, put Buster in the pickup and headed for Kalispell.

It was no good lately with Collin, and Willa knew it.

Things had only gotten worse with every day that passed since Sunday, the day he'd told her he didn't want the family over. Every day since then, he'd become more distant, more uncommunicative. And she wasn't sleeping well at night now. She kept waking up and staring at the ceiling and trying to lie very still so that Collin wouldn't notice she wasn't asleep.

Wednesday, she'd asked him about it, about what might be on his mind. He'd looked right in her face and told her there was nothing.

She'd wanted to believe him. But she didn't believe him.

There was a falseness now between them. And it was growing. She needed to break through it.

But how?

It was starting to seem to her that there was only one way to get through to him. She needed to put herself out there, tell him the hardest thing.

She'd wanted to wait a while, to simply be with him and let the closeness between them grow. But the only way they were growing since Sunday was further apart.

Yes, opening her heart to him was a big risk. She could end up without him. From the way he'd been behaving lately, she probably *would* end up without him as soon as she uttered those three oh-so-dangerous words.

But who was she kidding? In the deep ways, the ways that mattered, she was already without him.

So why keep lying to herself? She might as well go for it, might as well pull out the stops, put her heart on the line and accept the consequences. At least then she would know she'd given it her best shot.

On the way up the mountain Friday afternoon, she decided she would tell him as soon as he came upstairs from his workshop.

But when she got there, the house was empty. He'd left a note on the table: *Quick trip to Kalispell. Took Buster. Back by six.*

All right, she thought. She would tell him when he got back.

She could start dinner....

But no. Dinner could wait. She was much too on edge to think about food right then. She had lesson planning she could do, so she went to the spare room, where she'd set up a desk and computer, and she got to work firming up her choices for activities for the following week, making lists of materials she hadn't pulled together yet.

An hour dragged by. She finished at the computer and went back out to the kitchen to face the prospect of cooking something.

Anything to keep busy until he returned.

She was standing at the refrigerator with the door

wide-open, staring blankly inside, when she heard the crunch of tries on gravel outside.

Her heart gave a sick lurch inside her chest and then started beating so fast she felt dizzy. She shut the refrigerator door and turned toward the hall and the short entry area.

The door opened. She heard his boots on the wide planks of the hardwood floor, heard the door close, knew he would be pausing at the coatrack to hang up his hat.

Buster came bounding in ahead of him. She knelt and pressed her face to the warm, sweet scruff of his neck. He wiggled and made happy whining sounds—and then left her to lap water from his bowl.

Slowly, her knees feeling absurdly shaky, she rose.

And there he was. "Willa." He wore clean jeans and a blue chambray shirt rolled to the elbows and her heart just ached at the sight of him. "Come here…." He held out his hands.

She hesitated. She couldn't…read him, had no idea what was going on with him. He seemed to be looking at her so seriously, with such determined intention. "I…" Words simply failed her.

And then he was right there, so close. In front of her. He smelled of mountain air, of pine trees. He took her hand. "Come on…" And he pulled her with him, around the jut of the counter, into the main living area, over to a fat brown chair by the window. "Sit down."

She did what he told her to do.

And then he was kneeling at her feet, looking up at her, his jaw set, his full mouth a determined line. He had something in his hand.

And then he was sliding it on her finger.

A ring. A beautiful diamond solitaire on a platinum band. Exactly the kind of ring she would have chosen for herself. She stared at it, gaping. "Collin, what…?"

And then he said, "Marry me, Willa. Be my wife."

It was just what she'd hoped to hear him say someday. And for a moment, she knew the purest, most wonderful spiking of absolute joy.

It was all going to work out, after all. She would have her life with him. They would be married, have children. Be happy forever, just as she'd almost stopped dreaming they might be….

She opened her mouth to tell him how glad she was, to say how much she loved him and how scared she had been that it was all unraveling, all going wrong.

But then, before a single sound got out, she saw that it wasn't right, after all. She realized what he *hadn't* said. It was the part about how he loved her. He'd left that out.

And instead of saying *Yes,* or *Oh, Collin, I do love you,* what came out of her mouth was, "Why?"

He blinked.

He actually blinked.

And that was when she knew that it wasn't going to work.

To his credit, he managed to pull it together. Sort of. "It's the right thing. And I'm nuts for you. That's not going away anytime soon. It's the right thing and…"

She stopped him by reaching out and pressing a finger to his lips. "The right thing, why?"

He swallowed. "Well, we *are* living together. And I want to keep on living with you and I…" He paused, tried again. "Okay. I love you, all right? I love you and I want to marry you and all you have to do is say yes."

She laughed. It wasn't a happy sound. The laugh

caught in her throat and ended on something very much like a sob. "Oh, Collin. You're not telling me the truth. I know it. *You* know it. Can't you just say it? Just tell me what's going on with you, whatever it is."

He gazed up at her. He looked absolutely miserable. "You're not going to say yes to me, are you?"

She took off the beautiful ring. "I can't say yes to you. Not like this. I just can't." She reached for his hand. Reluctantly, he gave it to her. She put the ring in his palm and folded his warm, strong fingers over it. "You don't really want to get married, do you?"

He rose then. He gazed down at her, dark eyes so deep, full of turmoil and frustration.

She stared up at him and asked him again, "Do you?"

His mouth curved downward; his big body stiffened. And then he turned from her to the wide windows that overlooked their town. He stared out, showing her his broad, proud back. "What I want is you. What I want is for you to be happy, for you to have what *you* want. I don't want folks in town saying crappy things about you. I want you to have the best of everything. I don't really think I'm it, but you've told me over and over you won't marry that other guy, so it kind of seems to me that you'd better marry me."

"You *want* me to marry Dane?"

"No." On that, he didn't hesitate. "But you deserve the best. Is he the best? The way you talked about him the night of the flood, I guess so."

"I was stupid and small and petty the night of the flood. I wanted to get to you, to hurt you. I'm sorry I did that. It was wrong. Now, how many times do I have to tell you, Dane is not the guy for me?"

He didn't say anything. He only shook his head.

She tried again. "Who said crappy things about me?"

He still wouldn't look at her. "No one. I don't know. I just… I don't want them to, okay? And as long as you're living up here with me without my ring on your finger, well, they could, all right? In a small town like ours, they might. Especially the damn Crawfords. They'd do it just because I'm a Traub—the troublemaking, skirt-chasing Traub—and you're with me."

She got up then. And she went to him. When she stood at his shoulder, she said, "But they haven't."

He faced her at last. "Not that I know of." It was a grudging admission.

She wanted to touch him, to clasp his muscled shoulder, to lay her palm against his cheek. To lift up and press her lips to his, to kiss him until he pulled her close and kissed her back, until she forgot everything but the taste of him, the heat and wonder of him in her arms.

But no. Better not.

She said, "You keep evading the basic question. So I'll tell you what I think. I think you are a wonderful man—a much *better* man than you're willing to give yourself credit for. But I don't think that you want to get married. And you know what? I want *you* to have what *you* want. What you need."

He scowled down at her. "I don't like the sound of this, Willa."

Her throat clutched. The hot tears were pushing at the back of it. She refused to let them fall. "I love you," she got out on a bare husk of sound. "With all of my heart. And that's why I'm going to pack up my things and go."

Chapter 14

It was five minutes to eight when Willa arrived at the ranch that night. Buster leading the way, she came in the door carrying two big boxes full of her things. Her parents, settled into their recliners for a quiet evening at home, glanced over at her with matching expressions of surprise.

Her mom jumped up. "Willa. What in the world…?"

The tears broke free then. They streamed down her cheeks. "Collin asked me to marry him. He bought me the most beautiful ring. The perfect ring. And I said no."

Her dad got up, too, then. He came and put his big, rough, rancher's hand on her hair, pressed a kiss to her forehead. And then he took the boxes from her and carried them down the hall to her old room.

"Oh, honey…" Her mom held out her arms.

Willa went into them, into the kind of a comfort only a mom can give. "Oh, Mom. I love him."

"I know, I know…."

"But it's not… Oh, Mom. It's just…not…"

"Shh. Shh, now. It's okay. It's all right."

She was openly sobbing by then. She couldn't seem to stop herself. "It's not. No, it's just not…"

And her mom held her and stroked her hair and patted her back and kept saying how everything was going to work out. Her dad came back up the hall. Buster followed him out as he went to get the rest of her things.

After Willa left him, Collin went down to his shop and he went to work. He worked straight through Friday night. When the sun came up Saturday morning, he climbed the stairs, plodded down the hall and fell into bed.

He slept for a couple of hours, his dreams full of Willa. It was still morning when he woke up, by himself, in the bed that he'd gotten way too damn used to sharing with her.

In those first few seconds when consciousness found him, he forgot she wasn't there. He reached for her, but there was only emptiness on the other side of the bed.

That was when it all came flooding back. She was gone.

He got up and went back down to work.

Willa woke up early that Saturday. There was no summer school, but she went to town anyway. She wanted to talk to her brother before somebody else told him that she and Collin were through.

Gage was in his office.

She went in, closed the door and said, "I broke up with Collin. It's not what you think, so please don't try any big-brother heroics."

He was already looking thunderous. “What do you mean, it’s not what I think?”

“He asked me to marry him. I turned him down. I made the decision to move out, not him. He wanted me to stay—and do not ask me why I left, because I’m not explaining myself. All I’m saying is that he only wanted to do the right thing.”

Gage got up from behind his desk then. He came around and he took her by the shoulders. For several seconds, he simply held her gaze. And then he pulled her close and gave her a hug. When he stepped back, he said, “So what you’re saying is, you want me to stay out of it. You don’t want me to bust his face in. And you want me to keep him on the Recovery Committee, to treat him like nothing has changed.”

“Yes,” she answered softly. “That is exactly what I’m saying.”

Around five in the afternoon that day, Collin trudged back upstairs. He drank a quart of milk and ate a tuna sandwich standing up at the counter. Then he went down the hall and fell across the bed. When he woke up a few hours later, he returned to the lower floor and worked some more.

That was kind of the tone for the whole weekend. He didn’t bother to shower or shave or even use a toothbrush. He worked. When he started to feel like he might fall over or hurt himself with his own tools, he went upstairs, grabbed something to eat, fell across his bed for an hour or two—and then woke up, remembered all over again that Willa was gone and staggered back down to his shop.

On Sunday, his mother called twice. He let the calls go to voice mail.

He might have stayed on the mountain indefinitely, but on Monday morning as he stood at the counter, staring blankly into space, downing a mug of coffee, he heard a scratching noise. And then a whine.

He went to the front door and opened it.

Buster.

The dog whined again and wagged his tail. When Collin only stared down at him, he plunked his butt on the porch boards and whined some more.

"You're not supposed to be here."

Tongue lolling, the dog stared up at him hopefully.

"Fine." Collin stepped back and Buster came in. He went right to his water bowl and lapped up what was left in it. Then he sniffed the food bowl. "Oh, pardon me. I had no clue you were coming." Collin laid on the sarcasm. Unfortunately, it was wasted on Buster. "Okay, okay." He went and got the bag of kibble. Buster sat and waited as he filled the bowl. "Go for it." And Buster did exactly that.

Willa was probably worried about the mutt. He would have to call her….

His heart lurched into overdrive and his throat felt tight, his tongue thick and heavy in his mouth as he autodialed her cell.

She answered on the second ring. "Collin." A small voice, so soft. And then she must have realized why he'd called. "You have Buster?"

"Yeah. He just now showed up at the door."

"Oh. I'm glad. We were worried…."

"I'll bring him down today."

"You don't have to. I can drive up after—"

"I said I'll bring him. I have a meeting anyway." A

meeting he hadn't planned to go to, but hey. He couldn't hide in his shop forever. Life went on. Such as it was.

"I have summer school."

"Yeah, I know." He was aching for the smell of lemons, for that soft place in the curve of her throat. He loved to kiss her there.

"I'll call Thelma. She never minds watching him."

"But she's going to the meeting."

"It's okay. I'll ask her to wait for you. He's fine in the house without her. I'll pick him up there after school."

So, then. He wouldn't see her. That was good. Or so he tried to make himself believe. "All right, then."

"Thank you for bringing him…."

He tried to think of what to say next.

But then it didn't matter. She was gone.

Off the phone. Not in his house. Out of his life.

I love you, she'd told him. *With all of my heart.*

The bleak numbness of the weekend was fading. He'd started getting the feeling that he'd messed up bad, that he'd gotten stuck somewhere in his mind, stuck being some guy he really wasn't anymore. He'd thrown away what he wanted most because he didn't have the sense to say the things Willa needed to hear. It was all doubly discouraging because the things she needed to hear really were there, inside him, even though he'd gone and pretended they weren't.

He'd pretty much told her to go marry that other guy. The more he thought about that, the more disgusted he got with himself. It would serve him right if she took his advice.

Thinking about it all made his head spin. A spinning head and a broken heart were a real unpleasant combination.

He told himself that now, to be fair, he had to wait. He had to let her work it out with Dane Everhart one way or another. If she turned down the guy from Colorado, then maybe…

Maybe what? Seriously, what was the matter with him? What he needed to do was leave her alone. If there'd ever been any hope for him with her, he'd pretty much blown that by the way he'd treated her.

He scrambled some eggs and ate them, took a shower, loaded Buster into his pickup and drove down the mountain. He dropped off the dog and went to the meeting.

Gage was there. Once or twice, Collin caught the other man watching him. But Gage didn't say a word about Willa. They discussed the donations that were coming in—and how to get more. They talked about the volunteers who'd come in from Thunder Canyon and elsewhere and how best to put them all to work rebuilding Rust Creek Falls. The meeting lasted three hours and they were still only two-thirds down the agenda. They agreed to meet Wednesday, same time, and finish up.

Collin drove to Kalispell and stocked up on groceries. He went home and went back to work—and deleted, unheard, all the messages his mom had left him over the weekend and that day.

The next morning, there was Buster, big as life, waiting at his front door. That time he texted Willa instead of calling. It just seemed wiser not to talk to her. Not to put his overworked heart under that kind of pressure, not to give himself any opportunity to make an idiot of himself all over again by begging for another chance. He took the dog to Thelma's and went back up the mountain.

On Wednesday morning, he couldn't help expecting

Buster to show up again. But he didn't. They must be keeping a closer eye on him.

Which was good. For the best.

He was standing at the counter drinking his coffee, staring into the middle distance, wondering what Willa might be doing at that moment, when someone knocked at the door.

Willa?

He choked in midsip and his pulse started racing. Hot coffee sloshed across his knuckles as he set the mug down too hard. He wiped the coffee off on his Wranglers and made for the door.

It couldn't be her….

And it wasn't.

It was his mom, wearing tan pants, riding boots and an old plaid shirt, her straw Resistol in her gloved hands. She'd come on horseback, ridden her favorite mare, Sweetie, who was hobbled at the foot of the steps, nipping at the sparse grass.

"You deleted my phone messages, didn't you?" She asked the question softly. Kind of sadly. And that, somehow, was a thousand times worse than if she'd just started lecturing him as usual, if she'd called him her Last Straw and threatened to hit him upside the head to knock some sense into him.

He shrugged. "Yeah. I deleted them."

"Are you all right?"

"No."

"Sometimes you can be your own worst enemy."

"That's a fact."

"Not so much now as when you were younger, though." She almost smiled, but not quite. "I'll call that progress."

"You want to come in?"

She shook her head. "I'm just checkin' on you. I didn't check on you enough when you were little. Too late to make up for all that now, I guess."

"You're doing all right."

She put her hat back on. "You keeping fed?"

"Mostly."

"There's no law says you can't try again, and do a better job than you did before. Messing up is just practice for the next time, when you get it right." She turned and started down the steps.

"I love you, Mom," he said softly to her retreating back. The words felt strange in his mouth. He knew he hadn't said them to her enough. And this time she probably hadn't even heard him.

Gathering the reins, she mounted. "Love you, too." She clicked her tongue and the horse turned and started back down the road. He stayed in front of the open door, watching her, until she disappeared from sight.

About then, he heard a whine. He glanced over and saw Buster sitting in the scrub grass beside the porch.

For the first time in days, Collin smiled. He slapped his thigh.

The dog barked, jumped to his feet and came running.

That morning, Willa got the call she'd been dreading.

The one from Dane. "Willa. My God. I just came from the airport, just heard how bad the flooding was in Rust Creek Falls. Are you all right?"

"I'm fine. Really." *Except for the little matter of my shattered heart.* "I lost my house and my car, though."

"Oh, sweetheart. I'm so sorry."

"Dane. Listen. I need to see you. I'm coming to Boulder, right away." Shelby could fill in for her. And Buster had taken off again, but it was no mystery where he'd gone. Maybe she would just call Collin and ask him if he could look after the dog until she got back.

"Coming to Boulder?" Dane boomed. "Not on your life."

"But, Dane, I—"

"I'm coming to you."

"No. Really, I'll find a flight and—"

He interrupted her. Again. "Sit tight, honey. I've got a plan."

Lord. She blew out a long breath. "Don't you always?"

He laughed, a bold, booming sound. "I'll be there before noon, you watch me."

"We'll have to arrange to meet somewhere. As I said, my house is a total loss." And she didn't want to meet him at the ranch. Too awkward, with her parents there. . . .

"How about the middle of Main Street? You'll see me coming. I'll be the one in the CU helicopter."

"A helicopter?" How very, very Dane.

"Yeah. I'm getting the use of it courtesy of a generous alumnus. I'm coming, honey. I am as good as on my way. . . ."

Collin, Gage and the rest of the committee were finishing up their endless meeting in one of the town hall conference rooms when they heard a helicopter overhead.

Nathan frowned. "We're not expecting a visit from the governor."

But then the helo loomed outside the window, coming in. Apparently, it was going to land in the street out in front. It was black and silver, with a giant gold CU painted on the belly.

Gage leveled that steady gaze of his on Collin. "Looks like Coach Everhart is dropping in to see how Willa's doing."

Collin reminded himself that he had to stay out of it. He needed to let Willa figure out what she wanted for herself.

But then, he couldn't do it. He could not just sit there.

He shot to his feet and headed for the door. Behind him, he thought he heard a low chuckle from Gage.

Willa was waiting on the sidewalk as the helicopter touched down. There were people all around her, folks she'd known all her life. They'd come running out of the library, the church and the town hall. Others had halted on the street. Everyone stared upward. It wasn't every day that a helicopter flew down and landed in the middle of town.

Leave it to Dane to make his arrival an event.

The chopper touched down. Dane jumped out before the blades stopped whirling, bending low to keep his handsome blond head out of danger. "Willa!" He ran toward her, rising to his full six feet six inches as he cleared the slowing blades.

Dread and misery and a healthy dose of embarrassment formed a leadlike ball in the pit of her stomach. She wrapped her arms around herself and waited grimly for him to reach her. Paige had given her the use of her house so she and Dane could be alone when she said the things she had to say.

"Willa!" The wonderful, rough deep voice came from behind her.

She stiffened, gasped, certain she couldn't have heard right. And then she whirled toward that voice, her heart in her throat.

Collin.

He was real. He was there. He reached out and put his warm, strong hands on her shoulders and she trembled with happiness just at his touch.

"Willa…" He stared at her with such frank longing in those beautiful dark eyes. She blinked at him, hardly daring to believe, and a ragged, hopeful sound escaped her. And he said, "Willa, damn it. I want you and I love you. Maybe I've always loved you, since way back when we were kids and I used to spy on you playing with your Barbie dolls out in your dad's back pasture. Yeah, I know…" He tipped his head in the direction of the tall man behind her. "That other guy may be a better man. But there's no way he loves you like I do. And there's also no way I'm not trying again, no way I'm letting you go without pulling out all the stops." And then he dropped to his knees in front of her, the way he had last Friday. Only, somehow, nothing at all like last Friday. Because that had been all wrong.

And this, now, this moment? It was so very right.

He grabbed her hand and said fervently, "Stay, Willa. I'm asking. I'm begging. Stay here in Rust Creek Falls and be my wife."

People started clapping. Some shouted encouragements.

"You tell her, Collin!"

"Say it like you feel it!"

"Don't let her get away!"

There were whistles and catcalls.

Willa hardly heard them. For her, at that moment,

there was only Collin, though he was looking kind of hazy through her happy tears. She confessed, "You really had me worried there."

"I know. I messed up. But I swear to you, right here on Main Street, in front of God, the library, that other guy—and way too many of our friends and neighbors—that when it comes to you and me, I won't mess up again."

She tugged on his hand. "Come here. Up here to me." And he swept to his feet once more. "I love you, Collin Traub," she told him. "I will always love you. And yes. Absolutely. You and me. From this day forward."

"Willa..." He grabbed her close and kissed her, a real kiss, deep and long and sweet. Everybody clapped all the harder.

When he lifted his head, she blinked up at him, dazed with joy. "Buster?"

"At Thelma's." He bent to kiss her again.

"Ahem," said the man behind her.

Willa pressed her hands to Collin's warm, hard chest. They shared a long, steady look, one of perfect understanding. And then, together, they turned to face Dane.

As it happened, Dane Everhart was not only a great guy, he was also a good sport. He said wryly, "Looks to me like I don't have a chance here."

Willa answered gently, "You're a good man, Dane. And I was wrong not to be straight with you from the first."

Dane gave a low chuckle. "Sometimes I'm a little pushy when it comes to going after what I want." He nodded at Collin. "You're a lucky man."

Collin pulled Willa closer to his side. "You're right. And I know it. I'm the luckiest man alive."

Dane held out his hand to Willa. She took it and they shook. "Be happy," he said.

"I will."

And then he turned and ran to the helicopter. The blades started whirling again.

Willa threw herself into Collin's waiting arms. They didn't see Dane go. They were too busy sharing another long, hot, perfect kiss, one that sealed their mutual commitment to their town, to each other and to the future they would build together with their own loving hands.

They were married three days later, on Saturday, July 27 with Pastor Alderson presiding.

It was a simple afternoon ceremony in the Community Church. The whole town attended and there was a big potluck afterward. Willa wore her mother's wedding dress. Paige stood up as her maid of honor and Collin asked his brother Sutter to come out from Seattle to be his best man.

If people whispered about how the maid of honor and the best man used to be together, they didn't whisper for long. Paige and Sutter conducted themselves with quiet dignity and the talk quickly died down.

It was one of those weddings where all the guests were smiling, a feel-good kind of day. Rust Creek Falls may have suffered through the flood of the century. But now the sun was shining and love ruled the day. Everyone could see that the bride and groom were meant for each other. Willa glowed with pure happiness.

And the former Traub bad boy had eyes only for his bride.

* * * * *

We hope you enjoyed reading

RESISTING MR. TALL, DARK & TEXAN

and

MAROONED WITH THE MAVERICK

by *New York Times* bestselling author

CHRISTINE RIMMER

Both were originally **Harlequin**® series stories!

Discover more heartfelt tales of family, friendship and love from the **Harlequin Special Edition** series. Romance is for life, and these stories show that every chapter in a relationship has its challenges and delights and that love can be renewed with each turn of the page!

SPECIAL EXCERPT FROM

HARLEQUIN®

SPECIAL EDITION

Zane McLaren just wants to be left alone to deal with the demons his time in the army left behind. Fortunately, his service dog, Nell, has other ideas—ideas that include his pretty neighbor, Ashley Granger.

Read on for a sneak preview of
CONARD COUNTY HOMECOMING,
the next book in New York Times
bestselling author Rachel Lee*'s*
CONARD COUNTY: THE NEXT GENERATION
miniseries.

Things had certainly changed around here, he thought as he drove back to his house. Even Maude, who had once seemed as unchangeable as the mountains, had softened up a bit.

A veterans' group meeting. He didn't remember if there'd been one when he was in high school, but he supposed he wouldn't have been interested. His thoughts turned back to those years, and he realized he had some assessing to do.

"Come in?" he asked Ashley as they parked in his driveway.

She didn't hesitate, which relieved him. It meant he hadn't done something to disturb her today. Yet. "Sure," she said and climbed out.

His own exit took a little longer, and Ashley was waiting for him on the porch by the time he rolled up the ramp.

HSEEXP0517

Nell took a quick dash in the yard, then followed eagerly into the house. The dog was good at fitting in her business when she had the chance.

"Stay for a while," he asked Ashley. "I can offer you a soft drink if you'd like."

She held up her latte cup. "Still plenty here."

He rolled into the kitchen and up to the table, where he placed the box holding his extra meal. He didn't go into the living room much. Getting on and off the sofa was a pain, hardly worth the effort most of the time. He supposed he could hang a bar in there like he had over his bed so he could pull himself up and over, but he hadn't felt particularly motivated yet.

But then, almost before he knew what he was doing, he tugged on Ashley's hand until she slid into his lap.

"If I'm outta line, tell me," he said gruffly. "No social skills, like I said."

He watched one corner of her mouth curve upward. "I don't usually like to be manhandled. However, this time I think I'll make an exception. What brought this on?"

"You have any idea how long it's been since I had an attractive woman in my lap?" With those words he felt almost as if he had stripped his psyche bare. Had he gone over some new kind of cliff?

HSEEXP0517